CONVICTED

CONVICTED
Book 1 of the
Paradigm Shift Trilogy

RAVEN H. PRICE

**Cover design was purchased from SelfPubBookCovers.com
Artist: Asha**

Dedication
To all my sisters in Christ

Acknowledgments

I'd like to acknowledge my husband, Ralph W. Price III, who I love dearly. His love, support, and encouragement keep me going.

I'd also like to acknowledge three wonderful women, Jan Kane, Shannon Baker and Regina Hegwood, who helped me edit this book.

I also must acknowledge Curry and Robin Bushnell for creating beautiful pictures of me for the book cover. Curry's makeup expertise combined with Robin's photography skills, were awesome.

Disclaimer/Copyright

Convicted

This book is Christian Fiction and based on the author's
imagination and faith. No one is slandered or libeled in this work;
resemblance to other persons living or dead is purely coincidental
in nature and places where events take place are fake to the
author's knowledge. No portion of this book may be reproduced,
stored in a retrieval system, or transmitted in any form or by any
means-electronic, mechanical, photocopy, recording, scanning, or
other-except for brief quotations in critical reviews or articles,
without the prior written permission of the author(s). No part of
this book may be made into a movie without permission of the
author(s). All rights reserved

Print history
First edition published April 2015
Second edition published October 2016
ISBN-13: 978-0692649503
ISBN-10: 0692649506

Library of Congress Cataloguing-in-Publication Data

Contents

Reviews

"Convicted is a story about an abused woman, Hope, who sought support within the church she grew up with; desperate for peace and comfort. Hope is inspired by a female television evangelist, and she begins a spiritual and supernatural journey, one that unfolds in ways no one could ever imagine. This story is well written, and the pace is solid. I rate as five stars!" ~ S. Jackson, Author, *When Angels Fly*

"It was hard to put down this story of Hope's journey from fear and despair into revelation and relationship with the wonderful Counselor. So many books labeled as Christian fiction have no real depth. This book is rich. It is sure to inspire readers to want more of God and also encourage us to take our places in the kingdom as fully armored warriors, possessing our land and ready to stand in the gap for others. I loved how it showed how very exciting it can be! The author has a great writing voice and is an excellent storyteller. I really enjoyed Convicted and highly recommend it. Are your spiritual eyes open??" ~ Melinda Matthews

Prologue

After two divorces, Hope Anderson felt drained and very alone. The emotional overload was keeping her awake at night. Fear of her ex-husband coming around in a drunken stupor to beat her mixed with the joy of being free from him was making her crazy. The guilt of two unsuccessful marriages made her feel like a failure, but better a living, healthy failure than a dead, married pushover.

Seeking stability, Hope went to church to find a sense of peace. As a child, she had always been at church and had loved the way people accepted her. As a divorcee, she felt stares and judgment in the church where she sought refuge. The judgment came from an older woman who had given her comfort and guidance as a child. Seeking to fit back in, Hope had to deal with the pain of not being accepted. She had to learn to forgive people who didn't have a clue what it was like living in a loveless marriage or being too loved by a jealous drunk for a mate.

Returning to her roots, she had a plan she learned as a child. If Jesus was truly her Savior, it was time to give up and let Him take control, allowing Him to show her how to become something other than a needy, self-absorbed woman.

Giving Up

As a child, I was part of a loving church family. Mom and Dad were pillars of the church and were always helping with various functions. My young life was filled with love, joy, and acceptance from everybody.

As a teenager, I fell in love with the thought of love. I wanted what my parents had—love, stability, and fellowship. I couldn't wait to get married to my soul mate and start a family of my own.

As a twenty-year-old junior college graduate, I jumped at the chance to marry Teddy Barns when he proposed, even without understanding the meaning of true love. From day one, it was sex, sex, and more sex that kept our marriage alive. Neither of us knew the other's thoughts and feelings.

After the first year, the trials of marriage were very evident and taking their toll. Lack of money was the root of many arguments. We found we had nothing in common. We realized that we truly didn't love each other. Sex was great, but that was all we had. When Teddy told me he needed more only two years into the marriage, a divorce seemed inevitable. *More what?* I asked myself. I had my answer when I found Teddy in our bed with another woman.

After the divorce, I felt shame. I gave up on marriage and family. I started hanging around with other single women to get back in the dating environment. Many were divorced, but others had never been married. We seemed to gravitate toward each other for moral support while testing the waters. I was associating with bitter, lonely, and desperate women looking for the kicks of one-night stands and just having fun. Most were not interested in finding their true mates.

I can't deny hanging out with swinging singles was fun at first. I enjoyed dancing, drinking, and meeting other single people. It made lonely evenings bearable. I considered myself fairly attractive, so flirting was easy. Many guys wanted to associate with me. Some guys would ask me to dance. Most of the men wanted to get to know me outside of the nightclubs.

In time, I understood why so many of my new women friends were bitter. Each date would end up the same. I'd agree to a dinner or a movie then face the awkward time afterward of fighting off sexual advances. The guys expected payment for their time or services. I was a divorcee after all, and men had the opinion that all divorcees were sexually needy. After each experience, I felt dirty and cheap.

Then Sam Anderson came along. I met him in a nightclub, but he took things slow and made me feel special. He admitted he had been watching me for a while. He couldn't help noticing I liked to dance and have fun. His approach wasn't anything like the other guys who tried to baffle me with BS. He seemed straightforward and honest, which attracted me more than his looks. Don't get me wrong. He was cute, clean, well-dressed, and appeared to have money. Why not give him a chance? No woman in her right mind wants to date a man who looks like a bum.

One night, he asked me directly why I was never with the same guy twice. I told him the truth. Each one treated me like a slut or expected sex for dating services. He laughed at my answer. He told me I appeared flippant, and that was why he hesitated to get to know me. He didn't want the rejection. I assured him I expected to be treated like a lady but had not found a man with the same notion. So, he asked me on a date, and I accepted.

After that night, we ventured out. We went on picnics, boat rides, the occasional dinner, and movie. It was hard not to fall for him because all he wanted was to dote on me. We married six months into the relationship. Never once did he give any indication that he had a severe issue with trust; never once did he abuse alcohol in front of me. I had seen him drink on many occasions, but he never showed a violent nature until after we married.

The first time I experienced his violence was after hugging a male friend in front of him. One evening, we decided to go out to eat at a new restaurant in town. While waiting for a table, my friend, Joe, came over to say hello. Joe was a man I'd known from high school, and I hadn't seen him since we graduated. I was very happy to see him and hugged his neck before introducing him to Sam.

After too many drinks, Sam accused me of sleeping with Joe, running around on him and having orgies behind his back with Joe and several others. Voicing my innocence only ignited his anger, causing him to punch me with his fist.

The accusations and violence escalated. One night, after I had been so badly beaten, my family retaliated and pursued prosecuting Sam for domestic violence. After that, there was no way I could justify reconciliation because I was afraid for my life, so I filed for divorce.

It took three months to finalize the divorce. It took just as long for me to physically heal from the injuries Sam inflicted upon me.

Until then, my parents had been clueless about my difficulties. They were upset about Sam's abuse and anxious for my divorce. Repeatedly, I heard my mother thank God that He had kept me alive. They stood with me through the dissolution of my marriage, praying my emotions could withstand the mental torment that Sam was determined to evoke.

Even with court orders prohibiting Sam from coming near me, fear drove Dad to have protective provisions installed in my apartment. All the door and window locks were changed. He even threatened to have an alarm system installed when I was determined to live alone. He said he couldn't sleep wondering if he or mom would find me dead after a night of Sam's drunken rages. I assured him I was okay and that I wouldn't allow anyone inside my apartment until I was sure it was safe. I promised to carry my phone to my door in the event it was Sam so I could immediately call 911. A restraining order was enforced, and if Sam came near me, I was to call the police right away.

My body healed during the three months it took for my divorce to be granted. Now I needed time to recover mentally and spiritually. Mom and Dad, with my good friends, the Carmen's, encouraged me to go back to church. They felt my new single life needed a different path this time. They were lovingly watching my every move as if they didn't trust my decisions, and it hurt me that they had lost confidence in my choices. I was becoming painfully aware of the consequences of running with the wrong crowd.

If they only knew how determined I was for change. I took their advice because I realized two happily married couples, devoted to each other, were trying to show me the right direction.

I was raised on firm foundations with good spiritual roots. Going back to church instead of getting involved with the singles' nightclub scene was a better choice. There were singles in church needing to associate with like-minded, morally inclined people. After getting my mind, will, and emotions healed again, I planned to join them. We needed God's care.

That next Sunday morning was beautiful, sunny, and warm. Everything screamed for me to stay home and delight in the day. I needed all the resolve I could gather to steer myself toward church instead of the swimming pool to soak in the sun. I had to focus on seeking the Son: his sunshine could wait until after service.

I had not expected the mental energy, physical effort, and courage required to go back to church. My mind and heart stayed focused while my feet dragged me along. I knew I needed comfort. The only kind of comfort Jesus provided.

While driving, condemnation crept in, making me ponder on what had happened. *Where did my life go wrong? Now I've screwed up twice. What is wrong with me?*

Almost late for service, I ran inside as praise and worship were ending. I found a seat in the rear of the sanctuary that made it easier to slip in unnoticed. Condemnation had made me paranoid, and I didn't need the added stress of being watched at that moment.

I was surprised the old church was the same as I remembered. The stained-glass windows were gorgeous. The pews were the same wooden, stuffed, and padded seats that held many of God's faithful every week. One thing wasn't the same—the pastor.

This new pastor was impressive. His message touched my heart— "The one and only thing we need is the love of God." Listening to this pastor, my heart opened up and absorbed just what it needed. I was like a sponge soaking up this feeling of acceptance. Was this love just from the pastor, or was it also from the people sitting here? As a child, I had enjoyed such joy and peace. I instinctively knew it had never left me I just allowed it to go dormant. I was the one who drifted away from the love.

Condemnation was relentless. I was guilt-ridden and mad at myself. As I sat there, listening to this loving message, I began to cry. Embarrassed by my tears, I quickly wiped them away and fought to keep the sadness at bay. I knew this was a breaking point as well as a starting point. With everything in me, I had to fight the urge to run. I needed to stay and learn to forgive myself and love myself again the way God loved me.

As the service was ending, I remembered something I'd learned as a child. Jesus prayed to God, and He asked the Father to keep the evil one at bay for us. When the service was over, I said a quick prayer asking God for the same. "Lord, come into my heart and please keep the evil one from stealing this message of love from me. If I'm going to heal, I'll need this love to stay with me."

———⋙∘⊙⊕⊙∘⋘———

"Ah! Did you hear that?" Jesus asked the Father. "She is asking for me. She wants me in her heart. She finally needs our help! I love this one so much. I'm so happy she's been recreated, born anew. I've been waiting so long to hear this request. My hands have been untied. Oh, the plans I have for her. She will be molded to be of great use and for our purpose."

God replied, saying. "This conversion you are planning is going to be very painful and confusing to her. But after I sought her heart, I can see what you mean. This one is very valuable to us and the kingdom."

———⋙∘⊙⊕⊙∘⋘———

Satan also heard her prayer, and he had an idea. "I may be prevented from stealing the knowledge of that message from her, but I can make her doubt that it is real. I know exactly what will make her lose confidence—the threat of being physically hurt again by her ex. Mental anguish alone will cripple her. Nothing

14

drastic, just enough fear to take her mind off the protection she has under God's love. The fear I'll cause will dominate her mind so much that nothing will be able to penetrate her thoughts for a while. Isn't fear my favorite tool after all?"

———⚬⚬⚬⚬⚬⚬⚬———

When I returned to my apartment, unease overcame me the moment I realized the front door was not locked. I thought *this can't be right! I'm too careful these days not to have made sure my front door was locked.* My heart thundered in my chest as doubt racked my body. My mind questioned my actions. How had I forgotten to set the alarm? I couldn't have. That was the one thing I was now in the habit of doing. An unnatural panic was overtaking me. The need to run screaming was overwhelming. My mental feet were running, but my physical feet were frozen to the ground, paralyzed. My inner voice was shouting loud and clear, but my throat choked back any sound. *Get a grip on yourself,* I thought. But I couldn't. Fear increased with the knowledge that something wasn't right. Was I alone? Was someone lurking in my apartment?

I needed help. I closed my eyes and gathered my courage. Then I commanded myself, "Move! Don't take one more step inside! Slowly back out of the apartment and run back to the SUV." Back in the SUV with the doors locked, I asked myself, "What should I do now?"

Immediately, the answer was within sight as I caught the view of my friends—the Carmen's—coming home from church. "I'll drive over and ask for help. I won't take a chance going into my apartment until they can come with me to check it out."

These two friends, Mark and Judy Carmen, have been my rocks. They had been so supportive lately. Now that I was single again, it was a bonus to have them living two houses down from my apartment.

"Hi, guys," I called out. "Could I ask a favor of you?"
"What's up?" Mark asked.

A little embarrassed, I answered. "When I got home, my front door wasn't locked. I'm scared someone broke in and may still be there. Mark, would you mind going in the house with me to see if everything is all right?"

"No problem," he said. "Come on; let's see what's going on. Get your cell phone out and be ready to call the cops if I suspect anything, okay?"

Rather than leave my car at their house, I drove it to the apartment while Mark and Judy walked over.

During the hair-raising ordeal, I realized fear was not the only emotion I was having. Twinges of jealousy struck as I watched them walk hand in hand. I thought, *why can't I have a great marriage like theirs?*

"Stop it!" I commanded myself. "These are two of the finest people I will ever meet. Judy has been my friend since grade school. I should be happy Mark came into the picture to make her life complete. Like peanut butter to jelly or a hand to a glove, they are two parts of a whole."

———ᴡᴡᴏꙮᴇꜰᴏꙮᴇꙮᴏᴏᴡᴡ———

Seeing Hope fight with her emotions, Jesus intervened. He wouldn't let Satan's trick of fear and doubt last. Again, He would use Judy to get Hope's attention back on track.

———ᴡᴡᴏꙮᴇꜰᴏꙮᴇꙮᴏᴏᴡᴡ———

After parking my SUV, I got out and looked for Mark and Judy. They were waiting for me on the porch. Judy hugged me as she spoke, "Hope, it's going to be okay. I saw you at church this morning. I know you heard the same message we did. You need to remember and put in practice what Pastor Craig said. Jesus, Himself, asked his Father to keep and protect us from the evil one. Remember? So, don't you let the devil get you all worked up. God loves you! Even if Satan uses threats of any kind to torment you, it won't last long. God's free gift of grace will give you the faith you need to see the Word work in your life."

"Amen, sister, preach!" I agreed. "Believe it or not, I even asked the Lord before leaving the church to keep the love alive in me. I know you are right. He will not let me down."

16

Joining arms, we walked in after Mark. Everything was exactly as I had left it that morning before church. The only thing different was the blinking light on my telephone to indicate a message. Fear poked at me again, making me wonder, *was this the ominous thing making me fearful?* I played the message, but we only heard someone breathing on the other end before hanging up—no words, nothing to give us a clue.

Seeing the fear in my eyes, Judy encouraged and tried to comfort me the best way she could by saying, "Hope, let God heal you from this constant fear. Not every phone call or knock on the door is going to be Sam. He has court orders to leave you alone. Now you have God on your side. Pour out your heart to Him. Ask Him specifically to protect and heal you. Then trust in Him. We'll help you keep focused so you can have faith in what you asked of Him."

"I don't know what I'd do if you two didn't live so close. You are really good friends, more like my family than mere friends. I love you," I said tearfully.

"It's okay," Judy said. "We understand. We know that you lived in hell, and it's going to take time for you to feel safe again. We love you too, and it makes us happy to be here for you. Call us if you need anything, promise?"

Then Mark spoke up and said, "I'll keep a better watch on your apartment, and I'll also alert some of our neighbors to be on guard. If we see Sam's vehicle or one that resembles his, we'll call the police. It's not a secret about you and Sam, so a neighborhood watch might be a good idea. Several have expressed concern about you anyway. I know they will help protect you. Will that make you feel better? Come over anytime you get anxious and need to talk. I'll disappear so you and Judy can talk privately."

Watching them leave, I felt waves of love and compassion washing over me. It was time to get a grip on my emotions. Time to do exactly what "Dr. Judy" recommended and lay my heart open to God.

Sitting down on the sofa, I placed my Bible in my lap and prayed. "Lord, I give up. I'm a mess. I need a complete overhaul—

spiritually, emotionally and physically. Will you teach me to trust and live the way you want me to live? I can't go on like this one more minute. Please help me! I've let myself go. I'm a coward living in fear of Sam. I'm unstable, and I've gotten fat and unhealthy trying to cover up these emotions. Help!"

I found that reading the Word on my own was enlightening. For some reason, I was obsessed with the book of Esther. I loved how Esther was groomed for twelve months, being taught kingdom principles. She endured extreme pampering before she met the king. This is just the way I'd like to meet Jesus—beautiful and knowing his will.

The day seemed to fly by. It was time for bed, and I hadn't even had a meal since breakfast. I'd been totally engrossed in reading the Word and enjoying it so much I hadn't been hungry. Wow, that was a first. I'm always fighting with myself not to eat too much, but today, eating never entered my mind. I was feeding on his Word!

Going to bed on an empty stomach was never a good idea for me. Hunger pains caused me to have nightmares the same as eating too much. I decided to make a sandwich and have a glass of milk, which shouldn't be too heavy to sleep on. I needed to rest after all the stress I'd suffered earlier in the day.

While eating my sandwich, I surfed the TV channels. I stopped flipping channels just in time to catch the last few minutes of Kenneth Copeland's *Believer's Voice of Victory* program. I heard a lady minister explaining to the audience how she sometimes visited places in her spirit. Especially at night, she said, while she was supposed to be asleep. She would visit people or places only to wake the next morning knowing the journey had been real and not a dream. She even had people remember seeing her at various places later telling her about it. Even though she was on a spiritual journey while her body was at rest, people in the natural had seen and talked with her. It sounded fascinating.

"I'd love to have that happen to me," I said out loud. Praying, I asked, "Lord, could it be possible for me to experience the same thing? If so, will you please make it happen tonight?"

Be careful what you ask for. I went on a journey all right. Not like the lady minister's, but one I will never forget. A prayer asked is a prayer answered.

Hearing this, the Holy Spirit knew this was His time to show up and to show out. He was excited. Looking up to Jesus and the Father, He said,

"It's about time. I've wanted to help this little one for so long."

"I know," Jesus replied. "Hope has needed us but wasn't taught to depend on us. Go teach her what it is really like to be born again. Use parables to show her she can increase in knowledge and faith."

"I can't wait!" He exclaimed. "Oh, the joy of being set free to work in my beloved's life."

Jesus said, "It's a new day. It's also time to confound those who didn't teach her to depend on us. Correct their thinking by showing them divorcees can have a happy life with me. Hope will be my example. Quickly let her experience the bond with us so she can join her mind, will, and emotions with our purposes. Mold her to serve as I have called her. I can urge, but it will be up to her to choose the path prepared. Make it easy for her to do so. Don't waste another second. Get started now."

———⁓⦿⧜⦿⧜⦿⧜⦿⧜⦿⧜⦿⧜⧜⦿⧜⦿⦿⧜⧜⧜⦿⧜⦿⦿⧜⦿⦿⦿⦿⦿⦿⦿⦿⦿⦿⦿⦿⦿⦿⦿⦿⧜⧜———

Unable to sleep, I thought, *why did I eat? I should have had the milk and left the sandwich alone. What is keeping me awake? I need sleep!*

While tossing, and turning, I saw a light on the bedroom wall. It looked like a candle flickering. Focusing on its shimmer, I noticed it was also moving. Then I heard his heavenly voice calling, "Hope, come to me. I want to give you peace and rest."

My logical mind was telling me I was just tired and confused, seeing things that couldn't exist; but my spirit was urging me to reach out to the light. Hadn't I told the Lord I was giving up? What did it hurt to reach for the light? Didn't Moses seek a burning bush? This had to be the Lord because my spirit was so excited.

Getting out of bed to focus more closely on the light, I felt like a cat chasing a light. Extremely excited and wide-eyed, I watched it move. As I stretched out my hand to make contact, an amazing thing happened. The light began to pulse brighter. The air around me felt like it was pushing me into the wall. At first, I didn't feel anything when connected with the light. My body felt fluid as the light sucked me into another dimension. Instantly, I was flying or falling or spinning head over feet. Then I got motion sickness from the speed within the dimension. My head felt dizzy and my stomach felt sick, so I closed my eyes. My eyes were closed, but my mouth was continually screaming. I was at the breaking point. While screaming, I mentally prayed, *Lord, I can't take this! I'm scared! Please stop this!*

"Trust me. It's almost over," I heard the voice reply.

I was mentally preparing for a splat. I just knew I was going to land so hard that there wouldn't be anything left of me. I would be like Humpy Dumpty for the Lord to put together again. I wouldn't be dead because He was with me. There was no way around it. I was about to know more pain.

Then I felt a caressing touch on my skin. I was afraid to look. I couldn't bear any more of this. A few seconds later, I landed gently on a smooth surface, descending softly by his tender yet strong hands. The propulsion causing me to fall stopped, and I was frozen in midair before He gently lowered me down. Grateful the fall was over, I opened my eyes. Everything was luminous. Before I stood up, I looked down at myself. What had happened? I was naked and covered in blood. "Oh, my God! I'm hurt. Help me, I'm bleeding!" I shouted.

"Hope, you are not hurt," I heard the voice say.

I looked around frantically for the one speaking to me and asked, "Where are you? Who are you? Where am I? Why am I here?"

As my eyes adjusted to the brilliance, I saw what appeared to be a man coming toward me. He was beautiful. From his waist upward, He glowed a yellow-orange color—bright, like forged metal. From his waist downward, it appeared He was on fire. The aura around Him was like a golden halo.

Awestruck, I knew immediately who was in front of me. "You're the Holy Spirit, aren't you?' I asked.

"Yes, love, I am," He said. "The Father and Son have sent me to you. You've conveyed your heart to us. So, I've been assigned to be your Comforter, Counselor, Helper, Intercessor, Advocate, Strengthener, and Standby. I'll remain with you forever if you let me."

I must have looked dazed. I could barely comprehend what I was seeing; let alone what I was hearing. "What?" was the only word I could force out of my mouth?

Sweetly and patiently, He went on to explain. "Hope, you've been given a great honor by Jesus. I was granted the opportunity to give you the actual experience of being born again in Him. Most people only get to know about it. You have physically experienced how it feels in the spirit.

Still flabbergasted and confounded, I could again only utter one word. "What?"

"Don't be afraid of me, Hope. I'm here to answer your questions and calm your fears. Now that you know who I am and that I'm here for you, it's time to tell you where you are, why you are naked and covered in blood."

I looked down at myself again. "Yuck!" Another one-liner.

What was wrong with me? Was I so dumbstruck and spellbound that I couldn't talk? I was full of questions, to the point of bursting.

I took a deep breath and blurted out, "Why am I lying here covered in blood and naked? If I'm not hurt, why am I bleeding?"

Laughing so hard that it shook his body, He said, "When I was told to show you your new birth experience, I couldn't help myself. I have the need for drama at times. I gave you this awesome spiritual experience with your physical body as if you were a baby covered in its mother's blood, naked and cast out into a bright area. Only you experienced falling instead of pushing into your new environment. The blood covering you is not yours or your mother's, it is the blood of Christ. You were reborn through Him." "It wasn't funny! It was terrifying!" I blurted out.

"I'm sorry, Hope. Please let me explain why I chose this method to give you revelation. You need to understand the difference between the two births so you can appreciate the love we have for you," He said apologetically.

I couldn't help it. In the flesh, I was a little offended. Not only was the experience terrifying, but He was laughing about it. I managed to say as sweetly as I could at that moment, "I want to know all I can, but may I please get cleaned up and put on clothes first?"

"All in good time. I'm here to make sure the process is genuine this time. Let me show you what I mean. Then you'll be ministered to," He explained.

I asked, "What do you mean 'this time'? I thought I was baptized into Jesus when I was twelve. I thought I was already born again."

Sweetly, He replied, "Hope, you only went through the motions, and you only got wet. All the kids at that age went through baptism because they felt it was expected. You knew about Jesus, but you never truly gave yourself to Him until today. You made Him Lord over your life. Let me show and explain to you what I mean."

He tried to show me visual examples through the Word. He directed my mind to scriptures about angels and heaven. My mind was still so confused, and I didn't understand. He showed me the example of when Joshua asked an angel if it were there for him or his enemy; the angel replied it was there only because of the Lord of angel armies. He tried to explain that all of heaven didn't understand why God loved and wanted mankind to exist, but because He was sovereign, they bowed and honored his command. Their confusion was talked about in the Psalms, through David, as they wondered why man existed and why God gave man his authority.

I felt like I was being force-fed something hard and inedible. I could not wrap my mind around the fact that before I was reborn, all of heaven only helped me because God commanded it. The next reference from verses in Ezekiel 16 confused and disturbed me. It was a vision from a heavenly viewpoint about babies being born in their natural state on earth, which to them was abhorrent and disgusting.

Uncontrollable tears flooded my face. I was so disturbed, realizing that I was abhorrent and disgusting to all of heaven.

Because of my reaction, the Holy Spirit had compassion on my state of mind and stopped his explanation. He said, "All that I am trying to explain is past tense. Heaven obeyed God even when they didn't agree or understand. Mankind was God's love. Therefore, everything had to honor Him. I'm trying to relay to you that all of creation never helped mankind unless commanded to do so. Before Jesus was sent, I moved over the earth. I watched over all human births. When I passed by each one, I commanded them to live!"

Somewhat comforted, I was now curious, so I asked, "What confused all of heaven so much? Why couldn't they see or understand your plan?"

"All of creation in heaven and on earth minister to the Word. Mankind was created from dust not Word. Man was given God's Word to use, but he wasn't spoken into existence from it. Jesus, the Word made flesh, changed that. Without the Word in you, they only saw you as a being with no life—dying or leprous. Anything without the Word was not immortal. Mortal beings and deeds smelled like death or menstrual rags. They were nothing but polluted garments or dead leaves. Mankind was a thing subject to the wind's will because it was not grounded in God's Word," He replied.

Unsure of what He was telling me, I asked, "The wind has access to me? What does that mean?"

"Before Jesus, Satan was the prince of the wind. He used the curse of the law to toss mankind around and destroy because you weren't connected to God's grace. The curse, like the wind, can move you so far away from God's love that you self-destruct. Creation didn't see or hear any reason to intervene until Jesus.

Now, when the sons of God take their place, all creation responds." Then he gave me that scripture reference in Romans 8. I was still concerned, so I asked, "Am I okay? Didn't you say I was?"

"Don't fret, love. You've been born again. Look at yourself. You're covered in the redeeming blood of Christ—born from his side, made to partake in his grace. You've been freed from the curse of the law. That's why I wanted you to appear like a newborn baby, why you are naked, covered in blood, and cast out again into an open area. You've been reconnected to God and now mature enough for love. You can understand through Revelation's example the covenant blood, and you've been enabled with God's favor. Now you have us forever," He explained.

"Can the wind take me away from God? Can it separate us? Do I need to fear the wind when it blows again?" I asked.

"The wind will test you, Hope. You might not even know when it tries. From this point on, all you have to do is stand firm and declare verbally the name of Jesus. He is your root, the connector that gives back your relationship with God. It will be as if you had never left his kingdom," He explained. "Now it's time to clean up." The Holy Spirit then continued, "When we heard your prayers this evening, we knew you were maturing and ready for love. I asked the Father and Son if I could spread my skirt over you and cover your nakedness. Then we could pledge our troth to you and enter into a covenant with you. You would become ours—the Father's, Son's, and mine. We are one and want you to be one with and in us.

If you agree, I will have you washed with water, thoroughly washing away any filth from your mother's blood, and you will be anointed with the oil of God's grace. Now, Hope, I'm asking if you are ready to accept this offer and be ours?"

My answer was a firm yes. I'd never felt so humbled in my life. Then I went on to say, "I've wanted this with all my heart.

Please take over my life and show me the true meaning of what it is to be loved."

"It is finished! The vows have been spoken," He said. "I see a heart change. I am certain that you are truly born again."

His response astounded me. Did my ears really hear that? It sounded like we exchanged wedding vows. *Those were some of the most beautiful words I'd ever heard*, I thought.

All in Time

I had to change the emotionally charged atmosphere. I asked, "When do we start? I don't want to feel alone anymore. Please let me experience the comfort you promise in the Bible. Will it take long?"

"Here with me, time does not exist like it does for you in the natural. One day is like a thousand years, and a thousand years may seem like one day. It all depends on where your focus is," he responded. "Do you remember how time flew while you were reading the Word yesterday? Depending on your focus and determination, this process will seem like seconds, or it may seem like years. We know you are of flesh and need to rest and resume your obligations to the natural realm, so the process of your conversion will have to be done in stages." He paused then asked gently, "For now, I feel that it has been enough for you to see you are in my care. Look at yourself. What do you see?"

Looking down at my hands and body, I saw that I had been completely cleaned of any trace of the blood. My nakedness was covered by a white robe that appeared to be very sheer silk—dazzling, iridescent, and beautiful. Then it dawned on me; I never saw or felt anything happening to me. When did this happen? How did it happen without my knowledge? Gasping from excitement, I blurted out, "How? When? This is lovely!" I ran my hands down the robe.

"When did you clean me? And how did you dress me without me feeling it?" Laughing, He answered, "Sweet Hope, ministering angels have been all around you since you agreed to the terms. They didn't remove the blood of Christ. They rubbed it in with the oil of grace. The robe you have over you is our skirt. It is woven with covenant blessings from a rainbow. Do you like it?"

"Yes, oh yes! I love it! Do I get to keep it?" I asked excitedly.

"It is yours for eternity, to be like a canopy of divine love and protection—a royal covering stretched over you. It is a spiritual hedge of protection. I want you to always remember that this robe will be over you even in the physical realm when you return. Your natural eyes will not be able to see it; nor will you be able to touch or feel it. You must trust that it is there at all times," He informed me emphatically.

A little confused, I said, "Thanks for this robe. But it sounds like you're sending me back to reality now. I thought you were going to teach me all things and show me the way to understanding love."

As he was fading away, I heard his voice softly saying, "All you have to do is seek me, love. I'm here, and I'll never forsake you. Communicate with me anytime. You may not hear my voice, but you'll be able to sense me near. Seek my face within the Word when questions arise, and there you'll find me. We will have many more experiences like this, so don't worry. Though you are an adult, Hope, you are still very young and immature in some areas. Let me take you through training slowly. The more you learn, the more knowledge with understanding will be given. For now, your time here has ended."

———∿∽⊙⋆⊙⊙⋆⊙∽∿———

"**W**hat is that noise?" *Beep! Beep! Beep!*

"Monday morning! Ugh!" Rousing, I realized the sound was the alarm clock. It was time to get ready for work. Sitting on the edge of the bed, trying to gather my thoughts, I saw the empty milk glass and plate from the prior evening on my nightstand. Under the plate was my Bible.

Had I dreamed I went to heaven or was it a journey like the lady minister's? No, I was certain I had been in a place like heaven. I looked at the pajamas I had on; they were a far cry from the majestic robe I had been given.

In the back of my mind, I kept hearing, *it's still here, Hope. Trust in me.*

Okay, I needed some coffee. I needed to get my head together. First, coffee then a shower then to work. I had to focus. Duty called. I still had to pay the bills. Reality stank!

While waiting for the coffee to perk, I took my Bible and turned to its concordance. I have to look up the word *skirt*. Wasn't that what the Holy Spirit said the robe was? His skirt?

I found the scripture verse I was looking for. They were the same words the Holy Spirit had spoken.

'Now I passed by you again and looked upon you; behold, you were maturing *and* at the time for love, and I spread My skirt over you and covered your nakedness. Yes, I plighted My troth to you and entered into a covenant with you, says the Lord, and you became Mine.' Ezekiel 16:8 (amp)

"Wow! I've never seen this before. I wasn't dreaming. The Holy Spirit was telling me that I was ready for love. This skirt was my covering, mine!" I said happily.

Taking my unfinished cup of coffee to the bathroom, I undressed to shower and reflect further. I was naked but covered in blood. I felt sticky and funny. Then it dawned on me; I was naked in the presence of the Lord. I was stark naked! Horrified, I turned to look at my reflection in the mirror. I saw a short, fat, pale and unhealthy-looking body. What a presentation I must have made. I was a far cry from what He expected I bet.

"Time to go on a diet. Now! Maybe even start walking a bit. These legs are cellulite magnets. What did He think? My gut is sticking out farther than my breasts. I'm ugly. What makes me think that I'm ready to meet Jesus looking like this?" I was worried.

In the shower, I focused on last night's experience. The first thing I remembered was the flickering light. Next, being sucked into the light, flipping and spinning while screaming my head off. Then I remembered landing softly in this bright area, naked and covered in blood. That's when I'd heard his voice for the first time.

The sound of his voice had been so soothing and loving. His voice had been very masculine, low and deep but soft, with power and authority. Then I realized I hadn't been afraid of Him. He had made me feel at ease from the first moment. Oh my, I remembered. I had even been mad at Him. I'd been mad at God! Oh no! No one should ever be mad at God! What had I been thinking?

He hadn't been mad at me. He'd laughed and said He had a flair for drama. It was all coming back to me. He'd wanted to show me what it was like to be born in the Spirit. He'd wanted to teach me the knowledge of love and what it is like to be loved. He'd asked if I would allow Him to teach me. He'd asked for my permission. He was a complete gentleman. Awesome!

I had been cleaned up and given the most beautiful garment I'd ever seen. Yea, I had my prayer answered. I had an experience like the lady on television. Would I have another? He said there would be more to come. When?

After showering, I was more attentive with my makeup. I ironed my clothes, taking care to look more groomed. Next time, I wanted my appearance to be more presentable.

I've always eaten before going to work, but today, I decided to skip the toast and jelly. Instead, I settled for just coffee. The weight had to go.

What would I take with me for lunch? Think healthy. Looking in the fridge, I saw very little that could be considered healthy. All I had was eggs, bagels, cheese, butter, jelly, leftover pizza, and milk.

I'll go get a salad and fruit at the market down the street at lunchtime, I thought.

It wasn't long into my morning when my stomach growled and complained from lack of food. I felt like I was starving, and my head hurt. I was shaking and weak when lunchtime came. Once I got into the SUV and headed for the market, I was so overcome by hunger that I couldn't resist the first fast-food stop. Ordering two sandwiches and a milkshake, I ate with a ravaging appetite. After stuffing myself, the guilt set in. Condemnation was back!

I wanted to puke! "I hate myself." I berated. I have to get control over this eating. I can hardly move, and I know in a few minutes I'll be sleepy. "Lord, please help."

—⁓⦿⦿⦿⁓—

"What fun I'm going to have now," Satan said to himself. "She's let me get into her head a bit. She'll hate herself for failing Him."

With a raspy voice, he spoke into her ear. "Hope, look what you did. You'll never be worthy of Jesus's presence. He desires for you to be slim, fit, and healthy. At this rate, it's going to take you forever. You can't even get to the market or say no to a hamburger. Weak-willed and powerless, what makes you think you are so special and that you are loved? Didn't he promise to help you?" Then he laughed and said, "Where is your god now?"

———ᴡᴡ⋯ᴏᴏᴇʀᴏᴏʀᴏ⋯ᴡᴡ———

The Holy Spirit witnessed the mental anguish Hope put herself through that morning, and it made Him sad. He was learning that her fears stemmed from a severe lack of self-confidence. They loved her like she was. He would have to teach her that appearances mattered, but it wasn't what made them love her. Plus, she needed to be taught who really hated her—their mutual enemy, Satan. He was the source of everything evil and was only out to kill, steal, and destroy.

He was going to untwist many lies from the enemy. The first to untwist was her mental vision of herself. She needed to know they weren't looking at her physical faults. Those sins were covered by the blood, and God doesn't look at them any longer.

She also had twisted ideas about health because she had been programmed from an early age that men preferred skinny women. He had a tangled mess to unravel. He had to show her their love was unconditional.

———ᴡᴡ⋯ᴏᴏᴇʀᴏᴏʀᴏ⋯ᴡᴡ———

Disgusted with myself, I tried to focus on work. Sitting at my computer, I began to yawn, and I had to fight sleep. *This is torture*, I thought.

Then I saw the candlelight again. It was the same blinking little light, but it was on my cubicle wall, not at home. Could it be? Is it time? "Please, Lord, I'm ready," I begged, excited.

Reaching out, praying it would take me, I touched it. Just like before, it sucked me in. This time was different. I didn't fall, flip, spin, nor land anywhere; I was standing in the bright room. Out of fear, I immediately looked down at myself. I had taken care with my appearance that morning, so I hoped I was at least dressed. But no, I was naked again, not a stitch on.

Where's your robe little one?" I heard Him ask.

"At the laundry!" I responded, hoping to be funny. "I don't know what I've done with it, sir."

Responding back to me, He said. "Hope, let me tell you where it is. The devil has it."

"What? I didn't give it to him. How does he have it and why?" I asked, scared.

"It is a very prized possession. He stole it from you after your lunch. Do you remember belittling yourself? That allowed him to take it from you while laughing in your face." He continued, "I was there with you the whole time. I've been watching you from the moment you left me. When you woke up this morning a little confused about our meeting, I watched you fret."

"I'll never leave you, Hope. I'm your Comforter and your helper. I'll show you how to love yourself. But first, you need to know with certainty that we love you just the way you are," He informed me lovingly. "You are letting the enemy cause you to doubt and fear. Our enemy is your enemy. He is the devil. He hates you because we love you. He'll use your thoughts to trick you then use those very actions to make you hate yourself. Remember that!"

Crying, I said, "I'm so sorry. I don't understand. You must be mad at me for losing the robe."

Snapping his fingers, I was covered in the robe again. "See, Hope. Even though the devil may take this robe from you, He can't keep it. It was God's gift to you and for you only. We love you, and we are not mad at you. My job is to revamp your thinking. After the fall of Adam and Eve, mankind has never been perfect. That is the reason Jesus was sent. God sees you now through the Son. In his blood, you are beautiful, no matter how you look in the natural. He sees perfection because He sees His son's blood on you. You no longer see the blood, but it was rubbed into you, remember? But never fear love. God sees it, and so do we."

Happy now that I had the robe back on, I asked Him, "Who is the we you are referring to?"

Smiling, He told her, "They are the Father, Son, and me, with all creation. You are now living in the grace of God, in His favor and blessing. Our journey together will allow me to show you why Jesus came. This will be the washing by the Word I referred to earlier. You're going to have to wait for a while longer. You have to return, so our time has to end. Oh, and next time you want to eat healthy, look for the food God told Noah to eat after he got off the ark. Everything you need to know is between the two covers of your Bible. I'll show you how to properly divide the truth from lies. You must eat to live. Don't live to eat. I love you, and I'll see you soon."

———— ~~°∘♋○♋∘°~~ ————

Hearing someone call my name, I was startled out of my trance. "Yes? What do you need?" I asked, hoping to sound alert and focused.

It was Frank, my co-worker, wanting to know if I had a binder he could use for a project.

"Sure, I have one in my desk. Is a one-inch binder big enough?" I asked.

After Frank left my office, I used my computer to Google a biblical search engine to look up the word *food*. I needed to know what the Holy Spirit meant about food. What did God tell Noah to eat? To my surprise, there were thousands of references. To narrow the search, I looked for the word only in the book of Genesis.

There it is! I found it, I thought. Just as the Holy Spirit advised, I found God's instructions to Noah about eating after leaving the ark. He should eat any kind of meat, green vegetables, and plants. Jotting down the scripture verse so I could study it later, I made a mental note of what I needed. I'd go to the market down the street when I got off work to load up on lean meat, vegetables, fruits, and whole grains. Do plants include grains and fruit? They were both plants, weren't they?

Then I heard that raspy voice again. *Studying the Word on company time? You're cheating them and lying about working, Hope. Stealing and lying are sins, don't you know? You'll be punished because the Ten Commandments clearly states, "Thou shall not steal, thou shall not lie,"* he said mockingly.

"Get out of my head, you creep! You are not taking my robe again!" I shouted out loud.

"What?" Frank asked from the other side of the adjoining cubicle.

"Nothing. I was talking to myself," I answered.

Putting the piece of paper in my purse, I mentally justified my actions by saying in a whisper, "I give this company my personal time all during the week. It seems I work fifty hours instead of a forty each week. So, if I take a break from time to time, it doesn't hurt anybody or steal from the office. I've already accrued the time."

———ᴡᴡ∾ᴏᴗᴇᴛᴏᴏᴛᴇᴗᴏᴗᴡᴡ———

Angry, Satan said to himself, "Think you know what you're doing now, do you? Think again! I'm not finished yet. The rest of this day and all night are mine, and I'm going to show you what love is! Your memories are mine, and I'll destroy you with them."

Going away to work out his plan, he gathered her memories to review. Which ones could he use to keep her fear alive? He examined the memories that gave her recurring problems. Each time he reviewed them, he saw one that stood out and frightened her most. It kept repeating itself—her fear of Sam. Nothing or no one could jolt her into the dance of terror better than his puppet, Sam Anderson. Why not use Sam again? This time, it wouldn't be a suggestion of torment but the actual person who causes her agony. I will arrange for Hope to come face-to-face with Sam again. That should stir emotions not yet dealt with and destroy her for sure. "I love using people against each other." Leaving his sanctuary, he went off singing, "Division, division what a wonderful game."

The Thorn

With my food list in hand, I was excited about shopping and then cooking for myself. I checked the clock to see how soon I could start this new venture in my life. My new plan was designed by God long ago. I should eat to live, not live to eat. Who would have thought to begin in Genesis for instruction on what to put in your mouth? Even though I messed up at lunch, I was determined to get it right. I had less than an hour to begin again.

The local market wasn't a fancy supermarket, but it had the basics and was close to home. I entered, excitably steering my shopping cart toward the produce aisle first. The smell of the fresh items was intoxicating. "Why can't I enjoy the smell of this wonderful bounty given to us by God just as much as I love the smell of baked goods? I'm going to have to remember the signals of temptation and steer my nose to this awesome aroma from now on. I'm determined to love this new plan."

After loading up on apples, bananas, and peaches, I wheeled to the vegetable section. What appealed? I loved cabbage and broccoli, and I grabbed a head of each; then I placed carrots, lettuce, onions, and tomatoes in the buggy. These would come in handy if I want a salad or sandwich. Wait a minute. Were salads healthy if you put dressing on them? Dressing wasn't listed in the food group given to Noah. Ugh! Confusing! I decided to eliminate salads for now. I'd have to stick to whole foods until I was sure.

Meats were more of a challenge. I needed to choose those that didn't take long to cook, or I'd lose interest. Cooking for me had to be fun but fast. I needed to focus on quick meals. Fish fillets were a good idea. I was in the frozen foods to get the fish when I also noticed precooked chicken and steak fajita strips. Wonderful! These were just what I'd need for a quick meal.

I was happy with my selections, so I headed for the checkout. While unloading, I heard a familiar voice say, "Who are you cooking for? All this fancy food must be for someone special."

My heart almost stopped. It was Sam. Unable to run because I was trapped by my shopping cart in front and him in the back of me, I had no choice but to turn and respond the best way I could. "No one. I needed groceries for myself."

Out of habit from nights of abuse, I took a deep breath to determine if he had been drinking. Right now, he didn't smell like alcohol, but it was still early in the afternoon. Most times, he would be saturated by 7:00 p.m.; it was only 5:30 p.m. now. Oh, how I remembered the stink of beer on his breath after work. It made my stomach turn. It was sour, foul, and nasty-smelling. Right now, I didn't smell anything. Whether he was drinking or not, in my eyes, he was a drunk—and a violent one at that.

Then he said hatefully, "You don't cook for yourself. You like junk food. You must be entertaining."

"Leave me alone, Sam! Mind your own business," I said.

Trying to ignore him, I paid the cashier and strode out of the market as fast as I could. That's when he grabbed my arm. "Wait, we need to talk!" he said.

I screeched loudly, "No we don't! Don't make me scream for help! You're still under a court order, remember? You're not to get within one hundred yards of me! I'll do it, Sam. I mean it. I'll scream. Leave me alone!" I yanked my arm free, threw money at the cashier for my groceries, and practically ran to the SUV. I sped out of the parking lot as fast as I could without breaking any laws. I was shaking badly from just seeing him.

Panicking, I sped home to lock up. I did the one thing Sam hated most—embarrassing him in public. He would surely be in pursuit. I needed to expect his unnatural courage through alcohol and anger.

———ᴡᴡ◦ᴏᴇ❦ᴏᴏ❦ᴇ◦ᴏ◦ᴡᴡ———

The Holy Spirit kept trying to get her attention, but she was too panic-stricken. He blinked the light; he tried to talk to her. "Call on me, Hope!" Other than knocking her down and giving her an experience such as Paul's described in scripture, he couldn't get her to change focus.

36

When I got home, I kept fretting. "I hope he isn't following me. What am I going to do? He had that look! I just know from seeing his reactions that he wants to hit me. Why? What did I ever do to him to make him think such horrid things about me?"

I knew I had to get a grip on this fear. "Calm down, you're divorced. He is no longer a threat to you," I kept saying.

I knew he wasn't supposed to be a threat, but controlling that fear wasn't the same. I had to hurry, get inside under lock and key, and get these emotions in check.

In the apartment, as I unpacked the groceries, I reviewed the past. My mind started playing my memories back like a horror movie in my head. The mental screenplay started as I was putting the fish away. I relived the last time I tried to cook fish. Fish was on the menu for dinner the night Sam brutally beat me, the last time he would strike me. The beating almost killed me. It was the breaking point of my marriage, the proverbial straw that broke the camel's back. If I hadn't divorced him, my parents were going to kill him. No way was I returning to a life of hell.

⎯⎯⎯〰️ᴑᴐᴇᴦᴑᴑᴦᴇᴐᴑ〰️⎯⎯⎯

Satan was beside himself with laughter. He had her now, and he was letting her milk those memories for all they were worth. Pain, sorrow, fear, and torment were his specialty. "Wonderful!" Like all the others he'd tormented, she was her own worst enemy. He didn't have to say or do anything. She was doing a good job terrorizing herself. Her own emotions were making her unstable.

⎯⎯⎯〰️ᴑᴐᴇᴦᴑᴑᴦᴇᴐᴑ〰️⎯⎯⎯

When I'm nervous, I eat. At that moment, I didn't care. I just grabbed food. I ate a peanut butter and jelly sandwich, washing it down with a Coke. I was allowing my mind to revisit horrible memories of that last beating. I couldn't stop.

The movie in my head played on as I remembered the day. I was shopping for a few supplies when I saw a beautiful red sweater on the sales rack. It had been marked down from $25 to $3; what a deal. I just couldn't resist the purchase. I loved the sweater the moment I saw it. Plus, I was being thrifty. I also needed oil to fry fish for Sam that evening and decided to also pick up a cake. He loved coconut cake, and I was determined to have a romantic evening. It had been a few weeks since he had hurt me. He was trying to be nice as if he were trying to change. I was happy again.

He would always hate himself after hurting me. The next day, he'd act like a repentant puppy. He'd beg me to forgive him and try to make me happy. Each time, like a fool, I'd forgive him and tell him things would work out. Why hadn't I left when Mama warned me the first time he hit me. She'd said, "Respect yourself. He doesn't. No man should hit you and have you around the next day."

My thoughts continued with more about that evening. I'd been excited and in a hurry to start dinner. I unpacked the groceries, but I forgot to take the sweater into the bedroom. I left it lying on the kitchen table when I went to change clothes. I put on my old jogging suit and went back to the kitchen, eager to start dinner. My plan was to change into a nice outfit after I finished cooking. I wasn't ready for Sam to come home so soon. I had just started the oil warming to fry the fish when he arrived. The smell of alcohol came in the back door before him. I remembered my heart lurching and sweat breaking out on my brow. Oh no, he was drinking again.

I knew I was in trouble. Every nerve in my body was on edge. I remembered trying to keep my voice calm and words sweet so I wouldn't ignite his temper. He could get angry so fast over so little.

Trying to alter the ominous atmosphere, I said as calmly and lovingly as I could, "I'm making one of your favorite meals tonight and also bought you a coconut cake."

I was hoping to make him feel special. Depending on what was making him agitated, sometimes doting on him diffused his anger. Wrong move! Paranoia kicked in, and accusations took over his mouth. "What did you do? Why all the fuss?" he demanded.

His facial expression changed the instant he saw the bag on the table. He turned into a monster. "What is this? You have been spending my money on whore clothes?" he yelled.

"No, I found that sweater on sale and liked it," I replied.

"Who were you planning to impress with it? It wasn't me, or you'd be wearing it! Look how you're dressed for me. In old sweats!" he snapped.

"Take this thing back to the store now! If you didn't buy it for my eyes, then no one will see you in it!" he spits out.

"It only cost $3. I'd feel foolish taking it back," I tearfully replied.

"If you won't take it back, it's going in the trash," he said. He took it out of the sack and ripped it in pieces. Then he threw it at me. "There, whore! You have no sweater for your boyfriend to see!" he screamed.

"I don't have a boyfriend, Sam. I promise I've done all this for you," I exclaimed.

Without warning, the blows from both of his fists pummeled my head. Stumbling backward, my side slammed into the stove as my arm bumped the pan of hot oil still simmering on the stove. The pan was at smoking point, and the impact caused the hot oil to spill over my midsection. Screaming in pain from the burns as well as the blows to my head, I dropped to the floor sobbing. Infuriated, he began kicking me repeatedly. I felt a boot hit my back then my leg and stomach, each kick bringing sharper pain. My screams must have angered him because the more I screamed, the louder he screamed and the more he lashed out with his feet and his fists.

Suddenly, there was pounding on the back door. "Clayton County Police!" I heard a man shout.

"Help me!" I screamed.

Instantly, the door crashed inward. They grabbed Sam and pinned him against a wall. He was swearing at the top of his lungs. "Arrest that whore! That unfaithful whore!"

I was vaguely aware of Judy's husband, Mark, standing over me. I welcomed the numbing darkness overtaking me. I awoke in

39

the hospital. Hours later, I was admitted to a room. The family was gathered around me when I completely regained consciousness. A few minutes later, a doctor came in. He informed me that I had been burned and had several broken ribs, a broken nose, and what appeared to be a bruised kidney.

They'd know more after X-rays and tests results were returned.

"I can't see," I told him.

"That's caused by your broken nose. Your face took a severe beating, and your eyes are swollen shut," the doctor explained.

"Am I going to recover?" I asked.

"In time," he said sweetly and proceeded to praise Mark. "You are very fortunate your friend heard you screaming, or things could have been a lot worse." "My friend?" I asked.

"Your neighbor, Mr. Carmen, heard you screaming while he was walking his dog tonight. He used his cell phone to call the police for you. I think he and his wife are in the waiting area if you'd like to speak with them," he told me.

"Yes, please," I said.

When Mark and Judy came in my room, he shared how the police instructed him not to interfere but to wait on them. "I wanted to go in and beat the tar out of Sam, but they told me to wait on them. They'd be there soon. When they broke in and I followed, I couldn't believe the shape you were in. After the police called the ambulance, I ran to take the dog home and get Judy. We followed the ambulance and called your parents."

As tears ran down my face, I recalled just how much it hurt, but I was so grateful to have wonderful friends.

My mental movie stopped. My mind returned to reality abruptly as headlights flashed across my window from the driveway. Panic jarred me out of my trance. Full of adrenaline, I ran to the door, making sure it was locked. Remembering my promise to Dad, I grabbed the phone and had my thumb poised on the speed dial for the police.

Was this Sam? Lord, I hope not! I can't face him again. It's too soon. I knew without a doubt that he would be drunk and angry.

Out of a stress-induced habit and no particular focus, I mouthed to the Holy Spirit. "Lord, I'm scared!"

My heart was pounding so loudly; I couldn't hear a car door closing outside. If I heard anything at all, I was calling 911, even if it wasn't Sam. I wasn't taking any chances. I'd explain later if I was wrong. Safety is everything. For what seemed like hours rather than minutes, I realized no one was getting out of the vehicle. I didn't hear a door open and close. Gathering my courage to look out the window, I saw a car slowly back out of the driveway and go away.

Could it have been Sam? Had he reconsidered coming after me? I hoped it was a stranger and that I was just blowing this all out of proportion. Whoever it was had gone. But my heart was still in my throat. My head hurt. My hands were shaking.

High on adrenaline, I couldn't stop pacing from the front door to the back, fearful that Sam might burst into my apartment any moment. It was late, and I needed to go to bed, but I was too frightened.

About 1:00 a.m., I calmed down enough to go to the bedroom. Usually, when Sam drank, he'd pass out around 11:00 p.m. "Maybe I've worked myself up for nothing. I'm so tired," I said to myself.

Fully clothed and still wearing my shoes, I lay on the bed, tossing and turning as I replayed my past over and over in my head. When I finally dozed off, the *beep, beep, beep* of my alarm clock woke me up. It had only been two hours since I'd last looked at the clock. *I can't go to work this tired. I'm a mess, physically and emotionally*, I thought. I legally declared that I needed a sick day. I either needed to stay awake long enough for Joan to get to work, or I could call her at home. She was my friend before becoming my supervisor, so I decided I'd call her at home. She was fully aware of my past. Then I could go back to bed.

I knew Joan's phone number by heart. When she answered the phone that early in the morning, she was concerned, but she understood. I told her what had happened after work the previous day and why I hadn't slept. Compassionately, she agreed to have my workload covered and told me to let her know how I was doing that afternoon.

Before I rolled back into bed, I changed into my pajamas. I couldn't sleep well in my clothes. Now that it was daylight and I was calmer, comfort was an issue. When I sat on the bed, my attention was drawn to my Bible. Comfort had been lying on my nightstand all along. Help had been with me, but I didn't call on Him. This wonderful book appeared to be pulsing like a beacon of light. Emotionally drained, I burst into tears. "I did it again, Lord! He has my robe again! I just gave it away. Will I ever learn? When I wake up, please help me get it back. Please don't be mad at me."

Help Comes Running

I couldn't sleep after condemning myself. I lay in bed, fuming and frustrated. The Bible seemed to have accusing eyes. I looked at it and said, "Okay, already. I'll pick you up and read you!"

I sat up, turning on the bedside lamp for better light. When the light hit the opened book, the words *seek first* slammed into my eyes. Those two words were like a punch in the face. It felt like being spiritually spanked. Hadn't the Holy Spirit said to seek Him? Not making time for Him was my biggest problem. He sought me. Now I was going to seek Him.

I had an idea. I needed a vacation. I would call Joan and ask if I could take a week off from work. I wouldn't tell her the real reason was going on a spiritual vacation with the Holy Spirit. I needed training to be better equipped to face life. Condemnation stepped in again and said, "You've taken so much time off work lately."

I answered this time, "I have to try. Nothing lost, nothing gained. My training has to come first."

The spirit of condemnation kept nagging my mind, causing me to hesitate. The longer I waited to ask, the more nervous I became to receive Joan's answer to my leave request. It had been about an hour since I'd spoken with her. She would be at work by now and could check my leave balance on her computer. All I needed to do was call. Why was I scared?

———ᴡᴏᴏᴏ⌖ᴏᴏᴏᴏ———

There was a heavenly meeting concerning Hope. Jesus laid out his plan for the Holy Spirit. He explained the entire plan for Hope. "She has obtained our favor, and I've made arrangements for her to have time away from work. The time she requests will not be what she's expecting. Remind her that time is not an issue in the spirit realm. Much more can be accomplished here than in the natural. When she arrives, make sure her spiritual eyes and ears are fully open. Let her see and hear everything. I have called her to be an Intercessor, so she will eventually need to know what is in store for her. It is important that we don't let her know at first what our plans are. Let her get a feel of it on her own. She has to commit to becoming chosen. I know she will. She'll fit into the position without even knowing she is doing it. When she is ready, we'll let her know how extensive the job can be."

———⁓⁓•◦⟨◦⟩◦•⁓⁓———

I picked up the phone and called the office. My hands were shaking, but why? Joan was my friend.

When she finally answered, I nervously said, "Hi, Joan. I'm sorry I called you so early this morning. I was so tired I didn't think I could stay awake long enough for you to get to the office." "How are you?" she asked.

"I'm better, but I need to ask a favor," I responded.

"Sure, if I can help. What is it?" she replied.

"May I have a week off? I need to get away and regroup. My head is not where it needs to be. I'm having trouble focusing. Could you scan my accrued leave to see if I qualify?" I asked.

"Let me look," she said. "I don't think you can take personal days without prior notice. I'll have to read the company policy. It will take me a few minutes to gather the information, so let me call you back."

Time seemed to stand still as I waited for her to call back. While I waited, I kept chanting, "All good things come to those who wait. All good things come to those who wait." Was that in the Bible? I would check later.

When the phone rang, it startled me.

"I have some bad news, Hope. You can't take personal time without a written request at least a week in advance. However, you can have three sick days without a doctor's note. Will that be enough?" she asked.

"Will you approve time off for me as sick leave?" I asked.

"Since you requested sick leave this morning, I can extend it for two more days without needing a doctor's written statement. If you want more time, I'll work with you, but it has to follow company guidelines," she replied.

"I'll take the next few days to recuperate. Thanks, Joan, for everything," I said.

Okay, time to get started, I thought.

As hard as I tried, every line I read seemed to blur. I was so tired. I really wanted to beat this fear and face my worries. "Lord, I'm so sorry. I can't stay awake. I feel like such a failure. I've taken time off to be with you and seek your face like you told me. My eyes are not cooperating, and my mind is mush," I prayed. As soon as I closed the Bible, I was asleep.

———— ⚬⚬⚬⚬⚬⚬⚬⚬ ————

"Hi there," He said.

My eyes opened, and there He was standing in front of me. "Where am I?" I asked Him.

"You're in the kingdom of heaven. Your spirit is with me while your body is sleeping," He explained.

"Why didn't I remember that from the other day? My body was rested after the first time we met. When the alarm woke me up the next morning, I felt so refreshed," I said.

"We had to let your body take over. Your mind was everywhere except where it needed to be. Sweet Hope, do you know you've been fighting me all this time. From the minute you panicked yesterday, I've been trying to get your attention, but you resisted. When you realized this morning that you needed to seek us first, we were so pleased," He stated.

"I'm sorry. I keep letting you down. I gave away my robe again, didn't I?" I inquired.

"Look down, Hope. What do you see?" He asked.

I just knew from the past two experiences that I'd be naked. But I looked down anyway. My robe was lying at my feet. It hadn't disappeared. It was still there. I bent over and put it on.

"You didn't give it away this time. It fell off of your body because you didn't trust in what it represented," He replied.

45

"I don't understand," I said. "I want to understand, so I requested time off from work to be with you. Only one problem— I don't have much time, and we need to hurry."

He laughed at my dilemma and replied. "I can do all things. I raised Jesus from the dead in three days. What makes you think I can't teach you what you need in less time? In God's kingdom of heaven, time doesn't exist, remember?"

I was so relieved. My joy was immense. He knew how much time I had. There was an answer for me even before I said anything. "I don't know what to say. When do we start?" I responded.

"First I need to touch you, Hope. I've been ordered to give you spiritual sight and hearing that will enable you to see and hear everything in our kingdom. Be warned, though. Spiritual sight and hearing are not the same as spiritual insight. You've been granted an ability to see beyond human understanding into our reality. From now on, comprehension will be easier for you. The Lord Himself has called you for a specific purpose. You are taking the first steps of the process. Since you were born, this time has been specifically orchestrated just for you. We've been waiting for you to respond," He disclosed.

I must have looked horrified because He said, "Come here, child. I'm not going to harm you. You're going to have a blessing bestowed upon you that few have ever been given."

I stepped closer and felt immense power radiating from Him. He reached out, taking me by the shoulders, drawing me into his chest. I closed my eyes. I wasn't afraid. I was amazed and honored this was happening to me. He smelled so good. His scent was like a drug of joy overtaking me. I've never experienced such pure love surging through me. A mother's love couldn't even compare. Every person on the planet needs to feel this kind of happiness and peace beyond explanation.

I must have relaxed too much because he scooped me up like a child in his arms. "Open your new eyes, Hope," He said.

The colors were so vivid! The sights were awesome! Nothing was dirty. Everything was pure and dazzlingly beautiful, with such serenity. Then I saw an angel! I was seeing an angel! Looking around, I could see hundreds more. They were everywhere. So, beautiful! All alike, yet none the same. We were in a palace made of pearl, ivory, gold, and silver. The floor we were standing on was sparkling blue and contained transparent sapphires. The beauty of my surroundings was indescribable. Things regarded in the natural as precious were considered common here.

The sound was heavenly, everything humming in unison. "Joyful, joyful, we adore Thee, God of glory, God of Love." It was better than any white noise used to fall asleep.

I felt a slight tug on my arm and heard Him say, "Come with me now, Hope. You've got to get started. All of this will become normal to you soon, and you won't feel so awestruck."

As He led me into another room, I couldn't help gawking at the wonderful sights. Everything was ornate and beautiful. The seating area was elaborate with silk-cushioned lounges and chairs. Wool rugs were arranged on the jeweled floors, and beautiful tapestries adorned the walls. He pointed to one of the lounges and told me to sit.

He had to slap his hands together to get my attention. "Hope! Look at me!" He said. "How can I teach you if you're mesmerized? You need to be taught how to use your robe to its fullest extent."

That got my attention. What did He mean by using my robe? "Huh?" I asked. "How do I use your skirt?"

"You only looked at part of what your robe represented. You don't know what is available to you. You didn't follow through by reading all the verses explaining the depth of our skirt's capabilities. Your lack of knowledge left you unprepared," He said.

"I thought your skirt was a sign or symbol of approval. Like an engagement ring or something similar," I said.

"Yes, the robe is symbolic of our approval of you because you are ready for love. That is your symbol but also symbolic to the enemy when you use it. In addition, it is a canopy of divine love and protection. Its purpose is to be the hedge of protection given to you by God. When fear comes calling, you can cover yourself in your robe of love and know fear won't overtake your mind," He taught.

"Do you know what covenant means, Hope?"

"I thought I did," I replied. "But with two failed marriages, I must not know the true meaning. Please explain in detail what covenant truly means so I can understand."

"Covenant is a solemn pledge or promise given out of love. Our commitments are unconditional and can never be broken. Covenants are contracts made between two. Our skirt is the token of our divine covenant with you. When you wear it and use it as a covering, you agree to be ours. You're spiritually bound to us. When we see this robe, we earnestly remember our everlasting covenant made to the wearer."

He continued, "Using the robe against fear means you are depending on the love of God to protect and sustain you. It has tremendous power if used efficiently. When in use, it is a shield. There is no fear when in God's love. When He is your focus, dread does not exist. This full-grown love can turn fear out of doors, and it will expel every trace of terror. This robe is the symbol of love. When you use it, it is the shield of faith. However, it cannot remain on you unless you trust in the love of God. That is why the Word clearly says, 'Without faith, you can't please God.'"

I could feel liquid fire forming behind my eyes. Powerful tears fueled by repentance were burning my eyes. I had displeased God! I was putting my face in my hands to control the guilt when He said.

"Stop that now! There is no condemnation here. I'm just trying to teach you. You've been forgiven, Hope. You did not know."

"When you allow fear to enter your mind, it brings along with it the thought of punishment or death. When you belong to God, there is no longer fear of death because Jesus destroyed death with his flesh on the cross," He explained.

"This robe will help me be free from fear?" I asked.

"Yes," He said. "How do you see your robe now?"

Looking down at the material, I noticed it wasn't the sheer, iridescent material that it had been. It was bright red and appeared to be almost liquid. "I see a red flowing garment," I replied.

"Do you know what this is?" He asked me.

I knew. I don't know how, but I knew. "It's Jesus's blood, isn't it?"

"Yes! You understand! It is your eternal robe, the one you were spiritually born into. Remember you came to me in blood? Your angels rubbed it into you by the oil of his grace. The outer robe is the sheer, iridescent garment made from the blessings of the rainbow. You live in God's blessing and by his faith, which is the shield. It's just symbolic. It's temperamental and will not stay on you if it even senses fear in you. That's why it was on the floor when you arrived. The blood robe will never ever leave you after you are ours. In his kingdom of heaven, every creature can see the red one through the iridescent one, which is your faith," He informed.

"Doesn't faith come by hearing and from hearing God's Word preached?" I inquired.

"Faith is your robe, Hope. It is given to you by Jesus who is the Word. Faith is your conscious self. Being conscious of God makes you a blessed one," He answered.

"So it knows who I am by the Word? I think I understand better. I am a child of God," I said.

"The red robe underneath is God's robe of grace because it is made with Jesus's blood. God only gives it to his children. Using the power of your faith represented by the robe demonstrates to everything in heaven, on earth, and under the earth that you are conscious of God's love. You are dependent on his love. You know who you are. This is what pleases God. When you don't trust Him, it grieves us, renders your shield helpless. Satan has access to your mind," He said.

"So it is all about my mind?" I asked.

"Yes. Your mind is your soul. Every issue is determined by how and what you are thinking. If your mind, will, and emotions are controlled by the consciousness of who you are in Christ, then you can live in the light which is the kingdom of God on earth. But if fear, dread, guilt, and confusion rule your mind, then Satan has control, and you are living in darkness regulated by the world's system. That is why God's people perish for lack of knowledge. They have no understanding of how much they are loved and protected by Jesus through God's Word," He explained.

Waving His arms toward the wall, one of the tapestries changed into a visual projector. On it, Jesus was speaking to a city.

The Holy Spirit said, "I want you to see how unbelief or lack of faith grieves the Lord. Listen to his words as He speaks to Jerusalem. The ministers of the day were punishing the people and refusing his protection."

On the screen, Jesus was exclaiming this: O Jerusalem, Jerusalem, murdering the prophets and stoning those who are sent to you! How often would I have gathered your children together as a mother fowl gathers her brood under her wings, and you refused!

Behold, your house is forsaken and desolate (abandoned and left destitute of God's help). Matthew 23:37-38 (amp)

"Do you see the grief in his face, Hope? Under his wings is the same as being in his faith. Don't let Satan have your heart and mind, causing your life to become forsaken. We are here to help you. This battle is not yours," the Holy Spirit assured me.

Sightseeing

An urgent need of a bodily function forced me back into my physical state. It caused me to wake from this wonderful experience.

"Why did we have to urinate?" I was so aggravated by being awake that I was mad at myself. *Why was I taken from the Holy Spirit's presence by my body's need to pee?* I thought.

I'm still here, Hope, I heard Him say.

Every drop of blood must have rushed to my head in that instant, turning my face every shade of red imaginable. I was so embarrassed. I was sitting on the toilet of all places, muttering to myself about myself in the presence of the Lord.

"Sorry," I said. "I'll be finished in a bit." While finishing, I kept my eyes down because I was mortified beyond belief. My holy companion had to wait for me to finish urinating. At the exact moment, I had that thought, I heard Him laugh.

There is nothing hidden from us, Hope. Not a physical action or mental thought is in secret. We can see and hear everything you do, He said, still chuckling.

"Why are we so embarrassed about being seen in these circumstances then?" I asked.

Shame and self-loathing are two of the enemy's tricks. We like to know that your body functions work properly. It is part of being in complete Siloam, meaning nothing missing, nothing broken. There is no shame in getting rid of waste as a function of your body designed by your Creator, God, He said.

"Maybe no shame, but a need for privacy is important," I said.

Eager to change the subject, I asked, "Are we going back to the kingdom now?"

You'll be in the spirit realm but not in the palace, which was too distracting for you. I want to take you places and show you things. Where we're going, some of the scriptures you were taught in your youth will come to life for you. You'll understand why God's Word is considered alive and active, He said.

"Will I need to get my Bible?" I asked.

No, Hope. You'll see that all the scripture you were taught during your lifetime until now has been planted in your heart. When you have questions about certain things that are going to present themselves, I'll be with you to explain, He told me.

I said jokingly, "I'm getting to go on a Holy Ghost field trip." Then it dawned on me that my physical body was awake. "Will I be going in my physical body this time?" I asked.

As a matter of fact, you will because we are going to a natural place, one very familiar to you, He informed me.

He proceeded to explain, *I need you to remember that on this journey, you'll see and hear things with your new God-given sight and hearing. The things you'll encounter will be more real than anything you've previously experienced in life. Your reality will be a shadow of ours, or it can sometimes be a mirage or figment of the imagination instead of being real. We will be moving around in time and space in the natural realm, but we will be unseen by people. Be forewarned you will be seen and heard by creatures that operate in this same environment.*

"Creatures? What do you mean?" I asked.

You are going to see angels and demons, Hope. The purpose is to reveal how mankind is bound and how a person is set free, He said.

"I thought you were going to teach me all about love and why I feel so unlovable," I asked.

It all works together, Hope. You'll have to trust me. Are you ready? He asked.

"As ready as I'll ever be, but—" I responded but He interrupted.

Our first stop will be at the mall. I want to see if you can tell the difference between people who are saved and people not living in their salvation, He said.

The journey was swift. We were standing in the center court of a busy mall. People were all around us, but none acknowledged we were there. Good thing too because I was still in my pajamas. At least I wasn't naked. He hadn't heard my "but." I had been about to say that I needed to put on some clothes. Talking about being humbled! He certainly kept me humbled every time I turned around. I must be amusing because I heard a snicker as if He were suppressing a laugh.

"You did it to me again. You've made me aware of my appearance," I said.

What covering do you have with you, Hope? He asked.

Groaning, I meekly responded, "My robe."

I'm going to get used to this if it is the last thing I do. I stooped over, picked up my robe from its puddle at my feet, and pulled it up over my head, exasperated. If I was going to wear it, it needed to be over my head as well so I could remember it was there.

After straightening it, I was glad the robe was over my head. Right in front of me was the ugliest creature I had ever seen! When I saw it, I couldn't help screaming, "Oh my God!" Hearing me scream God's name caused the beast to look directly at me. To my surprise, it screeched and vanished.

"What was that?" I asked.

You've seen your first demon, Hope. You will see them everywhere now that you have been given spiritual vision. Don't be afraid of them. They are more afraid of you and God's name than you'll ever imagine, the Holy Spirit informed me.

"Why are they afraid of me?" I asked. I knew why they were afraid of God.

Because you can see and hear them. People who can't see demons are not aware of what they are doing, so they aren't afraid. When they encounter someone, who can see them, demons know their time is short because I am nearby, He said.

"*It's time to focus on the reason I brought you here. Don't pay attention to the creatures. I want to see if you know the difference in people*," He said.

Standing center stage of the mall, I could see all kinds of people. I was here for a reason, though—to discern a spiritual difference, not what race or sex they were. I decided to make it easier on myself by focusing on individuals I recognized as they shopped.

The first one I found was Cindy Grover, a girlfriend I once hung around with in the nightclubs. I admired her and wanted to be like her. She always looked stunning and attracted any guy she focused on. Expecting to see her lovely, well-polished features, I gasped when she turned and faced me. Her eyes were black; her skin was gray, dry, and almost cracking. She had on beautiful clothes and shoes, but she looked like a dolled-up corpse. I wanted to cry.

Remembering what the Holy Spirit said about being a dead leaf carried by the wind. I experienced for the first time the way angels saw humans who were cut off from God—leprous, filthy imposters. I prayed, "Lord, help her. She is dying, and she doesn't even know."

———*w-o-ᴏₑ⊦ᴏₑᴏₑ⊦ᴏ-o-w*———

Jesus just smiled. Thinking to Himself, He said. "I knew she would know what to do. Hope is a natural. It is not long now."

———*w-o-ᴏₑ⊦ᴏₑᴏₑ⊦ᴏ-o-w*———

The Holy Spirit asked me, *Hope, explain to me what you are seeing.*

With lips quivering, I replied, "I am looking at a dying friend! I thought she was so beautiful, but I'm seeing a walking corpse. I just asked Jesus to help her. She deserves better."

Good, Hope! Now you understand! You've witnessed someone without the Lord in their life. That is how everyone who is not born again appears in the spirit. They are dead before they have even lived," He shared. *"Now try to find someone you know who is altogether different.*

Looking around, I found Mr. Arnold. He was my gym teacher in grade school who retired. He was always so sweet and good to all the kids. He never had a bad word for any of us and would hug us a lot. He had to be born again. He was nothing but a kindhearted and compassionate person.

When he finally came close, I was expecting to see a robe like mine or some other symbol of salvation. Instead, he was surrounded by a dark cloud. His eyes seemed to be black. He appeared to be slimy, not dry, and very foul. I felt my head being turned by unnatural hands. I assumed it was the Holy Spirit causing me to look in another direction. As I did, I noticed what he was looking at. Mr. Arnold was watching a little boy crying in a nearby ice cream shop. It appeared he was looking lustfully at the little fellow. Then I heard his thoughts concerning the kid. Gross! He wanted to look at the little boy naked. He was fantasizing about touching the boy. My mind went to a very dark place. "No wonder he was always nice to us kids. We were his mental playthings. How revolting!"

"Lord, Mr. Arnold is sick and perverted. Protect children from him. Please direct him toward a mental health facility quick. he is twisted," I prayed.

"Holy Spirit, please take me to a different place. I can't stand here and listen any longer to his repulsive thoughts. I want to react," I asked.

He looked disappointed when I said that.

Keep trying, Hope. Focus, He pleaded.

"Please get me away from him. Let me look for someone else," I begged.

My judgment was way off base. I knew I needed to focus on another person quickly, or I'd mess this up. I would never have imagined Mr. Arnold was a pervert.

Then I spotted my old Sunday school teacher, Mrs. Lenney. She had to be born again. I resisted the urge to run to her. I needed to examine her eyes and body.

I was relieved that her eyes weren't black, and her body didn't look dead. However, I did notice her eyes were cloudy, and her body was pinkish and drawn tight. I couldn't be wrong this time, so I took a closer look. I saw she had a flicker of faint light behind her pupils. You had to look very hard to see it. Her body was stooped over as if she were carrying a heavy load. Her clothes were worn, almost threadbare. She had a robe, thank God, but she wasn't wearing it. It was trailing behind her like a veil. I listened with my new spiritual ears to her berating herself. She wanted a purse but didn't feel worthy of something nice. She kept thinking she didn't deserve a purse that cost $100. She was concerned about the hungry people with nothing that came around the church.

My heart went out to her. She was so special. I remembered she taught me in Sunday school many years ago that God wanted us to be blessed. I could still hear her saying to the class, "Be prosperous! Don't just have life, but have it more abundantly."

What had gone so very wrong leaving her to live like a pauper? Again, my heart cried out to the Lord. "Lord, please reward Mrs. Lenney. She has always been so faithful to your work. She deserves to know that she is worth much more than the price of this purse. She deserves a store of purses far more expensive than any displayed. You came and gave your life. By living in you, we have inherited more than rags and hand-me-downs. Please minister to her and love on her," I prayed.

It suddenly occurred to me that I was very much like Mrs. Lenney. I didn't feel I deserved to be loved as a young girl, and I still felt that way. Why?

The field trip ended as fast as it had begun. I was back in my apartment with my thoughts consuming me. I had so many questions. "Holy Spirit, what's going on? Are you showing me something about myself?" I asked.

Hope, what you just experienced was wonderful. Jesus, let you have a small glimpse the measure of his love for you. He wanted you to see the glory of your salvation in comparison to Cindy's loss. He wants you, as well as Mrs. Lenney, to experience his worthiness. In Him, you deserve greatness, majesty, and honor. There are not many people on earth that love themselves to the extent God desires. All creation is waiting for the children of God to come to this understanding, He shared.

I was excited by what He was telling me, but I was still so confused. I asked. "What is keeping us from accepting this love correctly? We are taught in church week after week about the love of God. What is preventing us from grasping it deep inside so it endures?"

Satan gives people mirages, confused mental messages, and attacks on the senses. People aren't able to distinguish the truth of God's Word from what Satan is presenting to them as real. Angels created for God's children can't help them unless they know the difference between truth and lies. Angels are bound unable to operate, unless they can hear positive energy from God's Word that is spoken in faith by believers, whereas demons and dark angels of Satan feed off negative energy from people's words, causing them to gain strength, creating a stronghold over a person.

Words are very powerful. Agreement with negative or positive can determine what controls a person's life's circumstances. Firm foundations are made with God's Word spoken for and over people. Same thing applies for negative words that establish evil strongholds. Over time, both are developed that may pass over from generation to generation. In the Old Testament, iniquities from evil words have only a limit of growth. God stopped evil iniquities after the fourth generation, but God's Word of blessing can last for thousands of years, He explained.

"Really? You mean words can keep you bound or set you free?" I asked.

Yes, Hope. But not just any words. It must be God's Word, which is like a two-edged sword. Only God's Word is alive and full of power. It can divide breath of life and spirit. It can expose and analyze every thought or purpose in someone's heart. Knowing God's Word can bless your life and break strongholds off you or around you, He instructed.

Equipped to Know the Difference

While Hope was pondering the images from the words she just received, Jesus had a quick meeting with the Holy Spirit.

—⁓⦿⁓—

"It's time to give her the baptism. Her appetite to help others has been whetted. Now offer her the power. She will accept you. With your assistance from now on, she'll be a force to be reckoned with. The two made one—my spirit, her will."

—⁓⦿⁓—

Hope, the Lord is offering you my baptism if it is your desire.

Tentatively, I responded, "I'm not sure exactly what you mean. I've been baptized, and didn't you say I was born again? Didn't you say you made sure?"

This is more than being born again. Being born again is making the Lord ruler of your life and letting Him dictate the circumstances around you. Being baptized in the Holy Spirit is becoming one, or a partner, with Him and changing the circumstances around you. It is giving the Lord your soul—that is your mind, will, and emotions— and receiving His, sharing in the works of the Father with Him. When He moves, you move. When you speak, it is Him speaking with your voice through your mouth. His Word is power. He wants to speak through you. You don't have the ability to speak in power without Him. Without His will and emotions, you would be only mimicking what you've read, not being what He says, He shared.

"I want to have everything He wants me to have, but I'm not sure I know what I have to do. Do I have to go somewhere to wait for fire to touch my head? Or do I have to prove to someone that you are with me?" I asked.

Sweet Hope, all you should do is submit your will to me and believe. Do you believe that you have spiritual sight and hearing? He asked.

"Yes, sir," I said.

Well, when you are baptized with me, it means that I've enabled you with the ability to speak God's Word, even when you don't know what to speak. All you must do is resist the urge to say whatever comes to your mind and give me your mouth to use. I'll speak words that need to be spoken through you. I'll use your mouth and voice to utter my words, even if it sounds like groans or gibberish. I know what to say to strengthen you up and to tear down your strongholds. Your trust and submission are all I need. You must die to your mind, will, and emotions this time instead of dying to sin. You are letting me take over, surrendering your control, making your thoughts the mind, desires, will, and emotions of Christ.

Usually, I will speak through you in another language or in moans. If you knew what I needed to say to change the circumstances or break down strongholds, your senses would cause your mind to wrestle with mine. You would let fear stop you from speaking altogether. I won't allow fear to enter, so I don't let you understand what you say," He enlightened.

He then said. *When I see a need, I'll direct you toward a situation, and you'll submit to my prompting, allowing me control of your body to serve another as well as yourself. During those times, I will share the meaning of what is being said so you'll relax enough to move into action.*

I wanted nothing more than to have Him take over the circumstances of my life. I yearned to be available to help someone else. Mostly, I wanted to be like a trusting baby again. I finally understood that if I allowed Him total control of my body, my mind, will, and emotions, especially my mouth, no weapon formed against me could prosper. I begged enthusiastically, "Take my mouth, my lips, my tongue, my throat, my whole head, and neck—everything. I need you! Why has it taken me so long to understand this? Give it to me now!"

I walked to Him expecting Him to hug me like He did when I received my sight and hearing. I wasn't ready for the impact that came. A warm comforting feeling began flowing from the top of my head and spreading throughout my whole body as his hands gripped me. Unspeakable joy flooded my mind and heart. I heard Him say, o*pen your mouth so I can fill it.*

I did as instructed and opened my mouth. I felt an incredible rush of warm air enter my lungs and penetrate through my soul. Then with a gush of my own breath, I heard the weirdest words coming out of my mouth. To my delight, the supernatural words I was speaking changed to words I could understand. I knew without a doubt they had authority, and that his breath which was transferred to me was giving them force and power. My mind had been given the evidence of speaking in tongues with understanding.

Through me, He said, "My Word is life, and with it, life is changed!"

He continued, *this time I let you understand what I said so your first experience would not be frightening. Don't ever worry about what is said. If you don't understand the words or sounds coming from your lips, remember you don't have to. I will be speaking even though you are vocalizing. I know the Father's thoughts for you; and I know what it takes to uplift, defeat, or break down.*

"I'm truly amazed, but I don't understand why you breathed in me. What was that all about? I thought you just wanted control of me," I asked.

Do you remember asking me about the wind blowing you away from God? Each time a person speaks out of line with God's Word; their breath is the wind that forces them away. I gave you God's breath again, mixed with the Word. His air forces evil away as you inhale drawing Him and all his blessings to you. This is breathing. Jesus, who is the Word, breathed on mankind before He ascended to heaven, but many have refused to breathe Him in and speak Him out, He shared.

I was overjoyed when He allowed me to go around the apartment for several minutes, muttering my weird words. It was fun knowing He was setting the stage of my life. I could rest knowing that his thoughts and plans for me were good. After a while, I began wondering, *didn't He say speaking over someone could change things for them?*

I asked, "Did you tell me that we could speak for others and angels would help them?"

Yes, if you allow me to pray through you for others, it does have the power to heal because I know how and what to ask God. So, yes, through you and me, angels will be able to help others, He replied.

"Do these people have to hear us pray for them in this holy language?" I asked, worried.

Don't be embarrassed that you pray in tongues, Hope. But to answer your question, they don't need to know that you and I are praying for them at all. That is between us and God. If you were to start praying in tongues in front of someone who is unlearned, it would frighten them instead of helping them. They'd think you were crazy. I understand your concern about someone hearing you. But if someone asks you to pray for them, you can say a quick simple prayer that they can understand, like asking God to grant their need or heal their body. That is all the assurance they need. Then in private, we can continue to lift their needs to God in words that make their angels free to help, He said.

I started thinking about praying for Cindy and Mrs. Lenney. I liked Cindy, even though she was the walking dead. She deserved to know God. Mrs. Lenney needed to know she was loved and appreciated.

Hearing my thoughts, the Holy Spirit interjected, *Hope, you want to help those that you like and who like you, but what about Mr. Arnold?*

I didn't know what to say. I had been so revolted and disgusted after hearing his thoughts that I wanted him to be punished. This man had completely fooled me into thinking he was an upstanding person in the community when he was really a pervert. So, I replied, "I can't speak favorably for him now. I want to report him to the police."

We love him too, Hope. You mustn't judge until you know what is happening. You heard his thoughts without knowing the

61

reason for those thoughts. We do, He said. *I feel the need to start the whole field trip over. You should see with your spiritual eyes the driving forces behind these three people. Looking deeper into the spirit realm will allow you to see the evil retaining Cindy and enslaving Mrs. Lenney. Then we'll move to see deeper into Mr. Arnold. I'm not leaving you to your own devices this time. Together, we will move and see the evil that needs to be confronted. Their example will teach you how to war against what has come against you.*

"We can go back in time? Great! That will be fun. I'm anxious to start praying for Cindy and Mrs. Lenney and, if I have to, for Mr. Arnold also," I said.

He explained, *"As I said earlier, Hope, time is not an issue for me. We may even have to go back further in the past to understand some of their thoughts and actions. You are going to come face-to-face with demons and possibly even face a dark angel. Demons are afraid of you, but dark angels are not. Don't worry! They are afraid of me. Are you truly ready for this?*

I knew He could read my thoughts, so I honestly said, "I'm scared, but if I'm going to learn, I need to see and hear the good with the ugly. Please don't leave my side!" *Never!* He said.

—————————

The Lord was really pleased. Hope was willing to experience on-the-job training, even if she didn't know what her job was yet. She was about to face true reality, encountering some of the mirages created by Satan in the world.

—————————

Preparing my mind for this new adventure, I gripped my robe of blessing as I grabbed the Holy Spirit's belt. Then I said, "I'm ready."

We were back in the mall but in an undisclosed bubble of sorts. I saw the same ugly creature, and it vanished again. When I saw, Cindy coming toward me, I looked at the Holy Spirit, waiting for instructions. He only nodded toward her.

Then He said, *Look!*

I looked but only saw the same thing I did the first time.

Look deeper! He instructed

I followed her into a dress shop, concentrating hard on her face. Reality seemed to shift, and I saw what appeared to be smoke all around her. It was completely engulfing her head. Then I saw it! A huge, fat demon was floating over her. The smoke engulfing her head was its breath as it exhaled damnation on her. As ugly as it was, it had a look of ecstasy on its face as it breathed in her energy. It was enjoying whatever it was doing to her. I wanted to scream! She didn't have a clue.

I wanted to start praying for her right then. He needed to whip this demon's butt! Or order angels to do it. But He read my mind and said, *Not yet.*

As bad as this looks, you need to know more. Praying through me will help, but knowing more about a situation will make your prayers more efficient. You will be more effective if you don't just go by what you see.

Then He asked, *what is she thinking and saying to herself? What is in her heart? Know what is making the demon so happy with her?*

"I'll have to get closer to that thing to hear her thoughts," I said.

Good! Remember what I told you, He answered.

What did He tell me? Then I remembered. Demons are afraid of people who can see and hear them. I was in its arena, so if it saw me, I could walk up and let it know I was watching and I didn't approve.

"Will Cindy know I'm there?" I asked.

She'll sense a presence, but it will not bother her. She is numb to being watched and judged. She has become hardhearted, He informed me.

I moved closer to Cindy so I could hear her while I focused on the demon. When I saw the anguish on her face, pity overwhelmed me. From that moment, it didn't matter that the ugly creature was around. My heart ached for her. She would choose a dress then start talking negatively about her body.

I listened closely and heard her say demeaning things. "I wish I could wear this, but it won't accentuate my bust. Guys like boobs, and I don't have any. Even with a push-up bra, I wouldn't have enough cleavage to turn heads." Then she looked at another dress and said, "This material would cling to my butt, emphasizing every dimple."

What dimples? I thought.

This girl was slender, with curves, and had just the right amount of bosom to be well-proportioned. Most women would love to look like Cindy unless they could see her in the spirit.

Then I heard her say, "Finally! I think this dress will work for my date, even though it's a little too tight."

"What size is it?" she asked herself, hunting for the tag.

When she found the size 4 on the tag, she remarked, "I'm wearing a size 6 comfortably now. I'll have to starve for the next few days, but it will be worth it. The dress will be tight enough to be sexy and show off what little I have going for me."

She had no self-esteem or self-love whatsoever. Cindy wanted to be noticed for all the wrong reasons. I felt so sorry for her. No wonder the demon was getting so strong.

Crying, I looked up to the Holy Spirit and said. "She is pitiful! I want to help."

Confront her demon, He said.

I took a deep breath, which made the Holy Spirit grin at me, and then I moved in closer. I focused on that hideous creature. I cleared my throat right in its presence. Startled out of its ecstasy, it peered wild-eyed at me. Then I spoke using God's breath, "I see you, you foul creature, and I forbid you stealing my friend's life."

As if it were choking, it grabbed its throat then vanished. The choking smoke disappeared almost at once.

"Now what should we do to help her?" I asked.

She needs the Lord, Hope. As you've noticed, she has no life. She is trying to whitewash a dead body. Nothing she puts on will change her. Anything she touches that God created to adorn his children will turn quickly to rags. She will even corrode gold.

Then He asked, *have you ever seen an abandoned house that was falling apart from decay?*

"Yes, I have seen several in the country just falling apart, overgrown with weeds and vines. I'd be afraid to go near because they are probably chock-full of snakes," I replied, shuddering.

Precisely! They had no life in them and were full of vermin. It is the same for a person without the life of Christ inside them. They will fall apart while being full of disgusting parasites, He shared. *Now you know what she needs instead of what she wants.*

At that moment, I knew what I needed to do! I bowed my head and said, "Speak, Lord."

I didn't have to know what was said. I allowed Him to pray through me with abandon as I wept. While I watched her, I asked her, with my mind, to seek peace and hope from Jesus instead of lustful attention from a man. I knew what was being muttered in the Spirit was for her benefit and inspiration, even though I had no clue what I was saying. Then the tempo of the language changed. The words became forceful and powerful and condemning. I knew they were directed at an evil force trying to prevent her salvation.

Abruptly, I finished. The need to speak left me. I had peace that circumstances for Cindy were soon going to be very different. I asked, "Is she going to find Jesus?"

From the moment, you begged for her salvation, a war began for her. Angels and demons will fight until a time is created for her to find the Lord, He said.

"So her angels are working for her now because of what we prayed?" I asked.

No, she doesn't have any angels willing to fight for her, Hope. The ones waging war on her demons are some of your angels. In time, she will be guided to the Lord. Remember, Jesus answers prayers. He will give you the desire of your heart for Cindy. He may even use you as the person to bring her to church or convince her to want a better lifestyle. Someone will give her a desire to

65

want what you have. Don't seek her, just let events fall in place. Jesus's timing and guidance are perfect. Wait and see, He said.

I'd like that. Cindy is a nice person. I'd like for her to get involved in church with me, I thought.

Then I groaned because I remembered who I saw next when we were here previously. I was going to have to face Mr. Arnold. Knowing his perverted desires still creeped me out.

Again, knowing what I had been thinking, the Holy Spirit spoke out; *Mr. Arnold is not our next mystery. I want you to see what's really happening with Mrs. Lenney. Do you remember what you saw the last time we encountered her?*

"Sure. She wouldn't buy herself something nice. She didn't think she deserved to have something when people were going hungry. I also remember that her eyes weren't black, but they weren't bright either," I said.

What were your feelings about her, Hope? He asked.

"Wait a minute! You know my heart. Why did you ask me that?" I asked. "What's going on? Is this a trick question? You know what I'm thinking and feeling before I do, so why are you asking me what I felt?"

You need to refocus, that's all, He said.

I had to stop and think for a minute. I felt sad. I felt she deserved better than hand-me-downs and wanted her to be rewarded. I remembered her as my Sunday school teacher and how kind she was. So, I responded, "I really like and admire this woman, and I want her to feel like a princess, not a pauper."

Then He asked a weird question, *do you remember how she dressed when you were in her class so many years ago?*

To be truthful, I couldn't remember. I tried to recall but didn't understand the purpose of knowing what she wore back then.

Smiling, He said; *Time to take a trip to the past to refresh your memory of Mrs. Lenney. Don't focus on anything but Mrs. Lenney. Notice what she wears and drives. After you are reminded, I'll take you on a quick trip of her life, to demonstrate why she is like she is now.*

I thought, *Cool! I'd love to have as much compassion as she does. Knowing what led her to be like Christ will be interesting.* "I'm ready," I said.

When I opened my eyes, I was watching myself as a seven-year-old, sitting at a little table with other kids and coloring a picture of Jesus. I had gotten up to sharpen a crayon when I looked out the window and saw Mrs. Lenney as she drove into a parking space in her new Cadillac. As she approached the building, I focused on how she looked. She was a beautiful and elegant lady. Her hair, makeup, nail polish, and jewelry were immaculate. She was wearing a lovely outfit with shoes to match. Even at seven, I adored her. But wait, this wasn't the Mrs. Lenney I knew today. This younger version was decked out in designer clothes and very expensive accessories.

"I'm confused," I said.

A mystery, isn't it? He said. Then He went on to enlighten me. *When you were this little girl, Mrs. Lenney was a newly married lady. She'd accepted Christ at eighteen after leaving home to attend college. Several years later, she met her husband while working at the local library. He had been a wealthy man who doted on her, giving her anything she wanted. He liked for her to look nice and made her feel loved and appreciated. She loved the Lord very much then and wanted to show her appreciation by loving as many children as she could. So, she became a Sunday school teacher.*

Back in the now, I asked, "What happened to her? Why is she acting like a homeless person almost?"

He replied *you'll understand soon. Let's see more.*

When was the last time you remember seeing her at church? What was she doing then? He asked.

"It had to be soon after my first marriage. I remember her helping in a food line during one of the holiday functions we were having. Even then, she seemed frail and unkempt. I remember the pastor urging her to sit down at one of the tables because she had worked so hard that day. He even brought her a glass of tea. She couldn't have been very old then, maybe in her late thirties or early forties. But she looked older. I thought, even that day, that she was such a saint. At that time, it didn't dawn on me she had been an elegant lady before. I had been blinded to it apparently," I said.

Then I remembered something He had said, so I inquired, "You said her husband had been a wealthy man. Are they broke now? Is that why she doesn't have any money and sympathizes with others like herself?"

No, Hope. Mrs. Lenney is still a very wealthy woman. Mr. Lenney died leaving her with millions of dollars. She has been made to feel unworthy of any of it, He said.

"Don't keep me waiting, and don't prolong this any further. Just tell me what happened!" I said impatiently.

There are many factors that played in her life, Hope. As a servant of the Lord, she came under severe attacks from the enemy. Someone on fire for the Lord was a threat to Satan, so he had to stop her progress. He knew her weakness and just how to hurt her. The strongholds from her past started working against her.

Let me start from the beginning. She was brought up by very rigid, religious parents who made her feel she had to earn God's love. She was never taught that God loved her regardless of works. After her parents both died from influenza, she left home. She was an only child who hated the farm, so she sold their property to her father's brother and moved to town. Afterward, she worked part-time while attending the local college.

She became the town's librarian and there, she met Albert Lenney, and you know the rest. He was older and very wealthy. Mary loved him with all her heart. Never had anyone showed her so much attention and love. She felt so good she wanted to share the feeling. What better way than to love on children since she didn't have any of her own yet. She taught them to love God and to work hard for Him, still under the impression she had to keep earning his appreciation.

One night after a lovely formal dinner celebration, Albert and Mary were walking to their car when a homeless man tried to rob them. Albert tried to fight his way out of the situation and was killed in front of Mary. The homeless man told her he was sorry. He hadn't meant to hurt them. He was just hungry. Then he ran away.

Fear, grief, and pity worked together, causing Mary to have a psychotic break and to be institutionalized. She stayed in the hospital until her uncle came to take custody of her. Back to the farm she went. Her uncle was a cruel man. He was like her father, very rigid, religious, and he hated her money. Satan's dark angels used his envy. He considered money coming from the devil, the root of all evil. He brainwashed her, belittled her, and made her feel unclean because she had money. He repeatedly told Mary her husband was killed because they were greedy and lusted after unjust gain. He often said God hated their hoarding; that God wants the homeless to eat. Then he used her money to sustain their needs.

Stuart Holmes was Albert's attorney, business partner, and friend. He needed to settle Albert's estate. He heard that Mary had moved back into her childhood family home, so he assumed she was well enough to discuss the estate. Everything Albert owned had been left to Mary and was waiting for her to take possession. All Stuart needed was her signature, releasing her inheritance.

When he visited the old family home, the uncle didn't want Stuart to talk with Mary. He told Stuart she was possessed by the devil. When Stuart saw Mary's condition, he called the authorities. Her uncle had her dressed in rags and tied to her bed. She was very thin because she wasn't eating. She couldn't eat because the uncle made her feel the as if the food was only for the homeless.

In her state of mind, Stuart took it upon himself to find a private nurse to take care of Mary. With proper care provided, he moved Mary back into the home she had shared with Albert. Slowly, she recovered physically, but her mind still hasn't fully restored. Stuart had to arrange for her finances to be controlled by an accountant after she was caught giving thousands away to strangers. Anytime the nurse purchased new clothes for Mary, she presented them to the homeless shelter and then bought items from the shelter's thrift shops.

The last time you saw her at church, she was stressed because she wanted the homeless to have a holiday meal. She had just given all her monthly allowance to the church, money that was placed in her account to pay necessary bills. It bothers her to know she has money for herself. Even though it is good to share, she is out of balance in her thinking. She can't know what she has, or she will give it all away. Her thoughts are consumed by the needs of the homeless, He told her.

So, overcome by Mrs. Lenney's story, I boldly asked, "Where were you when all this was happening? I know she was saved. You told me she accepted Christ into her life."

Hope, I was with her through it all. But she never knew about me, so I couldn't comfort her. She didn't know to ask for my help. The angels that have been assigned to her haven't been released because she is still governed by works, not by God's Word. She didn't understand that I could help her speak in line with God's Word. She knows of God, but she doesn't know what He wants for her. From an early age, her life was twisted by people who were warped in their thinking. Even after she accepted Christ in her life, she didn't really understand his Word. It's hard to break through strongholds ruling people's lives. Her life dramatically changed after her parents died and she moved away. She knew her life was being blessed, but at the same time, she thought she had to work to keep her blessing. There is still time for Mrs. Lenney. Why do you think you've been shown her plight? Together, we can pray for her. We can speak for her. I know what to ask for on her behalf. You need to speak for her using my knowledge. Are you willing?

Relieved, I said, "Let's get started. If it were me, I'd want someone to act on my behalf."

Are you ready? He asked. *You are about to sense a spiritual battle which can be very intense. That is why it is better to wait and look deeper into a situation before you pray for people. Not everything is as it appears. What you saw around Cindy was a demon. We are about to engage much stronger dark forces. Some*

70

of Satan's own angels were assigned the prevention of Mrs. Lenney's progression for God's kingdom.

"Am I about to come face-to-face with them?" I asked.

Maybe. There is only one way to keep your focus from derailment by what they say or do. Concentrate on your desires for Mrs. Lenney. Throw your robe around you, and stay in the love of God. Aim your thoughts at all the promises of God that you can remember, He instructed.

I mentally gathered my robe around me and closed my eyes before saying, "I'm ready, Lord. Proclaim what must be said through me. I'll be thinking about what I'd like to happen to and for my friend."

—⚬⚬⚬⚬⚬⚬⚬⚬⚬⚬—

While they were praying in earnest for Mrs. Lenney, Jesus was telling the Father how pleased He was with Hope. "She is fitting nicely into our plan. She has a compassionate heart and uses the emotion well. When she became frustrated with digging through Mrs. Lenney's past, she asked for wisdom to understand the truth rather than trying to find it out the hard way. It was good to see. The Holy Spirit's abilities are utilized best when people allow Him the chance. He was so pleased to be able to just tell Hope about Mrs. Lenney instead of wasting time showing her."

He continued even though his Father had watched it all. "During the battle itself, Hope hunkered down in her robe to focus on her childhood memory of Mrs. Lenney teaching Sunday school, praying for that awesome lady to return. Plus, she focused on many scriptures in her mind, mentally praying while we spoke through her mouth. Good job for one so new. It was wonderful to see the upheaval we secured against many strongholds. Mrs. Lenney's recovery is imminent. I've sent someone special to snap her out of her confusion. Hope will be rewarded for her help by witnessing a change in Mrs. Lenny soon.

Confusion

When the prayer for Mrs. Lenney was finished, I was exhausted. Even in the spiritual arena, I felt weak. We hadn't prayed for very long, maybe fifteen minutes, but it was very intense and purposeful. I knew that a sword had been wielded with power and force because my energy was sapped.

The Holy Spirit was aware of how I was feeling in my body and mind. *Hope, you need to be refreshed. It's time to go back into your own reality and nourish yourself.*

Now that I was out of the spirit realm, I opened my eyes and found myself already lying in bed. This was very disconcerting. I had been awake in the spirit in a mall but apparently asleep physically in my bed. This would bend even a strong mind if one tried to figure it out.

"Are you still with me?" I asked the Holy Spirit.

Yes, Hope. It is now Wednesday morning. You've physically rested for over eighteen hours. While we were on our journey, only three times did you have to visit your bathroom. I thought it best not to let you remember those times. He chuckled. *Now your spirit needs to be fed as well as your body. Get up and read the Word. Listen to teachers who are teaching the Word. Spend the day refreshing yourself then go to service tonight,* He said.

I sensed something was up. He was insistent that I eat and study. I asked, "Why are you telling me to study and listen all day?" *You'll know soon enough,* was all He would say.

Trying not to fret, I looked out my window and saw it was still dark outside. *What time is it?* I wondered. I looked at my alarm clock; it was three in the morning. It was going to be a long day. My stomach growled. I was really hungry but could wait a few more minutes to eat. I had greater need of a shower. The warm water felt good. I tried to remember everything that had happened in the last eighteen hours, but my brain was resisting. It seemed reality couldn't accept what happened and objected to the intrusion.

After showering, I pulled on jeans and a T-shirt then trotted off to the kitchen, ready to devour all the good food purchased earlier. I was famished.

I cooked several eggs, toasted bread, sliced an apple on cottage cheese, and made coffee. I hadn't eaten this much for breakfast in a long time.

I turned on the TV in the adjacent living room to see what was on that early in the morning when I heard a familiar voice. It was the same lady minister I heard before. While enjoying my food, I delighted in learning how she overcame shyness.

She had to speak to her fear on a regular basis. It had no place in her life, and she was determined to live her life free from insecurities. Boy! That was food for thought. I could speak to that little demon of fear now too.

After I finished my meal, I washed up the dishes and retrieved my Bible. I wanted to read the scripture verses she referenced that helped her know what to speak to fear. I needed those scriptures rooted on the inside of me. Feed my spirit was what the Holy Spirit told me to do. Knowing how to defeat fear through his Word was a good place to start.

The couch wasn't a comfortable place to study, so I made space at the kitchen table. I could still see the TV and needed space to spread out my paper and Bible. I was going to take time to study like I did in school. I was determined to make this fun and eager to start. I had my Bible, two pens, a highlighter, and a spiral notebook to take notes. I was ready.

I dated the first page of the notebook paper and titled it "Fear." Writing the scripture verses so I wouldn't forget them, I proceeded to find them in my Bible. I highlighted the verses in the Bible so the next time I came across them; I would know they were special. Then I read and reread them until I could almost quote the words exactly. On the notebook paper, I also wrote the word *ammunition*. I could use these verses as covenant promises to stand on when praying to help others.

During the day, I watched several speakers. Some were interesting, and some were confusing. It wasn't hard to determine which ones to listen to. If my heart agreed with their words, then I listened and took notes. I highlighted scriptures again so I'd be conscious of their importance when reading later. I was having so much fun that it was late in the afternoon before I even knew it.

I'd been instructed to attend evening worship services which started at 7:00 p.m. It was almost 5:30 p.m. when I put away my Bible and study material. I ate a quick meal, showered, and dressed. I was curious to see why the Holy Spirit wanted me to attend this service.

It dawned on me while driving to church that I hadn't heard the Holy Spirit since He told me to refresh myself this morning.

So, I asked, "Are you still with me?" *I Never left*, He said.

"You've been quiet today. Why?" I queried.

I wasn't quiet, Hope. You heard me speaking through other teachers today. You even recognized when I was speaking or when I was quiet, He told me.

"Really?" I asked, amazed. "I recognized some of the speakers were helpful and others weren't. I just knew deep inside which ones to follow."

Remember to utilize your new sight and hearing during the service tonight at church. Apply what you've learned so far. You'll see things spiritually that you would have missed without this knowledge. It's up to you to operate your gifts. If you don't, the enemy will make sure you can't see or hear, He warned.

"The devil can do that to me?" I asked.

Yes! He has the ability to deafen or blind believers. He'll hamper all your senses if he can. He will keep you from knowing the truth unless you are aware of his tricks, He replied.

"Is it going to be like it was at the mall?" I asked.

How real do you want it, Hope? He countered.

"I think I want it to go slow. I want to ease into the real if you know what I mean. I don't want to walk in there and see demons invading the place, sucking people dry. You haven't shown me any angels working for people yet, so I'm still timid and unprepared," I said.

74

Laughing at my analogy, He said, *Look for their robes. Listen to their hearts through what they say. What you see and hear will surprise you. That will be enough true reality for you tonight. Next time we pray together for someone, you have my permission to keep your eyes open. Then you'll see an angel work on someone's behalf. Most of the time, you just need to believe angels are working.*

"I didn't realize I closed my eyes when we prayed," I said.

Most people do it out of habit. It's a form of respect. But as an intercessor, you need to use your sight, hearing, and even touch to know how to focus. Leave the speaking to me. If something bothers your mind, will, or emotions, it is usually an attack against someone because it's against the mind of Christ now in you. Remember to focus on what is around the person, not on the person. You'll know what to come against. It won't ever be the person we attack, He said.

I parked my car and started to get out when I remembered to make a spiritual check. I had my robe on—yep! I had my Bible—my sword—yep! The Lord was with me, praise God! Why was I so apprehensive? What was I going to witness at church?

My steps were slow and labored as I moved toward the building. Something was trying to block my progress. It felt like I was walking through taffy. I pulled my robe up to my eyes and saw little demons trying to frighten me. I kicked out and said, "I see, you stupid things! Get away from me!"

When they realized, I could see them, they shrieked and vanished. The creatures trying to terrify me were comical, even though I knew they were evil.

After opening the front door of the church, I was greeted by Mrs. Anthony, a widow who had served the Lord a long time. I just knew she was going to be someone I could relate to. Remembering to focus with my new eyes and ears, I reached to hug her. Upon contact with her, I heard her thoughts. *The young girls always come back until they find another man. Poor things. When will they learn to trust in the Lord?* When I released her, these words came out of her mouth: "Hello, Hope, it is so good to have you back. We've missed you."

She hadn't missed me. She was condemning me under her breath. Why couldn't she have just said, "Hello, Hope," and left it at that?

I looked into her face and saw her eyes were not black. Thank God there was a flicker of light. She was saved even if she was judgmental. Then I looked for her robe. It was under her feet at the moment. I giggled and thought, *been there, done that.*

I found a seat closer to the front tonight. I had a reason to be in the thick of things. I was mentally gearing up for an experience. I didn't care who saw me. I wasn't there to be seen but to learn and help. I focused on looking for people with their robes on. It saddened me to see so many people not wearing them. The floor was a pile of robes. Their robes followed their owners around like toilet paper stuck to their shoes. No respect. *Done that also*, I thought. It puzzled me that some people didn't even have a robe. I made a mental note to ask about it later.

Since I'd arrived a few minutes before service started, I closed my eyes and listened to the conversations around me. I couldn't believe all the negative talk I was hearing. My heart started to ache, and the pressure in my chest made me a little concerned. I was almost afraid to look deeper. What would I see causing them to speak like that? I didn't want to see what was feeding off negative energy. How could demons be in church of all places? Wasn't any place sacred, protected from Satan's evil tricks?

Look! Hope, I heard Him command. *Someone is being attacked. Focus!*

I turned around, trying not to be noticed. Focusing on the attacker, I was worried what I would see. Mrs. Jacobs, my mom's friend, was sitting next to her sister, reciting a litany about all her aches and pains. She had no clue that a little toad of a demon was sitting at her feet, hurting her. I watched it poke her hard enough to cause pain then laugh when she would claim it. He grinned because she named the pain, giving him full rights to deliver the very thing she feared. Then I saw him clap when she gave him permission to keep bringing it on by saying the pain kept getting worse every day.

I knew what to do. I took another deep breath and cleared my throat. Instantly, the demon noticed me looking at it on the floor instead of Mrs. Jacobs or her sister. I didn't have to utter a word. Instantly, it screeched and left. I guess the sound of my breath and the fire in my eyes was enough to frighten it off.

"Good job, Hope. Mrs. Jacobs can receive from the service now without pain getting in the way," He said.

After that, the service started. I was awestruck immediately! The new pastor had on the most glorious robe. The radiance made it hard to focus on his face. When I got past the luminous beauty of his robe, his eyes mesmerized me. The light behind his eyes was dazzling. I couldn't help asking, "Lord? How? Why?"

It's not the man, Hope. It's me you see inside this man. I'm glad I appeal. I've overtaken him by the light of the Word. It is what is working and moving in him. Listen to the message and enjoy, He said.

The message was about David and the giant, Goliath. I finally grasped why I was here. I was learning battle strategy. I concentrated on David gathering stones for a weapon while speaking in the name of the Lord. It was interesting. I was gathering my arsenal as I studied scripture verses earlier. The promises were my ammo against threats.

Then I had a couple of revelations from the message. It only took one stone from all he gathered to kill the giant. Then David removed the giant's head. Thoughts and plans are living spiritual forces, so he removed the container from the body. The body without a head symbolized people being freed from Satan's thoughts and plans. We are dead to them. That's what it means by being dead to the law. We never could measure up to the law to receive the blessing, so the curse kept coming, which was Satan's plan. Now we are free of his plan. We've been given a better plan if we'll accept the mind of Christ. Awesome!

After copying a few new verses for my arsenal, I was startled by what I saw next. The Lord allowed me to witness a glorious sight—his four personal angels. They were beyond huge. The prophet Ezekiel didn't describe them very well. Let me rephrase that—they were indescribable!

I looked around to see if others were granted this blessing. Nope, not a person around me was awestruck. How different their lives would be if they could only see this amazing sight? These were church folks without a clue, another mystery to me.

Time flew! Had we really been in church an hour? As I was walking out of the church, I laughed because I remembered early this morning, speculating it was going to be a long, drawn out day. The very opposite described it. The day had not been long enough to truly satisfy me. I was enjoying my training and wanted more.

As I approached the exit, I heard a familiar voice say, "Hello, Hope."

My flesh started to crawl. The hair on my neck stood up as I recognized immediately who I would face if I turned around. It was Mr. Arnold, the pervert. I was angry he was at church.

When I turned, choking back the bile in my throat, I was bewildered to see he had a robe in the proper place, not pooled around his feet like so many others. His eyes were no longer black like I'd observed on my journey in the Spirit. The harsh words ready to vent suddenly froze in my throat. I was dumbstruck. I couldn't be cruel to him when I saw his spiritual state. I managed to croak, "Hello, Mr. Arnold." Ashamed of myself, I turned and darted out of the door.

By the time I reached my car, I was almost in tears. How could I have been wrong? Again? Hadn't I witnessed the truth in the spirit? Then I heard a wicked laugh behind me.

Breathlessly, I peered into the backseat. I was alone, thank God! I mentally pulled my robe tighter and drove home. It was my protection for a change. I trusted in that knowledge.

My intention on the way home was to consult the Holy Spirit concerning my confusion. However, shame, anger, and worry diverted my attention. How could I have been mistaken? What did I overlook? I totally neglected to ask my Comforter to help me understand. A cloud of condemnation engulfed my brain, making me revisit the visions of Mr. Arnold fondling the boy. I even remembered how he looked and smelled. I'd carelessly reclaimed my emotions, reeling with self-loathing for being so wrong.

I'd fallen for the illusion the Holy Spirit had warned me about. I was totally engrossed replaying it in my mind. The church was only ten minutes from my apartment, but time moved at a snail's pace now.

After parking in my driveway, fear gripped my heart. I anticipated turmoil in all my surroundings. I dreaded an unannounced visit from Sam ruining the rest of the evening.

Finally convinced that I was alone, I dashed in and locked the door behind me. Like a caring parent, I heard the Holy Spirit say, *Hope, you know we must deal with your fear of Sam.*

Ignoring the statement, I blurted out other concerns. "I have so many questions! I had a weird but awesome experience this evening. May I ask you about what happened?"

Always the gentleman, the Holy Spirit responded, *I knew you were going to have questions for me. You've only had a glimpse of what I see all over the world.*

"You mean what I saw is everywhere? Even in other churches? People judging, lack of faith, the resistance is everywhere?" I groaned.

Yes, sad, isn't it? If people would only rest in what was provided for them, the war would end so much quicker, He shared.

"Why doesn't your message get through to the masses? It was awesome. Your angels are remarkable, indescribable, and your glory is undeniable," I declared.

It gets through to some. You received it, and so did Joe Arnold, He replied.

Ugh! We're back to Joe Arnold again. I knew the subject was going to come up, but I wasn't ready just yet. I was still confused and didn't know what to say.

I wanted you to see Joe the way we see him, Hope. We love him and support him. He loves me like you do. He is a kindred spirit for you, He said.

Those words woke me up! He needed to explain, so I asked, "Kindred spirit? How? He's a pervert, or so I thought. Why did I see him as demon-possessed child molester at the mall, but at church, he was a saint?"

Before I answer your questions, I want to ask you a serious one. Remember, I'll know if you're telling me the truth. Don't open your mouth until I'm through speaking and you have pondered what to say, He said.

"Okay," I agreed.

Not everything you see, even in the spirit realm, is truly what it seems. We chose Joe Arnold for you to see at the mall for a reason. As an intercessor, you will need to learn how and why people judge others unfairly. Satan is the master of deception and twists everything for his plans and purpose. Do you want to know what he did at the mall to keep you from seeing the real Joe? How he distorted the truth about Joe? Question is, are you ready for this step? He asked.

He was right. I needed to think before opening my mouth. With everything He had revealed so far, was I ready for something so disturbing that He wanted me to be absolutely sure? Was I about to open a can of worms that I couldn't seal again? Was I ready for this or not? Curiosity was getting the grip on me, but before I committed, I had to ask, "More monsters?"

It depends on how you look at them. To a newcomer, yes, they will be. To me, nothing special. They will be bigger than anything you can imagine but no threat to me. Their evil destructive plans and purposes are nothing I can't repair. Are you going to accept this challenge? He asked.

I remembered the message I'd received at church—David and Goliath. The reason He insisted on my undivided attention was to prepare me for what was coming. Oh, my God! I wasn't David. I was this weak, fat woman who was recently born again. What have I gotten myself into?

———ᜃᜃᜃᜃᜃᜃᜃᜃᜃᜃᜃ———

While Hope was pondering the question, Jesus, and the Holy Spirit discussed her reactions. "This part of a conversion is always hard for my disciples. Releasing their minds is comparable to drowning. Receiving the baptism was the easy part. Totally surrendering their will is unnatural. She's wrestling with me, but I am prepared for it. It will be a while before she finally succumbs to me. But when she does, oh, the day! Hope will realize it's not her weakness, it's my strength. Through her brokenness, I will shine.

She is going to get a little hostile, overzealous, and totally out of balance with her new gift until that day. Continue to make her face her own fears before that happens. Keep reinforcing the need. When she realizes her mistakes, she will be victorious. I've been through the conversion of others many times. It's hard to watch their struggle but well worth winning the battle."

—— ᴡᴡ◦◦ᴏ◦ᴏᴏ◦◦ᴡᴡ ——

I considered every scenario but knew in my heart I couldn't withdraw now. The Cindys and Mrs. Lenneys of this area needed help. Who was I to deny the call? If only I could move inside the Holy Spirit, then I could be his David. I mentally spanked myself for entertaining doubt and fear. I was allowing them control. I gathered my courage and pronounced, "I'll do it."

Ah! You're catching on. Hope, I'm proud of you. You just disabled fear. I know this is more than your human mind can grasp, but you can do all things with me. Trust in the Word. Learn to rely on what it means. Remember the revelations you received tonight about David. Cut the enemy's plans off at the neck. You've been called by the Lord to join Him, He declared.

"I guess I'm still stunned by the fact He wants me to join Him in all this. Why me?" I asked worriedly.

People were created with gifts such as serving, others for leadership and encouragement, and some for intercessory prayer. You were chosen to assist the Lord in intercessory prayer. Your compassionate heart and desire to know the Word is evidence of your gift. You immediately agreed to the baptism by allowing me to pray through you for Cindy and Mrs. Lenney, demonstrating to the Lord your willingness. Now we must move into the next phase, He shared.

I needed to know, so I asked, "If I had said 'no thanks,' would I be like Jonah, running from my calling?"

You would have wondered about what might have been for the rest of your natural life, Hope. That's all. Jonah's self-contempt caused all his problems. The Lord, in the disguise of a whale, saved Jonah from himself. I've promised to never leave or forsake you. Refusing to accept our offer would only be a disappointment, He said gently.

"I'm just amazed and feel unworthy of such a duty. It's more than I prepared for and difficult to absorb. I want to be used, truly I do. Help me please," I responded honestly.

No person is ever ready in their own strength. That is why the Word reveals everything is possible with me. You have nothing to fear with me. I'm glad you think this gift is important. Intercessors will face awful things and frightening beings, but all creation is subject to me. The key is focusing on me and my authority, He said.

I relaxed, and it must have been obvious.

I see you're ready to get started. We must revisit the mall and look at Joe from a new viewpoint. I'll let you see why you couldn't discern correctly. We are about to face a giant, He informed me.

Giants Still Exist

"Before we go back to the mall, will you please tell me his story as you did with Mrs. Lenney? I don't need to go back in time unless it is necessary to observe what happened. With truth guiding me, I'll be better equipped to face what's trying to confuse me," I stated.

A very wise request, Hope. It will be like gathering stones. Seek the truth, and it will never fail you, He said.

Now, about Joe Arnold. Joe is an orphan in his sixties. His parents were killed in a car accident when he was two years old. He was passed around in foster care over the next five years until a couple agreed to foster him prior to adoption. If he fit in, they would consider making the arrangement permanent. All that was necessary back in those days was that a couple wanted to adopt. Background checks and unexpected visits by caseworkers were not required.

Harry Arnold, Joe's adoptive father, had a problem unknown to his wife. He had a lust for little boys. Harry molested Joe many times until the truth was revealed. The authorities that approved Joe's adoption stepped in.

Harry tormented Joe enough to make him cry. Then he consoled the child by fondling him to make him feel better. Perverted caressing will cause the flesh to respond against its natural intent. Joe's reactions to the caresses were the driving force behind Harry's lust. Do I need to clarify? He asked.

"No, sir, I know what happens to a man's flesh," I said.

Each time, the sexual experience progressed into something a little different until a neighbor caught Harry trying to rape the boy. Caught in the act, knowing he was about to be turned over to the authorities, Harry fled, leaving his wife and Joe all alone. Harriet Arnold was given the evidence and agreed to get Joe counseling. Humiliated, grief-stricken, and lonely, she committed suicide, leaving Joe with no one. Harry was long gone, so Joe was taken to a home for boys. He wasn't considered an orphan because Harry wasn't dead. Joe couldn't be readopted, so he stayed at the Boys' Home until he was old enough to take care of himself.

After Harry left, Joe went through psychoanalysis for a few years. Counselors worked with him primarily during puberty. We had taken pity on Joe and arranged to have a wonderful lady guide him back into God's line of conduct. She prayed for him every night, and eventually, Joe gave his heart to the Lord.

When Joe was old enough to leave the Boys' Home, he got a job as a coach in one of the local schools. He was always good at sports, and his natural gift made a way for him in life. He met his wife, Olivia, at the school. She has been by his side for forty years. They have two grown boys raised to be fine Christian men.

He still wrestles with shame over his body responding to being caressed by another man. He liked it, and it causes great embarrassment. He was too young to know what Harry was doing was wrong. It took many sessions with his doctor and social worker before he understood that he couldn't control his body's reaction.

When Joe sees a little boy in distress, it triggers bad memories. Harry used distress as an excuse to fondle Joe. The memory causes shame, which Satan's dark forces use as a tool to destroy Joe and his ministry. Remember? Seeing Joe like that repulsed you? If Satan can't destroy Joe, he will try to use someone else to do it. He saw your reaction and deceived you because you took the bait, hook, line, and sinker, He explained.

"You're right! I immediately wanted to report Mr. Arnold to the police for being a pedophile. I just knew he was stalking that little boy. If given the chance, I probably would have told someone about him. That's how horrible gossips destroy people, and I was about to become one." I shook my head at what I'd almost done.

Then I remembered something. I asked, "Why did you want me to see a little boy being fondled?" *I didn't, Hope,* He replied. "But you took my head and physically turned me around to face Mr. Arnold so I could see that happening to the boy," I argued.

That wasn't me touching you, Hope. It was the dark force wanting you to persecute Joe. Once he touched you, he controlled your mind for a short period. He caused you to see Joe's memory of himself, not something he wanted to do to the boy, He corrected.

I asked, "They can touch us even when we have our robes on? Why? I mentally made it a point to be wearing it during the trip. I had to use it to deny fear. I'd been scared out of my mind and needed to focus."

Precisely! He knew you were afraid. Fear in any degree, even minute, is still affirmed. Your fear allowed him to touch you. Evil can reach to any place it is given permission through fear. Fear exposes a person to evil manipulation. A dozen robes would not have protected you. Fear overrides faith, He warned.

"Come on! You can't expect someone who has been through what I have to be courageous. I went with you, didn't I? That was acting on faith, wasn't it? Why are you fussing?" I agitatedly asked.

Not fussing at you. I am simply trying to reinforce that faith must grow. I am very proud of you and how far you've come. I had to warn you to guard against fear appearing when you least expect it. You have the ability, with me, to force fear out. Allow love to overtake your heart, and fear can't survive, He taught patiently.

"I'm going, to be honest with you. I'm really afraid of what I'm about to encounter. So, if it only takes a little fear for evil to overwhelm me, I'd better wait, or I'll be a puppet again," I grumbled.

I know that, Hope. I've planned for you to watch what happened to you instead of going through the experience again. You will see everything that occurred as if watching a video of yourself, He revealed.

Breathing a sigh of relief, I relaxed considerably and then felt excited. What the Lord can accomplish is truly amazing. He knew my worries and the emotional roller coaster I was experiencing concerning this next step. He'd planned to keep me protected from my fear all along.

I didn't have to say anything. He knew I was ready. When He held out his hand, I didn't hesitate. I grabbed it, and we were off to the mall again.

Standing on the upper deck, looking down from behind the railings at the people in the center court of the mall, I saw myself approaching Mr. Arnold. What a weird sensation, watching yourself in an alternate reality while you are in that same reality.

Try to focus on the surroundings this time, Hope. Notice what approaches that you didn't see before. Everything will become clearer, and you'll understand why it happened, He told me.

I did as instructed and watched the whole scene. I could see the Holy Spirit was with me before, just like He was standing beside me now. Then I saw it! An enormous creature—so large that I wasn't even aware of it previously. What I thought was a dark cloud was actually his shadow overtaking us. I focused on its face and noted something odd. It was glaring at the Holy Spirit, taunting Him with a contemptuous grin on its face.

Looking in triumph at me, it engulfed Mr. Arnold with what looked like a shawl. It must have been the slimy and foul smelling creature's cloak I saw before. It had cast itself over us, forcing me to see Mr. Arnold in a different light. The creature's ugly coat covered Mr. Arnold's beautiful robe and concealed his true bright eyes.

Then I heard him taunt the Holy Spirit, *I've got her. She let me in so easily*.

That must have been when he turned my head to view the wicked twisted visions, making me think they were from Mr. Arnold.

Everything was becoming clear. I finally understood. The battle was always between the creature and the Holy Spirit. Mr. Arnold and I were just pawns in the game. Then something occurred to me. I'd forgotten the sadness the Holy Spirit felt when I wanted to withdraw from Mr. Arnold's presence. Evil had won the battle of wills through me.

I looked up into his glorious face and said, "I'm so sorry. I didn't know."

Immediately, we were back in my living room. The journey hadn't taken long. I'd witnessed all that I needed to know from that experience, and it was ugly. If we are pawns in the middle of this heavenly battle to hurt the Lord, we need the Scriptures for a weapon. There isn't any place or anything safe without the Word in your heart, accompanied by the Holy Spirit to interpret the Word by your side.

Hope! Stop fretting. Remember you were still very new when you encountered Mr. Arnold the first time. You were not equipped with the power instilled through spiritual baptism yet. There was a separation between us that evil used against us, but he can no longer conquer unless you allow it, He said.

"That's what it means in the Word when it warns us that the battle is the Lord's. Evil hates you, and it uses us against you. If we are abandoned, get hurt, or killed in the process, it's fine as long as you are grieved and wounded. Am I, right?" I inquired.

We never intended for mankind to come into contact with Satan and his followers. We wanted you to depend on the love of God alone and not know the difference between good and evil.

Unfortunately, you'll be tempted by Satan and his demons for as long as you occupy your physical body. Only when you are strong enough to allow us to fight will you comprehend the redemptive blessing given by Jesus. Jesus has overcome the world already. Make sure you never lose sight of that fact, He cautioned. *Tomorrow is the last day before returning to work. Get some rest. I'll show you the real Joe Arnold.*

I couldn't help myself. I needed to know. "Please let me ask you this. This whole time you've been teaching me about others' needs and battles. Does any of this have to do with my circumstances? I asked for help to overcome my fears. When are, you going to teach me the promises I need to conquer them?"

Get some rest, Hope. You'll understand soon, was all He would say.

—⁓⊙⊙⊙⊙⊙⊙⊙⊙⁓—

The minute Hope fell asleep, Jesus said to the Holy Spirit, "Frustrating, isn't it? Her last few questions are the result of being overwhelmed, I'm sure, but she is still missing the point. In time, she'll learn to accept that she has already been equipped with my blood covenant, my Word, and my Spirit. Waiting for the announcement of that revelation is so frustrating! Even in this state, she is still an awesome force for good."

Not only were the Holy Spirit and Jesus talking about Hope, Satan was also having his own little powwow with his followers concerning her. Satan was no dummy. This little pawn had too much baggage, and he knew how to use it against her. "I'll quickly break her usefulness. One more day, and I'll be back in her life. I'll bombard her with issues. She will have too many of my demons to handle. Plus, I'll assign a few giants to interfere. Can't let her rest! I'll wear out this so-called saint. The needs of her friends will exhaust her. She'll be so weak and depleted that it will be easy to move in for the kill."

———

I woke up early the next day feeling refreshed. I must have been worn-out because I was asleep the moment my head hit the pillow. I didn't even dream, which was unusual for me. I rolled out of bed, showered, and put some food in my belly.

I cooked another hardy meal because I didn't know what the day would entail. While cooking eggs and bacon, I listened to a television program on a Christian network. I was amazed at the good teachings available all this time, and I'd just ignored them. But let's face it. I didn't want to find them a few weeks ago.

Now I couldn't seem to get enough; it was like food for my soul.

Sitting down to watch the television, another local Christian program came on. It was my church's weekly broadcast filmed a few weeks prior to my re-connection. I turned up the volume and paid attention. I heard the pastor state they were visiting the local Boys' Home—one of their ministries. Standing next to him was Joe Arnold.

I grinned. This was not a coincidence. This lesson was prearranged for me to watch.

"I know you're doing this. You've set this up. This just can't be a coincidence. I know you are behind this, aren't you?" I asked.

Good morning to you, too, Hope, He said.

"I'm sorry, I didn't mean any disrespect. I assume you're with me all the time. So, I just started talking," I responded.

I am with you all the time, but it is always nice to bless a new day. To answer your question, yes, this show is something I've planned for you to watch. Be observant and learn more about this admirable man, He interjected.

The program was very emotional. It demonstrated hardships the Boys' Home faced each day. It showcased blessings given by volunteers and people in the church who supported this cause.

The main supporters and volunteers were the Arnolds. Their dedication to the home opened a door for the church to get involved. Their brave intervention on the home's behalf helped it receive the extra funding necessary to keep the home open and the boys' needs provided. Until recently, the Boys' Home was privately owned by a wealthy entrepreneur. The owner died, and due to the economy change, his estate didn't leave enough money to sustain the establishment's needs. That's when Joe Arnold convinced the church to step in and help. He used the platform that orphans were to be taken care of by the church. After many board and congregational meetings, the Boys' Home was purchased by the Christian Fellowship. Orphaned children are brought into this shelter, and area churches lend aid when rough times arise. This home is run God's way by providing the boys with a family and shelter but mainly love.

Wow! The church I grew up in has really changed. Their involvement in this home makes me want to show up and give support. I just didn't know what I could do. Then the Holy Spirit startled the wits out of me again. I don't think I'll ever get used to having someone living in my head. He spoke up and said, *do what you've been called to do, Hope. Pray.*

"It's a miracle I don't cuss out loud sometimes when you do that to me. It's like you enjoy sneaking up on me, purposely trying to spook me," I said.

No, I don't, Hope. I'm just using the time allotted to my advantage. After today, you'll have to seek me again. While I have today, I'm going to talk with you whenever and by whatever means, I can. I want to help you. I consider this time crucial. Tomorrow, your daily responsibilities will overtake your mind. I can't enter in unless you invite me, He shared.

"What? I thought you'd never leave me. That you'd always be with me?" I responded.

True, I'll always be with you. You'll shut me out unintentionally with your worldly daily activities because they aren't ministry-based, He explained.

Then a little exasperated, He asked, *are we going to waste this lovely day talking about tomorrow or are we going accomplish something?*

"Okay, now what? You've made your point showing me how wonderful Mr. Arnold truly is. What's next on the agenda?" I quipped.

Did you notice on the program that they are having an open house at the Boys' Home today? He asked.

"Yeah, why?" I inquired.

It's time for you to see firsthand how Joe used what the devil meant for evil and turned it around for good, He said.

"Oh, no! I'd be too ashamed to be in his presence, knowing what I know about him. My demeanor would give me away somehow. Can't I just go there in the spirit and watch?" I expressed.

Joe doesn't know you have knowledge about his past. Focus on the mission at hand—watching his actions and the joy he receives. To the best of your ability, forget the past and look at the now. Enjoy the moment. Engage him in conversation concerning the boys. Examine how he keeps his particular giant at bay. Now that you know the creature is always lurking about, trying to cast a bad light on things, you won't be fooled. Remember it is afraid

90

of me. You have me in you. I was just alongside the first time you encountered it, He advised.

"Will it be like it was at church the other night?" I asked. "That was fun. I got to socialize with the members utilizing my new sight and hearing."

When He didn't answer right away, I wondered. "Will I have these abilities after today?"

God never takes back a gift He has given, Hope. Only you have the ability to suppress it or use it. It's entirely up to you. That was his answer.

"Like my robe—available, but I must elect to use it," I responded.

It was already 8:00 a.m. I tried hard not to dwell on the fact it was the last day as I rushed to my bedroom to put on jeans, a shirt, and tennis shoes. I didn't bother with styling my hair or with putting on much makeup. I wasn't interested in impressing anyone. I wanted to enjoy my day, not waste it looking in a mirror. All I needed was to put my hair in a ponytail and apply mascara, blush, and lipstick.

I took a few minutes on my computer to look up the address of the Boys' Home. I wasn't even aware one existed in the area. I was shocked the home was only a mile from the church. The home had been operating longer than I realized because I just hadn't cared to open my eyes.

I took the time to change the channel on my radio to a station that only played Christian music. I wanted to stay focused and upbeat. Secular music has a tendency to sway your moods. During my ride, I praised and worshiped, singing to my heart's content with three wonderful Christian artists. I finally saw the large sign designating the Boys' Home. How had I missed it all these years? When I drove up, I noticed a large campus. It was like a school. It had a field behind the buildings, apparently for football games, with bleachers for spectators. There were four large buildings painted a lovely shade of blue. I was surprised the parking lot was almost empty until I remembered it was 8:30 a.m., a little early for most visitors or interested staff.

91

The moment I shut my SUV door, a lovely young boy, about thirteen years old, greeted me.

"Are you here for the open house?" he asked.

"I sure am. I watched the program concerning this place on TV this morning. I was really interested." Walking closer, I introduced myself, "Hi, my name is Hope Anderson. What's your name?"

"Bobby Sawyer," he replied.

A few seconds after the introduction, he was joined by several other small boys, all of them friendly, trusting, and no older than five. Suddenly, like a mother hen missing her chicks, Mr. Arnold came running out of the main house. "Hey, fellows, let the lady come inside," he hollered.

I couldn't help but notice the shadow instantly hovering over us. I knew what it was. When I looked up, it was glaring at me. The giant was here and looking point-blank at me. I didn't freak like I thought I would. I mentally gathered my robe up over my head and asked without speaking out loud, *Okay, you said it is afraid of you, so why is it staring at me?*

It is glaring at me, Hope, not you. I'm in you, remember? The battle is mine. Remove yourself from the altercation, He ordered.

How? I asked.

Ignore it. Pretend it doesn't bother you or matter at all, He directed. He didn't have to tell me twice. I focused on the kids and went inside.

"Hi, Mr. Arnold," I said, as I smiled and shook his hand.

"Hope, what brings you this way?" he asked.

"I saw the pastor's program this morning on TV. I had a day off and decided to see for myself what our church is doing," I replied.

"I'm so glad to have you visit. Come in and let me show you around," he said.

Love, God's Most Effective Weapon

I was escorted into a lovely huge main building that was warm and inviting. There wasn't anything fancy in the whole place, but it was clean and met their needs. The walls looked freshly painted; the seating area including a television that was well used. Nothing was extremely worn looking like I was expecting. Everything seemed orderly. There wasn't anything out of place or lying around to be stepped over.

Breathing in deeply, I couldn't help but make an "umm!" sound. The aroma of fresh baked bread hit me like a punch in the nose. The smell permeated the whole room.

"Smells great, doesn't it?" he asked. "Believe it or not, my wife, Olivia, teaches these fellows to make bread. The kids had her up early this morning because they wanted today's visitors to have some homemade sandwiches using their own bread."

Turning to answer him, I noticed his robe was on and his eyes were twinkling like the eyes on pictures of Santa Claus. Joe Arnold radiated love. My heart melted.

I answered his question by saying, "The bread smells amazing. Did you say the boys baked it themselves? I'd love to see them in action. Maybe even have a sample."

Then I felt a little hand take mine and start pulling me toward the kitchen. "That munchkin pulling on you is Tommy Grant," Mr. Arnold said as an introduction.

Grinning up at me, the cutest little fellow said in a little boy's slang, "Come on! Come on! Mrs. Arnold always lets me have a butt end. I'll get you one. You don't make samitches with them."

Looking at Mr. Arnold, I asked: "You and Mrs. Arnold live here?"

"No, we volunteer most of our time, though. She teaches the boys how to keep house, cook, and do their laundry, and I usually wind up playing ball games with them, coaching mostly. Since we've both retired from the school system, we needed something to occupy our time. We love children, and why not love on those that need it most? We love each one like they were our own. Our two boys are grown. One has a family of his own. With them grown and gone, our house is a lonely place.

When we were no longer working around kids and our boys moved out, we felt empty. God impressed upon us to enlarge our hearts to make room for these boys. It keeps us young, and the kids experience a loving relationship by witnessing how we respect and love each other," he shared.

At that particular moment, I was elated he didn't know I was aware of his history. I caught the meaning behind that last sentence very well.

I understand what you meant when you said Jesus uses the tools of destruction against the enemy, I communed to the Holy Spirit.

You're learning. Observe how Joe refuses the perversion Satan tried to inflict on him by showing these boys proper love and respect between men and women, He urged.

While talking, Mr. Arnold led me into an incredible kitchen. It had all the goodies any woman could wish for. Nothing was super expensive. It was just well equipped. Going over to the sink, Mr. Arnold planted a quick kiss on a lovely woman elbow-deep in soapy water, washing dishes. Then he introduced her as his wife.

"Pardon me. I didn't know people would arrive so soon. I'm Olivia Arnold," she said, after wiping her hands and offering to shake.

"I'm Hope Anderson," I replied as I took her hand.

Recognition flickered in her eyes. "I remember you. You're all grown up, but it's been a few years since you graduated from high school."

While I was looking into the face of this lovely person, not knowing how to respond, I felt a tug on my shirt. It was Tommy again. He got my attention by offering me a piece of freshly baked bread on a small paper plate. "Try it. It's great," he said proudly. "Bobby and Joseph made it this morning. Mrs. Arnold teaches the older guys how to do it. I can't wait until I'm old enough to bake bread. That way, I don't have to share. I can have all I want." He giggled.

I hugged his little body and said, "Thank you, Tommy, I'll love it."

"No, eat it! It's good," he said impatiently.

I did as ordered and was amazed. "This is heavenly. I'd love to know how to make something this awesome," I replied.

Then Mrs. Arnold shushed Tommy off, "Off with you! Go play, you little rascal."

Then she asked me, "Hope, what brings you to this wonderful place?"

"I've been away from church until lately. I didn't know this was part of the ministry until this morning. I had the day off and stumbled on the pastor's television program while eating breakfast. I was really moved by everyone becoming family for these boys, and I wanted to witness it firsthand, maybe even get involved somehow," I shared.

I couldn't tell her I came to be with her husband and learn from him. That would sound weird. I sat on one of their comfortable sofas, listening while she prattled on about the place and how much each child meant to them. Fifteen boys lived at the Boys' Home. Most were at school during the day while the four youngest stayed with volunteers at the home. There were only two people employed as caregivers. Each day was a challenge without the church volunteers. She had the same heart's desire as her husband, defining the reason they spent most of their time at the home. The boys' greatest needs were stability and love.

She patted me on the knee and said, "I'm going to let Joe take you on a tour of the grounds, showing you more of what goes on here. I still have a little cleaning to do before the open house gets into full swing. We can talk again, maybe before you leave. If not, I hope to see you Sunday morning at church."

Roaming the campus with Mr. Arnold, I remarked on how immaculate the grounds were. Flowers and shrubs adorned each building, framing them with beauty. Seeing my amazement, he proudly acknowledged, "The boys learn everything here. We

95

teach them to cook, clean, take care of their laundry, do yard work, repair toys or small engines. Before they leave, they will have skills and knowledge other kids may never get. Let me show you one of Olivia's pride and joys."

Rounding the main house, we came upon a garden. It was flourishing with every vegetable imaginable. They even had an area fenced just for corn.

"I love this! She has a vegetable garden for them. I just read in Genesis about God telling Noah what his family should eat—meat, fresh fruits, and vegetables. This is wonderful. They will be nourished with good, healthy food instead of junk food," I exclaimed.

"She taught them how to maintain a garden, so she doesn't tend it anymore. They love the food and are learning to take pride in what comes from hard labor. The house parents and older boys cook their meals. Almost every meal includes something from this garden," he said proudly.

"You sound like you really love this place. They are very fortunate to have you and Mrs. Arnold." I sighed.

He tearfully looked at me and disclosed, "Hope, I came from here. This place is part of me. I want nothing more than for these boys to be raised with proper values. Being an orphan isn't as bad as being a kid with parents who are cruel. The Lord provides their needs when He is allowed to get involved. All we have to do is provide the love. It is gratifying to watch them grow, become honorable men, and obtain happy healthy lives.

We teach them to respect each other, to honor and protect women. We stop cruel, self-indulgent behavior before it has a chance to take root. It's being a father again, which I feel is my God-given call."

I hugged him hard. "You're so special. I'm glad I had the opportunity to come today. I can't believe I have lived in this area all my life and never known about the Boys' Home," I said.

After seeing the garden, he showed me the shop where they repaired bikes, lawn mowers, etc. It also housed fishing rods and tackle, balls and bats, football gear and equipment. They had so much to be grateful for. Then he took me inside the barn, which had been converted to a gym. On the inside, it looked just like the one we had at high school. No wonder Mr. Arnold was good at sports. He grew up learning firsthand.

As we were walking back to the main house, a school bus pulled in beside the barn. A tall man exited, and Mr. Arnold smiled radiantly. "Let me introduce you to someone special."

He beamed. "Hope, this is my oldest son, Brent. He makes time each morning to take the boys to school before going to work." These two men glowed with the love they had for each other.

Brent smiled and held out his hand to shake mine. "It's good to meet you, Hope. I wish I could stay and take part in the tour, but I have a meeting at the office. I hope to see you again soon." Then he looked at his dad and said, "See you tonight."

While Brent walked to his own vehicle, Mr. Arnold warmly shared, "We are so proud of him. He has become a fine man. He spent six long years in law school and finally moved back to town where he is working for the District Attorney's office. We don't know where the interest in law came from, but it has made him happy. Our youngest son, Carl, coaches. He's a chip off the old block, can't get enough of sports. Carl met a fine girl. She was here doing social work for the county. They have two sons of their own. Olivia and I know Brent is lonely. He spends too much of his free time here with us and these kids. We pray every night that God will hurry and send him a soul mate."

More people were arriving for a tour, so I had to say good-bye to the Arnolds. Before I left, I had the opportunity to tell Mrs. Arnold how impressed I was with her garden. Then the Holy Spirit led me to bless them by letting them know how I truly admired them and how they were blessing this community.

In the SUV, on the way back home, I thanked the Holy Spirit. "I really appreciate the opportunity to see the home. There was more love there than most kids will ever know. Mr. Arnold is truly the special man that I thought he was before the creature warped my mind. I was glad that evil thing didn't make an appearance today."

It was there, but where loves rules, it doesn't have any power to interfere. Joe uses love to keep it at bay. The devil stole from Joe, but giving away what he was denied makes the evil one crazy with hate. He can't stop Joe from being a good father figure and a good example to create healthy lifestyles for each of those orphaned boys, He informed.

"Cool! I'll make a note to use what I've learned today to torment other giants. Love is an awesome weapon against them. Love makes them miserable. What else does?" I asked.

Satan was furious! How dare He show her!

"We are not weaklings! We are mighty and powerful and will not be denied. Hate, anger, envy are just as powerful. I can't wait for my turn to teach this so-called prayer warrior a thing or two. She'll be putty in my hands. Hurt the flesh, torture the mind. If I can't break her and make her hate all things, Christian, then I'll kill her and take her out of the picture. Talk about grieving the holy one. I'll twist up his plaything real tight, maybe even break her permanently. Ha, that will be fun."

"**W**hat's next on today's agenda?" I asked.

I want you to visit Judy. She is going to share some good news with you today, He said.

"Visit Judy? How is that going to teach me anything? I thought this was going to be a day to cram my head with as much about love and overcoming as possible?" I asked, confused.

You'll see, was all He would say.

I didn't even go to my apartment. I drove straight to Mark and Judy's house. What was the mystery? When I arrived at their house, I noticed a swing set in their backyard. They didn't have children, so why did they have a kiddie swing? Huh? What was going on?

I was about to ring the doorbell when Judy opened the door and greeted me with an awesome smile on her face. She looked like I was someone she hadn't seen in years.

"What's going on?" I asked.

She hugged me and said, "Come in, come in, we have the most wonderful news. You're right on time for us to tell you about it. Mark is due home with our little surprise."

"Tell me! Show me what? Don't keep me in suspense. I can't stand the vibes you are generating, so spill before you blow up," I said.

"We're legally fostering this awesome little three-and-half-year-old boy. If he learns to accept us, we may even adopt him. Our church has a ministry for orphaned boys, and I just fell in love with this kid. When he comes into my class on Sundays, he just lights up the room. Mark and I have wanted children for so long. While we wait for our own, we decided to share our love with one of these little guys," she told me excitedly.

While she talked, she kept looking out the kitchen window for Mark to come home. Finally, he drove up just as she finished telling the details of the foster care guidelines. I could see into the backseat of Mark's car. A little blond head was barely visible through the car window. When the door opened, I could hardly believe my eyes. The little boy was my new friend, Tommy Grant.

"No way! I just met that little fellow this morning. He is so sweet," I told Judy.

Tommy ran up to Judy and gave her a great big hug. Then I was able to say to him, "Small world. Do you remember me? You gave me a piece of your bread this morning."

"Yes ma'am, I remember. I'm going to live here for a while with Mr. and Mrs. Carmen. She's my Sunday school teacher, and Mr. Mark plays games with us kids. They are my bestest friends," he shared.

Mark asked, "You met Tommy this morning?"

"Yeah. I was visiting the Boys' Home's open house. I was real early and had a private tour with Mr. Arnold before the crowd showed up. You must have come while we were walking around the grounds or something," I answered.

"I had a few legal issues to wrap up with Greta Arnold, Tommy's social worker. Afterward, we packed his things and headed home. We must have just missed each other," he responded.

Feeling in the way, I said, "I need to get home. I can see you have fun things planned. Bye, Tommy. I'll see you at church Sunday morning."

I had a great morning. Now I felt depressed and didn't know why. My apartment felt lonely and oppressive. Little did I know that my own personal giant was trying to destroy my joy?

———♦———

Seeing Hope's negative emotions increasing, the Holy Spirit tried to get her to confront her own issues. Hoping she wouldn't allow this creature to dominate her mind, He asked her to consider letting Him help her. "It's time to deal with the reasons you don't feel loved, Hope."

———♦———

Unknowingly, I brushed off the issue and changed the subject again. "This day has been great. It was amazing to witness how God's plan weaves people's lives together, resulting in one big unit working in and through love. The whole family happily involves themselves with the needs of the Boys' Home."

"I can't wait to see if you're going to top this morning's experience. What's up next?" I asked.

Disappointed that she wasn't ready yet, He said, *take a while to ponder what you saw and heard today then let's pray for them. Each person you encountered today needs prayer. Use you're calling to help by getting the Father involved. Not a person on this earth cares more about children and those who help them in his name. The two of us praying allows Him to move. If you are interested in your petitions on their behalf, pray that he shows you the good work accomplished through your prayers. Always remember to ask for this blessing. Without being allowed to see some positive results from your prayers, Satan could use uncertainty to slow down and possibly stop progress altogether.*

"Okay. Can I search the Scriptures for guidance so I can prepare my mind? It helps me to know where to rest my thoughts while you are using my mouth," I asked.

Whatever makes you comfortable? Just remember that I am the Word. Even when you don't know how to think, I do. Just believe that I'm all you need. The promises are yours for all time. They are anchors for your soul, but the Word cannot be trapped. It needs to move freely to correct or remove the works of the enemy, He urged.

—⁓⁓⁓⁓⁓—

While Hope settled in with her Bible, Jesus and the Holy Spirit agreed to imprint one word in her thoughts so clearly that she would search out scriptures on the subject all afternoon. The word was *love*—what it means, what it does, how it affects, wins, and conquers. God's ultimate and divinely used tool is love.

Passing the Time with Love

Not only did I use my Bible, I retrieved my laptop so I could use a Christian search engine to help me find scriptures. One word was burning in my brain—love. Each person I met today used love's energy or sought out its comfort. Searching out scriptures on love was a good place to start.

———————

The giant of insecurity and pain writhed in torment as Hope feasted on the word the Lord imprinted in her mind. Each nugget she found pierced its evil heart with revulsion, causing it to search a hole to cower in. Its plan to use loneliness to force her out of the house was thwarted.

———————

I was amazed at all the scriptures in the Bible concerning love. The search engine I used found 566 verses on the subject. This was too much for me to remember, so I decided to get my notebook again. What better way to anchor my soul than study like I did in school. Some verses were lengthy, and others were short, but I searched for substance. Love alone was a subject worthy of my attention.

Two scriptures kept ringing true. The first one was to love thy neighbor as you love yourself. The other was to love the Lord your God with your mind, heart, might, and your entire being. Since I started leaning my heart on the Lord, I've never felt more loved. The ripple effect is to love others.

Apparently, it was true for everyone. These two scriptures seemed to rule each person I met or encountered today. Love was very evident.

My eyes read each scripture and kept going down the line of each reference until another would catch my attention. One held true for the Boys' Home. It plainly said that God executes justice for the fatherless and the widow and loves the stranger or temporary resident giving him food and clothing. This promise proved itself for me today. It was very evident. The home had adequate food. The boys seemed to have clothing and other needs provided. God was holding fast to that promise. He even provided a residence with Mark and Judy for little Tommy.

My appetite was whetted now. I couldn't get enough. Scriptures kept jumping off the screen at me, and I was having the time of my life writing down this awesome knowledge so I wouldn't have to look up the same scriptures over again. I came across how love and joy work hand in hand. Anyone who loves God's name will be joyful in Him and have high spirits. This was also evident today. Everyone I came in contact with was happy.

Then I came across an anchor. Words absorbed deep in my heart. God's love will follow me the length of my days, and in his presence, I will dwell. He will never leave me or forsake me and He will preserve all who love Him and destroy the wicked.

"Thanks for refreshing me again. I can never get enough of knowing you are with me and protecting me," I said gratefully to the Holy One.

You're welcome, He replied.

———〰️⚭⚭⚭〰️———

The Lord said to the Holy Spirit, "If she doesn't retain any other scriptures, I'm glad these have taken root. They will come in very handy when the time comes. It won't be much longer, but until then, times are going to get rough for her. It's part of the process. Keep trying to make her confront why she feels unworthy of love."

———〰️⚭⚭⚭〰️———

My neck and shoulders were getting tired, causing me to glance at the computer's clock. It was already late in the afternoon, and I hadn't eaten or done what I agreed to do. Taking a few minutes to eat and make a pit stop in the restroom before continuing my studies helped relax my body. I didn't want to stop. I was having the time of my life. I'd get to praying shortly, but my mind was hungry for all this love talk.

I came upon the scriptures that I learned the other day about being ready for love and how God covers us with it. It's like his skirt. We seem to think that things make us happy and enable us to feel loved. How foolish we are! It is his love for us. Wow! That's so sweet and comforting.

My heart ached a lot when I pondered on those words. I know my parents love me, but growing up, they never really showed me. I had everything I needed and more, but their time wasn't always available. Work, entertaining, and even church functions kept them too busy for me. I spent most of my time with sitters. I refused to dwell on those thoughts; that was a sore spot.

—◦◦◦◦◦◦◦◦—

Watching Hope, the Holy Spirit was glad she was opening up with herself. The Word will do the work as part of the cleansing process. Even sensing how much He cares can purge someone's wrong thoughts. It will cure the iniquities left from generational curses.

—◦◦◦◦◦◦◦◦—

I also read that we can grieve the Lord. We do that by forgetting his love, chasing after love from man instead. Been there, done that. I chased after guys and look what I found. I must have been crazy. That is why I failed so badly in my marriages. His was the only true love. Man's was conditional. Amen to that! If a woman isn't rich or sexy, most men aren't interested. I was looking for love in all the wrong places, like the old song. Then I read we are called upon to love and rely on God more than anyone in our family. Even a family's love isn't trustworthy, but God is always faithful—even unto death!

Focusing on God's love and protection causes all things to work together for our good. Man, cannot promise good things will always happen. But with God, all things are possible because nothing, not even death, can separate us from his love. This was heavy reading, hard-core stuff.

Then these words practically jumped off the screen at me. Love does no wrong to one's neighbor. Therefore, love is the fulfillment of the law. Love is all we need to practice, and practicing makes perfect. We need to make loving others a priority. No other work matters because only love can edify and build up. It encourages and helps someone grow. It gives courage and strength to be what God wants. His love helps us to endure because it is patient and kind. His loving spirit working in us is never envious or jealous of others, nor will it boast of itself and cause one to display haughty attitudes. His love helps us bear anything and causes us to see the goodness in everyone. His love never fails in us, through us, or for us. This was a mouth full to chew on, so sweet to the soul. That is why the Word tastes like honey.

Then I found scriptures to use against fear and doubt. God's love for us helps us to cast out fear. His love will not allow fear to have a resting place. Love will even cause dread to disappear. Hallelujah! Praise God! My mind was dancing, spinning, and leaping.

My hand was getting tired from writing. I wasn't finished reading all the scriptures concerning love, but my body was begging for rest. What better time to keep my promise? I let my mind wander over the day, recalling who and what I came in contact with. This day was extraordinary for me. Now I needed to do something special for the one who made it wonderful by praying for those He loves.

"Lord, I'm ready. My mind is so full of love and encouragement right now. Please use it along with my mouth to fulfill your desires for everyone crossing my path today," I asked Him.

Thank you, Hope, He said.

Laying my head back on the sofa, I allowed the Lord to use my voice. He muttered words through me that I had no way of knowing, let alone understanding. I just submitted my mouth and let Him talk. My mind stayed focused on the specific people I encountered today. Some, I prayed precise desires for; others, He alone knew what they needed and wanted. I knew everyone needed His love, mercy, and patient understanding.

When I finished, I was exhausted. However, I didn't forget the one thing He informed me to ask for. "Lord, please let me see some awesome results from our prayers. Don't allow the devil to ever keep me from praying with you."

I didn't want our time together to end. These three days were wonderful and enlightening, sometimes frightening, but altogether awesome. I hoped it wasn't a one time experience. I needed more days alone with the Lord. I needed to do this on a regular basis. To be totally in His world, never needing to work or answer to this world's system would be great, but that would be wishing my life here on earth to end. I needed to welcome every day as a new adventure, letting Him lead me to green pastures and making all things work together for my good. I wanted to discard the old me, always worried about tomorrow. I needed to thank Him again and let Him know how much He means to me.

"Lord, thank you again for our time. Help me please to never lose focus. I know you said that my attention would be taken away from you, but don't let it be for very long. It would feel like I was dying to be without your presence. I know I've never been happier than these few days with you."

It's been my pleasure, Hope. We'll have other days alone together. Remember, even in a crowd, I'm never far from you, ever. Call on me, and I will answer. Try to get some rest. Tomorrow is our new day, He said.

My body was tired, but my mind was racing. All night, I dreamed about fighting demons with love. I was superhuman, wearing a red suit, keeping the creatures at bay with a sword of light and words of love. I shielded the innocent with hugs and kisses and cleansed the lonely with companionship. Love never rested, love never wasted time, and love is never alone as it sought out the lonely.

———

Puffed up by pride with an evil plot against Hope, Satan took a few moments to inflict pain on her person. This new day belonged to Him. He'd use it to show this puppet of the Holy One just how outnumbered she really was. His invasion into her reality was going to be stupendous.

"She'll feel outmatched, outnumbered, and overwhelmed as she tries to fight. I'll have her spirit broken in a matter of days, if not minutes," exclaimed the enemy.

———

When the alarm clock woke me the next morning, my head felt like it was about to explode. My mind had been too busy. All night long, it was reacting to the information that had been crammed in that afternoon. It was no wonder my brain hurt. It was like how overeating makes you miserable. My brain was responding to stuffing it to the limits.

Because of the pain, I forgot a very important request from the Holy Spirit. It was just yesterday, barely twenty-four hours ago that He suggested I bless each day first by remembering Him.

My new day started in pain. I had to move and get ready for work. Determination kept me moving, even if I was slow. I didn't have any more leave to use. I took two pills for my headache and got some coffee before trying to focus on what to do next.

I thought to myself, *this work thing is a bummer. Going back to work on a Friday was insane. What in the world would I be facing?* Even in my current physical condition, I realized I was allowing fear and dread in my thoughts when I really didn't need to worry. Through the pounding in my head, I was barely able to convince myself everything would be fine.

I stared at myself in the mirror while applying makeup. It seemed like I hadn't had any time off. I was back on the wheel of life doing the same things. Had I really been on vacation at all? This pain was causing me to doubt that I even had a Lord, let alone spending time with Him. I had to get a grip. Pain or no pain, I was bound by rules and needed my job. I'd make it through the day somehow.

When I finished putting on my clothes and makeup, I went to the kitchen for a quick bite to eat before leaving. I wanted a Pop-Tart, reverting to my old way of thinking. Then I remembered I had fruit, cheese, and cooked eggs in the fridge. New day, remember? I need to eat right, get healthy, and treat myself better.

With that in mind, I fixed myself a bowl of strawberries and cottage cheese, grabbed a boiled egg, and went to sit down on the sofa so I could eat and watch TV. Then I saw my Bible and notebook. Instead of turning on the TV, I flipped through my notes, enjoying myself all over again with the promises of God's love. When I finished eating, I noticed my headache had subsided. I must have been hungry, causing such a painful headache. Now I could face the day full of the Word and good quality food.

I was glad I reread my notes. My mission field would be in the marketplace or at the office. I remembered I needed to use my gifts of new sight and hearing in order to love correctly. *Don't get in a hurry to pray until I've opened my heart to see or hear the truth*, I thought. I was a little hesitant, but at the same time, I was eager to know what had been lurking while everyone (including me) was going about normal activities. The Lord promised He would always be close by, so I'm never ever going to be alone again. *Don't forget the robe*, I thought. I needed to remember the covenant and the knowledge I've gained. Demons are afraid of me, and the giant creatures are afraid of Holy Spirit. The Lord and I are like pieces of forged iron, stronger together. I must never forget that everyone I come across needs love. Practice loving and being useful for the Lord was my purpose.

It was easier said than done. I was soon to find out that the world truly hates me.

People Are Rude

Satan sang, "My puppets, my puppets, come and play my game. Let's make Hope's day one of worry, fear, and pain. She won't have time to help those He holds dear. We'll make her lame. Keep her fighting and fretting and worried to boot. Before long, we'll own her and all her loot."

———〜〜∘◦◦◦◦◦〜〜———

Dread entered my mind again. I didn't want to face the work ahead of me. I wanted to be free to see and hear what I was called to do. I resented the mundane tasks required to put food on my table and keep a roof over my head.

The dark thoughts amplified when traffic snarled. Rude drivers pulled into my lane without warning. The unusual and crazy traffic caused me to turn off my radio so I could concentrate better. When I finally found a parking place a block from the office building, my fingers were stiff from tightly gripping the steering wheel as I tried to arrive safely. I had to take a moment to unwind and pry my fingers loose. *What had just happened? I don't remember traffic ever being so life-threatening before*, I thought.

Judging how far I parked from the building, I looked down at my feet and groaned. "Why did I wear these ridiculous new shoes?" I'd wanted to look good my first day back, so I'd primped more than usual. I'd parked in the same place for years closer to the building. Today, a truck had taken my space. Now I had to walk in mile-high shoes just to get to work.

Note to self, don't wear foolish shoes to work in the event you have to hike to the office. Most days, I could walk in, settle at my desk, and hardly move for the rest of the day. Today, I wore new shoes and forgot to pack a lunch. Now I'd have to trek back to the SUV to go after something to eat or just suffer the day hungry. *I don't think I can walk the distance more than twice today in these shoes. What if I can't find a closer parking spot when I get back from lunch? Then I'll have two more times walking in these stilts. Ugh! What was I thinking wearing these shoes to work before breaking them in? I won't have any toes left if I walk too much. Maybe I can get someone to pick me up something to eat at lunchtime*, I thought.

I wanted to cry by the time I got to my desk. My feet hurt, my head ached again, and the mess on my desk made me want to throw up. My desk is usually orderly. Everything is organized so I don't have to waste time. But not today! Files were everywhere! Pens and rubber bands lay on the floor or in my chair as if they had been tossed from the entrance. One of my plants had been knocked off my filing cabinet, and dirt was on everything. No one had bothered to straighten or clean up the mess.

Joan must have seen my office light because she stuck her head inside my workspace. "Wow! What a mess," she said first thing.

"Hi, Joan. I can't say it's good to be back, that's for sure," I snapped.

"Sorry about this. It's been crazy around here this week. I need your weekly and monthly reports turned in by 3:00 p.m. today. Since I'll be on leave Monday, I have to submit the information in case the managers have questions about the stats. Good to have you back," she said before practically running away.

I couldn't have heard correctly. Both reports by this afternoon? No way! It's hard enough to get information from my coworkers for daily statistics let alone weekly or the monthly stats. "Sit down, get a grip, focus!" I ordered myself.

First things first, I kicked off my shoes and started cleaning up the mess. I was never able to work in chaos. I needed order.

I swept the dirt, returned the plant to the cabinet, picked up the pens and bands, then neatly stacked the files. Now I could at least see my desk. Messages were piled next to my telephone, telling me to do this and that. They could wait. What to do first?

I opened my desk drawer and found everything out of place. Someone had rifled through my desk. Who had done this and why? No matter, I didn't need the dark thoughts ruling the day. Just focus on the work. Cleaning could wait.

When I finally found the folder containing the weekly stats done earlier in the month, I had my starting place. Monday, I had to compile information. Maybe it wouldn't be too hard, after all, to finish by 3:00 p.m. I needed the remainder of this week's figures. I poked around in the mess piled on my desk, hoping to find that my coworkers had turned in their work for the week. Five agents were in my area, but only one had completed work on schedule. The other four had ignored the procedure since Monday. Immediately, I fumed. "These aren't two-year-olds needing to be asked repeatedly. They know the deadlines!"

My first thought was getting on my computer and sending a memo to each agent about the importance of staying on top of daily issues to meet our deadlines. That wouldn't be very loving. I had to keep loving people. It was a critical command. I reminded myself that we needed to work as a team. I grabbed a pen and pad, put on my miserable shoes, and purposefully made an attempt to ask sweetly for the reports.

I jumped out of the frying pan directly into the fire! John was the first agent I came in contact with. He was already swearing when I walked up. When he saw me, he barked, "Where the hell have you been? Why haven't you done my legal notices? Joan is on my ass, and it's your fault."

My response was, "Well, good morning to you too." Then I remembered my same mistake this morning. Shamefully, I too had forgotten to greet the Lord first thing.

I continued trying to defend myself, "I've been on sick leave for a few days. I'll get to your notices as quickly as I can. Joan needs the weekly and monthly reports done by 3:00 p.m.

today. Have you gotten Tuesday, Wednesday, and yesterday's daily reports finished?"

He responded sharply, "I didn't have time to type them up, so I laid them on your desk last night. Everything is there. I don't have anything to report for today. It shouldn't take you long. Then get on my notices. I can't document that I've worked on any collections until notices are completed and in the mail."

"Oh, wait!" he commanded.

Turning back toward him, I reacted just in time to catch a file he was throwing at me. "Do this notice for me too?"

I noted on my pad that John's daily reports were on my desk, and Friday would be zero collections. Next, I hobbled down the hall, hoping Amber would have her reports ready.

She was polishing her nails when I entered her office, oblivious to anything going on around her. At least she said she was glad to see me. Then her tone turned nasty as she started complaining about me being off. She claimed she had to do my job. No one would answer the phones, the copier broke down, and she had to call a repair person. Dealing with office work wasn't in her job description. She and John couldn't get their collections done in my absence. She also left her reports on my desk to be completed when I returned. "Fair was fair," she claimed.

I made another note that Amber's daily reports were also on my desk. My first two encounters were bad; the last two were even worse. The other two agents were out of the office. Nothing on their desks resembled a daily report. I refused to plunder through their desk drawers. It felt like going through a home when the owner was gone. Both were working in the field, collecting taxes from employers disregarding the deadlines. Didn't they care about any responsibility besides collections? I would have to track them down to get as much as I could from a phone conversation. At least John and Amber had given me notes to type from.

Upon returning to my office, I located John's and Amber's daily reports amongst the files I'd stacked up earlier that morning. Everything was all mixed up. What made me think these people would help or work as a team? Uniting against one another but not working together as a unit. After typing their daily reports and compiling their figures to complete my projects, I tried to reach Tom and Martha on their cell phones. Neither was pleased with my call. Each blamed me for getting behind. Absorbing their verbal blows, I swallowed hurt feelings to complete the task. I felt like a punching bag. I was angry and hurt. My nasty thoughts were extinguished when both said their reports were done before leaving the office. I had to limp back to their offices to find the reports in their desks right where they told me to look. I was able to finish both projects on time.

I hadn't been able to slow down from the moment I stepped in the building. I thought I could relax a little once Joan received the reports. She took the reports without thanks, ordering me to finish typing John's notices, plus getting them certified at the post office so he could meet another monthly deadline. Great! Now I had to go the post office for him. Why couldn't he go? I resolved not to walk in my toe crunchers to my SUV before end of workday. I refused to let this get me down. I'd make the best of this situation. I could kill two birds with one stone and get some lunch after my trip to the post office.

By the time I finished John's notices, I was hungry, tired, and irritable. I didn't care how I looked anymore. I got smart and threw vanity out the window. I went to the ladies' room, removing my pantyhose. I walked barefooted to my vehicle, with letters and purse in hand. It was a warm day, so why not? If people looked at me strange, oh well.

I got to the post office but felt a little stupid going in barefoot. I put my high heels back on. Not a smart decision putting new shoes on blistered bare feet. The pain was almost unbearable. By the time I got back in my SUV, my toes were bleeding. Now, what? I sat back in my seat and cried. I needed something to cover my feet to finish the work day. I got my act together, found a dollar store nearby, and shopped for some form of footwear.

I looked like a crazy person, limping and grunting with each step inside the store. I found a cute pair of cloth shoes. They looked like ballet slippers but didn't bind my toes. I also picked up bandages and antibiotic ointment for my damaged feet. At the checkout counter, my stomach growled, so I grabbed a Cola, two candy bars, a bag of chips, and a couple of sausage strips to reduce the hunger until I could get some dinner. Not very healthy, but pain won the battle. I was either going to suffer or eat. I chose comfort and settled for any edibles.

Eating and driving is not a good idea, but I had no choice. I returned to the office in record time. I had an extra surprise. I parked nearer to the office. Hopefully, I hadn't taken someone's particular parking place like mine was taken this morning.

Sitting at my desk, I read the messages left beside my telephone. Some of the memos were no longer relevant. Others were silly. The last one puzzled me. It read, "Put the money in your desk drawer. Make sure a money order is purchased and the funds mailed to the district office." There was no signature, so I didn't know who made the request. What was I going to do? I'd been all through my desk today, and I hadn't seen any money.

My heart started to frantically race. This was serious! Some employers brought cash for agents to pay their employment taxes. Money orders had to be purchased instead of mailing their cash. The agents are responsible for receipting funds, buying money orders, and sending to the district office. Why was I given this memo? Who made me responsible for the cash? I didn't have a clue who had left me the memo or where the money was. I ran to Joan's office, memo in hand. This could be a firing offense if not resolved.

It was after 3:00 p.m., so I couldn't interrupt Joan and Frank in a meeting with the district office. None of the agents knew anything about the memo. I couldn't waste time waiting for the meeting to end. I hurriedly walked back to my office and diligently searched for the money. Each file on my desk got a thorough examination before stowing it back in the cabinet. Every folder inside my desk was emptied and searched. I looked under the desk and behind the cabinet. Anxiety didn't help digest my lunch. I was feeling sick. How much longer would Joan and Frank be in that meeting?

I was imagining all kinds of horrible things. I could lose my job. I would have to pay the money back and still lose my job. Everyone in the office was mad at me today for something. People here didn't stick up for each other. It was all about who does what to whom.

When I finally heard Joan's office door open, I grabbed the memo and ran. I saw Frank leaving, so I hollered, "Frank, stop, please!"

He stopped, puzzled at the reason I'd be screaming and running. When I caught up, I breathlessly asked, "Did you leave this memo on my desk?"

He looked at it closely and said, "Nope, I don't know anything about this. Sorry."

"Thanks," I said.

Joan was now my only hope to solve this mystery. I tapped on her door, asking if I could come in. When she looked up, I handed her the memo, pleading, "Please tell me you know about this. I've been searching for the money but can't find any in my office."

She didn't even apologize. "I put the memo on your desk and the money inside the drawer Monday night after you left. An employer dropped it off, but Amber was gone for the day. Your desk was on my way out, so I wrote the note as a reminder to take care of it. When you called in for sick leave Tuesday, I made sure the money got to Amber so she could get a money order and send it on to the district office."

Dumbstruck, I could only babble, "Okay, I was worried it was missing. I'm glad it's handled. I'm going home now unless you need me for something else." Thank goodness she didn't.

The entire trip home I battled each coworker in my mind. I practiced words I would say the next time I saw them. How dare they blame me for their lack of organization! Amber forgetting the money order was handled Tuesday. She boldly told me she didn't know anything about the money, making me frantic. I thought Joan would at least ask if I was all right. But no! All she wanted to do today was rule the roost with an iron fist. The only person in the whole office that hadn't had an issue about something was Frank. He deserved a gold star. Boy! I'm glad tomorrow is Saturday. I don't think I could live through another workday like I had today. It seemed like I worked a whole week in an eight-hour period.

Lesson Learned

The minute I walked into my apartment, the atmosphere changed. My mind welcomed my closeness with the Lord. It was like being on vacation. I was alone but not alone. Then I felt shame envelope me. Not one time all day had I made time for the Lord, not once. I read a few scriptures, but I didn't interact with Him. Why? I'd let everything else dictate my mood today.

"Lord, I'm so sorry. You warned me this would happen. I really thought I had learned to be more respectful. I'm still the stupid, self-centered brat that I've always been. Am I ever going to live up to your expectations?" I said.

It was hard to watch you struggle today. I knew it would happen. Fridays are always hard. People are tired and grumpy from a week of hard work. You noticed it more today because you lived in peace with me the last few days. You were out of the flow. If you had been at work with them all week, you wouldn't have felt the tension so strongly. Monday will be different, He said cheerfully.

"You're not mad at me? I failed the love test miserably. I did not feel love toward anybody, not even myself," I said.

You're still very new at this, Hope. It takes practice and determination. Falling down but getting back up again. No one is able to do it perfectly. We only want you to try. Keeping an open dialogue with me will help. We are never mad at you—grieved that you refuse our help—but never mad, He replied.

"How was I so easily sidetracked? Yesterday was wonderful. I was so full of your Word. What happened?" I cried.

What is your first memory of today? Let's break down thoughts, motives, and actions, He suggested.

I had to think for a minute. What was the first thing I did after I woke up? Duh! I had a bad headache. All I could think about was getting something to relieve the pain, making coffee, and getting ready for work.

I told Him this and asked Him to interpret what He saw.

119

Satan knew about our time together, so he was determined to dominate your first waking moments. It was his evil touch you were feeling this morning in your head. Human nature has been programmed to seek natural remedies for relief of pain. Your headache wasn't physical. It was spiritual. When did you sense relief? He asked.

"I swallowed a pain reliever but didn't feel any relief until I ate something. I assumed I must have been extremely hungry," I answered.

What were you doing while you ate? He asked sweetly.

"Oh my! I read over my notes about love. I remember feeling better. I think I even said something like good food for the belly and good food for the soul. It was the Word that gave me relief, wasn't it?" I commented.

Yes, Hope. Even written on a page, love is healing for your soul. It will drive evil away every time, He shared. *God is Love. Where God is, evil can't be.*

"I had the Word in my heart. Why couldn't I act in it today? I thought I wanted to," I said.

You knew the Word, but your heart wasn't submitted to the mission. Your rebellious nature wouldn't allow it. Dread, another one of Satan's tools, caused you to hate what you had to do today. Hate and love don't work together well. I want you to think. Remember how you talked with yourself this morning. You dreaded the workload. You wanted to be with me, but dread set the tone for the day. Depression, worry, resentment ruled your day, He explained.

I instantly got mad. I allowed a creepy little demon to prey on me today. He was sucking me dry, just like the one I saw feasting on Cindy at the mall. Yuck! Yuck! Why had I been so stupid? I didn't even try to use my gifts today. I had easily relapsed into life as usual.

"I did it again. I dragged my robe instead of wearing it. I allowed a varmint to feed off me," I answered angrily. "That stupid thing must be enormous after gorging on me all day. I gave it enough to share with several of its buddies. How can I keep this from happening to me again?"

Start slow. Make reminders to call on me. Position notes, signs or anything to get your attention at your apartment, in your car, and on your desk. Post simple reminders to keep me in your daily routine. The key is constant communication. It will require continued effort. That is why it is called practice. Try these suggestions until talking with me becomes second nature, He instructed.

"Mental conversations are okay, aren't they? I don't want my friends and coworkers to lock me away in a loony bin," I said.

Yes, just keep our constant communication going. Try not to allow anything to break it. Keep me tuned in while you are having conversations with others. It will get easier and easier. Trust me. Think of me as another person in the room. I'll be invisible but very much present. Don't let yourself be without me, ever, He urged.

"Okay! Point taken! Don't be without you in my head ever. You make it sound life-threatening or something. Are you trying to scare me? I thought you were always with me? I don't understand," I remarked.

I am always with you, but you must invite me into your thoughts daily. You welcomed me after opening your apartment door. I'm always knocking, but you have to open the door to your mind, will, and emotions. I will not push in where I'm not invited. I'll knock and beat on your subconscious, but I'll never ever force myself on you, He insisted.

"Finally, I understand. Thanks," I responded.

Today was difficult, but you needed the illustration. Now that you've suffered without me, let me ask you. Do you want another day like today? Or do you want me with you helping you through every situation?

"That's a no-brainer! Of course, I want you with me. My whole day was confusing, painful, and horrible. I'm certainly going to do all I can to prevent an encore," I responded.

Your gifts accompany my presence. Without me, you are not able to use them, He informed me.

Until He mentioned my gifts, I hadn't noticed their absence. It made sense now. I thought I always had the ability. Today would have been very different if I had opened my spiritual eyes and ears by allowing Him complete access. I wouldn't have been so critical of everybody. I would have recognized what was happening. Why can't I get this wonderful message inside my brain? It seems I'm being told repeatedly what to do or how to do it as if I'm being reprogrammed because my hard drive has malfunctioned or needs rebooting.

Feeling like a child instead of a grown woman, I took his hints to heart. I immediately walked around the apartment making mental reminders. I took lipstick and wrote on mirrors, "Talk with the HS." I did the same on sticky notes and tacked them on the fridge, the cabinet, the walls, and even my alarm clock. When I reached to turn off the alarm, I would feel the paper and be reminded to talk with the Holy Spirit. He told me to take things slow, but I was compelled to prevent any more miserable days.

"I've done all I know to do. Please remember I always want you in my heart and head from now on," I said. "You have an open and standing invitation."

Thanks, Hope, but you'll need to grant permission daily. Every day is new, He explained.

"Now what do you want me to do?" I asked.

That's easy. I want you to relax and enjoy your evening. Make yourself something good to eat, watch an enlightening program, or read more Word. Talk with me about what you see, what you read, etc. Get some rest. Don't over tax your mind this evening. Allow me to bring you sweet refreshing sleep, He said so sweetly.

I thoroughly enjoyed my evening. I made myself a simple meal with the chicken strips I'd purchased Monday afternoon, adding some of the vegetables. After that, I had a small bowl of fruit and cottage cheese for dessert. I watched a funny televangelist and then read a few scriptures again about love. I refused to pack my mind so full of the Word tonight. I wanted to rest body and mind. All evening, I talked with and thanked the Holy Spirit. I told Him how good his food suggestions were, how funny his minister was on TV, on and on. In the book of Psalms, I found the scripture promising sweet sleep. Before I turned out my bedside lamp, I asked Him to stay with me while I slept. I truly got the message to keep Him close and never allow myself to be alone again.

———✦✦✦———

Watching her sleep, blessed by rest, Jesus and the Holy Spirit were happy that Hope knew she was imperfect. Pride wasn't grounded in her spirit. They discussed the need to explain that cracked vessels can't retain water. Mankind without Jesus will always be cracked. With Him, she is being mended and molded hourly for his use. Like a child, she will need to be told things over and over. She might get exasperated being continually reminded, but it will mold her into an awesome tool.

———✦✦✦———

I woke the next day fully rested and energized. I didn't forget to say, "Good morning, Holy Spirit." *Good day to you*, He replied.

When I went into my bathroom, I saw my note. It reminded me to let Him know how good I felt. "Thanks for the sweet sleep you gave me. I don't remember being this rested in a very long time. I'd like to have this kind of sleep every night," I proposed.

The best place to start receiving the kind of rest you need is remembering to feed on the Word in the morning and again read an encouraging Word before going to bed. Eventually, you'll see it will set the tone of peace in your soul. Remember the anchor? Same principle. It will ground you to me, the prince of peace. As you study more of my Word, you'll discover we want to nourish you with the meat of the Word, morning and evening. The more your soul is at peace, the better rest your body will have, He shared.

I took his advice and picked up my Bible. Then it occurred to me to ask Him what He wanted me to learn rather than to start reading from page one. I humbly asked, "Lord, where do you want me to study? You know what I need, and you know what will help me today."

After a quick consult with Jesus, the Holy Spirit replied, *Start with the first few chapters in the book of Ephesians. You'll see the conversion process and understand our feelings about you all along.*

I would not have started in that specific book. After taking his advice, I felt empowered and appreciated. I felt I could face the world, knowing that all is well with me.

On Saturdays, I usually cleaned the apartment and did my weekly grocery shopping. While I cleaned, I talked with the Lord. I even asked Him to sing along while listening to music on the Christian radio channel I found recently. I was singing joyfully and hoped He was okay with listening to my horrible singing voice. When I finished the household chores, I went shopping with Him. He showed me things in the grocery store that caused me to wonder how we could eat and be healthy. Items most people thought healthy were nothing more than sawdust— powdery versions of what was real. While we were walking down the grocery aisle, He made a statement that made perfect sense to me. If God's Word isn't at the base of an item, it wasn't created by Him; man made it. God didn't say let there be pizza or pie or candy. He must have seen me shudder and become disheartened when understanding dawned. That's when He made a point to explain He wasn't forbidding me to have these items; He was just suggesting that I *rarely* eat them.

Sunny, Fun Day

I was pondering on my lunch options as I was putting away my groceries. I heard my doorbell ring. Peering out the window, I saw a little blond head. It was Tommy. *What was he doing here?* I thought.

I opened the door to greet him and was startled to see Judy. I made a mental note not to open the door from just glancing out the window. The window didn't reveal the complete picture.

"Hi, guys. What's up?" I greeted.

"Tommy wanted to invite you to come with us to the barbecue. The church and Boys' Home are sponsoring a fund-raiser. There will be food, games, and fellowship," she offered.

Tommy chirped, "Please! We need to hurry! The game is about to start. Mr. Mark wants me to pitch. Ms. Judy needs a buddy to keep her company."

"I'd love to go! First, let me put away purchases. You go ahead so Tommy can play. I'll eat a quick lunch and meet you at the home, okay?" I suggested.

"That's great!" Judy said as she was being pulled away. "Let me get this scoundrel to the game before he pulls my arm out of its socket. If you don't see me right away, I'll be in the main house helping Olivia."

Watching them leave, I interacted with the Holy Spirit. "Thanks for putting Tommy in their life. He is so cute and sweet." Having barbecue later, I decided not to eat much for lunch. I cut up a small apple and a peach over some cottage cheese. I thought it would be enough to satisfy me until the dinner meal.

Moving to the bedroom to freshen up, I decided to change into a more festive outfit. I also snatched a lightweight sweater if the evening got too cool. I pulled my hair into a high ponytail, put on light makeup, and decided to wear a new short set that I'd bought recently. Looking in my closet for shoes, I came across the little cloth ballet shoes I'd purchased yesterday.

"Thanks, Lord. These shoes are perfect. My feet hurt from wearing running shoes this morning. Compliments from yesterday's romp in stilettos I suppose." I felt really pretty as I stepped out of the apartment.

Riding to the home, I asked the Lord, "Do you have anything to do with the invitation to this event? What's going on?"

Hope, we always try to go before you to make your life pleasant. At the fund-raiser, you'll have an opportunity to serve others while enjoying yourself. Being with family, whether you're own or your church family is better than being alone. Expand your thinking to include time for fellowship. Use the time with me to learn how to help. You've been called to pray, so get busy seeing and hearing what to pray for. You don't have to be on a spiritual journey, like with Cindy and Mrs. Lenney, to accomplish the goal. Remember how we worked together at church Wednesday night? With me, life itself can be a journey, He shared.

I had fun at church Wednesday night. I enjoyed the message and was able to use my gifts. It's amazing how much my life has altered in such a short time.

———⁓⁓∘⳾⳾∘⳾⳾∘⁓⁓———

Satan didn't like what he was hearing. His plan for Hope was slipping further and further away. Overworking her so-called gifts was the only thing he could do. He ordered his demons to populate the place and terrorize as many as they could. There were many little boy knees to scrape while they played games.

They also could cause confusion and compel the children to start fights. He would cause her to worry about discord ruining their lovely event.

———⁓⁓∘⳾⳾∘⳾⳾∘⁓⁓———

I was glad I'd worn my new shoes. The entire area was crowded, with no parking places close to the main house. Looking around for Judy, I caught a glimpse of dad and Mr. Arnold cooking the meat. I waved to them and asked, "Have you seen Judy Carmen?"

126

"Yeah, she's with your mom and my wife in the main house, making potato salad. I'm sure they could use some help," Mr. Arnold answered.

"Thanks," I replied as I changed direction.

Laughter pealed from the main house. Joy and love spilled out of these people. Seeing Mom as I walked in made me feel like I was home. Mom came over to hug me and exclaim how happy she was that I came. Then Olivia, bless her, asked me if I was comfortable helping before thrusting me into the work zone.

"I'll do whatever you want," I replied.

She said, "We need tea made, also pies and cakes cut into slices. Which task would you prefer?"

"I've never made tea in large quantities before, so I'll slice the desserts. I don't think I'll mess that up. I know I can slice cake and section off pies." I also then added jokingly, "They smell and look so good you might not have any to serve because I'll be the culprit who ate them all."

That made her laugh. "You and me both. Why do you think I'm avoiding this area?"

While cutting a cake, I heard a conversation between my mom and another woman. They were talking about sweets being their downfall. The weight on their thighs was from cakes consumed on days gone by. They kept on tearing themselves down about being fat and having no willpower. I immediately got angry. I knew what I was about to face. I turned around, knife in hand, to face the little monster head on. Floating over my Mom's head were two creepy demons, each feeding off the insecurities spoken by these two women.

Without saying a word, I banged the knife on the table hard enough to be heard but not loud enough for someone to question. It had the desired effect, though; it made the creeps look in my direction. Seeing me glaring at them, they realized with eyes bulging that they were busted. They screeched and had the sense to leave.

I had to ask, *Lord, why are these stupid things always messing with our heads? No one is safe from them. It seems people can't even talk innocently about issues without a demon trying to steal their energy. When will this end?*

Before the Holy Spirit was given a chance to reply, the door to the main house burst open. Two big teenagers were carrying two little guys who had been fighting. One had a bloody nose and skinned knee; the other had a split lip. Each was fussing and fuming over who tagged at first base. Demons were enjoying the commotion and fighting, giving them a feast.

I couldn't keep from shouting at the demons (not the kids), "That's enough! Stop that right this instant!"

The demons fled, and the boys got quiet. I had the attention of the whole room. Good!

Lord, you've got control. Please speak through me. He did, by taking my voice and commanding demons and people alike, "This is supposed to be a fun-filled day, not a fighting match!"

The effect was like a sonic boom in the spirit realm. Demons in every corner fled, and Satan growled and spit. His plan was foiled again.

In my spirit, I heard a wonderful compliment from the Holy Spirit. *Good job Hope! You are learning to allow me to take charge of a situation.* Praise my God! I wouldn't hear or see a creepy demon the rest of the day because He had voiced a command for us to have a fun-filled day.

Judy and I were almost finished putting wrapped slices of cake and pie on the barbecue plates when the front door opened and in walked Mrs. Lenney. My mouth almost hit the floor! She was beautiful. She was wearing a new pantsuit, her hair was fixed, and she was carrying that expensive bag.

When she got close enough for me to greet her, I noticed her eyes were bright. She was radiant. Flabbergasted, I spiritually asked the Lord, *did we do that? Did our prayers work so quickly? What happened?*

Many in her church's congregation have been praying with me. She is a beloved patron. Your prayers helped. You've just been rewarded visible evidence of how prayer is being answered for your friend, He informed.

I almost cried at the dramatic change.

He went on to share, *Mrs. Lenney's caregiver convinced her to get the bag later that afternoon after we prayed. Once she had purchased it, a yoke was destroyed from her mindset. She remembered her past and longed for her old self to return. It took only a few hours to restore her mind, will, and emotions.*

Due to this change, she was allowed the blessing of financing most of the necessities for this barbecue. Stuart Holmes, her lawyer and friend, observed her new mental condition. He made arrangements with her financial advisor to use her money. Now the proceeds from this barbecue can go to good use, giving her much happiness.

Mrs. Lenney and Lois, her caregiver, waved to Judy and me. "Off you go young'uns. Let us take over. You go enjoy the games."

Happy for a break, Judy and I went outside to find Mark and Tommy. We were just in time to watch their T-ball game. Finding a seat, I turned to watch a young version of Joe Arnold coaching the team. I remarked to Judy, "That has to be Carl Arnold. He looks just like his dad."

"Yeah, Carl is the spitting image of his dad, but Brent is more like Olivia," she replied.

I remembered Brent from the other day, the lawyer. I wondered if he was here amongst the crowd.

After the game, it was time to eat. Remembering there would be a fee for the meal, I hiked to my car for some cash. I'd stuffed my purse in the trunk so I wouldn't have to tote it around. On the way, I was worried about what I could eat. Even if I didn't eat much, I still needed to buy a plate. The funds being raised were for a very good cause.

I was ready to pay for my meal when I heard a familiar voice say, "I've got this." It was Frank Addison from work.

I was floored! "Thanks, I didn't know you liked functions like this."

He replied, "I've been a church member since I moved to town last year. This is my favorite charity. Whenever my schedule allows I volunteer to help the boys."

I was very grateful for my meal but wanted to sit with Judy and Mark. "I'm a guest of Judy and Mark Carmen. They are expecting me to sit with them. Would you please join us?" I asked.

"Sure, I know Mark and Judy," he remarked.

Looking down at my meal, I realized there wasn't much on the plate that was considered healthy eating. I mentally asked the Lord, *what can I do? I know this isn't good for me, but Frank bought it. I don't want to hurt his feelings by not eating.*

So, understanding, He replied, *I bought you the meal. I just used Frank to pay for it. Enjoy the day, the food, and the fellowship.*

With peace in my heart, I thoroughly enjoyed every bite. We were all having a good time. Frank remarked about my ordeal yesterday, "I felt so sorry for you having to take the blame for incompetence. That's why I volunteered to participate in the district meeting with Joan. I knew you might need backup, and I didn't want one of the others to throw you under the bus."

I wanted to cry. "I wish you had told me. I was having a horrible day."

"No problem," he said shyly.

Watching his face while he spoke, I was impressed by his blessed eyes—a true sign that God was in his life.

The four of us were watching the bigger kids play when a large van drove into the area loaded with television equipment and a large antenna on top. My eyes were fixated on the vehicle. As I watched, I recognized a familiar silhouette exiting the van; it was Cindy Grover.

I had to interject with the Holy Spirit, *No way! Is she another part of your plan?*

I'm setting the stage, Hope. She needs love. What better place and with what better people to find some? He replied.

Right away, she spotted me among the crowd. I must have been the only person she knew, so she gravitated my way. Attractively dressed in a business suit and high heels, she was a lovely sight, but I knew the real Cindy on the inside.

I welcomed her. "Hi, Cindy. I didn't know you worked at the television station. Why are you here?"

She replied, "It's good to see you. It has been years. We're doing a follow-up from the program aired earlier this week. I'm supposed to interview Joe Arnold. Do you know where we can find him?"

Frank spoke up, "Hi, I'm Frank Addison. Joe is in the gym, setting up for another type of game this afternoon. Come, I'll take you to see him."

Thankful I didn't have to do much walking with my sore feet, I said, "It was good to see you, Cindy. I hope we'll get to talk again soon."

Grinning to myself, I interacted by mentally saying, *you're sneaky. You've got something up your sleeve with Frank and Cindy, don't you? I noticed how fast he jumped in to help her.*

Maybe, was His only comment.

The day was rapidly ending. I was full and weary from all the fun. I said my good-byes to Mom and Dad, Judy and Mark, and a few others I'd met. Then I noticed Cindy and Frank sitting together. The television van was long gone. Smiling, I knew something good was happening. Walking up to them, I said, "It's good to see two fine people getting to know each other. I'm going home. I'm tired and want to go to bed. I hope to see you soon, Cindy. Frank, I'll see you Monday if I don't see you at church tomorrow."

They both said good night as I walked away.

I was about to pull out of my parking space when a car drove into the area. The driver getting out was Brent Arnold. He looked exhausted, and he certainly wasn't dressed for an outdoor event. He must have come straight from work but on a Saturday? I wondered earlier why he was missing this special event. Oh, time will tell.

Finally home, I got ready for bed. But before I lay down, I remembered to take out my Bible and interact with the Lord. "Holy Spirit, I want to thank you for a lovely day. It wasn't too hard to keep you with me. I want my life to be this peaceful every day. Is there a scripture you wish for me to read before I close my eyes?"

I had a good day also, Hope. I'd like for you to read Matthew 6. It will tell you not to worry about tomorrow. Trust me. Good night."

Like Minds

My dreams were comforting. I don't know why, they just were. I kept seeing a protector, defender, and companion always near. Many times, I'd thank the Lord and find that my protector wasn't spiritual, but a man. The Lord came in the flesh. It had to be Him. He will never leave me.

I woke up rested and anxious to get to church. Mark and Judy explained their Sunday school class was wonderful, and I'd learn from the teacher.

I remembered to greet the Lord, putting in a special request, "Good morning, Lord. I'm so glad to have this day with you. I never again want time to lapse so long that I'm embarrassed to attend church. Yesterday was wonderful. I want more, please."

Good morning to you too, Hope. Allow all things to work together for your good, He said.

Before taking my bath, I checked my closet for an outfit to wear with my soft shoes. My toes were healing, and I didn't want to cause more pain by wearing uncomfortable footwear. When I found a smart sundress and jacket in the same colors of the shoes, I breathed a sigh of relief.

I washed my hair and shaved my legs while singing the song with the phrase the Lord just shared with me, "All things work together for my good."

When I finished blow-drying my hair, putting on makeup, and dressing, I looked as good as I felt. I knew all would be okay.

It was still too early to leave for Sunday school, so I decided to make myself some steel-cut oatmeal, with honey and almonds instead of eggs. When it was finished cooking and in a bowl, I thanked the Lord for such a good meal. I also thanked Him for showing me how to determine when the food came from Him. When I tasted it, it was heavenly.

On the way to church, I asked the Lord, "Will I have to deal with creepy demons again today?"

Probably, it's part of your calling to keep watch so you'll be available for prayer. Keep your robe on, He shared.

———〜〜○〜○〜○〜○〜〜———

He hadn't wanted to scare her. Yesterday, He'd witnessed Satan growling at Him as He spoke through her. Without her robe being acknowledged, she might fall into a trap.

———〜〜○〜○〜○〜○〜〜———

"**O**ops! Remember my covenant, thanks" I said.

I recalled our church had a prayer room, so I was on a mission to find it. It made sense that I would need to use it often if I'm called to be an intercessor. When I located the room, the door was ajar. Inside, I saw a man sitting on a bench with his head in his hands. It appeared he was in deep prayer. When I opened my spiritual eyes wider, I recognized Brent Arnold. I also saw an awesome sight. His robe was beautiful. He had it completely engaged, and the beauty was overwhelming. He must have been praying the covenant blessings over something because he looked so engrossed. I decided I wouldn't interrupt. I could come back to the room later. Instead, I searched for Judy to direct me to the Sunday School class.

Mark saw me coming and motioned me into a room. The room was large, with chairs arranged in a circle so we could easily discuss the lesson. Sitting next to Judy, I eagerly shared how much I enjoyed yesterday. A deep voice interrupted, addressing me directly, "You're Hope Anderson, the lady I met the other day, aren't you?

I looked up to see Brent and responded, "Yes, it's good to see you again."

He asked, "Do you mind if I sit next to you?" "No, please do," I said.

We didn't get to chat longer because our teacher walked in. To my astonishment, it was Frank. Judy giggled when she saw my expression.

"Would you have joined us if I told you Frank was our teacher?" she asked.

"Probably not," I answered honestly.

Already feeling a little out of place, I was even more embarrassed when Frank acknowledged me in the class. "We have a new attendant this morning. Would you please tell everyone your name? Most of us know you, I think. Please make sure by standing and telling us your name."

I glared at him but complied. "Hi, everyone. I am Hope Anderson. I'm not new to the church. I've been a member here since I was five. My parents are Martin and Sue Joiner. I've stopped attending regularly until recently. I plan to be a familiar sight from now on."

Frank winked at me and smiled, knowing I would get even with him later for putting me on the spot. Then he asked everyone in the room to introduce themselves to me. It felt like first grade all over again.

I didn't have a lesson plan to follow. I couldn't read with Judy because she shared with Mark. I tried just paying attention until Brent noticed and pulled his chair closer, offering to share his. Suddenly, a chill filled the room, causing my spiritual eyes and ears to snap to attention. It didn't appear anyone in the room was being affected but me. I knew what it was. A demonic giant was trying to overtake our class. I was about to call on the Lord when I heard Brent lightly stomp his foot. It wasn't loud enough to cause others to notice, but I knew what he'd just done. I looked into his eyes to see if he was glaring at the specter.

I immediately engaged the Lord, *He has the same gifts I do, doesn't he?*

Yes. His are similar but not the same. He's been at this a little longer than you. I'm helping him with the situation. The message is powerful, and Satan is trying to interrupt. He sent a distracter. Brent is standing ground for me. All is well. Don't worry, He replied.

I have a comrade. This is great! I relaxed as the Lord suggested and tried to stay focused on Frank's lesson. It was good. He shared how important it is to maintain a strong faith regardless of what we see or hear. God's Word is truth. Satan only tells or shows us lies. The thirty-minute lesson was just enough, not too long that people lost interest. Afterward, we were offered coffee and donuts. Everyone was talking about the barbecue at the Boys' Home yesterday.

I wanted to talk with Brent but kept having people asking me questions. When the bell rang to indicate Sunday school was over, I walked to Brent. "Thanks for sharing your lesson plan. I didn't want to cause a scene by asking for an extra after he started."

"No problem. Let me see if we have another lying around here somewhere before you go," he replied.

After he gave me the plan, he asked sweetly, "Do you mind if I sit with you in church? I feel a little silly sitting like a kid with my parents."

"I know the feeling." I groaned. "I was either doomed to be the third wheel with Mark and Judy or sit with my parents. I'd love to sit together."

Truthfully, I wanted to study this man's reaction to the pastor. Last Wednesday night, I was in awe, listening to the Holy Spirit preaching through him. When his angels appeared, time quickly passed. I wanted to watch Brent without staring at him to see his reaction. The Holy Spirit said Brent had been gifted longer, so I needed to observe and learn. I felt strange about my response Wednesday night, and I was curious to know if it showed.

I was a little disappointed when I didn't have the same experience. Brent's expression never really divulged anything. The sermon was very enlightening and helpful, but something was missing.

I said goodbye to everyone after the service, feeling the need to be alone. On the way home, I asked the Lord, *what's going on? Why didn't I have another experience like Wednesday night?*

Simple, you would have if your focus had been on me instead of Brent. What Brent has is between him and me, not you and him. You have a friend with the similar gifts, but time with me is private until you are called to act together, He informed.

"Why do I want to separate from everyone right now? I have this urge to withdraw and read or something," I asked.

You're craving more of me. You went to church to be spiritually fed. You didn't acquire what you needed due to your divided focus. Watch a few Christian teachers on your television or read a few scriptures to relieve your sense of emptiness, He said.

"May I at least ask you a few questions about Brent?" I inquired.

He responded by saying, *You may. But I won't promise to answer them. Like I said earlier, some things are private.*

A little hesitantly, I continued, "I won't ask anything personal. I was curious about seeing him in the prayer room. My spiritual eyes were aware he was engaging his robe in deep prayer or something. Do I have to do that when I want to pray?"

Good question. Brent was relying on covenant promises as he prayed. Your robe is also engaged when we are praying together, He explained.

"Really?" I responded. "It was beautiful! It glowed so brightly it appeared ready to burst into flames. Thanks for sharing."

It was a good thing I had consumed a good breakfast before Sunday school; otherwise, the donuts offered after class would have been a problem. Now I was hungry again. It takes effort to eat healthily. Normally, I would've eaten junk to fill the void. I looked in my fridge and pulled out a bag of salad, chicken strips, and a tomato, assembling a quick salad. I took honey and mustard, mixing them together with olive oil for my dressing.

With salad and a glass of water in hand, I went to my living room to watch television as instructed. It didn't take long to feel spiritually full as well as physically full. Now my body was crying for a nap.

I had the same silly dream. I was a superhero dressed in a red suit, protecting the innocent with hugs and kisses while fighting demons with a lightning bolt. *What was that?* I thought.

It had to be my subconscious working overtime again. I eventually felt the need for company. Not wanting to butt in at Mark and Judy's, I decided to visit my parents.

Mom was pleased to see me but concerned at first that something was wrong. Puzzled, she asked, "Hope, honey, are you okay?"

"Sure, I just got lonely in the apartment and decided to come see you guys. I haven't interrupted anything, have I?" I said.

"Not at all. Dad is on the patio, trying to cook steaks for supper. Would you like us to take out another for you? It won't be a bother," she asked.

"Please don't. I don't need to be out long. I didn't get to talk much with either of you yesterday at the barbecue. I wanted to tell you I had a wonderful time. I'm grateful you and Judy convinced me to go back to church. I'm beginning to feel I have a purpose for my life again. I loved helping out at the home," I told her.

After thanking mom, I had to admit I really liked helping at the Boys' Home. Working with the kids is helping me overcome fear of rejection. Then again, I knew something else was also influencing me. Was it a need for children or was it just a need for companionship? I was thinking this through when Mom sent me a teasing question that jolted me out of my thoughts, "Have you got a boyfriend or possibly two boyfriends? I saw you sitting with Frank Addison and Brent Arnold yesterday." Her teasing upset me. "Come on Mom! They are just friends. I work with Frank, and I just met Brent on Thursday," I argued.

Exasperated, Mom said, "I've been praying for God to send you a Christian man, and both of those guys fit the bill. Pick one."

"Mom! Please let me find out who Hope is before wishing me on someone else," I pleaded.

"You can't blame me for wanting to hear the sound of little feet. Of course, I want you happy! I also want some grandchildren before I get too old," she prodded, trying to get a reaction.

Dad arrived in time to overhear the end of our conversation. He started right where Mom left off, making me bristle defensively. "Seen you with two fine boys lately. Which one do you like?"

I felt my throat constricting as if I was being strangled. My mind kicked into overdrive down a familiar old dark path. Another marriage was inconceivable, so soon. Why were they pushing me for grandchildren when they never found time for me growing up?

Needless to say, I didn't stay much longer. That topic was choking me. No matter how hard I tried to change the subject, both parents kept babbling about how sweet Frank was or what a good breadwinner Brent would be. The air was thick, oppressive, and uncomfortable, so I made an excuse to leave.

In my SUV, alone with the Lord, I found peace and true acceptance. I could breathe again, so I vented. I loved talking with Him while driving anyway. "Why are my parents pushing me so hard to date? And what is this about grandchildren?"

It's human nature. Your parents are getting older. They want to see their seed, meaning you, multiply. Tolerate them, Hope. They love you and just want you to be happy, He said.

The rest of the evening, He and I chatted while I watched television. Before going to bed, I consulted Him about a scripture verse I didn't quite understand. I refused to overload my mind. I needed to rest and didn't understand why I had that same dream again. I'm no superhero.

———⟶⟶⟶———

The Holy Spirit chuckled because He knew that her dream was symbolic to her calling. One day soon, she would become the noble tool Jesus designed her to be.

Practice, Practice, Practice

As soon as my alarm clock began to beep and before I even opened my eyes, I started greeting the Lord. I was not taking any chances. He directed me to practice his presence, and I wasn't going to let Satan get the upper hand. Today was Monday, and I refused to have another day like last Friday.

"Good morning, Lord, help me, help me, help me! I won't be able to breathe today if you aren't around! It's Monday! I'm still reeling from Friday's ordeal, so please keep verbal contact with me today," I begged.

He quickly answered *I'm here, Hope! Stop fretting! We are going to enjoy the day. You'll still have that sense of security and accomplishment from working there. We want you to feel comfortable and secure at your workplace. No person is trying to hurt you. Satan is the enemy. Now that you know who was behind the actions Friday, you'll be better prepared to ignore the petty issues.*

With a sigh, I said, "Okay. Just wanted to make sure we were on the same page. You have my permission today to butt in, interrupt, or whatever it takes to keep my attention. I need smooth sailing please."

He must have thought I was joking because I could have sworn I heard Him snicker.

"I'm serious. Friday was a nightmare," I said, grimacing as I remembered.

After I made sure all was well with Him, I read my Bible for a few minutes then proceeded to get ready. Instead of trying to impress, I was going for comfort today. I chose a pantsuit with a comfortable pair of loafers. I would still look professional, just not glamorous.

Next, the most difficult decisions—what to eat for breakfast and what to prepare for lunch? On my fridge door was a note to self—turn on TV and listen to preachers while getting ready and interact with the Lord while listening and cooking. It took about two seconds to make that happen then I was back in the kitchen. I wanted more steel-cut oatmeal with almonds and honey for breakfast; it was wonderful yesterday. As it was cooking, I looked in the freezer for my quickies—beef strips and a steam bag of broccoli. I put the meat in a plastic container and heated up the veggies. After they were finished steaming, I also put them in the container and sprinkled a little cheese on top. That was easy, and the aroma made my mouth water.

All the while, I talked to the Lord and listened to preachers on television. Multitasking was fun. The speakers would make humorous remarks, which made it easy to converse with the Lord. I was aware He probably knew all about me since He created me, but it felt like I was conversing with a person.

It takes a while for steel-cut oatmeal to cook. When it was finally ready, I had to scarf it down hurriedly. It was tasty, but I didn't have the time. I had Sunday to savor every bite I forgot to figure how long it'd take to cook and get my other items ready. This little bit of distress caused me to make a request. "Lord, help me to remember to set my alarm tonight to wake me a few minutes earlier so I can relax with you and eat before work."

He answered, *Very well, Hope. You are catching on quickly. Most people can't relate to me as a person. Continue this kind of interaction and nothing will faze you today. I want to go before you as well as be your rear guard.*

I was letting Friday's experience affect me too much. When I got behind the wheel of my SUV, I almost started to panic. Nope!

I'll stop this now, "Hey, Lord. Please take care of the traffic issue for me. Let's enjoy the ride this morning, okay?"

Cast my cares! I had to remember He cares about the little things also. Before I put my SUV in gear, in faith, I turned up my radio so I could sing. I arrived at the office without a single crazy or frightening incident. My usual parking spot was waiting for me to take possession of it.

I'd cleaned and put things away in their proper places on Friday, so I knew I wouldn't have that mess to face again. The only thing I hadn't tidied was my desk drawers. When I opened the middle drawer, the first thing that caught my eye was a pad of Post-it notes. I whispered to Him happily, "Lord, I'm making little reminders to practice your presence even in here. These cute little colored notes stuck all over the room will do the trick. They'll be our secret. I'm making sure they are inconspicuous and illegible to all but me. Like you said last night, our conversations are private."

Amused at my efforts, He said, *You don't have to whisper. I can hear your thoughts. That way our conversations will stay private.*

Gosh, sometimes I felt like an idiot, I thought. He's human to me, even though I know He is a spirit. I keep forgetting to interact with my mind.

When I had my office in order, I decided to fetch a cup of coffee from the break room before I started my daily tasks. When I walked in, it was like being in an alien movie. Little creeps everywhere—on the counters, at the cooler, in the middle of the tables, making themselves at home, and waiting for their meals of the day.

Immediately, I mentally asked, *Lord, do you see this?*

Yes, what are you going to do? He shot back.

I didn't want to cause a scene for people to witness and talk about afterward, so I kept my mouth shut. I straightened my spine while walking to one sitting on the counter. I sat my coffee mug on the counter harder than usual. I made sure I got the creep's attention. Like every other time, the minute it realized I could see it, the thing had the sense enough to leave. When it vanished, I turned in a circle, making sure the others knew I wouldn't tolerate their presence either.

Very good! I heard Him remark.

Frank's office was on my way back, so I decided to say hello. Just knowing I had a brother in Christ in my office was great. After this weekend, I felt we had grown closer. He had been my friend all along, but now, I knew why he was special.

I knocked on his door and entered when I heard, "Come in."

"Good morning. I hope today will be a hundred times better

than Friday," I joked as I entered.

"Hi, Hope! I agree! Today is going to be much better. We both know who is going to see to that don't we?" he joked back.

Then he asked, "Hope, how well do you know Cindy Grover? She seems like a nice person, and I'd like to get to know her better."

"You want the truth?" I asked him seriously.

"Yeah," he said.

"Okay, first of all, I want to say that Cindy is a real sweet lady. She is very friendly and outgoing. I know this because I used to meet up with her and a few friends when I was single. She liked to party, but I think she is tired of that lifestyle. You would be a very good influence on her. She needs to be with people she can trust and who can treat her like a lady," I answered.

I couldn't tell him that I saw her as the walking dead or that she was very insecure.

He replied, "I want to date her. We had a connection at the barbecue Saturday that I want to keep going. I could tell she knew you, so I am asking your opinion."

I knew something was brewing. The Lord had answered a maybe to my question about them on a potential date Saturday night. I replied, "Frank, Cindy is an awesome person. She is attractive, funny, and honest. She just needs the Lord. Who better to lead her in the right direction than someone interested in her as a person as well as a possible sister? Do you know what I mean?"

"Thanks, Hope," he said happily. "I'm going to ask her for a date soon."

When I got back in my office, I interacted with the Lord. *Was I correct encouraging Frank to date, Cindy? I felt you were bringing them together Saturday night, so I urged it along.*

You painted Frank a lovely picture of your friend. You gave him something to think about when you told him she needed me. With that information, he'll sense a purpose, as well as male attraction, for Cindy. You've done your job. Don't do anything more, he coached.

I decided to use my smartphone to listen to music at my desk. I kept a charger with me so I wouldn't risk running down my battery. I was in love with my newfound Christian radio channel. Having soft music playing in my office while I worked was wonderful. I'd have to remember to buy a small clock radio for my desk the next time I went shopping.

Before I knew it, lunchtime arrived. The first half of my day sped by peacefully. Even angry people on the telephone hadn't bothered me. Today, I'd remembered to focus on who was behind their harsh words. Each time I had a mean customer on the line, I'd mentally tell the Lord, *you have a customer*. I'd take a deep breath and let Him speak to them through me. Somehow, he could be so patient with people while using my skills as a secretary to help them. Remembering to let Him handle my issues wasn't easy, though. I had to keep saying to myself, "Practice, practice, practice."

After the incident in the break room this morning, I didn't want to eat lunch there, so I quickly heated my container of food then strolled to a park across the street. The city equipped the park with picnic tables arranged under trees or in the sun for people to enjoy their day. I chose one in the shade. I hadn't been there long when Frank arrived, asking if he could join me.

—⁓◦◦◦◦◦◦⁓—

Jesus and the Holy Spirit were orchestrating a plan for Hope to receive emotional healing. What better way than showing her what it was like not having a mother or father in her life. Using Frank to motivate her toward children in need will be just the push she needs to overcome.

—⁓◦◦◦◦◦◦⁓—

In our new comfort zone, Frank and I were able to have deep conversations while enjoying each other's company. During those few minutes, I learned he had a passion for teaching and sharing his knowledge. He fulfilled that need by volunteering at the Boys' Home.

He shared, "I like to volunteer whenever the boys have science projects to complete. Science is my specialty. Other patrons take turns helping in other ways but most assist school-age kids with homework in the evenings. Olivia and Joe are retired teachers, but fifteen kids spread them pretty thinly."

Insecure in my abilities, I asked, "Is there anything besides helping with homework that someone like me could do?"

He grinned at me as he chewed. When he finished the mouthful, he said, "They all need mothering. Ladies showing them kindness and attention means more than you can imagine."

Then he asked, "Would you be interested in helping the house parents when one of the little ones needs special attention?"

"Yeah, I can do that. They are so cute. How do I get involved?" I inquired.

"Let me ask around this evening and get with you, okay?" he said, excited.

———— wwₒₒₑₓₒₒₑₒₒ-ww ————

Satan was extremely angry with Hope's progress. He was about to have his way very soon. He was using Sam at this very instant to start trouble.

———— wwₒₒₑₓₒₒₑₒₒ-ww ————

Hope and Frank didn't have a clue they were being watched. Sam was parked a few feet away, glaring at them, fretting over Hope having a new boyfriend. He kept muttering to himself, "No way is my wife going to sleep with another man. I vowed—until death do we part. She may think we are divorced, but I take vows seriously. One way or another, she'll be with me again."

———— wwₒₒₑₓₒₒₑₒₒ-ww ————

When Frank and I walked together into the office building, it caused a small stir. Amber noticed we were having a good time and thought it was more than it really was. She started singing this silly song, "Frank and Hope sitting in a tree k-i-s-s-i-n-g. First comes love, second comes marriage. Next, we'll see a baby carriage." How dumb!

"Get off it, Amber! Two church friends can have lunch together without being in love," Frank contended.

Practice, practice, practice, I mentally thought. Then I begged the Lord, *please don't let me say something bad. Put your hand over my mouth.*

Look at her, Hope. See how she really is. Then you'll be able to show another emotion, he shared.

Doing as He suggested, I opened my spiritual sight to see another dead person walking. Amber was pretty to look at but dead on the inside. He didn't want her like that, and at that moment, neither did I. After I had my emotional correction, He went on to state; *she is lonely and dissatisfied with her own life. She strikes out childishly at others when she thinks they may be happy. Don't hold that against her. Satan has her mind. Soon, you will allow me to help you pray for her. Walk away for now. Our time will come.*

Saddened by what I experienced, I changed my heart. I recognized myself a few days ago. Being lonely and dissatisfied with life was not a happy place to be.

Praying from the heart, I asked, *Lord, should I start befriending Amber outside of work? I know what she's feeling.*

Maybe she needs a girlfriend that cares enough to steer her in the right direction. If I'm not that person, please let me know.

Start slow. Invite her to lunch with you during the week. Make friends with her here at the workplace before trying to engage her in things away from this environment. A prideful spirit grips her heart. At the moment, she feels you are not her equal. Remember her in your prayers with me this evening. Then watch and wait for the right moment to offer your friendship. I'll make it crystal clear when the time is right, He shared.

The rest of my work day passed as quickly as the first half. When it was time to go home, I didn't feel the usual physical exhaustion. I didn't want to go home lounging on my couch doing nothing, so I detoured to Judy's house. Since she and Mark decided to foster Tommy, Judy chose to be a stay-at-home mom until he was older.

Judy was going to be a great mother, and I needed ideas on mothering little-orphaned boys. Watching one in action was a good place to start.

Every time I visited, she welcomed me with opened arms. Even though we are not blood relatives, Judy has been like a sister as long as I can remember. There wasn't a finer lady on the planet.

Judy is an immaculate housekeeper, but today, her living room was turned upside down. You could definitely assume a little kid was on the premises. I smiled and asked, "What's happened in here?"

"Tommy has been playing fort. Can't you tell?" she replied.

He had a sheet draped over chairs, with toy soldiers and animals lined up around the room. The minute the front door closed behind us, his little blond head popped out of the makeshift fort.

"Hi, Ms. Hope! Want to play with me? Ms. Judy says she's tired and needs a break. She's the animals, and I'm the soldiers. We were playing war."

Judy spoke up and said, "Tommy, Hope came to see me. You have fun. Mark will be home in a few minutes. You and he can play outside, okay?"

She really was tired. I was hurried into the kitchen so she could have a breather.

She asked, "You want something to drink? I need something."

"Sure, I'll have whatever you're having." Then I asked, "Is everything okay? Looks like you've got your hands full."

She replied, "Everything is great! Tommy doesn't like being alone. He loves it when we play with him. It's either play or have him underfoot while I'm doing chores. You should have seen the

147

house yesterday. He and Mark had chairs turned over, making all kinds of noises, playing cowboys and Indians. We made it a family cleanup affair before getting ready for bed. I'm not accustomed to a mess all the time. I have to adjust my emotions."

I chuckled. "Yeah, the moment I came in, my first thoughts were 'Judy is usually an immaculate housekeeper.' I would bet your need to be clean complicates playtime."

She giggled. "You just don't know. I never considered myself stiff and formal until Tommy came. The first few days, I was killing myself cleaning up behind him. After yesterday, I gave up. The three of us had fun last night, making a game out of putting toys away. Mark even made the comment that it felt like we were a family."

"How is Tommy fitting in?" I asked.

I saw her expression alter slightly before she answered. I knew she was carefully considering what she was about to share. "During the day, he is a fun-loving, energetic little boy. At night, he gets needy and whiney. He hasn't told me, but I think he is afraid to go to sleep. Every night, he has horrible nightmares. One of us has to reassure him that all is well. The next morning, he pretends nothing happened. I don't know if I need to talk with Greta about this or not."

Trying to comfort her, I said, "It's probably nothing. He's just adjusting to his new surroundings. He hasn't been here a full week yet."

"You're right. I think I may be overreacting. I just want him to fit in so badly. Hope, I love him already, like he is my own child. Mark and I have claimed him as ours. I don't want this to be just a practice run. We want Tommy if we can't have a child of our own. If this fails, I think I'm done trying," she shared.

I knew she was tired and tense. My spiritual ears knew that my friend's faith was being tested. I left a few minutes after Mark arrived. I could see they didn't need me to overstay my welcome. They were working out a few kinks that needed straightening in their new lifestyle.

Loneliness was an issue with me these days. I had a companion. He and I had some praying to do.

Emotions

Full of evil and liquor, Sam parked down a block from the apartment he and Hope had shared in order to spy on her. He was confident she wouldn't recognize his new vehicle, so he fearlessly monitored her without fear of the cops coming after him. He tried to let Hope go, but after seeing her today, he could not bear the thought. He had vowed "till death do us part," and he was going to make certain she would never be with another man. He would stay in his car night after night until he could figure out a way to have her in his life again.

———∽∽∽∿⊙⊱⊙⊰⊙∿∽∽∽———

In the apartment, it felt like I had a roommate. The Holy Spirit and I conversed, sang, and watched television together. Even while cooking meals, He motivated me to try different flavors. To my surprise, I really liked natural, non-modified food better than their counterparts. It might take a few minutes longer to cook a fresh potato compared to a pack of dried potato flakes, but the taste was far superior. Who knew that a nine-minute microwaved acorn squash with honey, cinnamon, a dash of salt, and a splash of vanilla extract would be like a custard—a perfect dessert.

Feeling full after a lovely dinner of fish, potatoes, cucumber salad, and squash custard dessert, I entered my bedroom to change clothes and get serious. I had many issues to lay on God's altar tonight.

I'd made mental notes throughout the day of who I would bring to Him. First, I needed to pray for Cindy to find the Lord then a great guy like Frank. Second, I needed to pray that Frank didn't rush into a volatile relationship. Cindy needed respect but might not be able to accept it after too many fake relationships. Then there was Amber. I knew what she faced each evening. Been there, bought that T-shirt of loneliness. I understood how envy and jealousy could unknowingly produce bad behavior.

The most important prayers of the evening were for little Tommy, Mark, and Judy. They needed all the help God could give them to make their new family succeed. The Carmen's were great people, and Tommy was very fortunate to have found them.

Talking with Him lately was as easy as breathing. I just started praying, "Lord, I know your Word tells me that you sent it to heal every problem. You've told me lately on numerous occasions that the promises were for me to use as weapons against Satan's attacks. I need a clue where to look for promises that could help Cindy, Frank, or Amber. One thing I certainly know is that without you, I'd be right there with them—lonely and miserable. You are the Word, so you know exactly what they need. Can I just submit my heart and mind to that truth and trust that all will be well with them?

"Cindy has always been nice to me, and most of all, I want her to know you. Frank is a new brother to me, and I don't want him to be hurt. I fear his goodness may be misunderstood by Cindy. Sexual flirtations are expected, but if she doesn't get them from Frank, she may wound his spirit. You know all about my club life. Every guy I met had one thing on his mind. I know for a fact that Cindy expects the same treatment, perhaps even needing it to feel beautiful and whole. To be very truthful, Lord, I don't want to be involved in their relationship. I just want them happy with or without each other.

I was really angry with Amber this afternoon until you opened my eyes. Loneliness can be a destructive force. Finding you is the only way for them to shatter their strongholds. If I never see Amber or Cindy at church, at least let me know that they have you in their hearts. I know they are in yours. You draw with love and kindness. Please let them be unequivocally drawn to you."

His response was, *That was a huge request, Hope. I truly want Cindy and Amber to know me as much as you. Relationships between a man and woman are trickier. Frank's influence on Cindy will be good, but whether they would be good together is yet to been seen. Amber needs love. If you are willing, I can pray for them through you. Remember, you don't need to know what I'm saying. Just trust me.*

I hadn't even asked Him to pray for Mark and Judy when he interrupted my train of thought.

As for the Carmen's and little Tommy, all is well. This issue has already been prayed through. Angels have been working, and no devil in hell will prevail.

Sighing with relief, I leaned my head back on my pillow, closed my eyes, and offered the Lord my mouth. "I'm yours, Lord. Put in motion what is needed."

I hadn't been in prayer long when the phone rang, startling me out of the moment. I couldn't be angry because the Lord can do all things with little time. Whatever he said was enough.

I reached to answer the phone, hearing Frank's voice on the other end. "I didn't wake you up, did I?"

I responded, "No, I hadn't turned off my lights yet. You must be calling about the Boys' Home."

"As a matter of fact, Mrs. Elder, the housemother needs help tonight. She has two little ones in need of love. Is there any way you could come over?" he asked. "Consider it a dress rehearsal to determine if you want to volunteer for this need."

"Can you give me a clue what I'll be facing when I get there?" I asked.

"Two tummy aches but not enough laps and huggers in the building to hold them through their pains," he said.

It took me about a second to reply, "I'll be there in about thirty minutes. I have to throw on jeans and a shirt first. Tell them I'm coming."

———

Sam watched as Hope left. It was nine o'clock in the evening. Where was she going? Furious that she may be meeting the guy he saw in the park, he tried to follow. Too drunk to focus on traffic, he lost sight of Hope within a few minutes. Fearful of being caught driving drunk, he decided to go home for the night. Tomorrow

152

night, he'd stay sober. He couldn't allow this relationship to develop. One way or another, he would stop her or that guy from spoiling his plans.

—⁓⁓⁓⁓⁓—

On the way over to the Boys' Home, I kept wondering if I was doing the right thing. I hadn't been around small children much, but I loved them. Letting the Holy Spirit know my concern; I was encouraged to stop fretting and let Him love the little fellows. First, I was his mouthpiece, and now, I was his arms and lap. This must be what being a servant of the Lord was all about.

Frank was waiting for me in the yard when I arrived. He was such a nice guy. He was at my SUV the moment I parked. Walking to the main house, he shared, "Greg is the little fellow you'll be helping tonight. He hasn't been with us long and is scared and a little uncertain. Lately, his stomach hurts after he eats. The nurse thinks it is anxiety and nothing dangerous. See if you can get him to open up to you. The elders are having problems getting him to respond."

"Okay," I sighed. "But I thought there were two?"

"Johnny has already fallen asleep. One of the older boys already tucked him in," Frank explained.

When I saw Greg, my heart broke. He was no more than three, with a sad and lost look on his face. I introduced myself to the lady holding him. "Hi, I'm Hope Anderson. You must be Mrs. Elder." Patting Greg on the back, I said, "Is your name Greg?

Would you like me to read you a story? Mrs. Elder needs to finish her chores, so it will be just you and I cuddled in this big old chair with a good book, okay?"

The minute our eyes connected, I knew all was well. Could he be seeing the Holy Spirit in my eyes? I don't know what he saw, but he reached out to me instantly.

Mrs. Elder commented, "Well, I'll be. That's a first. I'm very pleased to meet you. It's good to have your help. Frank tells me he works with you and that you'll be a great substitute mom. Olivia gave you high marks as well. She said you came from good stock."

As soon as I had Greg cradled in my arms, Mrs. Elder was called to attend to an urgent matter. "We are acquiring another child in a few minutes. Greta reported we're about to be overwhelmed by a hysterical little man. He's just witnessed his parents' murder and has no relatives to assume custody." Eyes on the ceiling, she breathed, "God, please give me strength. These are so hard to handle."

I settled in a large rocking chair with Greg as I talked with him. He was a lovely little boy with big brown eyes, rosy cheeks, and honey-colored hair. "How can I help, little man? Mr. Frank told me you have a tummy ache and can't eat or sleep. Will you tell Hope what's going on?" I inquired gently.

His little head lay against my chest. He appeared fascinated with my hair, constantly weaving it through his fingers. I heard him speak around the thumb in his mouth. "You look like Mommy. Mommy read me bedtime stories."

Thank God, my Comforter was near. I prayed fast, *Oh Lord; this three-year-old thinks I look like his Mom. It's breaking my heart. He's so sweet but so lost. How can I make him feel loved and appreciated?*

Remember how you craved your mother's hugs, Hope? At this moment, he craves a touch more than food. Be his mother, even for a few minutes, until he relaxes enough to fall asleep. I'm with you, and I'll guide what to say and do, He shared.

I gathered Greg tighter in my arms and started sniffing his hair and around his neck. Then I said, "Greg, you smell so good. Have you bathed in hamburger juice or something? I could eat you up!"

This made him chuckle and hug me, saying in his little slang, "I not eaten anything, so I not smell like food."

Trying to coax him to eat something, I suggested, "I'm hungry. Would you find me something to nibble before we start reading? Right now, I think my belly growling would be louder than my voice. Please show me to the kitchen to find something we can munch."

His eyes twinkled at my suggestion. Then he jumped off my lap. He grabbed my hand, leading me to the kitchen.

"What do you like to eat, Greg?" I asked.

His quick reply was, "Peanut butter samitch."

"That sounds good to me too. I'll add some jelly to make it sweet or maybe cut up an apple," I suggested.

"I'd like an apple please," he said excitedly.

I was on the right track. If I could get him to eat a little, maybe he would relax enough to fall asleep.

When we walked in, Bobby Sawyer was putting away the clean dishes from dinner. "Hi, Bobby, I'll try not to mess your spotless kitchen. I'm hungry, and Greg thinks he wants to eat something with me." I really wasn't hungry, but I'd do anything to get Greg to eat something. I asked Bobby, "Where do you keep the peanut butter and bread? I think we'd also eat an apple if you have one."

He replied while pointing, "The apples are in the refrigerator. The bread and peanut butter are over there in the pantry. We have some milk in the refrigerator if you'd like some." "That would be great! Thanks," I responded.

Fixing one sandwich, I cut it in half then peeled and sliced an apple. After pouring Greg a glass of milk, I asked if we could thank God for our food. "Thank you, Jesus, for this good food and my new friends."

I watched Greg bow his head and heard him say, "Thank you, Jesus, for my samitch and for bringing a new lady."

He ate his half of the sandwich, plus all the apple sections, without declaring his stomach hurt. When we finished, I quickly cleaned the dishes, putting them on the drain board so we could go read a bedtime story.

Returning to the great room, Greg found the story he wanted then motioned for me to sit in the big rocking chair so he could climb up in my lap. I was captivated by this little boy, who was so full of love, needing an outlet of affection. As we were reading a story about Noah's ark, I felt Greg go limp as his breathing changed. I quietly said, "Thank you, Lord! Getting his belly full did the trick. He has finally relaxed."

I was about to ask someone to take him to bed when I heard a ruckus. Greta Arnold and Brent Arnold came in with another small boy who was crying so hard he was hiccupping. This must be the emergency Mrs. Elder mentioned earlier.

Not wanting to risk waking Greg, I hugged him tighter while we rocked. My heart was heavy with the emotions flooding my soul. These precious children would never know parents again. They were forced to rely on strangers like me to give them attention. My eyes flooded with tears. I sobbed as I reprimanded myself for hating my parents for leaving me. At least I had parents. They may not have been close by every waking moment; but they loved me, provided for me, and gave me just about anything I wanted. I had hugs when they were there. Why had I made such a big deal out of their actions? I had parents only by the grace of God. I could have been like little Greg—alone with no parents at all.

———ᘛ⠀ᘚ———

Jesus was elated, shouting to the angels standing around, "It's done! She has healed! Now we can provide her with the love she deserves."

———ᘛ⠀ᘚ———

Standing in the doorway of Mrs. Elder's office, Brent watched Hope holding the small boy. His heart melted from seeing the lovely sight. Could this woman he'd met only a few days ago be the one? Then he noticed she was crying. Although compelled to rush to her side, he stood firm because of the current situation. Work was always first. The new child's placement had to take priority. He'd find time to talk with Hope later.

———ᘛ⠀ᘚ———

I didn't care if it was eleven o'clock at night. I needed to talk with my mama. I called her as soon as I got in my SUV, before even starting the engine. I knew if they were asleep. I'd probably startle them senseless, but I couldn't wait a minute longer. When Mom answered the phone, I exclaimed, "Mom, I love you! I thank God for you! Please forgive me for calling so late. I've just spent several hours at the Boys' Home and realized how privileged I am to have parents like you and Dad. Please tell Dad I love him. It was imperative to tell you after witnessing these boys coping without parents of their own."

She quickly replied, "Good grief, Hope! You scared me to death! We appreciated you for thinking of us. I'd much rather have calls like this than giving us bad news. We love you, honey, and don't ever forget that. Do you need to come over? We are here if you're upset and need to talk."

I resisted, "No, Mom, please try to go back to sleep. I'm just overwhelmed with emotions. Thanks for offering, though. I'll call you tomorrow with details. I promise."

Sounding Board

The apartment was dark and quiet, which usually made me uneasy. I was tired and overcome by what happened tonight. All I could think about was climbing in bed.

My first instinct was to just let sleep overtake me, but I refused to be tempted. I needed to appreciate my Lord before closing my weary eyes. The only way to accomplish that was to pick up my Bible, asking Him to show me his comforting words; they were food for the soul and rest for my mind. He had to be my main focus for life, sleep—everything.

I had been sleeping so soundly that I had trouble responding to my alarm. Rousing enough to reach over to turn it off, my fingers felt the reminder to interact first thing with the Lord.

"Good morning, Lord!" I yawned.

Joyfully, He greeted me, *Good morning to you too, Hope.*

After crawling out of bed, I staggered to the kitchen for coffee before getting ready for work. Along the way, I kept seeing my little reminders greeting me with their cheerful colors; the words *practice his presence* or *talk with HS* grounding me as I shook off the cobwebs of sleep.

Preparing for a new day required taking care of normal body functions. It was still hard for me to grasp that the Holy Spirit didn't mind how or where I studied his Word as long as I made it a priority. I decided to take advantage of this time to saturate my mind and heart. Others read newspapers to catch up on events. I planned a better purpose. I had to giggle at the visual image of flushing sins into a "sea of forgetfulness."

Reminded of how good yesterday had been, I chatted with the Lord, giving precise permission to guide me again today. I certainly didn't want a repeat of last Friday. We talked while I showered, cooked, ate breakfast, and prepared lunch. He was my constant companion. I loved every minute of it! I'd spent the majority of my life without Him. Why had it taken me so long?

On the way to work, I had the incredible urge to let Him pray through me. For about ten minutes during the drive, I just let Him babble. After we stopped, I was curious enough to ask what had occurred. "Could you give me a clue about what I'll be facing today? Must be something important for you to want to pray like you did. Could I please have a little heads-up?"

We were just setting the stage for today's activities. I'd like you to think you are working for me today while at your job. Who did we discuss yesterday? Who needs a friend? Ponder on those two questions, and you'll have your answer, He shared.

We'd talked about a lot of things yesterday. But the one thing at the moment that was heavy on my heart was how Amber behaved? Could she be my assignment today? How did He want to use me to help her? I worked for Him last night with Greg. He must have something lined up for me to do for Amber. Frank didn't need a friend, and Cindy had too many friends, so it had to be Amber.

"Is it Amber?" I asked.

You're catching on. Follow my lead, Hope. I'll show you what, when, and how, just like I did last night for Greg. Let me love on her through you. She needs to feel appreciated and wanted, He informed.

I had a mental image of me and Amber in an embrace, and it frightened me a little. "You don't want me to cuddle with her, do you?" I asked hysterically. "That would be too weird!"

I got a one-word reply. *Maybe.*

"You have got to be kidding! I'll be her friend and confidant, but I don't think I ready for snuggling," I argued.

Laughing, He responded to my hysterics, *You will not be expected to do something out of nature, Hope. Sisterly love is all that will be required. Your job is to comfort her the way I comforted you. Be there to guide her to the truth. Show her a means of entertainment other than bar hopping. Help her see how I want people to treat her.*

"I can do that, I think. What else will I be facing?" I asked.

The usual. Look for something feeding on her negative energy and get rid of it. Make sure your robe is in place so you will not be overtaken by the force. Some people get sucked into the negative vortex and can't get free. Don't let that happen! With your robe in place, understanding covenant rights, you'll be able to fight it off. I'm with you. Don't forget that! If we need to pray, I'm always ready. Do not engage Amber until I prompt you. Watch and listen for clues of brokenness, He said.

What in the world was I about to encounter? It must be something unnerving for Him to warn me about wearing my robe. Sometimes, I don't feel qualified for the tasks ahead. But today, I must say, I'm a little excited. I know what it's like to be lonely. I wish someone had been there when I felt abandoned and miserable for days.

I walked in the break room to put my lunch in the refrigerator. The creeps were back. This time, no one was in the room but them and me. I made a scene. They pushed my buttons! My mouth loaded and locked, so I blasted them. "If you don't stay out of this building, I'm reporting you to the Father. You won't ever have a place to go ever again." I know it was childish and a little stupid, but it worked.

I had just finished my hissy fit when Amber walked in to get coffee. I was not supposed to engage her, but I didn't want to be rude. I would at least say hello. "Good morning, Amber." "Yeah, good morning," she grumbled.

I could see she was already in a sour mood. Time to pray. "Lord, you know what she needs, so here I am."

I opened my mouth for a faint-whispered prayer, muttering what was needed for the moment without caring what He declared or commanded. I trusted Him totally. Like a good shepherd, He wanted goodness and mercy to follow us all the days of our lives.

The morning was extremely hectic. My mind and body needed a break. I planned to enjoy lunch in the park again today. The warm air and sunshine would clear my head. I had to pass by Amber's office going to the break room. When I did, I heard her sobbing. Was that my clue?

"Lord, is this the time? I hear her crying," I asked.

160

Not yet. Linger in the break room a few minutes, He said.

I didn't want to hear that. I was looking forward to my lunchtime outside. I had to obey, though. I had committed to helping her regardless of the timing.

I was reaching in the refrigerator for my lunch when I heard Amber sobbing uncontrollably. I knew instantly this was the moment to interact. She needed help.

"Amber, what's wrong? Sit here before you fall over," I suggested.

She was embarrassed, humiliated, and detached, lashing out at anyone in her path. "You don't care! Nobody cares! You with your perfect life. How could you understand?"

"Amber, I know you are upset. Please let me help," I begged.

She put her face in her hands and just cried. That's when I did it. I couldn't believe I did what I said I couldn't do. I hugged her like a crying baby. We even rocked in the chairs a little bit while I patted her back and smoothed her hair out of her face.

I took her hand. "Come with me. I was going to have lunch in the park across the street. I have enough food for both of us. I think the fresh air will do you good. We can talk out there without the rest of the office eavesdropping. Right now, you need a shoulder to cry on, plus I have big ears for listening."

She was like an obedient puppy at the moment. When we found a secluded table in the park, she refused to eat; she said she felt sick. I knew the timing was right to offer again. "Amber, I promise I will keep our conversation confidential. I want to help in any way. Obviously, something has badly upset you."

I could see she considered sharing everything with me. She was very agitated. I knew the moment she made the decision to accept my offer. She faced me, squaring her shoulders and posturing for a fight. Then she blurted out, "I'm such an idiot! I met this good-looking guy last night at Sandy's Pub. We seemed to hit it off. After a few drinks and dinner, I discovered he was a traveling salesman visiting a branch of his business for a few days. After dinner, he asked if we could go back to my place to watch television. I was very flattered. He was so cute and had impressed me by spending so much on our dinner. One thing led to another, and he spent the night. When I woke up, I found him hurriedly trying to leave. He said he had an early meeting. He needed to return to his hotel room to get ready. I should have recognized the warning sign, but I didn't.

Midmorning, I thought I was being clever, calling him on his job. I knew he was a salesman but risked it all. I really wanted to invite him back to my place tonight for a home-cooked meal. I regret my effort now. I wish he hadn't been there, leaving me with a memory of our good time together. But no! My luck isn't that good. I got him on the phone all right, and he was rude. Do you know what he had the gall to say to me! He said, 'No thanks.' He told me I should check my counter for the money he had left me to pay for our lovely romp in the hay. Rubbing salt in the wound, he said I was a cheap hookup because he usually spent a whole lot more on a professional escort. He ended the call by telling me never to call him again because once was enough."

She cried for a few minutes and then continued. "Hope, I feel like a slut. He paid me like I was a whore, and a cheap one according to him. I was giving him my heart on a platter, but all he wanted was—" She was too distraught to finish.

After hearing her story, I could hardly eat. My heart pounded in my chest because I hated verbal abuse. Each time I took a bite, it felt like the food was sticking in my throat. I was furious with the unknown man. I knew her pain; she didn't deserve that from anybody. Then his warning flashed like a lightning bolt. *Put on your robe! Stand on your rights! Don't get captured!*

Wow! My spiritual sight had been clouded without a hitch. When I reclaimed clarity, I saw two small demons attempting to feed on my angry thoughts. I had almost been sucked into their trap. Her negativity and hostility were very contagious. Without her knowledge, I mentally sent up quick thanks to the Holy Spirit, followed by an expelling of the creeps hovering around us.

With the demons banished, I attempted to change the subject and atmosphere. "Let's do something together after work tonight. Neither of us needs to be alone. I know we can find something fun to do. Let's think about it. I'll drop in later. Right now, you need to go in the ladies' room and freshen up. This stays between the two of us, but your red face and puffy eyes will raise questions."

As we returned to the building, we saw Frank juggling his briefcase and several bags. To avoid a calamity, I offered assistance.

Knowing Frank's kind heart, I didn't want him asking questions. Amber ducked into the ladies' room as I grabbed two sacks full of items from a local craft store.

"What's all this?" I asked.

He laughed. "Things to help the boys with their science projects tonight. I didn't want to leave this in my car, getting hot and making a mess. My attempt to carry it in all at once was failing miserably. Thanks for lending a hand."

As promised, the Lord helped me with Amber by directing my eyes to an interesting flier sticking out of one of the sacks. It advertised a ceramics and pottery class tonight at 6:00 p.m. This was perfect! Except for the cost of supplies, the admission was free for this good, fun, and entertaining event.

Having a few minutes left of my lunch break, I took off to find Amber. I knew Amber liked to draw because I'd seen several of her sketches lying around. I hoped she would like ceramics or pottery as well. No! I was going to be positive. If the Lord led me to it, then his plan would succeed.

I stuck my head in her office. "Hey, I've got the perfect thing for us tonight. Go home, change into old jeans, and T-shirt, and I'll pick you up at five thirty. I'm taking you out for some fun and junk food. My treat! Tell me how to get to your place."

With directions to her apartment in hand, I was proud of myself for not giving her a way to bow out. I knew what would happen if she stayed home alone tonight. Depression would overwhelm her, and she might do something stupid.

Compassion for Amber filled my heart. The Lord was making this job easy. I had to give thanks. "Thank you, Lord, for guiding me and paving the way. The hard part will be convincing her she is special. Please speak through me, letting her feel your presence, revealing the need for her to seek your face. I know how empty life is without you, so please do for Amber what you did for me."

Filling a Void

The anticipation of the pottery class made the rest of the afternoon drag. Time always slowed when there was an exciting event planned, but time zipped by while in the event.

When 4:30 p.m. finally arrived, I tried to hurry out of the building, but someone needed something from me at every turn. Even Frank stopped me. "Are you coming to the Boys' Home this evening?

Not wanting to be rude, I said, "Not tonight. I plan on being there Thursday night. Tonight is girls' night out. Give Greg a hug for me and tell him to look for me Thursday night. I'll be there early enough to have dinner together. See you later. I have to hurry."

I let the Lord pray through me as I drove home. I was comforted, knowing he was in control. Amber's soul was our mission. If I was to be a light to her, then he would have to shine through me. I didn't have a clue what to say or do. Trusting Him was all I had at the moment, underlined by a sense of urgency.

Then it hit me. The Lord was alerting me to get to Amber as fast as I could. She didn't need any lag time between work and our outing. I would dress her if I had to. I wouldn't let her give me any excuses. We had to get away from her apartment and any reminders of last evening lingering to torment her.

I must be on the right track because I heard his sweet voice say, *When you arrive at her apartment, offer her your hospitality by inviting her to stay with you tonight. We'll let her know the reason without frightening her. Treat her special tonight for me. I'll make sure all your needs are taken care of, so don't worry about the expense.*

I got the cue. Amber was about to become a sister in Christ. Awesome! And I was going to be the tool. She would be my first convert.

I didn't waste time getting ready. While programming my GPS, I noticed an old car I'd never seen before parked just around the corner. That was strange. Brushing off the thought, I pulled onto the road and headed for Amber's. I was excited. I hadn't had a night out with a girlfriend in a long time.

———๛๏ๅॐฺ๏ॐฺ๏๛———

Satan continued to use Sam. He had to ruin or annihilate Hope before she got much stronger. His hate for her escalated to destructive passion. His preference would be to kill her, getting rid of her once and for all. This puppet he was forced to use was a dreadful human being, mean-spirited, lazy, always drunk, and totally inefficient for his plan. He'd have to send some of his more murderous demons into amp things up a little.

———๛๏ๅॐฺ๏ॐฺ๏๛———

Hiding from Hope then hearing her SUV pass by, Sam sat up, "That was close! She almost saw me. Where is she going tonight? Hiding cost me precious time. Now I'll risk being recognized if I follow her."

———๛๏ๅॐฺ๏ॐฺ๏๛———

Amber was not ready when I arrived at her apartment. She was seized by another crying jag. She let me in, and I calmed her as much as possible. "Come on, Amber. This isn't solving anything. While you're changing clothes, pack a bag with some things for work tomorrow. Plan to stay the night with me. Being here while your emotions are so raw only causes you to feel worse. Trust me. I know from experience how memories can torment. After our class, we'll get something to eat then veg out in front of the television or maybe play card games."

She looked stunned. "Why are you being so nice to me? We've never been the best of friends. In fact, we hardly speak at work."

I replied sympathetically, "I've been in your shoes, Amber. I know how bad you feel. I wish someone had offered comfort and assurance to me during those times. Maybe I wouldn't have messed up my life so badly."

Then I lightened the mood. "Come on, girl, hurry up. I've been excited about this all afternoon. I know it will be fun. I can't let you stay here alone. You'll let self-pity defeat you and feel worse tomorrow."

While she dressed, I went into her kitchen to wait. I engaged the Holy Spirit about his plan. *Now that I've got her motivated and moving forward, what is next?*

Faithfully, He replied, *Do you remember the story about the potter and the clay?*

Sure, the vessel was marred in the potter's hand, and He had to remake it, I answered.

Good! Use the events tonight to teach Amber without her realizing she is being taught. While you and I are working on your piece, talk to me without reservations so she can see our relationship. Let her experience firsthand a relationship in action. Don't get involved in too much chitchat with me. Have just enough words to let her know you can't do the work without me. What seems like a one-sided conversation will pique her interest enough for the two of you to have a discussion about me later tonight.

She's coming. Thanks for the heads-up. I can hardly wait to get started. She'll be my first convert, I replied giddily.

I wasn't shocked to see she was willing to stay the night with me. She was dressed and packed. Now I needed common ground to talk with Amber. As she pointed out earlier, we weren't the best of buds.

I prayed to myself. *Lord, please don't leave me now. Amber and I need something to talk about. Don't let silence make her uncomfortable.*

Praise Him! He knows how to start a conversation. When will I learn not to sweat the small stuff? We were in the SUV a few seconds when a Christian song grabbed Amber's attention. She remarked, "That song is lovely. I've never heard it before. What station are you on?"

It was a beautiful old song by Ron Kenoly, "You Are the Love of My Life." It was a love song to Jesus, but to a non-believer, it would seem like any other love song.

"That's Ron Kenoly, a Christian music artist. This song is one of my favorites. After my divorce, Mom and my friend, Judy Carmen, talked me into listening to this Christian station. Now all my preset buttons are tuned to it. The music and hosts are always upbeat and inspiring. Listening to them while driving soothes me. I especially love singing this song. It makes me feel happy. As a matter of fact, I purchased the CD not long ago.

Music was the topic of conversation during the ride to the craft store. In no time, we arrived and I could hardly wait to go inside. The ad for the class was successful. There was a long line from the door. When we finally got inside, a lady behind the counter asked which class we wanted. I spoke up first because I'd been prompted by the Holy Spirit. "The pottery class please." Amber agreed, "Me too."

Then the lady said, "The class is free, but the supplies for the class will be $50 for each of you."

Amber gasped. "That's $100 dollars! I wasn't expecting this."

I smiled and said, "My treat! I didn't expect you to pay. I knew about the expense before I invited you. You can't back out now! I won't take no for an answer."

"Thanks, I'll owe you one," she conceded.

When Amber and I entered the room, there were two side-by-side turntables remaining. I snickered to myself, knowing they were reserved for us by the Holy Spirit who prepared the way.

"This is going to be so much fun. I've always wanted to make something out of clay but never had the opportunity until now," I babbled. "Have you ever done this before?"

"When I was in college, I took a few classes. It's harder than it looks. I usually made a figurine instead of a bowl or vase. I never could get them to turn out right," she replied.

"Hum, I still want to try," I countered.

We watched about an hour while the instructors made everything look easy. After they completed a bowl, vase, or figurine, it was moved to a drying track to be put in a kiln later. Then they proceeded to show us individually how to operate the equipment and place the clay.

After my few instructions on operating the equipment, I turned the wheel on, took a lump of wet clay, and began the process of making a vase. Time after time, I'd mess it up. As expected, it wouldn't stand correctly, or it would be lopsided. Each time, Amber looked up and giggled at my attempts. "I warned you. It's not as easy as they make it seem."

"Okay, maybe I need some help," I admitted.

I submitted to the plan and interacted with the Holy Spirit. "Lord, this is hard. Show me what to do. Please help me get it right."

A simple request of my Lord in her sight and hearing was all He required from me. Now God's hands were turning the wheels of curiosity, which had nothing to do with my pottery wheel. The Lord was drawing her, causing cogs to turn and ideas to form in Amber's mind.

I was having a blast, spiritually and physically. My latest attempt at making a vase was shaping up well. The base was flat and heavy; the sides were rounded and standing on their own. I was very pleased and said for both Amber's and the Holy Spirit's ears, "Thanks, Lord! This one turned out pretty good." Only my ears heard, *You're welcome. I had fun too.*

A thin wire cut the clay from the wheel. My vase kept its shape, so the instructor placed it on the drying rack alongside some they had done earlier.

Amber made a fabulous horse that also was placed on the rack for drying. After our pieces were numbered, we received a ticket indicating when to pick it up. We had the option to attend another class for glazing them. At that moment, I could only say, "We'll see."

Amber spoke up, "I'll get yours if you can't attend the next class. I want to finish mine."

We were both famished when the class ended. We decided on a buffet to avoid waiting to be served. Amber was a health nut. Her choices were very similar to items the Lord was directing me to select. We devoured baked chicken, vegetables, and fruit for dessert. When we got to my apartment, we only wanted to sprawl on the couch and watch television.

As soon as I turned on the set, a Christian channel came to life. I'd been watching that particular channel before going to work. I was expecting some kind of catalyst to get our conversation started about the Lord; I wasn't expecting it so soon. I felt sick from the unexpected pressure. I was on the spot to answer the same kind of questions that I had recently for the Lord.

She pushed, "Is everything you watch or listen to Christian?"

The only reply I had for her was, "Honestly, it is all I want to watch or listen to lately."

"Why?" she prodded.

I sent up a quick verbal prayer for her and the Holy Spirit to hear. *Lord, you have to help me here.*

Taking a deep breath, I started with the truth. "Until a short time ago, I didn't have a relationship with Jesus Christ. Now that I found Him, I want to learn, know, experience all I can to make Him Lord of my life. I need to know how to live a better life to honor Him."

It was my turn to ask questions before she had time to comment. "Amber, have you ever been to church? Has anyone ever told you that Jesus loves you?"

She hesitated but finally answered, "I've been to church a few times, but I never felt welcomed. I know about Jesus and think I know why He came. I just never understood all the emotion and hoopla."

She finally said what I was expecting. "I didn't understand until I watched you tonight. You and Jesus talk with each other, don't you?" She didn't give me an opportunity to answer. "It wasn't weird at all. It seemed very natural to you. Then I watched you work on your vase and saw for myself that you didn't have an issue asking Him for help. The vase turned out lovely. It was at that moment I realized that there is an assurance to believing in Him."

"There is, Amber. A relationship with Him is more real to me than ours at this moment," I replied.

"Why?" she persisted.

"He loves me and will never leave or forsake me. Humankind doesn't have that ability. Their love and attention are conditional, subject to change on a whim. Jesus is the same yesterday, today, and forever. That is why I want to know all I can about Him. So, I can be loving and care for others like Him," I shared.

I saw tears in her eyes just before she asked a serious question, "Doesn't He judge you for being bad? For doing things He doesn't approve of?"

I honestly answered, "Not anymore. God sent Jesus to take away everything bad that we have committed or ever will commit. Instead, He took away the punishment of death, hell, and the grave, giving us His forgiveness and eternal life. We are like vases without Him, already dead, unable to stand or hold water. When we accept what He did on the cross for our bad thoughts and behavior, He gives us the opportunity to live a life filled with good things and joy unspeakable."

Then she asked, "What is the devil then? Doesn't he try to destroy you or something?"

"Satan still exists, and his fight is with God. He uses us or things against us to hurt God. He tries to prove God's Word is not true. He will never be able to do that if you belong to Jesus mind, spirit, and body. You have to submit to what God says, believing it is the truth no matter what you see or hear. That is why I constantly keep his Word in my face and going through my ears. I don't want to be sidetracked by Satan's lies," I told her seriously.

"It sounds hard," she shrugged.

"It can be. I'm constantly reminded to keep God in the loop of my life. To stay in contact with Him so Satan doesn't stand a chance. He told me all we need to do is practice that He is with us. Eventually, it will become second nature," I shared.

I watched her for a few seconds, wanting to see if she was ready to receive Him. When I saw the tears ready to spill on her cheeks, I knew that was my cue. "Do you want to have Him come into your life?"

She didn't say a word. She just bowed her head and nodded.

Then I asked, "Amber, would you like to pray with me and ask Him to come into your heart, teaching you what He has taught me?"

"Okay," she said shyly.

I started the prayer. "Lord, this is Amber, and she wants to pray with me. Please welcome her and show her how much you love her. Okay, Amber repeat after me. Jesus, I believe you are the Son of God who died for all my sins. I need forgiveness. My life without you is a mess. Please come into my heart and change me. Show me how to live and honor you. Make me a new creation, able to love my brothers and sisters the way you would have me to. Show me how to forgive myself, as well those who have hurt me or offended me. I can't live another minute this way. Amen."

After we prayed, she relaxed and looked up. "Thanks, I never would have been able to come to Him without help," she confessed.

"You are so very welcome, Amber. I'm honored to be the one who led you to Him," I replied.

I felt the Lord urge me to warn her about the enemy. "One thing I want you to remember with all your heart—you have an enemy now. Satan is after your salvation. He will try to prove that God does not exist, that what Jesus did is a lie. He will not stop there. Keep your focus by believing what the Bible says no matter what. Stand firm on what it says. Don't react to anything heard or seen that doesn't line up with it. You don't have to prove anything or do anything but believe. The battle is not yours. It is God's. He proves Satan wrong every time. All you have to do is believe and wait on Him. He will never let you down."

I frightened her. She looked alarmed. "I don't own a Bible. What if I have questions or something? How will I know what to believe in? I don't have a clue what to look for," she admitted.

"Stop worrying," I soothed. "We'll get you a Bible, one you can understand. God will direct and show you the way. I find a lot of help through this Christian television channel and by listening to Christian radio. Trust me, he will not forsake you. Lean on Him. Talk with Him. He talks back," I affirmed.

She was too new for me to try to tell my story. Even though we shared similar things, our journeys would probably be totally different. Plus, the Lord said that our personal relationship with Him was private. I thought my job was done. I had a new sister and new friend.

The rest of our evening was lighthearted and uneventful. We played CDs, and I gave her the Ron Kenoly CD she loved. We even watched one of my favorite evangelists on TV, Jesse Duplantis. He was hilarious and made Amber laugh. I think his message helped her.

I was exhausted, needed rest, and knew Amber probably needed some time alone. I assured her she was welcome to watch television all night if necessary. I explained my kitchen was open for anything she craved. I programmed the coffee maker so coffee would be ready in the morning and showed her where I kept the coffee mugs. Then I laughed at myself for being a lousy host. I'd forgotten to show her to the guest room. Her things were still piled just inside my back door. Apologizing for my lack of hostess skills, I showed her the guest room and guest bath. Then I gave her some towels and toiletries to use. After that, I bid her good night as I went to my room.

I couldn't help wondering if she was about to take a journey with the Holy Spirit that would change her life forever. I mentally reprimanded myself; it was none of my business. Now that I was certain of her salvation, I needed prayer time with the Lord.

I prayed, "Lord, thank you so much for allowing me to be your servant tonight. It was a marvelous experience. I know you have Amber's best interest at heart. Show her she can rest assured in the truth I told her. Reveal yourself to her as you did to me. She is a blank slate needing to be covered with your Word. I am physically and emotionally drained at the moment, but I know you are not. Please use my mouth now to set wonders in motion for Amber."

After I said my mind, I opened my mouth and let Him use it. Again, I didn't have a clue what He was saying but knew whatever it was would be for good.

—⁓∘⦵⧟⦵∘⁓—

Jesus and the Holy Spirit were grateful for Hope's servitude and willingness. It concerned them that she still wasn't asking for any blessings to come her way. Without her permission or request, they blessed her anyway.

Baby Steps

The next morning, I was awakened by the sound of running water. It frightened me at first, then I remembered Amber spent the night. I rolled over to look at my alarm clock, groaning. It was only 5:00 a.m., and it was not scheduled to beep until 6:00 a.m. I tried going back to sleep but couldn't. I lay there but the sound of running water was forcing me to get up and take care of business.

I waited a few moments until Amber turned off the water before I used the toilet and jumped back in bed. With it being so early and my brain fogged with sleep, I was glad I hadn't forgotten about the water issue in the apartment. If I had, my guest would have been scalded. The plumbing was weird. You couldn't flush and shower at the same time. Flushing caused the toilet to use all the cold water, leaving only scalding water for the one taking a shower—not good.

Lying there, chatting with the Lord while feasting on His goodness by reading His Word, I became anxious to see how Amber was faring. Why was she up so early? Did she even go to bed? Surely she would have awakened me if she was scared. Then something dawned on me. I was worried about Amber like she was my child. I thanked the Lord for that vision, and I quickly got a robe and went into the kitchen to see if she needed me.

To my surprise, she was dressed, ready for work, seated at my dinette drinking coffee and reading one of my Bibles. Curiosity overtook me, and I had to look at her with my spiritual sight. There it was! She had a covenant robe. It was pooled around her ankles, but all that mattered at the moment was seeing it. She would learn about her covenants soon enough. She was just a baby Christian.

She heard me shuffle into the room and greeted me with beautiful sparkling eyes. "Good morning! I hope I didn't wake you too early. My cell phone alarm woke me at my regular time, so I took my shower quickly to avoid fighting over the water."

I had to ask, "Why on earth do you get up so early?"

She laughed. "I usually go to a ladies' gym for a workout before going to the office. I take my clothes and makeup to get ready after exercising. It's been a routine for me since college graduation. I found if I didn't make time for exercise, I gained weight. When the school's exercise equipment was no longer available, I had to join a gym," she explained.

"Wow!" was all I could manage before coffee.

I didn't want to seem rude, so I sat at the table with her for a few minutes while I sipped my hot coffee. When I noticed that she was reading a King James Bible, I had to comment. "That Biblical translation is too hard for most to understand. Let me get the Bible I study from. You can take a look at it while I get ready for work," I recommended.

I gave her my Amplified and New American Standard dual translation explaining how to compare the verses. "See which one of these reads better to you. If you don't understand one translation, try reading the same verse in the other. Don't get upset if you don't understand at first. If you have any questions when I get out of the shower, just ask and I'll try to explain. I found it easier to start with the book of Romans. Anything before Jesus went to the cross confused me. The book of Acts was worrisome because it edified the suffering of Paul. Reading Paul's letters explained a lot. That may work for you also."

In the shower, the Lord said, *You know, Amber is going to have a lot of questions. Be patient. She is like a sponge at the moment and needs you. When I gave you the feeling of motherhood earlier, it was for a reason. Your responsibility to Amber isn't over until she is comfortable enough to walk inside a church as well as being on her own. Help her with her baby steps. Don't abandon her to find her way alone.*

My flesh wanted to scream no. But I submitted and listened to His request. I liked the humble and new Amber, but the old Amber, not so much. When He urged me to guide her, I wanted to run. I thought all I had to do was introduce them after she was saved, and He would take care of her training. At work, she had a tendency to be shallow and condescending, which made it hard to be around her. Then He gently reminded me of what she was about to face on the job. That did it. Motherhood kicked in again. I

176

thought of the demon-infested workplace that could change her from humble to a greedy, self-centered witch again in an instant. I couldn't allow that to happen. I'd keep Him on guard every second of the day if I had too. Satan wasn't about to lure my first convert back to the dark side.

Ready for the onslaught of questions, I exited my room dressed and ready. She was still absorbed in reading. Then I remembered He said she was a sponge. She was soaking in exactly what she needed, so I kept quiet.

The quiet was short-lived. "What's with all the Post-it notes stuck everywhere?" she asked.

I giggled because I hadn't expected that question at all. I was ready to instruct her from the Word. Then I heard a sweet whisper, *Be truthful but don't elaborate.*

I responded by saying, "Do you remember me saying I keep Jesus involved in my day? Well, I had to work at it because talking with Him wasn't natural to me. I remind myself with visuals like these Post-it notes to speak to Him, share with Him what is going on, or mentally engage Him in my thinking. When I do that, my day is so much easier and happier."

"What I saw and heard you doing last night seemed natural. You talked to Him like you talk to me," she said.

"It has gotten easier. Life, in general, will keep you from putting Him first. I had to figure out a way around that, so I put up reminders for myself. I even have them at the office and in my SUV," I shared.

I was braced for more questions, but none came. As I packed my lunch, I asked if she would like some cottage cheese and fruit for her lunch, but she declined. She did ask if I minded taking her home so she could get her car.

Even during our ride, no doubts were expressed. I was beginning to get concerned that I was missing something. The Lord said there would be many questions. All we did for the entire ride was listen in silence to the radio. I wasn't seeing or hearing anything alarming with my spiritual gifts to indicate an underlying problem.

When we arrived at her place, she thanked me again for everything and said she would see me in a few minutes. Alone again, I inquired, "Lord, what just happened? I was ready for questions, but she didn't have any."

She will. You are her safety net for the time being like I am to you. When things start getting tough, she'll come running. Don't shoulder her burden. That's my job. Turn her toward me and my Word as much as possible. She needs to learn to stand on her own feet. Show her how, then watch. If she starts to fall, encourage or comfort her. Never judge. I will prove myself to her, but she has to learn to trust in me, not you, He informed me.

I felt a sense of panic, so I begged, "I haven't been born again myself for very long. I'm a little scared of taking on someone's salvation issues. I still have many of my own. Will you send help with this until I gain experience? I want to help, but I don't want the full responsibility."

I plan for Frank to help you. Encourage her to go to church with you tonight and get Frank involved. The more people she gets to know as brothers and sisters, the easier it will be for her to learn and trust me.

She needs to see that you are not the only one who has a relationship with me. Don't let fear in. Tell it to leave, He encouraged.

I couldn't believe I had an invisible creep trying to steal my peace. That was why I had suddenly panicked. I felt the little monster hovering somewhere while I was driving. I hollered loudly in my SUV, "In the name of Jesus, fear, and panic, leave me alone!"

At the office, I went into the break room to put my lunch in the fridge, checking for demons in the area. No creeps. They must have gotten the message where I was concerned. They probably come only when their food sources are in the room. Negative energy is their favorite snack; if it isn't available, they stir it up.

I had just walked back into my room when Amber came bounding in. "Where can I buy a Bible like yours? I have to go out this morning to collect accounts. I thought if I was near a store I'd use my break to buy one for myself."

"I got mine at Gateway Books on Century Street," I answered.

Then she asked, "Can you tell me how much it costs? I may want to buy more than one type if I can afford them."

I had an idea. I made an offer as I answered her question, "Mine cost about $40. If you can't get by Gateway this morning, why don't we go shopping after work? Then you can go with me to church tonight." I saw apprehension in her eyes as her face paled.

"Don't be a chicken. The people at my church will welcome you. I promise I won't desert you."

God was on cue because at that moment, Frank walked in. "Hi, Frank, tell Amber the people in our church are nice." Nothing like putting him on the spot, but he was a godsend, prepared and ready without even knowing.

He cheerfully joined the conversation and assured Amber, "I think you'll have a great time. There are a lot of people our age. Not all are old and judgmental." He looked at me and said, "Bring her to my class Sunday morning." Then he winked at me and jokingly added, "She'll get a kick out of seeing the all-knowing and all-powerful side of me."

I don't know what piqued her interest more and made her laugh, the fact that everyone wasn't old or Frank's last comment. Either way, we had her attention. "I'm going to try it tonight with Hope. I really need a positive outlet to hook up with. This may be the one."

The three of us had to get back to work. We decided to meet for lunch in the park. After Amber left, Frank poked his head back in and grinned. "I talked with Cindy. We have a date this Friday night."

I squealed. "Great!"

179

Satan convinced Sam to spy on Hope again during her lunch break. He tortured Sam with the idea that she was dating the man he saw her with previously. Fury, jealousy, and suspicion were some of the demon tormenters available for times like this. Sam was just a pawn for Satan to maneuver in his efforts to destroy this opponent.

———————

Frank met me outside a few minutes before Amber could join us. It gave us some time to discuss what he really had on his mind— his date with Cindy. He told me his plan to take Cindy somewhere nice for dinner then maybe to a movie unless something more interesting became available for them to attend together. I was so excited that I hugged him.

———————

The demon of fury had Sam by the throat. He was making Sam angry enough to kill the guy she was cuddling. Suspicion and jealousy set in motion a plan for that to happen. They didn't care where Sam's anger was aimed. They were happy gorging their current meal of rage. Satan cared! The idiot was focused on the wrong person, causing Satan to change tactics.

———————

Tonight was going to be fun! Frank had decided to go shopping with us. He'd volunteered to pick us up so we could make an evening of it together. He'd said, "I'd like to tag along. Let me pick both of you up so you can ride in my new car. We can grab a quick meal before church."

God is so good to His Word. He didn't hesitate in getting Frank involved with me and Amber.

I hurried home to change clothes and wait for Frank. I had just finished combing my hair when I heard my doorbell ring. Looking out the window before opening my door, I was surprised to see

Frank. As he walked in, I anxiously said, "You're here early. What's up?"

"I thought we needed to talk before picking up Amber. I was curious. Is she legit? Did she really accept Christ last night?" he asked.

Confidently, I responded, "Yes, I'm certain of it. I wish you could have been with us. It was a beautiful experience. I felt the Lord guiding me the whole time. Why?"

"She is so hard-core," he explained. "I've known her for years. Nothing I ever said or did seem to penetrate her self-obsession. Don't get me wrong. I'm happy for her, but I'm concerned you may be in for a neurotic, stormy time with her as she grows. She might be a handful. The tug to change her ways may cause her discouragement. I've seen many new believers fall back into their old comfortable lifestyles. I'm wondering if you are ready for the challenge. Do you realize the burden as well as the joy of your undertaking?"

"I've prayed about it, and I know deep in my heart that I need to see this through. The Lord explained to me that it would be like teaching a baby how to walk. I asked for help. Guess what?

God sent you. Are you ready for the challenge?" I jokingly replied.

"I stepped into that one, didn't I?" he retorted.

Evil was having a field day while Hope and Frank were talking. Frank's innocent visit was giving the demons of suspicion and jealousy a weapon to suck the life out of Sam as he watched from the sidelines. These lesser demons disregarded their master's focus on the girl. They cared about getting to feed. Joined now by the demon of rage, their plan was wreaking havoc with Sam's mind. The evil emotions were killing him slowly on the inside as excessive drinking clouded his thinking and numbed his body. Sam thought the alcohol would be a salve to calm him, but evil influence fueled his torment. He was consumed with rage. Hate helped him plot ways to get rid of Hope's lover. In a state of intoxication, he was willing to risk getting caught. He knew he was violating the restraining order Hope had placed on him. He approached the complex property to get a closer look at the man's vehicle, a new white BMW.

After seeing the make and model of the car, jealousy caused Sam to assume Hope was being lured by the man's money. Sam thought he needed to scare him off. If that didn't work, Sam would take more drastic measures.

Sam barely made it back to his old car before Frank and Hope left her apartment. Seeing them together didn't help. The way this man opened the car door for Hope convinced Sam there was more to their relationship than he truly wanted to know.

Hope and Frank tried to think of ways to guide Amber from being so self-centered. How were they going to get her to unburden herself rather than demand attention? They decided to pick her brain for answers during dinner. They needed to know if she had any knowledge of God other than what she had received within the last twenty-four hours. They also needed to find out her interests. There had to be something she cared about more than herself.

Hope giggled. "This feels like gathering stones for our slingshot. The slingshot is Amber."

"How do you figure that?" Frank questioned.

"She has to be the weapon used against Satan. When we help her find her way, she can hit that evil beast right between the eyes with her new life. Childish, I know, but sometimes, that's how my mind works," Hope quipped.

I noticed Frank's reaction after my comment and knew he liked the way my mind worked. It was good to know his thoughts ran along the same lines as mine.

When we pulled in Amber's driveway, she came bounding out of her door as if she had been waiting for us to arrive. At first glance, we were shocked at what we saw coming toward us. She had on casual and very, very revealing clothes. We both had the same reaction and said in unison before she opened the car door, "Oh, boy!"

I threw a quick prayer up to the Lord in my mind. *What do I need to do? I don't want everyone in the church to have the same reaction we just had. I don't want to hurt her feelings either. Help!*

Hope, Amber is used to sexual innuendos. A joke about her appearance will flatter her but at the same time get your point across. I've already told Frank to be still, keep his mouth shut, and let you handle this, He advised.

I was on my own! I said the first thing that came to mind when she opened the car door. "Lord, blind this man before her boobs do!"

She laughed. "Bit much? Do you think I need to change?"

"We have time if you don't mind. Frank has to be able to focus on driving. You will save lives simply by changing clothes," I joked.

She took the hint gracefully. "I won't be but a minute, sorry." I heard a sweet voice say, *Good job.*

Frank looked over at me and sighed. "Thanks!"

Minutes later, we were on our way, with Frank's eyeballs back in place, his sanity restored, and Amber properly dressed.

Parenting

Our first stop was Gateway Books. When we went to the Bible section, Amber was amazed at the different translations available for believers. I showed her my favorites, but Frank had a better idea. He suggested a New International Version with a built-in concordance. She could look up subjects and find related scriptures faster.

Amber asked, "Would it confuse me if I bought one like Hope's and this one also?"

Frank and I looked at each other, and grinning, I replied, "Not in the least. It helps to have different references. One will always give the answer you need if another one doesn't. What's the old adage? 'Different strokes for different folks.' God wants people to understand. I would own a Bible in every version if I could afford it."

Excitedly, she chose Frank's suggestion in addition to the one she'd read at my apartment. Now she was loaded for bear with three translations and a concordance.

Next, we headed to the buffet so we could pick her brain for clues. There had to be something other than man-chasing that this girl liked to do.

On the way to the buffet, I suddenly remembered my depleted bank account. I spent a large sum on art supplies last night. Worried about using my debit card, I started digging through my bag, searching for cash to buy something to eat. Amber saw me digging out bills and change, and she reached over the seat to hand me something while explaining, "I was going to give you this after church, but I think you need it now."

I looked down to see $200. My mouth dropped as my fist clenched. God was good to His Word; He'd provided. "Thanks, Amber," I whispered.

She murmured, "It is most of the money that jerk left me the other night. I used some of it to buy my Bibles. I was hoping you'd take the remainder. It's the least I can do, considering you saved my life by introducing me to Jesus. Made the devil pay, didn't we?"

I responded, "You're so sweet. God is truly going to bless you. You took what the devil meant for harm and changed it to something good." Without even realizing it the other night, I'd set in motion seed, time, and harvest. I planted and received a harvest, and so did she.

———∿∽∾☙❦❧☙∾∽∿———

Jesus nodded toward the Holy Spirit. He was pleased that Hope was catching on to His ways nicely.

———∿∽∾☙❦❧☙∾∽∿———

Brent was waiting at church for Hope to arrive. He couldn't get the vision of her cradling the little boy last Monday night out of his head. Could God be answering his heart's cry for a special mate? He had prayed for someone who loved the orphans of the world as much as he did. When she finally appeared, his heart leaped. She was a vision of beauty, but she was with Frank. Now he was confused. Were Frank and Hope and item? The lawyer in him had to know.

As he watched them find a seat, he noticed another woman with them. Acting like a schoolboy, he was almost giddy to watch the woman position herself between Frank and Hope. That assured him Hope wasn't with Frank or they'd be side by side.

Without hesitation, he proceeded to move toward Hope.

———∿∽∾☙❦❧☙∾∽∿———

The Holy Spirit arranged the seating as part of a secret plan. He'd make everything smooth and easy for all involved.

———∿∽∾☙❦❧☙∾∽∿———

I was getting situated when I looked up to see a familiar face. It was Brent. "Hi there." I smiled. "You want to sit with us? We have plenty of room."

185

"I'd love to," he said as he edged in beside me.

It was unnerving, having Brent continually stare at me. He was usually talkative, and it made me feel strange. I had to break the tension. "Why are you staring at me? Do I have something on my face?"

Apologizing with a reddening face, he replied, "I'm sorry. Nothing is out of place. You just look extra beautiful tonight."

Taken aback, I spurted, "Wow! You don't waste words. You get right to the point with come-on lines."

"I don't waste time or words, Hope. I think you are lovely, and I'd like to get to know you better," he asserted.
We couldn't continue the conversation due to the starting service. "We'll talk later," I mumbled.

I was looking forward to hearing another wonderful message from the pastor, but now my head was jammed with flattery and confusion. I wasn't ready for a relationship. I didn't need a man in my life. Why did a nice guy like Brent have to hit on me? I didn't want to hurt his feelings, but I couldn't see a way around it.

Agitated and upset, I rebuked my thoughts and prayed, *Lord, help me focus on you instead of Brent's comments. You are all I need or want. Help me. Help me get out of this mess without hurting a good person in the process.*

The Holy Spirit's silence was causing me to mentally beg. The service seemed to be flying by. Soon, I'd be faced with Brent's attention again. During the whole service, I hadn't even focused on Amber. Was she receiving what she needed? I'd planned to seek God for her if she was having problems. I should have been watching her reactions, but I couldn't. I'd been thrown an unexpected curveball. My mind was scrambling. Hopefully, Frank was filling in the gap so she could get her training plus companionship needs met.

Without help from the Holy Spirit, I decided to be kind and go with the flow. I would not hurt this man with rejection. I'd find another way to let him know I was through with involvements.

Two failed marriages were enough. I never wanted to risk being hurt or hurting someone again.

Just as I'd expected, Brent followed me to the car. He said, "Hope, would you be interested in seeing me?" I quickly prayed, *Okay, Lord, help me here.*

I took a deep breath and replied, "Can we take this slow? I've committed my time to the home. I'm just now finding my way again after a bad divorce."

"Well then, I'll be seeing you at the home. We'll get to know each other while helping the kids," he answered cheerfully. "You get to know someone working together toward a shared goal. If slow is what you need, slow it will be."

———

Brent's heart was bursting with joy. Hope was committed to the Boys' Home. What better place to get to know her and work for the Lord at the same time? *Thank you, Jesus*, he prayed.

———

Why had I said that? Why did I give him an opening, even if it was only a crack? Why didn't I just say I was only interested in friendship? What made me say we needed to keep things slow?

Where was your help in this? I asked the Lord.

At Frank's car, the subject changed, thank God. Brent started jokingly accusing Frank of being a copycat. "You had to buy the same car that I drive, even the same color." Peering inside, he conceded, "No, wait, you have cloth seats. Mine are leather. You're not a copycat after all. We have good taste."

They shook hands. Then we said our good-byes and left. In the car, I was surprised when my spiritual senses took over, especially since I'd been so engrossed in other matters. I felt a chill overtake the inside of the vehicle. Then I noticed a blackness making the night seem even darker. We were being overshadowed by a giant. Something was drawing it close. I immediately looked over my seat to see Amber crying. "What's wrong?" I inquired.

She sobbed. "Hope, I can't be alone tonight. My heart is breaking, and I'm afraid I'll do something stupid."

Then Frank chimed in worriedly, "What do you want us to do?"

"Frank, I don't want you to feel shut out, but this is a girl matter. You've been terrific, making me feel special tonight. Something the pastor said depressed me and I need Hope's help, I think." She sniffled.

I knew from experience this was seriously heavy. There was no reason for a giant to hover unless it was anticipating access to Amber, possibly jeopardizing her new salvation. What had the pastor said that could have upset her so much? Why hadn't I listened instead of getting agitated over Brent?

I offered, "You can stay at my place again tonight. You're more than welcome."

She countered, "No, I need to show you something at my place. Please stay with me. I know you're not prepared, but if you don't mind, I'll lend you something to sleep in. I can take you home early in the morning."

I had an idea, so I said, "You are the only ones who know I wore these clothes tonight. I'll wear these same ones to work tomorrow. I have makeup and a hairbrush in my bag, so all I need is a toothbrush. Do you have a spare?"

She nodded her head to confirm. "Thank you, Hope."

Frank was a dear. After we got to Amber's apartment, he didn't hang around or insist on knowing what was going on. He simply said, "I'll be praying. See you guys tomorrow." Then he drove off.

Inside the apartment, Amber escorted me to her guestroom. She laid out a gown, pointing to the bathroom stocked with towels and a toothbrush. Then she offered me something to drink.

I made her aware I didn't drink alcohol any longer but that a diet drink would be good. I also told her I understood if she needed something stronger. I'd have another chance to talk to her about living holy. Tonight wasn't the proper time; she was too distraught.

She poured herself a glass of wine, brought me a diet drink, and started crying again.

"Amber, I can't help you if you won't tell me what's wrong," I pleaded.

Looking at her glass, she proceeded to say, "Tonight, the pastor said we were all designed to be like God, that he was a good, loving, and gentle parent. It broke my heart that he wanted a family and would do anything for us. I'm nothing like Him. I'm a bad parent."

Did I hear her, right? Bad parent? I didn't know she was a mother. I didn't want to offend her, so I carefully suggested, "Tell me all about it, Amber."

I was confused when she abruptly got up and went to her room. She returned, handing me a photograph. "This is my daughter. She will be three in two months. My mom had to raise her because I couldn't. I wasn't ready to be a mother or accept the responsibility. After tonight, I feel a hole in my heart from giving away a gift from God. I know God is mad at me because I'm nothing like what the pastor said. He said God wants us to be like Him—loving and caring."

I knew I was in a very sensitive position. I couldn't speak because my tongue felt glued to the roof of my mouth. I could hug her though. I moved next to her, putting my arms around her and holding on while she cried.

Praying while I rocked her in my arms, I begged the good Lord, *please speak through me. Help her know all will be well. I can't. I haven't got a clue what would help. Please pray through me so I know you want me to submit and let you help her.*

I didn't hear a verbal response, but I felt a rush of air—my clue he was near, breathing into me. I deeply inhaled Him, closed my eyes, and submitted my heart and mouth to Him. Through me, He said, "Amber, God is not mad at you. He knew how you would respond to this before your child was born. He has softened your heart tonight to change your thinking. Don't feel guilty any longer. Do something about it and start raising your child. It's never too late to form a relationship with her. You came back to Him. Now go back to her."

I knew the words hit the mark. She looked into my face and started to smile. "You're right! I went to God. He is going to help me go to Lacey. He'll help me be a good mom, won't he?"

We talked for hours about her boyfriend, Lacey's father. He dumped Amber when she got pregnant. She didn't have the courage to abort the baby. She explained how her mother, widowed and lonely, volunteered to raise Lacey with Amber's financial help. I could tell Amber loved the little girl but had been too self-absorbed to be what the baby needed. God was truly doing a wonder in her heart. I felt honored to be a part of this transformation.

I encouraged her to visit Lacey tomorrow night after work, getting to know the child she birthed using her Bible. I guided her through His Word to promises God made to families and the instructions of Paul on raising children. I shared with her the importance of moderation, as sharing too much Bible knowledge with her mother could backfire. Her mother had to witness the change in Amber. She needed time to come to terms with this newfound desire. She had to see that Amber was sincere and willing to be a good parent. Time would heal both women. They would be awesome parents for Lacey. At this point, Amber would have to share responsibility with her mom because the attachment was too great. I also reminded Amber that she was Lacey's mother. God didn't take that from her.

We finally exhausted ourselves with conversation and went to bed. My head was reeling from this wonder. Thank God I had my Bible. I praised my Lord and read His Word before I closed my eyes. All memories of what happened at church were forgotten but would be resurrected the next afternoon. Right now, I was too happy for Amber and excited about Lacey getting to know the real mother God was making of Amber.

At work, the next day, Amber and I were business as usual. I didn't have a vehicle, so I asked Frank if he would pick me up something for lunch, and I'd pay him back. We agreed to meet at noon at our new lunch area in the park. I couldn't wait to tell him about the miracle that happened last night. He needed to know because he was instrumental in getting Amber to church in order for God to work in her heart. I trusted him with the information. He could be discreet and very supportive.

———∿∿∿∾∘⋐⋗∘⋐⋗∘∿∿∿———

Sam was still Satan's puppet. Sam was almost insane with jealousy after staying confined in his car for hours last night, waiting for Hope to return. At midnight, he gave up and drunkenly drove home, resolving to spy on her at lunch again. He had a feeling that if he waited, he would see her at that park. He had the twisted idea that he could make her see that he still wanted her. Sam was willing to risk it all to convince her of his desire to reconcile their relationship. He would do anything, maybe even agreeing to detox if she would just take him back.

When Sam parked his car close enough to see the picnic table, Hope was already there as he expected, but she was not alone. She was with that same guy. Sam suddenly realized that Hope wore the same clothes she had on last night. He was convinced that she hadn't returned home because she had spent the night with that jerk. Sam, certain that Hope had slept with this guy, decided it was the only explanation that she'd still be dressed in last night's clothes. As Hope and Frank laughed and enjoyed themselves, Sam was seething with anger and hate. He was crying, driven into a raging maniac while his demons happily feasted.

Taking It Slow

I hated being without a vehicle. It made me feel needy, dependent, and insecure. When my workday ended, I didn't know what to do. Frank and Amber were on assigned employer field visits. *They've forgotten about me*, I thought.

Without my SUV, I needed a way home. Since Amber was the one responsible for me being in this predicament, I called her cell first. The call went straight to voicemail. *She must be in a meeting and had turned off the phone*, I reasoned.

I called Frank next. After two rings, I heard his cheerful voice, "Frank Addison."

"Hi, Frank, it's Hope," I said. "Are you headed back to the office?"

Answering, he said, "I'm almost there, why?"

"I'm stranded, remember? Amber didn't answer my call. Would it be too much trouble to take me home?" I begged.

"No problem at all. I'll be there in a jiff," he responded.

On the way home, I was pondering what I could do for the boys at the home. I had some extra cash thanks to Amber's one night stand. I shouldn't show up again empty-handed. What could I do?

"Frank, would it be inappropriate for me to buy sweet snacks for the boys? I don't think I've ever seen doughnuts, cakes, or pies lying about. Are sweets off-limits to the boys?" I inquired.

"Come to think of it, Hope, I've never seen them eat desserts either. I don't know how to answer your question. Give Mrs. Elder a call and ask before you bring anything. It might not be in their budget or possibly some kind of state regulation," he suggested.

I gratefully replied, "I'll do just that. I'll call her or Olivia beforehand. I want to share my blessings by giving to the Boys' Home."

Once I got in my apartment, I looked up the number for the Boys' Home. Mrs. Elder answered immediately. "Hi, Mrs. Elder. It's Hope Anderson. I plan to come out this evening to entertain the little ones. I wanted to know if I could bring everyone a dessert?"

I could almost hear her smiling through the phone. "Hope, that is so thoughtful. Do you realize how many mouths you'd be providing for?

I answered her honestly, "No, ma'am. How many should I bring?"

She hesitated. "With boys plus the volunteers, we usually have about twenty to twenty-five to feed every evening. Will that be a problem?"

"Not at all!" I whooped. I'll stop by the doughnut place and get several dozen assorted flavors."

After our conversation, I gulped a quick sandwich then took a shower to freshen up. Even though it wasn't officially summer yet, I'd been hot all day. I decided to wear shorts and a tee shirt so I could play with the kids. I needed to be ready to play rough, considering they were all boys. I pulled my hair into a ponytail and applied light makeup again. Nodding at my reflection in the mirror, I thought, *Not bad. I'll have those little fellows eating out of my hand in no time. I'm ready to tomboy with the best of them.*

———◦◦◦———

Satan was having fun tormenting Sam. Sam was such an easy puppet to manipulate, persuade, and guide into sinful thoughts and actions. Satan couldn't wait for the day his plan would finally come to a head.

———◦◦◦———

Sam wouldn't accept the fact that Hope could live without him. The revelation that she could possibly have feelings for another man so soon infuriated him. He would have to insert himself back into her life. There was only one way available to him at the moment. She wouldn't agree to a meeting, so he would have to pay her a surprise visit. He would humble himself, begging for another chance. She loved him once. She would love him again. He hated courtship, being romantic wasn't in his nature. He would try approaching her clean, sober, and peacefully offering to show her that he'd changed. Not wanting to risk her seeing his new vehicle, he drove his old car.

By the time he turned onto her street, he arrived just in time to see her driving off again. Timing was his enemy. Following her in this car would create problems. He couldn't live another night wondering where she was or what she was doing. He was thinking irrationally. It was time to take action, even if it was destructive. He went home to plan his attack.

———⁓⁓⊙⊙⟊⊙⊙⟊⊙⊙⁓⁓———

The Holy Spirit knew Satan was up to something. Keeping Hope spiritually progressing was His main goal as he showed her how good things could really be.

———⁓⁓⊙⊙⟊⊙⊙⟊⊙⊙⁓⁓———

Standing in line at the doughnut store, I thought about how current events had played out. The Lord had promised to provide if I agreed to help Amber. He kept His word in the moment of my need. Mentally, I thanked Him again. In my heart, I genuinely prayed my thanks with commitment, *Lord, I'm so glad that you take such good care of me. Knowing you're here gives me joy and peace. I've never been this happy. You've proved to me that your Word is good. I can depend on what you say. Not only did you make sure I had enough until payday, you've blessed me with extra so I could share. It means a lot. You're better to me than a hundred husbands. I don't ever want to be without you.*

Never doubt me, Hope. No one and nothing can ever give you complete peace, He said.

———⁓⁓⊙⊙⟊⊙⊙⟊⊙⊙⁓⁓———

He knew the last statement He made would soon cause Hope confusion. Little did she know that her life would be changing again—for the better. It wasn't good for man to be alone. His plan was in motion now. She would be making another visit to paradise very soon. The bridal supper was scheduled in a matter of weeks.

194

The news about dessert coming must have spread through the home. I was greeted by several smiling faces after parking my SUV. My little buddy, Greg, came running to me. He was a beautiful child. He was so glad to see me that his hug nearly knocked me off my feet.

I greeted him cheerfully, "Hey there, little buddy! Don't knock me over. I don't want these doughnuts to fall in the dirt."

"Love you, Ms. Hope," he squealed.

The simple greeting brought tears to my eyes. The lump in my throat made it hard to keep my cool. Putting the boxes down on the hood of my vehicle, I leaned over, picked him up, and hugged him hard. His honest emotion caught me off guard, and I didn't know how to handle it. I could only confess, "Love you too, buddy."

A deeper familiar voice behind me offered, "I'll get the boxes. You've got your hands full." It was Brent.

Now, I had to contend with the emotional upheaval from Greg, plus remembering all that was said and insinuated last night. I was dealing with one little fellow and a big one at the same time, both seeking love from me. *Hadn't I just declared the Lord was all I needed?*

Greg held on tight as we walked into the main house. When I tried to put him down, he seemed afraid to let me go. I could feel the tension in his little body. Was he trying to tell me something without words? Was he afraid? Why? I would have to ask if Mrs. Elder could enlighten me.

Dinner at the home was always served at 6:00 p.m. Strict schedules had to be observed to maintain that many kids. When I arrived with dessert, the dinner dishes were in the process of being washed, dried, and put away. Good thing doughnuts didn't need plates or forks. Sticky fingers were easy to clean.

Brent situated the boxes of doughnuts on the counter, and a swarm of male hands in all sizes grabbed up the treats. By the time

195

the swarm subsided, only a few of the tasty treats remained. I was thrilled that my offering was such a hit.

Seeing Mrs. Elder in her office, I excused myself from the masses to talk with her about Greg. His reaction earlier really concerned me. I knocked on her door before entering.

"Mrs. Elder, may I ask you a question?" I inquired.

Puzzled, she replied, "Yes, if I can help."

I probed, "I'm concerned about Greg. From the minute I arrived tonight, he has been very clingy. I picked him up to hug him, hello, but when I tried to put him down, he held on tighter and whimpered. Has he still been having problems eating and sleeping?"

Sighing, she answered me truthfully, "Greg's problems are not rare. He is young and trying to deal with loss. We call it the curse of being an orphan. Attachments to them seem fleeting. He has a deep-rooted fear of being abandoned. Last Wednesday morning, when he woke, you were gone. He looked for you, but you weren't here. You bonded with him the night before, and he thought you'd be here for him the next morning. It caused him to cry when he realized you weren't here."

Heaven forbid! I didn't want to cause Greg more pain. Shocked, I responded apologetically, "I am so sorry. I only wanted to help. If I'm hurting him, I'll stop coming."

"No, child! He needs attention at this young age anyway he can get it, as often as he can get it. When Frank told me that you would like to volunteer in a motherly role, I was ecstatic. The youngest boys—Greg and three others—need a loving female in their lives, even if it is moments every few days," she explained.

"I'm not hurting them?" I inquired.

"No more than when you were left alone growing up. It teaches them to cope. It helps them develop and become strong men. They need lessons when they start school. They start developing bonds with other children and don't need adults so much," she said.

I thought for a moment about what she said. Why had she referenced me? How had she known that I was the same as a little girl? I developed a hard shell over time when my parents left me in the care of other adults. The only difference was that I grew bitter for nothing; I had parents that came home every evening. I had their love, even though I thought they didn't want me. I felt abandoned, but I never really was. In my mind, it seemed I had been a burden, something preventing their happiness. All along, I was the source of their happiness. A spirit of condemnation was trying to sneak into my mind to accuse me of wasting so much time being bitter. I felt it the moment it touched my thinking. I was getting good at recognizing evil trying to get an upper hand. Mentally, I ordered the little creep of condemnation to scram.

Instantly, it occurred to me that God had put me here for a reason. If I knew from experience how Greg was feeling, then God could use me to help. It was a revelation knowing exactly how to respond. I was equipped with the knowledge of how and what to say to reassure them that everything would be okay. *Thank you, Lord.*

After my epiphany, I made a point to respond enthusiastically to Mrs. Elder. "I see what you mean! I think I understand now. I'll try to come as often as I can."

Then two other things occurred to me. If Greg was having abandonment issues, Tommy might also be having problems. I'd have to share this with Judy. The other issue was about Greg's mother, which I'd totally forgotten.

"Mrs. Elder, Greg said something to me the other night that may be part of his problem. He said I looked like his mother. Do I?" I asked.

Before I had an opportunity to object, she called Brent into the room. Brent walked in, a little confused, especially when she asked him to close the door. She took a deep breath and asked, "Brent, do you remember much about Greg's parents?" Now I was confused. Why had she asked Brent this question?

It must have shown on my face because she addressed me, "Hope, Brent works with the District Attorney's office and has dealt with many of the cases that involve these children. I think he would be the one to answer your questions."

Before Brent started talking, he stepped over to a filing cabinet located behind Mrs. Elder's desk. When he found the file he was looking for, he opened it on her desk so we all could see what it contained.

Then he started talking about Greg Hines as if he were an object instead of a little boy. "Subject is a three-year-old male, and father unknown. Mother consented to adoption. Mother incarcerated for child trafficking and drug possession with intent to distribute."

I was annoyed and sputtered, "Wait just a blooming minute! This is a precious little boy, not a block of wood or something. Why are you acting so insensitive?"

He responded, "It's my coping mechanism, Hope. I have to remove my heart from the equation as much as possible or be tempted to injure someone instead of being impartial. I was just reading from Greg's file. What was your question?"

"Greg made the comment the other night that I looked like his mother," I answered. "I was hoping to get some insight to help him through this adjustment period without causing him grief in the process."

He understood, smiled, and replied, "There is a mug shot of Amanda Hines in this file. I don't agree she looks like you. She has dark hair like yours and is about your size, but that is all." "Can I see the picture?" I asked.

"Sure!" he said while handing me the photo.

I gasped. Amanda Hines looked horrible. A poster example of a meth addict—dark circles under her eyes, rotten teeth, and gray-toned skin. Why would Greg associate her with me? That was something the Lord was going to have to show me.

"I see what you mean," I said as I handed the photo back to Brent. "She gave Greg up for adoption?"

"Yes, according to the file, she signed all rights over to the Boys' Home," Brent replied. "I remember this case! This woman was selling her child for drugs when the cops busted her. That's the reason we prosecuted her for child trafficking. She wanted to trade Greg for a large quantity of cocaine to sell on the black market. Poor little guy!"

If my heart was broken earlier, it was shattered now. This precious little boy hadn't been deemed worthy of attention, let alone love. I had my work cut out for me. My job is to show Greg and the other little guys how much they are appreciated.

I said to Brent and Mrs. Elder, "Thanks for showing me this. It helps me understand. Now I think I can better serve you and them."

When Brent and I left Mrs. Elder's office, I had a teary-eyed little fellow waiting for me. He looked dejected until I knelt and opened my arms for him.

While holding him, I asked if he ate a doughnut before they were all gone. He nodded and said he got a chocolate one, his favorite. I was glad.

—————ww∼e⊗⊙⊗⊙ww—————

The Holy Spirit loved watching a puzzle fit together. He saw the moves before any players involved ever did.

—————ww∼e⊗⊙⊗⊙ww—————

Watching Hope among the little boys as they played with Legos and Matchbox cars, Brent knew he could wait. Patience had gotten him this far. If Hope was the one, God would make it happen. Right now, it appeared that God was answering his heart's desire. Brent would wait and watch to determine if she truly loved these children as much as he did.

At 8:30 p.m., Hope was assigned to prepare Greg and Johnny for bed; as bunk bed mates, it made sense. She was told the little guys showered in the morning so the older guys could shower at night. All she needed to do was make sure their faces, hands, and feet were washed before putting on pajamas and that their teeth were brushed before tucking them in at lights out.

Both little boys complied with everything she requested, making it easy. When she had them in bed, she tucked the covers around them and kissed each one lightly on the forehead. Before leaving, she told them, "I'm going to try to come back tomorrow night. God doesn't want me to promise because something could happen to prevent me from coming and I would never intentionally disappoint you. I want you to know that I really enjoyed spending time with you, and I want to come again soon. Can you accept that?"

The boys replied that they could. Then in unison, they said, "Hurry back!"

This was the best job ever! I was exhausted but in a good way. I was ready to leave when I noticed two big guys, Frank and Brent, lounging in rocking chairs on the porch, eating the leftover doughnuts.

I couldn't help laughing, "You two look like worn-out kids, sitting there stuffing your faces. Don't you ever leave?"

Frank answered around a mouthful of doughnut, "Shortly, I've got to get as much beauty sleep as I can tonight because tomorrow night I plan to be out real late."

"Oooh, I remember. You have a date with Cindy. Yeah, it's going to take a lot of sleep to keep up with her," I replied jokingly. "See you guys later. I'm bushed." I turned to walk away.

—◦◦◦—

Brent's lawyer instincts narrowed on the exchange between Frank and Hope. They must be good friends. Who would know Hope better than one of her friends? To open the door for a conversation about Hope, Brent used his skills, remarking, "She seems like a keeper."

Taking the bait, Frank responded, "Yeah, she's great. We work together, so I know she's funny, loyal, and very supportive. We've become closer in the last few weeks since she started coming back to church. We just seem to have a new connection."

Frank was no dummy. He could read between the lines. "You're interested in her, aren't you? You sly old goat! Why don't you just admit it?"

"Yeah, I'm interested. She made it clear last night that she wasn't ready. She said something about taking it slow. Frank, I'm nearly thirty, and I'm ready to settle down. I've asked the Lord to bring me someone who could love these kids and my lifestyle. I don't want to waste time chasing skirts. When I watch her with the little guys, my heart melts. She's lovely to look at, compassionate but feisty. She appears to be what I've asked for. Now I have to wait." He moaned.

Frank chuckled then stated soberly, "You've got it bad, my friend. I agree. Hope is a prize. But she has been hurt beyond our understanding. To my knowledge, she was severely abused by her ex-husband, Sam Anderson. She still has an active restraining order on him, so things may be very sensitive. If you want to know more, ask Mark Carmen. He and Judy are two of Hope's closest friends. They've been by her side through all of it."

Restraining orders were something Brent could research. Being in the District Attorney's office had some advantages.

Getting to Know

Lying in bed, Hope reminisced about the night's events while talking with the Lord. "Lord, even though I had an emotional breakdown tonight, I felt honored that you led me to help those little boys. I knew in my heart that you sent me there because I would understand what they were feeling. I don't know if I will ever be a great mom, but I can be a good friend. I want to prevent these little ones from growing bitter like I did. Show me and guide me in the right direction. It doesn't appear having my own children is your plan. I am content being a substitute parent even on a part-time basis. Thanks again for a wonderful day and night."

Thanks for loving them for me. You did great. You're learning to trust me even without discussion, He replied.

———⁓⁓●⦿⊶⊷⦿●⁓⁓———

A few blocks away, Brent was also reminiscing while talking with the Lord. His discussion was inquisitive, leaning toward investigative. He wanted to know more about Sam Anderson. *What man in their right mind could beat up on a woman as fine and lovely as Hope?* He thought. Supplied with tools of the trade, Brent had access to reports of abuse that led to restraining orders. When he found Sam's name, he wasn't surprised to find Sam had a history of violence as well as some drunk and disorderly charges. He studied the face of the man who beat this lovely woman. Brent wanted to be prepared for action if Sam appeared.

Two things made Brent angry—something that hurt children and anyone that beat up on the weaker sex.

He'd make it a point to find out more details Saturday if he saw Mark Carmen at the kids' ball games. The more information he had on Hope, the better. He could see getting to know her was going to be difficult without some outside help.

———⁓⁓●⦿⊶⊷⦿●⁓⁓———

In the morning, the Lord had my focus totally turned from the previous evening. After devotions, breakfast, and coffee, my thoughts were consumed with Amber and Lacey. Had their visit gone well? I wanted to call Amber but assumed she was probably at the gym. I could hardly wait to hear all the details. The good Lord had orchestrated their visit, so it had to be productive.

From the moment, I turned the key in my SUV, I knew something was wrong. The motor started spitting and sputtering. Hesitantly, I put it in gear. Worried that I would be stranded by the side of the road, I prayed, *Lord, please don't let this vehicle break down. Please make sure I arrive at work safely.*

It was a jerky, shaky, and spasmodic trip, but the SUV made it to the parking lot. It hadn't died on the side of the road. My prayer was answered! Now I had to find someone to look at it before venturing off again. However, my vehicle was not a priority now. I went to Amber's office. We almost collided in the hallway; each intent on finding the other. I wanted to know results of her night, and she wanted to tell me. I could see on her face she was happy.

"How'd it go?" I asked.

Smiling from ear to ear, she said, "Fantastic! The three of us had a wonderful time. Mom, Lacey, and I had dinner together and talked about everything they were doing. Lacey showed me some of her drawings and dolls. She let me hug her a lot. Mom wasn't even suspicious about my change. She seemed overjoyed that I was attempting to get to know Lacey."

"I knew God had plans. He set you up," I said.

She continued, "I'm taking them to the jazz festival and carnival tonight. Not only am I getting to know my little girl, I'm getting to know my mom too. Something clicked for me last night. I felt like I belonged with them."

I was so grateful for the restoration happening for them. "I'd love to meet them one day. I bet you look like your mom. I bet Lacey is your Mini-Me," I guessed.

She giggled and replied, "No, she looks like her dad, but she has a petite build like me."

We agreed to meet soon to talk more. Right now, we both had jobs to do. I'd forgotten about my SUV problem until I reached into my handbag for a piece of gum and felt my keys. At times like this, I needed a man. I was clueless about fixing car problems or who to call for assistance.

The Lord stepped in with the answer as I was mentally listing my options. He gently recommended in His sweet soft voice, *Call your dad.*

Since my divorce, nothing pleased dad more than hearing from me. The reason didn't matter. He just loved to help me and talk to me. Whatever was needed, he was happy to comply. At first, I thought he was motivated by guilt. Until recently, I wouldn't accept a different explanation. Now I knew the truth. My parents love me and will be there for me. Retirement allows more availability. When I was younger, Dad and Mom both worked to provide a comfortable lifestyle. Working with the Boys' Home helped me finally understand.

The Holy Spirit was right; Dad was delighted to help when I told him about my SUV. He and Mom came to my rescue. Dad suggested taking the vehicle to a trusted mechanic to diagnose the problem. He would drive with Mom following, in the event that the vehicle had to stay overnight. If that was the case, they agreed to stay in town to take me home after work. I was a kid again; it felt great having them lovingly plan my afternoon. It was pleasurable watching our relationship grow.

When they returned several hours later, I was overjoyed to learn my car was ready to drive. Giving me the keys, Dad made an unusual comment, "You had water in your gas tank, Hope. They had to drain the tank. Where did you fill up last?"

I replied, "I filled up where I always do. I don't understand why it didn't give me any trouble until today. Shouldn't it have caused a problem three days ago when I filled the tank? I'm confused."

Dad repeated, "I'm just the messenger. Bill, the mechanic, assured me it would soon be humming again. He thinks catching it this quickly and changing the fuel was all that was needed. I trust his judgment. I've been taking my cars to him for several years. Bill has always been honest and fair."

When I asked for the service invoice, Dad refused. He said it wasn't enough to fret over and to consider it a gift.

I thanked them both for taking such good care of me. I assured them I'd come and visit them soon. Then I offered to eat with them after church Sunday if they wanted my company. That comment made their day. I was glad to see the delight on their faces.

—⁓⁓⁓⁓⁓—

Satan loved being evil. He could torture two at the same time. He didn't care who. Pain was gain to him.

—⁓⁓⁓⁓⁓—

Sam was sitting on the sidelines while pondering his situation and waiting for Hope to leave work and head home. Due to his constant tardiness and apparent drunkenness on the job, he had received a pink slip that afternoon terminating his employment. Unemployment benefits were his only alternative, but at this point, he didn't want to show up where Hope worked, asking for a handout. He'd have to find a detour around that issue.

Today was supposed to be a turning point in their relationship. He was confident his scheme would work, and all would soon be well. He couldn't let other issues get in the way. He'd wait for her after work, following her closely (but not too close), waiting for her SUV to malfunction. He was sure what he did to her car would cause her to pull off the road in need of assistance. Still trying to worm his way back into her good graces, he'd planned to be her knight in shining armor, coming to her rescue. When that didn't happen, he became even more furious. His plot had failed. He'd needed a different strategy. He certainly had uninterrupted time now to devise a new plan. He already decided it would not include spying on her each night.

—⁓⁓⁓⁓⁓—

The Holy Spirit was happy Hope had been spared the distress Satan had planned. He knew the time was coming when she would have to deal with Sam, but not yet.

———∿∿⦿⧫⦿∿∿———

I was so grateful my vehicle didn't sputter going home. Car trouble always made me uneasy. "Lord, you always take what the devil means for evil, and you turn it around for our good. I enjoyed seeing Mom and Dad today. My revelation has awakened a deeper appreciation for them. That bitterness burdened me for so long, dragging me down until you showed me how good my life really was. You opened doors for us to get better acquainted. I know that sounds strange, but I caused myself to miss out on a loving relationship by staying away out of baseless spite."

Wanting to keep my promise, I hurriedly dressed and ate so I could go to the home. Upon my arrival, I was surprised to see Mom and Dad's car parked next to the Boys' Home barn. Why were they there? Duh! Hadn't I asked for more time with them? God works fast. *Quit analyzing! Walk over to see what is going on*, I thought.

Dad and Joe Arnold were setting up equipment for a ball game while Mom was in the garden with Olivia. When Dad saw me, he smiled. "Hi there again. What brings you here?"

"I'm a volunteer. I'm helping Mrs. Elder with the youngest boys," I replied.

"Great! Your mom is helping Olivia pick a few vegetables from the garden. I'm helping Joe get ready for tomorrow's ball games. Don't let us keep you from your duties. I'll come see you later," he offered.

Waving me off, he went back to helping with the gear. I gestured to Mom because she heard me talking with Dad. I told her I'd be back in a minute. It was a nice evening to bring the guys outside after they finished eating.

My timing was perfect. The four had finished eating and clearing their dishes. When Greg and Johnny saw me, they were ecstatic. Their little faces beamed! "Hi, guys. Let's play outside while we still have light," I suggested.

All four boys—Greg, Johnny, Mark, and Shawn—joined me outside, wanting to play a game of hide-and-seek. As a child, I had hated that game. Always, I felt like I was the one having to find the others. Tonight, I took that dreaded feeling away from the boys by being the seeker, trying to catch the hiders. Being an adult had its advantages. I could deal with the pressure; they probably couldn't.

I chased little boys until I thought I'd drop. They were fast and slippery little varmints, which made them all the happier. I made it a point not to find any boy, so they could have the fun of hiding. We ran and ran until it was getting too dark to see well. They didn't care about the time. They were full of unending energy. We decided to catch lightning bugs after calling the hide-and-seek game over. I told them to wait on the porch while I went in to get everyone a clear plastic cup for the bugs they caught. They could see the light without harming the bug. On the way out, I also grabbed a few napkins to cover the tops of the cups to keep their prey trapped.

When I opened the door to return to the porch, I had a much larger child present. Brent held out his hand, wanting a cup so he could play with us. He said, "We need to hurry. These guys need to be ready for bed in about an hour."

"Spoilsport!" I joked as I handed him a cup.

I hadn't tried to catch a lightning bug since I was a little girl. It was hard. Not everyone was successful, but those who captured a bug let the others see their prize. They knew how to share, which helped a lot. I've seen other kids more fortunate fight over the smallest things, but these little guys didn't have a problem at all.

Of course, time flew, and we had to wrap up our game before any of the boys were ready. Rules were rules, and I wasn't allowed to deviate.

I was glad for the help, even if it was Brent. These four little guys reeked worse than any billy goat I'd ever been around. No way was I putting them in bed this dirty, sweaty, and smelly.

Being in a boys' facility, I asked Brent to check the bathroom for older boys occupying the sinks. Ten older kids have their regular shower times in the evening.

He quickly returned, reporting, "Rules! There are guys wall-to-wall and shoulder-to-shoulder. You'd get an eyeful, trust me."

"Where is the laundry room?" I asked. Surely, there is a sink in there.

Grinning, he replied, "Go to the kitchen and take a right. I'll get some washcloths and towels."

He didn't completely answer my question, but I took what he said as compliance and herded the stinky little fellows in that direction.

All four looked confused when we found the laundry area. Aha! There was a large sink. Perfect. I squatted to their eye level and said, "I want each of you to remove your shoes, socks, and your clothes. Don't take off your underpants because you are not bathing. You'll shower in the morning. You need to wash so you don't get grit and body odor all over your bedclothes."

Brent came in with washcloths and towels just in time for me to ask him for help. "Will you take two so I can work on the other two?"

"Sure," he agreed. "What do you want me to do?"

I explained, "Turn on the tap, get the water running warm, then sponge their faces, arms, and feet. We can leave their nasty clothes in a neat pile by the washing machine."

The boys thought this was great fun. It was like a new game. When we had them mostly clean, I wrapped each in their towel, parading them up to their bedrooms. They soon had on their pajamas. Next, they needed their teeth brushed before turning in for the night.

I could see they were still a little wired, so I had to get firm. "Guys, Brent and I are tired. It is time to get in bed. You have ball games planned for tomorrow, so you need to get your rest. You want to win, don't you? Then get to sleep, and I will see you later. Good night."

———∿∾◦❀◦❦◦❀◦∾∿———

Brent watched in fascination as Hope negotiated with the kids. She'd be a good mom. He was learning a lot about her by just listening and watching.

When I turned off the lights and closed the adjacent rooms' doors, my body almost gave in to exhaustion. How did women all over the world manage work, home, and a family day after day?

Brent saw my pain and made a suggestion, "Why don't you and I get a glass of tea and sit on the porch to regroup before you go home?"

"That sounds fantastic! My throat is parched, and those rocking chairs are calling my name," I replied.

We weren't the only ones wanting to rest on the porch. Mr. and Mrs. Elder, Olivia and Joe, and my parents already occupied the chairs. Dad made a funny comment when he saw our faces, "Age before beauty. Our bones are older," he joked.

Like a little kid, I stuck out my tongue at him then pouted my lower lip. "I'll sit on the steps and lean against the railing so I can listen. I don't think I can stand another second."

Joe said, "We were planning a summertime school's out celebration for tomorrow. We could use some fresh ideas."

I was too pooped to join in their conversation. I just sat there listening as he shared the plans they had so far, describing the schedule and type of games they could play. Olivia suggested the women make sandwiches for a picnic outside. Then Mom volunteered to bring their ice cream churn to make fresh ice cream. Mrs. Elder said that they also had a churn. With two more churns in the main house, there would be plenty of homemade ice cream for all to enjoy.

It sounded like great fun. Words started running together as I dozed off. The next thing I knew, Brent had me by the hand and ordering, "Come on! You need to get home before you pass out on the ground. Do you think you can drive?"

"I'm just tired, but I don't live very far. I can make it, thanks," I answered.

He insisted on walking me to my SUV, even opening my door as I climbed into the seat. I felt claustrophobic, sensing he wanted more than I was willing to give. If I hadn't already been through two unhappy marriages, he would be someone I could be interested in. He was a Christian, charming, good-looking, and extremely nice. He was too good to be strapped with a woman who was damaged goods, and besides, I wasn't willing to give my heart away again to a man. I'd given my broken heart to my Lord.

Looking at me with gorgeous blue pleading eyes, he asked, "Will I see you tomorrow?"

I was taken aback by the question but answered honestly, "I don't know. I hadn't planned to come to the games. Saturday is my cleaning and shopping day."

"Please come," he begged. "I had such a good time tonight. I haven't felt this free in a long time."

"Let me think about it. Right now, I'm too tired to make any plans," I countered.

As I was ready to leave, I looked at him and shared my feelings, "I had fun too."

Crazy Dreams—or Were They Warnings?

If it hadn't been for bright car lights shining in my face every few minutes, I probably would have fallen asleep at the wheel driving home. My whole body felt violated. What had possessed me to try to keep up with three- and four-year-old boys? I hadn't exercised in years, so my muscles were screaming from abuse.

When I finally staggered into my apartment and locked the door, my bed started loudly calling my name. I didn't care if I smelled like a goat or had dirt from head to toe, I'd bathe tomorrow.

I started undressing before securely locking the door. I kicked off my shoes and pants. I unfastened my bra, pulling it through my tee shirt without removing the shirt. I'd sleep in my tee and panties. My tank was empty.

———————

The Holy Spirit tried to get Hope's attention before she completely succumbed to sleep. He used the light on the wall trick, but she didn't see. He whispered for her to wait, but she didn't hear. She shouldn't go to sleep with negative emotions swirling around her head. She was leaving the door open for the enemy to torture her mind while her body tried to rest. She had learned to keep practicing His presence and held Him close for many days. Tomorrow, if she was in a better frame of mind, He'd have to warn her about getting too tired. An exhausted, vulnerable animal is a lion's meal. Tonight, He would have to watch from the sidelines as His enemy tampered with her emotions.

———————

Satan laughed and verbally responded to the Holy Spirit's concerns by letting Him know he was right. "Ah! You know me so well. I knew if I was patient, your little plaything would weaken, giving me a shot. Now you'll get to watch as I masquerade as you in her dreams. I'll call her a whore. I'll make her so ashamed of looking at a man that she'll be afraid to leave the apartment, fearing punishment if she did. I can be very persuasive, you know."

———ᴡᴡ◦◦ᴏ◦◦ᴡᴡ———

The Holy Spirit refused to acknowledge the attack. He was convinced that Hope knew His voice and would not listen to another. Blocking the joy He was experiencing at that moment from Satan was easy. Satan had unwittingly divulged his plan. Wouldn't he ever learn that his plans for evil would backfire? Hope may get confused tonight, but He'd make sure that she would have joy in the morning.

———ᴡᴡ◦◦ᴏ◦◦ᴡᴡ———

My dreams were fitful with illusive visions. The Lord kept appearing and disappearing as if he were indecisive. When he finally stabilized, I could see him clearly, but something about him wasn't right. The radiance I loved to gaze upon wasn't glorious. It was disturbing. I struggled to keep him in sight, but he evaded me at every turn. When I touched him to get the attention I craved, his whole being exploded into a flame. I wasn't encountering love; all I was seeing and sensing was rage.

With my heart in my throat, I asked, "Why are you so angry? Who are you angry with?"

Without a word, he pointed his finger at me. I was the one being judged! From that point, his eyes were too furious to look into. I fell to my knees in horror! What had I done? When he finally spoke, I was confused. His voice sounded raspy with condemnation, not soothing as before. His voice was always a loving symphony. The transformation made me cower in fear. My eyes assured me this was my Lord, so I lay at his feet in tears. I was witnessing firsthand how anger changed even him. I couldn't sink low enough to escape his rage and disapproval.

My heart longed to know how to make things right again. I begged for him to tell me what to do. I beseeched, "What is it Lord? How have I displeased you? Please let me make it up to you!"

"Whore!" he yelled. "Why would I ever want you back? You couldn't control your lustful thoughts."

What? I couldn't have heard right. I hadn't been unfaithful to him.

He kept screaming, "Whore! You unfaithful abomination! Allegiance doesn't mean anything to you!"

"Lord, I don't know what you mean. Show me please!" I begged.

"You want to see! Then see you will!" he snarled.

In a flash, I was caught in a whirlwind of images—scenes from last night of Brent smiling at me and me smiling at him. The Lord even let me see my thoughts. He replayed my thoughts— the thoughts contemplating Brent's good qualities and wishing he wasn't interested in me—throwing them in my face. My life was damaged.

"I see the future as well as the past. Your loyalty has changed!" he shrieked.

After that statement, he displayed visions of me partying and drinking. Then even more disturbing visions of me in bed with men, not a man, but men, in plural. In my future, I apparently had chosen flesh over his love. Why? How could I? What isn't he telling me! What made me turn completely around?

To my horror, I was seeing bloody swords next, indicating a slaughter. I was leaving a path of destruction everywhere I went because I'd made him so unhappy. My parents were disgusted with me, wanting no part of me or my associations. I couldn't get them to even acknowledge my presence; I was disowned. The church that held its arms open to sinners wasn't welcoming me. In fact, when I tried to attend service, windows and doors were slammed shut, barred, and locked.

Something in my subconscious knew this wasn't right. My spirit was not willing to accept any of this. But the Lord kept playing horrible images of me over and over while screaming accusations.

I awoke before daybreak in a tangled mess of bedclothes. Instantly, I knew I had experienced a nightmare. Nothing about it was true. My mind swiftly readjusted, but my body was still in

213

panic mode. My breathing and heart rate were ragged and swift. His presence was the only thing that could calm me, and I immediately called His name, "Lord, I need you!"

Good morning, Hope. I'm here, He replied comfortingly.

"Oh, God, I wish you would hold me! I had the most horrible dreams. Please assure me that what I witnessed through them wasn't true or would ever become truth," I begged.

I didn't feel arms around me, but I sensed a peace that was past understanding. Calmness flooded my heart when He said, *You're right. Nothing you witnessed was true.*

I sat straight in bed so I could recover. When the peace of my heart spread throughout my body, I began to relax, like a wound healing from the inside out.

"What happened, Lord?" I asked. "Why were my dreams so accusing and condemning? If they weren't true, then were they some kind of warning from heaven?"

He laughed, but I knew He wasn't being judgmental. He was just amused that I was worried about failing.

Sweet Hope, I am happy that you would be concerned with displeasing me. Fear not, you can't. You may grieve me from time to time, but you will never displease me again, He assured. Then He helped me understand. *You were too tired last night. Fatigue allowed your body to dictate your actions. You failed to close your day with the peace that only comes from me and my Word. Being too tired is a cue to Satan that you are falling behind, easy prey. Without my Word to protect you before falling asleep, our enemy was allowed access.*

"It's like being without my robe, isn't it?" I asked.

Exactly! The Word activates covenant power. As you sleep, the covenant promises are still at work. It's part of the canopy of divine protection," He explained. *"Through your dreams, Satan tried to fool you into believing I was the one attacking you. He is a master of deception and used your own fears against you. I am pleased you realized something wasn't right from the beginning of his torment. Can you recall what?*

I tried hard to remember, replaying the horror in my mind. "His appearance wasn't right. His voice wasn't right," I replied.

Correct! Satan can only mimic. He has no true light. He only tells lies your spirit could not follow, He shared.

"Then why could he make me cower and bow?" I asked.

He uncovered something that we need to deal with once and for all, He answered.

I was confused. "What?"

Your guilt. Your shame from having more than one mate. Your insatiable desire to be loved by a man, He stated.

I couldn't deny He was right. It truly bothered me that I couldn't satisfy either husband. The first wasn't content with just having me; the other wanted too much of me. He wanted my soul. I yearned to be desired and to love freely, unhindered, without rules or fear.

"What can I do to change?" I asked.

In simple terms, what does being born again mean to you, Hope? He countered.

His question about being born again disturbed and worried me. I remembered clearly when He said my salvation was complete. I thought I was past the basic part of my salvation. He wouldn't have asked me this question, though, if I wasn't lacking in understanding. I replied as truthfully as I could, "It means knowing I'm a sinner and giving my life to you. Living for you or dying for you if needed."

You are partly right. Live for me, yes. Die for me, maybe. The assertion you are still a sinner, no! You were a sinner. Now you are righteous. Stop referring to yourself as damaged goods. That implies from birth that you were flawed. Born again means new, you were given a chance to start over. All your past sins have been forgiven. Why do you want to continue harboring the shame from your prior life? From the start of this journey, you've craved self-acceptance as well as mine. It is time for you to learn, He directed.

I finally comprehended that I wasn't honoring my new creation. I kept seeing myself as who I was and instead of who I could be.

This silly question kept cropping up in my mind. I was timid about it but decided to ask anyway. "Can I start over my life as if I were a virgin?"

Now you understand. In my mind, you already are one, He said joyfully.

I was overjoyed. My life was really new again. I could start over fresh, without baggage. I would not allow myself to be fooled ever again by a love that wasn't sincere. The love that I had found with my Lord was all I needed or wanted.

Reading my thoughts, He interjected with a light rebuke, *Hope! Let others love you. Allow others to love me through you. Don't let your love stay bottled inside your heart, preventing the flow to others.*

What He said was sobering. Love was giving Him, not just receiving Him. I surrendered, asking for help and patience, "I'm new at this. Will you help me be what you need me to be? I don't think I can fearlessly receive love until you show me how. I am a new creation in Christ, but my memories are old. Right now, I don't think I'm capable of a romantic relationship."

Fall in love with yourself. Loving yourself is loving me. When you look or think of yourself, know that I am in you. To get to me, you have to care for yourself. Don't allow any form of attention other than respect and compassion near you. I respect those I love. I have compassion and mercy on them also. If you don't sense these characteristics from someone, then I am not in them. Judge according to righteousness. Love is patient, kind, joyful, merciful, long-suffering, and self-controlled, He instructed.

The rest of the morning, I cleaned the apartment, listened to praise music, and considered the new information in my heart. I knew I was allowing God to use me so He could help others. I didn't realize He wanted to love them through me. Further puzzling was the thought that He wanted to love me by others. I was just now allowing my parents to care for me. These were people who should love me unconditionally. Where could I start this flow? I had to start giving and receiving where I was, right? My scope of relationships at the moment were small—work, church, and the Boys' Home.

With the command in my heart, I decided to go to the picnic after finishing my weekly shopping. I was fairly good at love's outflow, but receiving might be hard.

New Perspectives

Brent was at the Boys' Home early the next morning. Big plans had been made for the day—games, picnic, and ice cream. He was mostly excited about the possibility of seeing Hope again. While he helped his Dad with the boys, he contemplated what Frank said about Hope harboring a deep hurt. He knew he couldn't rush her, but the reason plagued him.

Excusing himself, he went for a walk. He needed to talk to his Lord. His best friend would guide him better than any person ever could. He'd introduced Brent to a lovely woman; now he needed insight on how to win her heart.

The Lord didn't share personal information concerning Hope. The Lord did recommend treating her with respect, honesty, compassion as if she were a treasure. Brent was also encouraged to let the process flow unhindered. People, as well as all creation, worked together for the good of those the Lord loved.

When he returned to the campus, he saw that Mark and Frank had arrived and were in deep conversation.

Acknowledging Brent's presence, Mark motioned for him to join them. "Frank tells me you're interested in Hope. I couldn't be happier. She needs someone like you in her life."

For the next hour, Mark shared with Brent all he knew about Hope's two failed marriages. He especially highlighted the nightmare she lived through with the last one. God was using Mark to inform Brent about her deep-seated fear of being harmed again by Sam. In Mark's opinion, Sam was completely unstable, a loose cannon. Because of this, he had arranged for several other neighbors to help keep watch over Hope's place as much as they could. Hope was easily spooked; they tried to give her a sense of security.

Brent made a mental note to do more investigative research on Sam Anderson when he got to work Monday morning. He needed to know what could possibly be Sam's next steps. Brent included himself as part of the team watching over Hope.

All the negative information didn't change Brent's mind about who Hope really was. He'd seen firsthand her kind and honest nature when he watched her with the orphaned boys. He was saddened to hear that someone so good had gone through such hardships. No wonder the Lord suggested that he treat her like a treasure. It was evident God was working in her life; it was another reason he was so attracted to her. Until she developed into what God was calling her to be, he'd have to follow the Lord's advice.

―――∽∾◦⊙◆⊙◦∽∾―――

The Lord and the Holy Spirit excitedly watched the stage being set, thankful their enemy's plan finally backfired. Once the giants were removed for good, bringing Hope and Brent together— Brent's spirit of justice and Hope's intercessory abilities, two of the Lord's divine characteristics at work—would be great asset to the kingdom.

―――∽∾◦⊙◆⊙◦∽∾―――

While at the market, I decided to call Mom to see if I could contribute items for the picnic. Her suggestion to make a big batch of sandwiches encouraged my spirit. The Lord was showing me how to allow Him to participate in the festivities through giving. It was amazing how even little gestures of love pleased Him.

Mom told me to keep it simple. She recommended preparing pimiento cheese or peanut butter and jelly. Talking to Mom while shopping was fun. When I found soft drinks on sale, I asked if they were needed. At first, she hesitated then said if I could afford it, two dozen more assorted flavors would be appreciated. I assured her that it was no problem; God knew how much I had to spend and continually provided. He was finding bargains for me as well as the picnic.

I quickly constructed sandwiches then stored them in a large plastic container to stay fresh. Next, I iced down the canned drinks.

I couldn't help talking excitedly with the Lord during the drive to the home. "Lord, this is fun. With the new perspective, you gave me, I grasp how you are able to show love through my physical obedience. When I removed myself from the equation,

218

you bought items, prepared the items, and now you're delivering the items. If I wanted to get weird, I could say you're a body snatcher, but in this case, I've given you my body to use."

It is fun, isn't it? Now I have a request. Please sit back and enjoy others caring for you. Don't lift a finger after delivering these goods. Find a comfortable seat and enjoy the fellowship. Today, I want to show you how I love you by using others, He said.

I couldn't believe what He requested. I wasn't one to sit back and do nothing. Little kids needed assistance.

My thoughts rendered a light rebuke from the Lord. *Hope! Do you remember when I allowed the woman to rub the expensive ointment on my feet, kissing my feet as she wiped them with her hair? I had to learn to let the Father love me the same way I'm asking that you allow me to show you, my love. Receive everything as if I were personally serving you, as I watched my Father do it for me. Let me continue in His service.*

"Lord, I remember the story. You were rebuked harshly for allowing such affection. Now I know why, so you could use it to explain love," I answered.

Sit back and enjoy all the events of today with your spiritual sight and hearing. Wear your robe proudly and with confidence. You are a child of the Living God, deserving love in every aspect, He said lovingly.

Mentally, I submitted. As soon as I parked at the Boys' Home, I purposely concentrated on my robe. Covenant commitment was an awesome thing. I was ordered to be proud of wearing the robe and knowing who I was. I was nervous about His request. I'd always been the servant, not the recipient. I was jolted by the revelation. I'd just admitted my weakness about receiving. The confession was accompanied by a shadow engulfing me, even though I had my robe on. The giant responsible for my problem in being a gracious receiver was present. Strong covenant determination came with insight; this giant's stronghold would be destroyed today. If God ordered me to do something through the covenant robe, he would see me through. The battle was on between God and this giant. I was stuck in the middle.

219

I walked to the back of my SUV then reined in my actions. He said to deliver the goods. Was I supposed to carry them inside or not? Pausing to see what would happen wasn't easy. I pretended to look for something in my purse to avoid appearing stupid, just standing at the back of my vehicle. A few seconds later, I heard a strong familiar voice I'd been trying to avoid.

Not Brent! I thought to myself. Why did the Holy Spirit want to use him?

Mentally, I prayed, *Okay, Lord, here goes. Just please keep romance out of the equation. I am not ready for that.*

Brent asked, "Do you need help?"

"Yes, please. I have sandwiches and a cooler of drinks to bring inside," I answered.

"You go ahead. I'll bring in everything. I think your Mom is expecting you," he said.

"Thanks, you're sweet," I replied.

I felt so guilty. I felt I was using him as a slave to carry the load. How could this be fair? It didn't feel right, but I had to submit. A war was on, and my twisted morals could not get involved. I had orders. What could I do?

Hearing my distress, the Lord whispered, *softly pray in the Spirit.*

I should have thought to do that in the first place. Rather than scolding myself for not thinking of it, I started praying while walking to the main house. Instantly, I saw the little demon trying to feed off my guilt. When I scornfully glared, it was startled then it screamed loudly before vanishing.

Prayers worked! It opened my eyes, allowing me to see my negative emotion. Now I was able to change it to joy. God was carrying my load through Brent.

Inside, the women were working. One was gathering plates, cutlery, and cups from the cupboard; another was arranging sandwiches on platters and chips in bowls. Mom was in the laundry room using the big sink to get the ice cream churn ready. Watching her fumble with the heavy bag of ice without offering assistance was difficult. I wanted badly to help her. As soon as I had that thought, I reproved myself. The correction allowed God to use Dad to help her.

I stood motionless and watched them hug and kiss as if they were newlyweds. It was so sweet seeing their love for each other, still strong after all these years.

"Hi there," I greeted. "Don't you two look lovey-dovey?"

Mom was a little embarrassed until she saw it was me standing in the doorway.

Recovering, she said, "Hi, sweetie, I'm glad you're here. I was just about to find a seat to watch the games. Do you want to come with me? I think Dad has this churn under control and will join us in a minute. He needs to plug in the motor and make sure the churn works now that it's packed with ice."

I noticed something special; Mom didn't have a problem letting Dad love her. She didn't flinch about leaving him alone with the churn. She was confident in their love. I would have worried about everything. I would have helped pack the ice and plugged in the motor. I realized I would have denied him pleasure if I had been Mom.

The softball game for the older boys was already in progress. Mom and I saw Judy watching Tommy and Mark preparing for a T-Ball game by throwing balls to each other. I suddenly remembered I needed to speak with her about orphan anxiety. I excused myself from Mom for a few minutes.

"Hi, Judy," I greeted. "How's it going?"

She grinned. "Wonderful. It's good to see you," she replied.

I asked, "Have Tommy's moods gotten better? You were concerned the last time I saw you."

"It's getting better," she answered. "I think he is adjusting to being with us."

"I'm asking because I learned something from Mrs. Elder the other night that may help." I advised, "She explained the little kids have problems with abandonment. They have a hard time adapting to being orphaned. They crave security, so when the relationships they have aren't rooted, it breaks their hearts.

Until they get older, they are constantly trying to form a stable attachment with someone. It could be that Tommy is trying to overcome the fear of losing you. He could be worried that what he has here with you will not last."

With tears in her eyes, she hugged me and whispered in my ear, "Thanks for sharing that. I had no idea he could be struggling with that fear. This gives me a new perspective on my little man's heart. He must love us. This explains his anxiety when we want to come out here some evenings. He doesn't want to come unless it is for a game," she confided.

I affirmed, "I'm glad I remembered to tell you. I come out sometimes during the week. I stumbled on the information while trying to help last week."

"What do you do?" She asked.

I thought she would laugh when I told her. I giggled. "I mother the youngest boys."

She calmly stated, "You know you'd be a great mother."

"Thanks," I choked.

Emotions wouldn't allow me to hang around after that. These orphaned boys were going to be my kids. It must not have been in God's plan for me to have my own. I made an excuse. "Mom is waiting for me. Will I see you later?"

"Yeah, we'll be here awhile. Tommy's game doesn't start until after the picnic," she said.

"See you then," I replied.

I found Mom sitting with a few others from church, watching the softball game. It was good that Mom, Dad, and the church were involved in organizing teams with kids from church to play with these orphaned boys. When the weather gets warm, their committee arranges outdoor events like these games and picnics once or twice each month. Family days were important. All involved were happy and welcomed. People are entertainment junkies; if proper outlets aren't available, they seek other forms that could lead down dark paths.

With that thought in mind, I speculated that my parents got involved with this ministry after observing the choices I made that eventually led to Sam. I was thankful something good resulted from that disaster after all.

Aware of my approach, Mom motioned for me to join her. She had saved a seat for me. I knew Mom loved me, but today, the Lord asked me to look at everyone, everything, and every action with my spiritual vision. Mom loved me through Him today. The moment I sat next to her, she lovingly patted my leg. I closed my eyes, picturing His loving hand doing the patting. His reassurance through touch overwhelmed me with unconditional love.

The day was a roller coaster ride of emotions. At the moment, I was relishing in being loved unconditionally. I was experiencing the love of the Father.

I was lost in my thoughts, oblivious of Frank's presence. I was startled when he touched me with a cold canned drink, saying, "I thought you'd like something to drink. It's hot out here."

"Thanks! It is hot, and I am thirsty. How do you know what I like?" I replied curiously.

He snorted. "I've watched you drink the same thing every time we had lunch together. Mind if I sit here? Thought you'd like to know about my date."

I definitely wanted details of his evening with the socialite queen. But something deeper was happening. He was offering brotherly love—two people enjoying each other's company with no strings attached. One more way the Lord can use people.

I snapped out of my moment of relishing another perspective of love to demand, "Spill it! I'm all ears."

"We went to the jazz festival," he said.

"You took her to a carnival?" I laughed in disbelief.

"Yeah, what's wrong with that? It's where she wanted to go," he asserted.

"Okay, now I'm even more bewildered." I giggled. "You had a date with a woman I know prefers expensive dinners with dancing. You are telling me she wanted to go to a carnival. It's a little hard to believe. Did you win a stuffed bear, buy cotton candy, and enjoy the rides with her also?"

"As a matter of fact, I did all the above. We had a wonderful time." He pouted.

"I'm sorry, Frank," I apologized. "I wasn't making fun of you. I'm just amazed. I really like Cindy, but she is considered high maintenance. She likes expensive things. She wants to be doted on. I imagined she would ask you to take her to the most expensive club in town, order the most expensive fare on the menu, drink the most expensive wine, followed by dancing the night away."

Thankfully, Frank took my teasing in stride and replied, "Nope, we talked a lot during the week. I told her I didn't drink, so drinking was not an option. I might have enjoyed dancing, but it usually includes an unwholesome atmosphere. I've come too far in my walk be tempted by that again. Our conversations made it clear that her usual kind of date wasn't an alternative."

"Are you going out again?" I asked.

"As a matter of fact, I'm seeing her again tonight. We're going to get a burger then go to a movie," he shared.

I was truly happy for them. I knew Frank would be good for her. Maybe Cindy would discover there are good guys in the world who want to treat her like a lady. Most men from the clubbing scene were willing to go on an expensive date but expected a particular payment in return. I was sure Frank's perspective on dating was throwing her for a loop.

The two of us joked and watched the game until it was time for the picnic. He had duties to perform and left me again with Mom. I reveled in her company, but I was feeling useless. I was anxious because I wasn't doing anything to help. Sitting around doing absolutely nothing wasn't my nature.

I had been commanded not to lift a finger. How was I going to eat? Did the Lord mean not to make me a plate? Was I taking His instructions too literally? Lost in these thoughts, deliberating these questions, I heard a familiar voice behind me ask a question, "Mind if I eat with you?"

I didn't want to be rude, and I really liked Brent. "Sure. The company would be nice."

His response was unbelievable. "I'll get us a plate of sandwiches and some drinks. You find us a place in the shade."

I was stunned! The Lord had meant I wouldn't have to lift a finger. I responded by saying, "Okay."

He smiled and asked, "What kind of sandwiches and drink do you prefer?"

Intrigued by what the Lord was doing, I used my spiritual vision to respond to this new perspective. I knew he was using Brent. I happily replied, "I'd like pimiento cheese and a diet drink, please.

As Brent walked away to get our lunches, I realized the giant's dark shadow was gone. The Lord had won the battle! When? Was it when I submitted to Him through Brent? Yes, it was! What a great surprise.

———— ∞∞∞∞∞∞∞ ————

The Lord laughed. Hope was catching on nicely.

A Connection

I was on a mission to find a picnic table out of the sun. Tables had been set up in various locations, but most weren't completely shaded. I finally found a small one isolated from all the others underneath a large oak tree next to the barn. I wondered why I was being drawn there because I didn't want to be alone with Brent. What were we supposed to talk about? All we had in common were orphaned boys and our church. I was no dummy. I knew the Lord was setting me up. This abrasive experience was happening for a reason. I inquired what to do and said, *Lord, what can I talk about with Bent? It is obvious you want me to get to know him. You know I feel uneasy with him because he wants more from me than I'm willing to give. My emotions are too raw, and he is salt to my wounds. Please tell me what to do and say.*

I heard Him say, *what intrigued you about him? What fascinated you the other day? When you remember, start asking him questions. You'll be surprised at the answers.*

He did seem to be listening to my plea about romantic situations. Seeing Brent coming toward me made me frantic. Why was I making this so hard? I took a deep breath, closed my eyes, and concentrated. When I opened my eyes, I saw the clue for my fascination. It was bright as the sun—Brent's robe. In that flash, I remembered why I'd been intrigued. I had been amazed watching him in the prayer room at church, using his ability to engage his robe while in prayer. It had captivated me so much that I couldn't focus on the message. I also remembered the Lord's reprimand for not paying attention to the pastor.

Now what Lord? Should I ask about his robe or the prayer room? I prayed.

What does the robe represent? Where was he? Keep it simple, He whispered softly.

Covenant! Prayer room! I had my answers. *Thanks, Lord!*

I couldn't simply ask about his spiritual robe. He might think I was crazy. This could be trickier than I thought. Rather than working so hard, I decided to put the labor in the Lord's lap.

Start the conversation for me Lord. I'll mess things up, I pleaded.

He chuckled. *I thought you'd never ask.*

When Brent arrived, he said, "I was hoping you'd find this place. I strategically set a table here the last time we had an event, out of the sun and away from the noise. I could watch everything but still relax before the festivities resumed."

"So you admit to being a loner?" I remarked.

"I guess you could say I need a bit of privacy from time to time," he agreed.

He sat the plates and drinks on the table then sat on the bench across from me. It took my breath away when he clasped my hands as he bowed his head to bless our meal. His prayer was different than what I usually heard spoken over food.

"Lord, thank you for this day, for this bounty, the friends, and family to share it with. Your blessings are amazing, and we will be forever grateful. Amen."

The prayer was the opening for a conversation. I took the Lord's cue and simply asked, "Brent, your prayer was sweet and different from any I've ever heard spoken at meals before. Can I ask you why?"

He had taken a bite of sandwich, so he motioned for me to wait while he finished chewing. He soon replied, "I pray to my God as if he has already gone before me, provided His best for me—the cleanest and most wholesome. I treat everything as already blessed. If he has gone before me, then what should I fear? All I need to do is thank Him."

"It takes confidence to pray that way, doesn't it?" I remarked.

He apparently suspected asking questions instead of eating meant that I had something on my mind. He stopped eating, giving me his undivided attention. Brent's qualities were very familiar; his patience sweet, like someone else I knew.

He looked at me very seriously then stated, "I take my covenant rights very personal. If I'm a child of God's, why would I be given anything to eat that could harm me? If an attempt were made to harm me through food, I expect Him to intervene on my behalf. For example, if I drop a bite of something on the ground, I

227

take that as telling me I wasn't supposed to eat it. If a drink turns over before I have a swallow, I take that as a sign I wasn't supposed to have it. I make things simple in my mind and live by His loyalty to His Word, which promises to take care of me."

"Thank you. Your views are so simple and easy. That's what God meant by having childlike faith," I responded.

I had more to say, but I was afraid to watch Brent's expression. Bowing my head, I revealed, "I talk with Him like you do."

I felt tender fingers under my chin as his deep voice said calmly and sweetly, "Hope, look at me."

When I did, he looked me straight in the eyes, confirming, "I talk to Him with childlike faith all the time." Then he grinned and asked, "Can we eat now? I'm hungry."

I was so relieved! Could it be I had someone with whom I could share my supernatural events? I couldn't rush in. I needed to wait and see. I would let him direct our conversations, knowing the Lord had control. Suddenly, I had a raging appetite. I needed filling—but why?

Since I've allowed Him access to my mind, He always heard my thoughts. He explained, *You poured out your heart a few minutes ago. You let someone have a part of you that was very personal.*

When Brent finished his sandwiches, he started asking questions, "How long have you known the Lord?

I braced myself. I wasn't prepared for his directness, which must be the lawyer in him. I could think of no other reason for him to be so blunt.

"A few weeks," I replied.

"Do you have the evidence?" he asked.

I knew he was being as subtle as he knew how (typical male), but I answered him anyway. "Yes, the Holy Spirit presented Himself to me and gave me gifts."

"Great! He gave me a discerning spirit and a spirit of justice. When we pray together, he uses me in the most amazing ways," he exclaimed.

He was talking to me as if I knew! He does understand! He won't think I'm crazy! Still, I'm going to take things slow. I wasn't ready yet to divulge my journeys or my ability to see creepy demons and giants.

I did share, "He uses me to pray for others."

"You're an intercessor! Hallelujah! Our church is in dire need of another generation of prayer warriors," he whooped.

"What do you mean another generation?" I asked.

He laughed. "Most of the intercessors in our church are old ladies who carry the load. There are a few men, but not many, and they are old too. God may be calling you to be the beginning of His next generation of warriors. Why else would we be having this conversation? Would you be interested in getting involved in the prayer group?"

"Why don't you help them?" I questioned.

He replied, "I do on occasion, but my spirit of justice needs privacy—time alone with God to seek the truth."

I wavered. "Let me pray about it. If it is what he wants, he will let me know."

"If you feel directed to be part of the prayer group, come to the prayer room tomorrow around 8:30 a.m. I promise I will be there, so you won't be alone facing everyone," he offered. Then he changed the subject. "Want some ice cream? I'm going to get me some before it is all gone."

"Please!" I consented.

———

The Holy Spirit was very pleased. He had shown two people a link that could be a stronger bond than marriage—their love for Him. The connection was developing according to plan. He knew together they could energize the church, encourage others their age to get involved in sensitive areas and help the church family grow. It was time His current warriors had some relief; they'd been faithful for so long. It was also time to renounce one or two who shouldn't have been involved.

Hope would soon find herself in a new position. She would have to battle against an old order. She was about to encounter judgment based on her past. With her newfound strength in Him, she would make it evident that she was His new creation. It was time the old condemning order was discarded.

—⁓•ᴏⱰᴇⱰᴏⱰᴇᴏ•⁓—

While Brent stood in line for the ice cream, his joy was unmistakable. He knew he was beginning to care for Hope, and now he knew why. They had many things in common, but the most important was having the same knowledge of God.

He knew it was the Lord who guided him to be so direct with her. He was very glad that he obeyed. The insight opened an entirely new area of interest beyond her concern for the kids. She had the Holy Spirit! Brent could sense her excitement when he told her about himself. He'd discerned she was hesitant about sharing her newfound strength. In time, she would learn to trust him. Giving her time and space was only part of treating her with respect and making her feel special.

He truly hoped the Lord would encourage her to take part in the group. They needed revival. It wasn't his place to vent, but some were too critical and judgmental to continue in the prayer group. The Lord had shown him long ago that the time would come when things would change. He was convinced he had an important part in that change. Someone was coming that would cause it to happen, but he would be the one to see it through. There had been a time when judgment and sifting were necessary, but not today. Grace must abound. It had to be enforced within the church, not condemnation.

When he returned with their ice cream, he planned to have a deeper discussion with Hope, but she was no longer alone. Greg was in her lap. Brent couldn't help staring. The sight of her holding a child was beautiful. He regretted they couldn't talk privately, but God would make more time for that. He had to keep reminding himself to take things slow, not to get impatient, and not to force issues, even if he thought it involved her in prayer.

Brent was thankful God allowed him to watch Hope relax as she learned to be comfortable in her surroundings. Her sense of security was an important part of her healing. If Greg was assigned to play a part in that healing, Brent would have to learn to share. With that in mind, he remembered something Hope said earlier— childlike faith. Laughing to himself, Brent assumed, with childlike faith, that he and Greg would share her like a new toy. Somehow, he'd learn to keep it simple just like Greg.

Uncoiling

Greg was overjoyed that I was going to watch him play ball. He was excited that he had been selected to play shortstop. He considered shortstop a key position and being chosen to play it was like a grown-up winning the lottery. He was trembling with the need to tell someone. He had spotted me next to the barn and left the group of boys to share his excitement.

Greg was so animated that he could hardly speak plainly as he tried to explain the important position he had been chosen to play. He was a buzzing with pure joy until Brent walked up. He looked as if he had been caught doing something wrong. His little body stiffened in my lap, causing my motherly instinct to kick in.

"What's the matter, honey?" I soothed.

He looked into my eyes and said, "I need to go. I didn't ask to leave."

"Sure, I'll be watching you play. I promise," I assured him. Brent hadn't even sat down before Greg bolted. What was that all about?

When Brent extended his hand with a bowl of ice cream, I couldn't believe my eyes. My bowl could have fed three people. I was at a loss for words. How was I supposed to react? The Lord was using Brent to serve me today; he was the one handing me this large bowl of ice cream. Was I supposed to be watching what I was eating and eating healthier?

I quit trying to analyze and just accepted what he offered. "Thanks, Brent. I hope you got two large bowls because you were hungry. I can't eat all this," I admitted.

He replied laughingly, "I tend to have a heavy hand when I serve others. If you don't think you can eat it all, I'll be glad to finish it, if it isn't too soupy."

Pushing my bowl in his direction, I stated jokingly, "Take some of it now. I eat slowly, so it's guaranteed to be soupy before I'm finished. I've watched you eat. It won't stand a chance of melting before you're through."

While we ate, I felt comfortable enough to ask him about Greg. Maybe Brent would know why Greg had suddenly become apprehensive. Remembering to keep it simple, I asked, "Do you have any idea why Greg left a few minutes ago as if he were afraid of you?"

Brent frowned in deep thought. Then he grinned and replied, "I think I do. I've been having some difficulty getting the little guys to ask permission when they want to go somewhere. It isn't right for them to just disappear without letting a grown-up know where they are headed, or if they can go somewhere unsupervised. What did he say or do that makes you ask?"

That must have been it! I repeated what Greg had said, "He told me he didn't ask permission. You're right. He must have left the group when he spotted me. He was so excited about his ball game; he probably didn't think to tell someone. Your teaching must be getting through because he tightened in my lap like he had been busted."

Another question instantly came to mind. "Do you ever spank them for misbehaving?"

"Never have and never will. I will give them a firm lecture and stern look, though," he pledged.

Something inside me melted. This huge man had the heart of a lion and the nature of a kitten—one authoritative and the other playful. He reminded me of someone, but I couldn't decide who. I had very few male friends, no brothers or male cousins, so who did he remind me of? Then it hit me! No! It couldn't be! This was not funny! It was time for our little outing to come to a halt. *I'm not ready, Lord. Please don't take me there*, I begged.

I excused myself, using the promise I'd made to Greg, "Thanks for the lunch and ice cream. I had a good time. I need to leave in time to keep my promise to Greg to watch his game. If I'm not mistaken, he and Johnny are playing with Tommy and a few other church kids. This should be interesting."

I picked up my trash and started toward the ball field. I looked for a trash can, hoping Brent wasn't following me. I refused to be rude, but I needed some distance, immediately.

I guess he understood or sensed my agitation because he gave me the breathing room I desperately needed. The only response I got from my abrupt exit was hearing him say, "I enjoyed our lunch too. See you soon."

The hot sun, plus a full belly, was playing havoc with me. Or was it my thoughts combined with a sense of guilt? Brent had been nothing but kind and supportive. He and I had connected. I no longer felt alone with my spirituality. I was delighted to find someone who understood, but that was as far as I wanted our relationship to go. In my mind, the only thing I truly needed was space away from a man. My heart belonged to my Lord, and I wanted it to stay that way. He never failed me, never left me, never disappointed. I was prepared to do anything necessary to keep my flesh from ruining our relationship, even if that flesh also knew Him.

I appeared to be watching the games, but I really wasn't. My eyes were focused on the ball field while my mind was in deep conversation with the Lord. I sat in a crowd of people, but I was alone spiritually on the bench. We were having a discussion about the events of the day. I appreciated every second of being loved His various ways. It was utilizing Brent that caused an issue.

Why, Lord, are you using Brent? You know I'm trying to discourage his advances. I want to maintain a friendly and professional relationship, but you keep throwing me curves. What am I missing? Please help me understand? Please make it plain and simple, I begged.

Rest assured I hear you, Hope. You are not ready for romance. Time is a great healer, though. Let me heal you through it. You need male friendships. You need male companions. I insist that you allow my brethren access to your heart. Stop fighting and let things flow. Don't consider every gesture or word as sexual. Brent is cooperating with me. Allow this friendship to grow. I need the two of you working together for me. All my brethren have my same characteristics. That is why you are attracted to Brent. You are attractive to him for the same reason, He explained.

As I contemplated His interpretation, I felt something in me uncoil. I had emotionally overreacted to something simple yet overwhelming, but the Lord was very complex. I was afraid of men, especially of one with Jesus' influence written all in his nature. I knew Brent wasn't Jesus; he just had the same qualities of the Jesus I loved.

For the sake of the one I loved, I was willing to submit to God's will. There is a purpose for Brent getting close, so I will quit fighting. The Lord understood that I didn't want romance, thank goodness! His need for us to work together must relate to intercession.

Lord, are you calling me to the church's prayer group? I inquired.

Yes. I want you to get involved. Brent will be your guide, He responded.

I was curious to know more. Brent had said something that made me wonder about the group. *Brent said all of them were old ladies, and you may want to change things. What does he mean?*

Brent is right. Change has to happen. There is a wolf in sheep's clothing among the group that needs realignment. Your presence will make that happen, He answered.

What! I don't like confrontations. I can't do that! I screeched inside my mind.

A wolf, to me, signified someone mean and violent in nature, disguised to cause destruction of God's people. I couldn't combat someone like that. Until lately, I ran from battles. I folded like cheap chairs under pressure. The Lord fought my giants. Why was He requiring me to do this? This wasn't a demon; this was a person.

I said the wolf had to be corrected not dissected. Brent and the pastor will do that. You just have to stand your ground during the meeting. Together, you and I will defeat the giant behind this problem. Go through the motions. The battle has already been won, He assured.

Oh, my! He just revealed my future! The incident was prearranged and already won in heaven. I could relax and walk it out, even if it appeared difficult. Tomorrow was going to be interesting, maybe terrifying, but victorious just the same. Another thought occurred to me. Was this wolf a threat that needed to be kicked out of church? What was my role in that issue if Brent and the pastor were steering?

Is the wolf going to be removed from the church? If so, by whom? I asked.

This spoiler will be given a choice—confess, repent, obey me or leave. It has exercised power over the body for too long. A rebellion will happen but not until the cause of the uprising arrives. You are the cause, but not the one to offer options, he answered.

He restored memories of how it felt when I returned to church. The condemnation and judgment I sensed the first morning. The second time I attended, I'd heard with my spiritual ears the truth from Mrs. Anthony who greeted me at the door. Could she be that pretender? Or was it someone who shielded their identity?

My past shouldn't determine my status. I was the victim. Was this ugliness considered the cause? My former life was none of their business. God has forgiven me and has called me, so none can stand in His way. A sense of excitement mixed with trepidation overwhelmed me. Tomorrow wasn't going to be fun, but it was necessary for the benefit of church growth. In today's society, there are too many lonely divorced people needing acceptance and love from Jesus. Strongholds and barriers must be removed. Give me an ax, a sword, any weapon. I was ready to fight now that I knew the reason.

I could finally discern the Lord's need for Brent and me to work together. My job was to stand in the gap for all divorced people in our church, with Brent doing the advocating. Would I be the first? This lost sheep had come home, and I had God's guarantee to be welcomed. I wanted to be a light for others to follow.

The tension inside me uncoiled even more. I felt empowered and strong because I had a calling, not only to intercede but to change the game. I was going to be the Lord's example that he loves the broken and abused, and he wanted to use us in church service. I was more than ready and willing now; I was pumped up! Brent and I had to be close to win this for our Jesus. He had to know.

Where was Brent? That was funny! The hunted has become the hunter. God Himself requested I be Brent's helper, so, where was he? Greg's game was over. I could safely search without causing the child grief.

Then a thought came to me. Where would Jesus be? What would Jesus be doing? He'd be helping, teaching, defending, or healing. With that in mind, my quest included people cleaning up the picnic or helping with the kids.

When I found Brent, he was helping some ladies put away tables and chairs, a gentleman to the core.

My approach must have startled him. He almost dropped a table when I said, "Hi, can we talk?"

Laying the table down, he replied, "Sure, I'm at your service."

It was my turn to respond. "I just want to thank you again for our lunch. It meant a lot. It's good to know I have someone who understands. While I was watching the game, I inquired about intercession. I wanted you to know I'm going to accept your offer to meet in the morning. Can you wait for me outside so I won't have to walk in alone?"

I watched as a glow overtook his face. He was thrilled with my decision. "Sure! I'll be happy to make your first visit easy. I'll meet you in the parking lot tomorrow so you can't change your mind."

Then his expression of joy changed to one of concern. He must not have been sure about what I said or my expression because I felt his eyes lock on mine, searching my soul. Then he used words as probing instruments to make sure I understood the operation. "Do you understand that the group must agree for you to be involved? Your first visit will be a test. Will you be all right with that?" he asked with concern.

Knowing the outcome, I was fine with tests; bring them on. The Lord assured me this test was already won. I was able to answer Brent truthfully, "I understand fully."

He must have suspected from my direct answer that I had been updated by our Lord. My eyes declared more to him than my words ever could. He was seeing confidence and victory. With our eyes locked, he probed deeper for the clue that God had unveiled the plan to me, the plan he had prearranged, and the plan that bound us together. Three words—not a question but a statement—finalized the probing. "He told you!"

I shook my head in confirmation. Bear-like arms grabbed me and drew me into an embrace. I could have sworn I heard him sob. I couldn't see his face to verify it because I was being smothered by his intense hug.

"Brent! You're hurting me!" I choked.

He immediately released me and stepped back. "I'm sorry! I'm so happy, Hope! The Lord showed me long ago this was coming. Time for change! I've waited then, wondered if I had misunderstood. Until today! It wasn't until we talked earlier that I knew you were the one. My sister, my friend in Christ, we are about to have an awesome adventure."

Brent and I spent the rest of the afternoon and part of the evening discussing what was to come. He didn't know who the wolf was exactly, but he had a suspect. I shared in detail what the Lord told me, and he did the same. The only thing omitted was my discussion with the Lord regarding romance. I'd been assured He understood; therefore, I didn't need to address it with Brent. My understanding of the relationship was the Lord forming a professional contract for Brent and me to work together. We were to make sure His desired plan was accomplished—that was all.

Brent suggested we end the evening by going to our individual homes to rest and prepare. Tomorrow would be exciting, soul-stirring, difficult but necessary. I was in total agreement; sleep was definitely needed to defeat the deceiver.

Dressed for Success

The atmosphere in my apartment was almost oppressive. It felt like something was missing or lost. I knew the Lord was present, so that wasn't it. I tried to keep our conversations steady. I hadn't had any dinner, so I was hungry. After such a fattening lunch, I couldn't afford to eat much. I needed to eat and decided on a slice of turkey, a wedge of cheese, and a cup of chamomile tea. Turkey would help me sleep, and so would the tea.

After eating, I dressed for bed and proceeded to read my Bible for a few minutes. My phone rang. Who would be calling? *Just about everyone I associated with lately had been at the picnic*, I thought.

I answered the phone and was greeted by Amber's excited voice. "Hi, Hope! Am I calling too late? I tried your cell a few times today, but it was either turned off or not with you. I'm just too excited to wait. I had to tell you today."

"What's got you all worked up?" I asked.

Cheerfully, she responded, "I'm moving back home to live with Mom and Lacey. These last few days have been amazing. Mom said she could see a difference in me. I told her everything, and she was so happy for me. She had been praying for me to change for a long time. She was grateful to see her prayers answered. I never knew she was a praying woman. I didn't even know she was going to a church until today."

Amber continued, "I explained to her how the Lord awakened my desire to be a mother and how much I needed her and Lacey back in my life. Then the most amazing thing happened. Mom asked me to move back home with them. She didn't see any reason for me to spend money on another place. Hope, I'm going to do it! She assured me that if I want to date, she didn't have a problem with it. She just wants me to be careful."

"Amber, I couldn't be happier. See how God works!" I hesitated. "Does this mean you'll be going to your Mom's church?"

Amber quickly answered, "Oh no! She plans to come to our church. Mom said if a pastor could get my attention, then she wants to meet him. I told her I hadn't joined the church yet, and I didn't know the pastor. She said that didn't matter. We would get to know him together."

I echoed, "Great! I'll see you tomorrow then."

I knew she was wired and needed to talk, but I needed to relax and meditate with the Lord. I had a very important day coming. I politely excused myself but agreed to another night of pottery before hanging up. I loved my new friend. I was also happy the Lord allowed me to be a part of this wonderful change.

My meditating didn't take long, nor did my studying. The tea and turkey were working. I drifted off to sleep without a problem but I still had my recurring dreams. I was still fighting dressed in a skin-tight red jumpsuit. The difference this time was I was holding a sword dripping in blood. Hugs and kisses hadn't been the weapon for this battle.

When the alarm clock beeped to wake me, I sprang out of bed. Of course, I greeted the Lord first; I had to have Him engaged in today's plan.

With the memory of my dream very vivid in my mind, I walked to the closet before brewing coffee. I had to find the dress I'd purchased when my divorce was finalized. I had the need to make a statement that I was free, and the dress screamed defiance. Mom, Dad, and the Carmen's had planned a fancy dinner to celebrate, and I needed to feel powerful. I'd been timid for too long.

It wasn't a red jumpsuit, but it was a short-sleeved bright red sheath dress with a squared neckline; it was definitely a power statement. I knew whatever I selected wouldn't matter to the Holy Spirit as long as I was decently covered in public.

After drinking coffee and eating a hearty breakfast, I took a long shower, washed, blow-dried, and hot-rolled my hair. I gave great attention to applying my makeup. Everything about me had to speak volumes of confidence. Jewelry had to be understated because it was daytime. I chose gold loops for earrings with a gold choker. My shoes were dyed red pumps, especially purchased to wear with this dress. When I put the dress on, I had another pleasant surprise. It fit better today than the last time I wore it. I had lost weight. Now I looked good and felt better; I was dressed to kill.

I gathered my handbag and Bible, ready to head out the door for church when I heard His commands.

Halt! Sit down! He ordered.

My body was immediately paralyzed in place. Now I knew how a horse must feel at the end of its master's reins when the master said *whoa*. I didn't know whether to sit on the couch or plop my fancy, dolled-up butt right on the floor where I stood. I had been ordered to sit—now. I did what would humble me most. I crossed my ankles, sinking to the floor. I had obviously done something wrong.

"What is it, Lord? Why are you angry?" I asked.

I am concerned, Hope, not angry. You're unprepared, He answered. "Pardon? Unprepared how?" I faltered.

Your confident attitude is correct. Your desire is correct. Your battle plan is faulty. You are going into this by your own strength, He replied.

I still didn't understand. I was fully intending to let Him use me and pray through me. My body and mouth were at His disposal. So how was my battle plan wrong?

"Lord, please explain. I'm confused. Make it plain and simple for me," I begged.

Until today, you've allowed me to use you to fight spiritual battles. Those battles were for other people. Today the battle is against you. We must change roles.

"What? Change roles how?" I implored.

You allow me to step into you and use your mouth and body to help others. Now you must step into me and use me to overcome your enemy. Put me on like armor. Use my body and mouth to win. Remember the dream I gave you! The skintight red suit was my blood. When your enemies see you wearing it, they see me. When you speak, they hear me. The sword in your dream was my victory, He informed.

"Why is the suit as tight as my skin?" I asked.

241

I will allow only you inside me—no materials, just you, naked, He answered.

My mind was trying to comprehend. I started to condemn my choice of clothes. Condemnation wanted me to apologize for my prideful attire. I began rising so I could change clothes.

He sharply corrected, *Hope, stop condemning yourself! Didn't I say your attitude was correct? Use whatever makes you feel strong as a point of contact with me. Before you leave this apartment, read about my armor. Instead of going inside the church with just your covenant robe on, you must also have my armor on this time. I'm allowing you to see through me, hear through me, and when the time is needed, to speak through me. You'll be able to see the wolf, hear the wolf, but standing against the giant behind the wolf's mind, will, and emotions is harder. The wolf is an innocent, being misguided and misdirected by the giant. We will overcome the giant while Brent convinces and redirects the wolf.*

While I sat on the floor, I opened my Bible looking for the word *armor* in my concordance. I found it in Ephesians 6. Nowhere in the chapter could I find a reference to clothing. I read about the breastplate of truth, helmet of salvation, shoes in preparation of the good news, shield of faith, and sword of the Spirit.

My heart was full of the truth of His Word, promises that I could stand on. My mind was being controlled by His, like a helmet. My feet worked only because they were covered by the good news of victory. My protection was His faith; all was well from start to finish. My sword was His words spoken with my mouth. I could do this through Him. I've learned from experience how to humble myself and let Him step inside of me. Now I had to control fear and step into Him.

He saw something in me that I was unaware of until this moment. I had a desire to be brave. He was giving me the chance. I picked myself up from the floor and mentally stepped into Him. I straightened my clothes and held His head up high. I might look like a debutante on the outside, but on the inside, I was all Him.

I drove to church with praise and worship music guiding me. This is the day that the Lord has made. I will rejoice and be glad in it. Today, I was entering the enemy's camp and taking back what rightfully belonged to the Lord.

Brent kept his promise. He was waiting for me outside, propped up against his BMW in the parking lot. I watched his expression change as I exited my SUV. His eyebrows shot up as a wide toothy grin appeared. I could tell he was pleased with my choice of clothing without any word spoken, but what he was really seeing was me dressed in the Lord. He dressed every day in a power suit and argued because his job required it; today wasn't any different for him. I wasn't shocked in the least when he asked, "Got your armor on?"

I answered confidently, "Guaranteed."

"You look great! But I bet you feel even greater, don't you?" he continued.

I looked at him and responded, "Stop beating around the bush, Brent. Remember we said we'd keep things simple. Quit fishing."

He took the hint and replied, "Okay! Did you and the Lord come to an understanding about today? Did He give you insight on what to do?"

"He gave me vivid dreams last night. This morning, He told me to step into His armor. That's why I dressed up," I answered.

"And in red no less!" he stated.

I agreed, "You got it—the color of His blood. I bet it's the same reason you're wearing a red tie."

He just grinned and said, "We're coming to know each other so well."

Remembering what the Lord explained to me during the ball game about being attracted to each other because of Him, I responded to Brent's remark by saying, "No, I think what you mean is that we both know Him very well. We think and act like Him."

Before we headed toward the church, I had a sudden urgency for prayer to go forward, to lead Brent and me inside. The Lord was directing me to make this request of Brent instead of me praying in the Spirit.

243

Following the Lord's guidance, I stopped and faced Brent. "Brent, the Lord is impressing upon me to ask you to pray us forward. Do you mind if we join hands and pray as a team, with you as the lead?"

He didn't hesitate. He motioned for me to put my Bible and bag on the hood of his car. Then we joined hands where we stood while he prayed, "Lord, Hope and I come with you this morning. By you, this morning, we move and speak. You prearranged this day to happen. We are here to see it through because of you—your vessels, your plans spoken. Cover us now with power to be the weapons needed. Give us your forgiving heart and guiding hand while your Spirit defeats our enemies. Thy will is done. Amen!"

He had prayed with such confidence and grace. It brought tears to my eyes. The Lord wanted me to hear that Brent was totally committed and under His control. Brent's prayer had affirmed that the Lord had us both covered with His full armor. We were ready.

My Advocates

Something amazing happened after Brent's prayer. We were joined by two heavenly companions because we were walking in the Lord instead of Him walking through us. My companion was His mighty eagle-faced angel. Brent's escort was the angel with a lion's face.

The Lord previously allowed me to see these angels when the new pastor had been preaching. It was the night I was so amazed by the pastor's appearance and the Lord explained that it was Him.

Inside the church, my spiritual vision and hearing were also heightened. I was seeing people dragging robes all over the place. The sound of negative emotions being spoken everywhere was feeding little demons; no wonder the Lord was grieved so much by His family. Most of these people were the ones in service who should know better. They should have been using His faith.

Service workers were always early to prepare for classes, nurseries, sound and media, administration, or for intercession.

When Brent and I entered the prayer room, most of the team had already arrived. He began introducing me to everyone as Martin and Sue Joiner's daughter. Most knew who I was. Some had participated in my Christian education. The few who groomed me as a child still had their loving demeanor.

While we were talking, and getting reacquainted, my spiritual sight allowed me to see who was robed well and who wasn't. Of the ten participants in the room, only four wore their covenant robes properly. One had their robe draped over their shoulder, another robe looked limp as if it hadn't been ironed or honored, and the rest looked tattered and dirty. I mentally inquired of the Lord; *shouldn't your warriors be better dressed?*

I wasn't talking about what they had on. Clothes didn't matter. What I thought I was seeing through His eyes was disrespect of their covenant garment until He corrected me.

He replied, *These warriors are old and worn-out. They have fought many battles for me and need rest. But not many of the younger generation want to step into the call. It is not that they are disrespectful, but they are tired of carrying everyone else's load. Being an intercessor has its drawbacks. It's not that their faith is small. It's the people they are praying for who aren't receiving my grace because their faith is too weak. Watching the people's failure to receive prayer after prayer, time after time, about the same issues drains the intercessors, leaving them sad and brokenhearted. You will come to understand.*

I was grateful He had corrected my thinking, I had better respect for their faithful service afterward. Even though I was seeing their robes worn in various disarray, I wasn't hearing negative talk. Not being among negativity was like breathing fresh air. This small room was like a capsule, separated from evil forces that were barred from entering, or so I thought.

The leader, Mrs. Jonesboro, explained that prayer would begin when two others arrived. In the meantime, she informed me that after my first visit, the group would have to meet and discuss my qualifications to be an intercessor. She explained that during the actual intercession process, one of their petitions would be for God to show them if I had been called by Him. His answer, which they counted on more than any other, was first and foremost. Secondly, they considered if the new person appeared to be mature enough to handle private and sensitive issues.

The meeting took place immediately after prayer among the current intercessors, and the new person was excused to go to their Sunday school class. Their practice was to inform the new person of their decision no later than the next service. I should know something by evening service tonight.

My understanding of the process pleased Mrs. Jonesboro. I assured her Brent had already detailed the process for me. She was such a sweet lady, but I could see the administrative duties of the church's intercessory leader had taken a toll on her over the years. I was glad I wouldn't be one she would have to deny entry; I'd already been approved. A few moments from now, she and the others who heard from God would also know.

My opponent must be one of the two late arrivals. What was the deal with this one? How had a wolf been allowed in the prayer group if they made sure he approved of each of them beforehand?

I hear your concerns, Hope. It wasn't always the case with this person. I had called her. Her beginnings were humble and upright. In time, money, financial power, and influence dulled thinking, causing wrong motives and actions to seep in. Now the prayer that comes forth from her mouth is not from me, but a form of mimicking, which causes a break in the ring. I have to spiritually stand in that break so evil can't manifest within my group. I am the chief intercessor. Therefore, I'm responsible for making sure my group is whole, no matter who is warming a seat. Today, the group will side with me and see a need for change. Sadly, this trial has to occur. Righteous judgment occurs today. The outcome will not be pretty. Remember what I told you, it is not the person but the evil giant in the background. This person will be broken severely by night's end. My desire is for brokenness to allow humility to emerge as pride and cruelty are discarded. You'll know how to pray and what to do. Even though I'm covering you outside, I'm still very much inside of you. You will do the right thing, He informed.

I was about to ask Him about the ring when the door opened, and the other two we'd been waiting on came inside. With my spiritual vision, I instantly knew who the wolf was. My heart broke, and my head felt heavy. I could hardly believe who it was. This woman had been my perfect example. I adored her. I'd placed her on a pedestal.

Mrs. Victoria Reynolds was who I wanted to be. She was beautiful, successful, prim and proper, financially secure. Her daughter, Anna, was my best friend growing up, so I was often at their house, drooling over what they had. Anna had married as soon as she graduated high school, leaving me almost friendless for a time. Then I went to college and met Teddy. For as long as I could remember, I wanted to be part of their family. I even fantasized about marrying her eldest son, Luke Reynolds, when I was a teenager.

Mrs. Reynolds had always been nice to me, but then I remembered she was critical of my upbringing. She hadn't approved of my parents leaving me with sitters so often; she said it left avenues open for bad morals to corrupt me.

247

So, my idol was now my spiritual enemy, my opposition. This was going to be painful for me to watch. The characteristics I most admired had to crash and burn—her confidence, power, and demeanor.

I watched as her eyes focused on me while I was still dealing with my shock. Without seeming to stare, I looked quickly for her robe. It was under her feet. At least she still had it. Then contempt and judgment-filled her eyes. At that moment, I felt my ears burn. My first instinct was to grab them to make sure they were not bleeding. Immediately, I remembered my spiritual hearing was also activated, allowing me to hear her thoughts and criticisms.

What is that slut doing in this sacred place? She'll corrupt us all! Her parents allowed evil communications in their house, and now we have to clean it up! This little tramp has slept with no telling how many perverts. She thinks she's good enough to be in our prayer group? Never! God forbid! I haven't kept myself and my family's honor pure for this long so she could come in and try to take what rightfully belongs to the faithful. My children deserve a seat in this group, not her. Our money established this church. John and I have created stable families to take over in our place. Our children honor marriage and commitment. I'll just have to petition for the Lord to remove her instantly.

I felt her thoughts as if they were physical blows. In the same instant, I heard the Lord say, *Let the reproach come on me. I'm taking the hits, not you. All you feel is the reverberation of the blows bouncing off my face.*

I wanted to cry because my Lord was taking blows directed at me. I couldn't cry without signaling my enemy that she could upset me. I loved my Lord too much for that.

Mrs. Jonesboro began sharing all the prayer requests while explaining the process for my benefit. After reading each petition, we were asked if we had others to add to the list for prayer. When she was satisfied the list of needs was complete, scriptures were read and applied as declarations for salvation and redemption.

Looking at me, she explained reading scriptures before prayer and confessing the promises as already done in Jesus's name empowered us to pray more effectively. Not wanting to appear rude, I quietly listened. I understood the procedure because I'd been doing that with the Lord already. Then she extended her right hand to the person next to her until all hands were grasped together, forming a ring. She prayed with her interpretation of scripture, "In your name Lord, ride on triumphantly for the cause of truth, and let your right-hand guide you to do tremendous things for us."

At that moment, the Lord spoke to me, *My ring of covenant! God's right hand empowering the others until they realize their right hands are nothing without grasping His left hand. Mrs. Jonesboro's leadership presence stands for the Father's hands.*

What a beautiful image we must be to the Lord. All were joined in Him as one. I glanced briefly at Mrs. Reynolds before closing my eyes for prayer. I was disgusted to see her holding the tips of Mr. Abernathy's and Mrs. Farly's fingers as if their hands were dirty. She hadn't grasped their hands at all. The Lord had to step in, seizing their hands to complete the ring's power.

Brent's right hand held my left. When the scripture spoken by Mrs. Jonesboro was completed, a surge of heat enveloped me. My tongue loosed causing me to pray in my heavenly language. I assumed the person at my right was experiencing the same thing because she started praying in her language as well.

All the prayer requests placed before me started coming to mind. I knew the Lord was dealing with each issue through our combined petitions. Then I focused on Mrs. Reynolds, asking God to forgive and help her to change her heart.

After a few minutes of honest petitions for her, I began to feel pain. The reverberations were a lot stronger than the last time. Through her prayers, my Lord was taking the onslaught of a beating meant for me. The power behind each complaint felt like an actual blow and must have been excruciating. Every time she lashed out, He countered with words defending me. She's forgiven. She's clean. She has my grace. She's been redeemed. She's my daughter. It went on and on.

This time I couldn't control my tears, not for what I was feeling, but for what he was receiving. My Lord was being hurt, and I couldn't stand it. With each of her petitions bouncing off

Him, she attacked with hostility. By now, I was physically sobbing and moaning in the ring. I kept praying for her forgiveness because I knew it was what He would do, even though I wanted to strangle her for abusing Him.

I had to remind myself that He still loved her and wanted her to change. Hadn't He asked God, in the midst of His personal agony on the cross, to forgive them for they knew not what they were doing? It was no different for Mrs. Reynolds.

When the prayer ended, I had no doubt that the team saw compassion in me. They didn't know it was for my Lord. It broke my heart that he was willing to suffer so much for me. I was the object of her vengeance. I should have been the one receiving the force of her anger, not Him.

The atmosphere in the room was thick. No one wanted to break the ring except Mrs. Reynolds. She took it upon herself to override Mrs. Jonesboro's leadership by arrogantly saying, "Hope, you have to leave the room now. We must vote whether you can join our group. Someone will let you know soon."

Brent still had my hand as he helped me from my chair. He could tell that I was physically shaken by what had just occurred. As he walked me to the door, I turned and said to all involved, "Thanks for an awesome experience. I will never forget it."

Before Brent closed the door behind me, he looked into my eyes and said, "It's my turn."

I couldn't stand it. I ran to the ladies' room. I had to go somewhere to be alone, even if it were just a bathroom stall. I couldn't stand the thought of Brent also taking a beating for me. But wait! Brent wasn't going to be punished. He was my advocate, my defender.

The Lord spoke, *Hope! The battle isn't over. Look up!*

Looking up, I could see our giant enemy. It was grimacing and growling, thinking it had me cornered in the bathroom stall.

Instant instructions came from the Lord. *Stand your ground, Hope! Do not fear! You are in Me. He is growling at me. He is baffled because His physical blows had no effect on Me. He watched as I took the blows directed against you and listened to My orders of salvation. He couldn't harm you, and it has made him extremely angry. He is going to try to attack you physically. When he does, my angel and I will cut him down.*

"Yes, sir! I'll stand!" I exclaimed.

After what He had just gone through for me, of course, I would stand. I needed to know what to expect. Would I have a clue when the giant was about to attack? Would I need to duck or something? So, I asked, "How will I know when he is attacking?"

The moment you hear the prayer room door slam, start praying through Me. Then it will be over. I will have the giant's head, He informed me.

"Is that all? All I have to do is pray? Then what?" I asked.

He instructed, *Yes, all I want for you to do is be still and pray. Keep asking for her forgiveness. This time, seek the Father's mercy because she is doomed unless she changes. By leaving the group and slamming the prayer room door behind her, she physically attacks me with her statement of defiance. She will be going to the pastor, prepared to buy him off if necessary, to have you removed. Her plans have already failed. This pastor can't be bought.*

"Oh, my word! She is going to try and bribe the pastor to kick me out. If money makes you this mean, I don't ever want to have more than I need."

In the prayer room, Brent was in his element, defending attorney to the core. By his side stood the Lord's angel of justice spiritually. He had an answer for every word and accusation that came against Hope. He was very grateful the Lord had Mark share everything that had happened to Hope. The whole group listened while he and Mrs. Reynolds argued for nearly an hour.

He explained that Hope had been the victim of adultery by her first husband. She had been led astray by the wrong crowd because she was too embarrassed to come back into the fold. Guilt accused and convinced her that she was responsible for her failed marriage.

Then her second husband physically abused her, almost killing her the last time around. It was her parents and the Carmen's who encouraged her to come back to the loving arms of

251

the church. Hope had made her way back with the help of loving friends and family.

Before the vote, he made a final point, one that should mean more than any other. He asked if they had individually heard what he heard. God had spoken on Hope's behalf during morning prayer. Brent had heard God say "Forgiven, clean, favored, redeemed, as well as calling her daughter." Plus, they had witnessed her gift of tongues during the prayers, followed by signs of compassion. The moans and tears coming from her hadn't been fake.

Mrs. Reynolds hadn't heard any such thing! Ignoring Mrs. Jonesboro's leadership, Mrs. Reynolds snarled, "This is ridiculous! Can't you see he is trying to push his girlfriend in here? I vote no! Who's with me?"

No one agreed with her. Mrs. Jonesboro took command, stating, "It seems it is unanimous. Hope is in the group. Brent, I would like to thank you for helping us see how Hope was a victim of circumstances. God had His way. We knew Hope had a good foundation. Some of us helped establish it when she was a child. Proverbs 22:6 (amp) clearly states 'Train up a child in the way he should go [and in keeping with his individual gift or bent], and when he is old he will not depart from it.' I am glad she has returned to His graces."

With everyone overruling her, Victoria Reynolds pushed away from the table, gathered her bag and stormed out of the room, slamming the door behind her. Mrs. Reynolds couldn't believe this slut would be allowed to pray for sinners when she was one of the guiltiest.

At the thunderous sound of the door, the sword of truth and justice sliced the giant's head cleanly from its body. The angel of the Lord that followed me had subdued the giant, allowing the Lord the honor of cutting off its head. Victoria was operating in her own ugly power now, free from that giant's dominance.

"Father God, please have mercy!" Hope prayed fervently.

Vindication Belongs to the Lord

Satan couldn't believe it! He had just witnessed one of his better warriors slain, cut down, humiliated. Satan no longer had a spy in the inner sanctum. But so, what if the puppet was exposed? He had others in various places. Satan could care less if God annihilated her.

———w·o·o·o·o·o·o·w———

God, the Father, was definitely focusing on Victoria as she stomped off to confront the pastor. He kept hearing intercession on her behalf. Through the power of His Son, Hope was pleading for mercy. He would have to stop and listen to His Son's request before destroying this violator.

"Father, please wait! Victoria is your child and part of me. She has been a victim of our enemy for too long. I prearranged long ago for this day to come, and victory is mine. Not only have I been vindicated, but the circumstances have been diverted.

Watch how my pastor redirects her thinking. Witness my plan unfolding as the weapons her family wielded for Satan are exposed not only in the church but in the community. Public humiliation will be Victoria's reward. Through this, she will come back to me cleansed."

———w·o·o·o·o·o·o·w———

Pastor Craig had settled down to meditate over the message again while he and the Lord communed. Alone time with the Lord was important before any service. All of a sudden, the door of his office flew open. He could have sworn that he'd locked it; that was his usual practice. When he saw how agitated this woman was, he didn't have the heart to ask her to leave.

After a few seconds, he recognized her—Victoria Reynolds, wife of Johnson Reynolds, the wealthy businessman who constantly pushed his weight around in church business affairs. It appeared she was also accustomed to having her way. He couldn't be rude, so he let her speak her mind.

Her complaint was about a young woman who wanted to be an intercessor. In Mrs. Reynold's opinion, the young woman was corrupted, vile, and dishonorable. She had ruined her family name and shouldn't be involved with the inner dealings of the church. He sensed there was more to this story than Mrs. Reynolds was divulging. It wasn't his business. It needed to remain private between these two women.

He couldn't believe his ears when she commanded him to kick this young woman out of church. Refusing her request only fueled the fire. Denunciation of him and the church started gushing from her lips. She threatened to withhold funds from the latest building project if her demands weren't fulfilled. She reminded him that salary increases within the church would be in jeopardy if her husband found out she had been denied.

Before ever agreeing to accept a ministry, he promised the Lord that he would never take bribes or buckle under a financial threat. Money didn't rule him and never would. Now he was being put in a position to defend someone he didn't know. He did know if the Lord called this young woman to be an intercessor, nothing could stop it except the woman herself.

Politely, he asked Mrs. Reynolds to stop ranting so he could share something from Scripture. He wanted to warn her that if she were coming against a plan of God, she was fighting a dangerous battle. If she continued accusing and acting prideful against God's plan, she could be in jeopardy of her accusations coming back on her and her family. He had to change her thinking before it was too late.

Of course, she refused to listen. Nothing he said applied to her or this situation. No one in her family had been swayed by a bar hopping, partying spirit. Neither of her children slept around nor divorced even one time. What made this young wimp of a pastor think he could tell her anything?

Leaving his office, the same way she entered, she planned to go home to tell her husband everything that transpired that morning. Confident Johnson would share her rage and confirm her indignation; she drove home to get him. Since neither of them attended a Sunday school class, that was her usual practice every Sunday after intercession anyway. They went to church service together but weren't interested in patrons trying to teach them anything.

———~~~oᴏ⊙ᴏⵀⵀoⵀo-~~~———

Brent was concerned when he couldn't find Hope anywhere. He knew she was there since her SUV was still parked outside. He was sure she was feeling stressed and drained. He wanted to be there for her. Unable to locate her, he did the only other thing he could; he walked to Sunday school class to wait.

Relief flooded his heart when Hope walked in the room. Sympathy gripped him as well. The beautiful, confident woman he escorted this morning now looked like a combat survivor. Her makeup was almost gone, her skin was ashen, and her face looked haggard. She was in desperate need of being fed God's Word; she'd been depleted.

When they locked eyes, though, he knew she was only exhausted. He didn't realize his part in this morning's upheaval wasn't over. His cell phone vibrated furiously in his pocket, not once but many times. He decided it must be very important for someone to call him on Sunday morning. He answered and learned he was needed immediately to deal with a problem concerning the District Attorney's office. Hating that business demanded his attention, he excused himself from class.

He was to report promptly to the home of Johnson Reynolds. A late-breaking event had occurred requiring involvement by the District Attorney's office. Since he was located first, it was his responsibility to make an appearance. He couldn't believe that he would have to deal with Johnson Reynolds today. He would soon know the reason.

Upon arriving, he was surprised his office wasn't the only one called to the scene. The sheriff's office, state investigative services, and the FBI were also present. On site, he discovered the reason as he watched Johnson Reynolds being ushered handcuffed to a police car.

Johnson had been embezzling for years. Motives had not been divulged yet. The FBI would only share with Brent that Johnson's fraudulent actions had been excessive and worthy of a federal arrest. At present, all the Reynolds' assets were frozen due to ongoing investigations. Virginia was being watched by the sheriff's deputies, allowing her to pack. She couldn't stay in their home until a painstaking search of the property, including computers and confiscated records, had been completed. It could be days before she could return.

Inside the house, he found Virginia in total disarray. She was a broken lady. When she saw Brent standing in their den, she ran to him, demanding that he do something. Her husband was innocent. They were victims of something evil.

At this point, he didn't know what he could do. He was certain their affiliations wouldn't allow him to get involved with the case. The moment his boss discovered that he knew these people on a personal level, he'd be taken off the case permanently. When he explained that to Virginia, she collapsed in sobs.

While she wept, she complained about not having anywhere to go. Her children were out of town, she wasn't allowed to leave town, all her accounts were frozen, and she did not have the cash to stay in a hotel. What was she to do? He suggested she stay at one of her friends' homes. She quickly rejected the advice. Couldn't he see she was clearly too embarrassed to ask a friend for help? He did the next thing that came to mind. Pulling out his wallet, he gave her all the cash he had. At least she could stay somewhere overnight until one of her children arrived to take care of her.

It was even sadder to witness a policewoman refusing to permit her to drive her car. She had to be driven to her desired lodging. Even their cars had been confiscated.

He stayed with Virginia for a few hours while police, investigative services, and the FBI interrogated her. He didn't have the heart to ask her any questions that involved Johnson. All he could do was his job, be a presence representing the department, taking notes when necessary.

That evening, Virginia was trying to relax in the cheap motel that she had to endure. She finally had a chance to ponder all of the day's events. That morning, she had been so self-assured of her status in life, now she didn't know who she was. Then she remembered what Pastor Moore tried to tell her. If she didn't alter her thinking, God would put her in a humbled position.

She recalled how she had acted that morning, so condemning and judgmental. She had even prayed against Hope. Now Virginia knew how embarrassment felt. Now she understood why Hope couldn't come back to church for so long. What would people think about her? What were they saying? Virginia also had been a victim beyond her circumstances. That revelation produced healing. She fell on her knees, asking God for forgiveness and strength. She prayed not only for God's help through what her family was facing but for restoration to her roots. She had been a lonely, poor, young woman when Jesus called her. It wasn't until she met Johnson that she started changing and becoming hard-hearted. She wanted to feel like God's child again instead of the wicked and dirty person she was today.

Changes

Over the last month, many wonderful, as well as hurtful, things have taken place. The painful part was the whole community watching Johnson Reynolds being taken into custody and booked for extortion on a grand scale. The deception involved people in other states and other countries, not just the local area. The television media exploited Johnson and made a public spectacle of his entire family. Gifts that had been purchased for family members and friends were confiscated; cars and boats were repossessed.

With the Reynolds' children living out of state, Virginia had to deal with most of the aftershock alone. Caring church members were concerned for the family's mental well-being. Rumors were spreading all over town that Virginia was humiliated to the point of being suicidal.

Our intercessory group prayed continuously for God to intervene. Brent and I knew what happened to Virginia was for her good. Jesus wanted the old Virginia back and assured us her redirection would make that happen. Confidence in the Lord's plan kept us praying in line with Him. We came against the naysayers who wanted to ruin and destroy the Reynolds family. We prayed for the Lord to find a way to get Virginia back in church as quickly as possible. Shame and fear could prevent her return.

Even though Brent was forbidden involvement with the case, he kept the pastor and intercessory group informed the best he could. Knowing the truth smothered gossip before it got out of hand.

Three weeks after Johnson's arrest, our prayers were answered. With the encouragement of some close church friends, Virginia came back to church. When Mrs. Lenney reached out to her, I was elated. Mrs. Lenney is a testimony to overcoming mental stress by God's grace. Grace is always sufficient. Mrs. Lenney gets to live the life Jesus and her husband intended for her to live.

After Mrs. Lenney's welcome, I could testify Virginia was humbled. I felt her pain. I knew in my heart that I needed to go to

258

her. I asked the Lord what to do. "Lord, should I? Should I physically go to her and show support? Would my presence be a slap in her face?"

His very profound answer surprised me. *Hope, your forgiveness will drive away the shame and guilt. She needs forgiveness to heal.*

I didn't wait. I immediately reached out to her. I knew what it was like to feel rejection in church. I could not allow that pain and deception to grow.

When I touched her shoulder to let her know I was there, I was stunned by the look in her eyes. She appealed to my heart for forgiveness without saying a word. She stood up, and I wrapped her in my arms, extending my Lord's love and forgiveness.

After that day of acceptance, Virginia came back for each service. Our intercessory leader, Mrs. Jonesboro, told Virginia that she was still considered part of the group. However, because of the stigma of the indictment, Virginia needed to give herself time before coming back. There had been harsh complaints and wicked finger-pointing by those who judged her unfairly for something her husband had done. Still, Virginia said she understood completely and didn't want to jeopardize herself or the group.

The best part for me was feeling completely accepted in my church. I finally understood being part of a body. I studied the inner workings of the church. It was a vast system of mercy and care for the community. Every aspect was covered and supported with prayer and supplications. I learned from the elder intercessors what to expect, what not to fear. In the process of my education of the church functions, I watched them change as well. I was sure my presence was vitalizing the group. Those I originally complained about to the Lord were wearing their robes proudly now. When I asked the Lord about it, He gave me a lovely viewpoint to ponder.

He said, *The old ones are reassured their kind has not perished. They have prayed so long for other intercessors to join them, younger and stronger, to carry their torch. Years went by, and only one appeared. However, he couldn't commit as an intercessor for every service. Brent's abilities were given to him for seeking justice in the physical realm. I allow him access to the group so they can have the power of agreement when needed. You, sweet Hope, are like their new child. They want to pour into you as much as they can as fast as they can. By doing that, they've strengthened themselves in the process. They knew if one arrived, others must be coming. Their faith has been renewed.*

My days were overflowing in a good way. Until recently, I'd complained about being lonely, with nothing worthwhile in my life. Now, every day and night were booked with places to go and people to see. I was either with Amber at a pottery class, at the Boys' Home caring for the little ones, or at church. Being committed to intercessory prayer, I was constantly called away. I purposely kept myself away from everything for a time to pray for requests. I was with the Lord while interceding, but something was missing. I enjoyed the kids, the pottery classes, Wednesday night services, and Sunday services, but I needed to be exclusive with my Lord.

I longed for the times when He and I talked and reminisced about the week's adventures. I missed those moments very much. Now, my days were a flurry of activity. Mornings were spent praying for other people while I got ready for work, instead of chatting or learning from Him. I dreaded the chore of coming to work just so I could pay the bills. I once enjoyed working as a secretary, but now, I'd rather be helping at the Boys' Home or at the church. I knew my heart was grumpy, and I needed help.

The Lord heard my heart's plea and knew I needed to refocus. Even though I thought I was doing His will, I was missing the most important part. I needed our time together. The only way He could get my attention was by allowing small disasters the way He did before I became part of the intercessory group. It wasn't very funny.

For weeks, I had allowed people to use me. Every day was full. I'd work five days a week then volunteer at the Boys' Home or at church or with Amber and Lacey. I'd let family members or other close friends claim my weekends. I kept up my Bible studies in the morning and a little at night. I greeted the Lord every morning. I hadn't been talking with Him. I had been using Him when I needed to pray for someone. I was constantly feeling guilty about it but couldn't seem to get off the fast-turning wheel of my life. Apparently, He had had enough of it.

Sunday arrived with the clock beeping for me to get up and start my day. First thing was the trek to the bathroom. My first disaster showed up in the form of no toilet paper. I dealt with it while chiding myself for not doing my weekly Saturday shopping in over three weeks.

After my shower, I proceeded to get breakfast. I was looking forward to eggs and fruit. I had one egg, but it was cracked, so I was afraid to eat it. I also had one peach, but it was almost rotten, so it went in the trash. I decided on cereal instead, only to find the milk had soured, leaving me dry cereal for my meal. More reminders I had failed to do my weekly shopping.

The Lord tried to get my attention through the pastor I was listening to while eating my dry cereal. My complaining mind was louder than His voice. I was very angry at myself.

The straw that broke the camel's back came when I went to my closet to find something to wear. I had my mind set on one particular lightweight pantsuit then remembered it was still at the cleaners. It dawned on me I hadn't done any laundry in nearly three weeks. Most of my clothes were either dirty or at the cleaners. Relieved to find an old forgotten dress in the back of my closet that I wouldn't be too ashamed to wear, I then faced another dilemma. No clean underwear.

I analyzed the problem. I could wear a dirty bra twice without being revolted, but I could not wear panties more than once. I didn't have time to rinse out a pair and get them dry before I had to leave. I had two options—go commando or wear pantyhose. It was entirely too hot to wear pantyhose, so I cut off the legs. Being covered was the point.

I was scolding myself relentlessly about being forgetful and unorganized until the Lord finally made me examine myself. He allowed me to see myself spiritually in a mirror while complaining. In the reflection, I not only saw myself but also a hideous frog-like demon that was on top of me, riding the waves of my reproach, sucking me dry of all positive energy.

That image infuriated and disgusted me. I had no one to blame but myself. Tapping the mirror to get the little creep's attention, I frightened it away. I instantly made the decision to stand my ground and quit allowing another Saturday to be taken from the Lord and me. I realized I needed one day alone with my Lord.

I wouldn't feel guilty when people called or if I declined their invitations. I'd finally gotten off the merry-go-round, and I refused to jump back on. Saturday would be our day. We could have fun, just like before, even if it was cleaning and shopping. I loved fellowshipping with Him, singing and dancing while I cleaned the apartment. I loved His help shopping for groceries. He was my one true mate, and I'd missed Him so much. Even though the day He got most of my attention was a Sunday, when I left church it was the start of our new week. We crammed as much time together as possible that day. I took my phone off the hook and then turned off my cell phone. He and I cleaned the house, did the laundry, and went shopping. We had a lovely dinner and talked. I got comfortable with Him on my sofa, reading the Bible before going to bed.

The next day, I could tell my grumpy heart had been healed. Our relationship had been renewed. It amazed me how we could be our own enemies while doing what we thought was right.

Brent was not forgotten. We had become close but nothing romantic. I shared more with him than most people. I still haven't disclosed my gifts of seeing and hearing in the spirit. Our relationship is as comfortable as an old shoe. I can laugh and be myself around him. Brent makes me feel secure and appreciated.

On the nights we plan to be at the Boys' Home at the same time, he insists we ride together. He argues we live too close to each other to drive separate vehicles. However, he never lets me drive my SUV, he always has to drive. I can't truthfully say I object. It is nice knowing I'm being protected until I'm safely inside my apartment.

To be honest, before Brent came up with this plan, I was a little fearful unlocking my apartment door in the dark. I always felt I was being watched. I asked the Lord why. His reply was to be sober and vigilant; it was part of being a warrior. I felt something was amiss, though I couldn't put my finger on it. I just chalked it up to my alert spidey senses.

—ᴠᴠᴠ◦ᴏᴏᴏᴏᴏᴏᴏᴏᴏ◦ᴠᴠᴠ—

The Holy Spirit was glad that Brent was on top of things. By using His discerning spirit, Brent had followed up on some of Sam's activities.

—ᴠᴠᴠ◦ᴏᴏᴏᴏᴏᴏᴏᴏᴏ◦ᴠᴠᴠ—

Each night, Brent took Hope home, waiting in his car with headlights blazing until she was safely inside. He didn't want to alarm her. Mark had informed him that someone in her neighborhood had seen a man fitting Sam's description snooping around her apartment while she was away. Brent invented the carpool idea to guarantee Hope's safety on the nights she was at the Boys' Home; that way he could safely escort her home. He would have been glad to take her anywhere she needed to go, but he had to settle for the few nights she permitted.

The Monday after Mark had alerted him, Brent decided to use some of his spare time investigating Sam Anderson. His ties with the District Attorney's office granted him access to files and lives of criminals. One of those resources was the state's probation office. Working closely with these officers had produced friends that also helped him out with cases. One of those friends was a probation officer named Bonnie Fowler. She was in charge of some of the roughest probationers in town; multiple offenders dealt with his office as well.

As always, when Brent called on Bonnie, she didn't let him down. He was truthful with her about wanting to know Sam's whereabouts and lifestyle. He confessed he had fallen in love with Sam's ex-wife, Hope Anderson, and was concerned for her safety. He explained that Sam had a court order forbidding him to

263

approach Hope, but someone in her neighborhood's watch program had observed a man that looked like Sam snooping around her place.

Bonnie hated domestic violence and child abuse cases the most, even though they had led her to pursue criminal justice as an occupation. When Brent shared the reason he wanted help, she broke a few rules to look into the situation. Even if he hadn't been honest, she wouldn't have thought twice about getting the information. It was part of working with the DA's office. Since it was a personal request concerning someone he cared about that involved one of her probationers, she couldn't deny the request. An innocent person could be victimized.

Domestic violence probationers usually had other issues, and Sam was no different. His lifestyle matched the usual pattern, causing incompatibility with general society. She disclosed that Sam had recently lost his job, had been evicted from 708 Hillcrest Drive, and hadn't informed the office of his current whereabouts.

Sam was also behind on his payments to their department, which could be his reason for hiding. Bonnie appreciated Brent's alert of Sam's activities; otherwise, he could slip through the cracks of her extensive case load. Sam was about to receive extra attention, as Bonnie would personally put him under a microscope.

———ⓦⓞⓒⓔⓣⓞⓒⓣⓔⓞⓦ———

Satan was ecstatic! Sam was playing right into his plan. Insanity had almost taken over. It was only a matter of time before possession was complete. Then Sam would self-destruct, taking out that goody-two- shoes, Hope. Satan could see it all now. He loved playing chess with people's lives.

———ⓦⓞⓒⓔⓣⓞⓒⓣⓔⓞⓦ———

In a city twenty miles from home, Sam stood in line at a Department of Labor office. He hated driving so far to get what was due him, but he had no choice. He didn't want Hope to see him in this humiliating unemployed position. In addition, he had that stupid court order preventing him from getting anywhere near her. Court orders didn't care one way or another whether he needed assistance. Sam knew he could be arrested, even if he had a legitimate need to be at her place of employment.

He had a rotten life. He'd been kicked out of his nice apartment, his new ride had been repossessed, and now, he had to live in his brother's old jet stream camper. Sam hated the space. It was pitiful, with only the bare necessities. Sam's brother, Marty, loved it because it was all he needed for weekend fishing trips next to a lake.

Funds were limited, and Sam needed all he could get. He was hoping for money when he called his brother for help. Instead, he was offered short-term lodging at the lake place. Sam was infuriated when his brother insisted the electricity bill be paid while he lived there. Sam was a family member in trouble.

Why couldn't his haughty rich brother give him money instead of moving him to that dismal little camper, expecting him to pay their bill? Sam had to grovel and accept the crumbs thrown his way. One day, one day, all would pay!

Sam felt forced to accept Marty's offer. He couldn't afford another new ride to continue spying on Hope. Now he had to do the best he could, gambling that no one would recognize him. Every night that he was able, he parked his old car in the nearby woods then moved close to her place so he could watch for an opening to present itself so they could talk. Hiding in bushes, watching her comings and goings was in vain night after night. The same jerk in the white BMW picked her up and brought her home. Sam knew that once she was inside, he wouldn't stand a chance if he approached the door. She'd have cops on him in a heartbeat. He had to find another way. As each day passed, he was losing her, what they had, and who he was. If he couldn't have her, then no one could.

The Outing

The fourth of July's celebration and festivities were one for the history books that year. I couldn't remember ever having so much fun. On the second of July, nothing had been planned yet for the boys. Sad faces were everywhere because they usually had fireworks or a barbecue. It didn't seem to be happening.

Mr. Arnold returned from a church meeting with a surprise, long after we'd put the boys to bed. One of the wealthy businessmen that belonged to our church had provided free passes for all the boys to go to a new fun park located about an hour from town. This was a big deal. The facility was new and had everything—rides for all ages, a water park, and even a petting zoo. On July fourth, they were having a grand opening with food vendors and a Christian concert after fireworks. All they needed was the adults to buy their tickets and plan a picnic. The adult volunteers could take a break from having to set up a barbecue, and the boys could ride and swim all day with supervision and then enjoy a picnic later.

Even Mr. and Mrs. Elder thought this was a great idea. They hadn't had an outing in a long time. It would be fun for everybody, but it required six adults to accompany the boys. I raised my hand. Brent did the same. Then Olivia and Mr. Arnold joined us. We had the six.

I was so excited! I volunteered to buy supplies for sandwiches. Brent agreed to purchase the drinks. The others agreed to make sure the boys packed swim trunks, sunscreen, towels, and extra clothes.

Even though it was late and we had to work the next day, Brent and I decided to go shopping before heading home. We drove to a local supercenter. This would be fun! On the way, I remembered that neither of my husbands or even my daddy had ever gone shopping with me. The only male I had ever shopped with was the Lord. *Stop it!* I reprimanded myself for comparing again.

Lord, why am I constantly doing that? I asked Him.

Peas in a pod. He laughed.

I snickered to myself at that remark because it was so very true. Brent was a wonderful person.

Inside the store, I had a moment of confusion. What do you feed fifteen boys? I knew I needed bread, but what to put between slices of bread had me stumped. My mind and body froze. I hadn't thought this through. Panic started raising its ugly head as the magnitude of feeding fifteen boys and six adults struck me. My vow was going to cost me a weekly grocery allowance. I swallowed hard, plodding slowly forward as I realized my error in judgment. I couldn't back out. There was only one option. I had to use my credit card.

I prayed mentally, *Lord, you own everything on this planet. I'm going to have to trust that you'll help me pay this bill when it is due. I made the pledge out of love for the boys.*

Done! I heard Him say.

With that problem solved, I asked the big boy with me for ideas about what to buy. "Brent, what kind of sandwiches do you think I should make?" He could eat! Brent had a hollow leg when he consumed food.

"Meat! Boys love meat. We'll eat salad spreads, but we prefer the real deal. Add a little cheese, and we are happy campers," he replied.

Thinking bulk to save money, I went to the meat coolers for a selection instead of buying the meat in small packs. We found precooked ham and turkey loaves. Finding the luncheon meat, I needed to know how much to buy. That was the next question I had to ask Brent. "How many of these loaves of meat do you think I'll need?"

"Fifty sandwiches should be enough so get two each," he responded.

"Fifty sandwiches? What army is going with us?" I asked, flabbergasted.

He exclaimed, "Think about it, Hope! Boys eat a lot! I'll eat three sandwiches. Is that going to be a problem? I'll help you make them."

"It is not a problem making sandwiches. The quantity surprised me. Boys are pigs! Lovable pigs, but still pigs," I answered jokingly.

Waiting on the butcher to slice the meat, I realized I didn't have enough bread, so I made a mental note to get more. Next, we headed to the cheese section. Still thinking in terms of bulk, I counted out packs that had twenty or more. I needed equal amounts of cheddar and Swiss.

I picked up large bottles of mayonnaise and mustard, grabbed four more loaves of bread, and then headed for the chips section. Brent suggested keeping the chip selection simple by buying all the same packages to eliminate fighting. Regular chips were the solution. I could buy the store brand, getting six large bags for the price of two of the fancier brands. At least I could see savings there.

Then Brent had a question. "What are we going to feed them as a snack in the afternoon? It will be a long time between lunch and the picnic."

Looking at him stupidly, I countered, "What do you suggest?"

"Do you really want to know?" he asked with a wicked grin on his face.

"Yeah!" I bantered. "I might as well get what we need while I'm here."

Like a little kid, he pointed to a large bag of jerky. I rolled my eyes and said, "You're joking, right?"

"We love meat." He shrugged.

"Okay, get a few packs, and I'll pick up a few bags of cookies too," I replied.

Brent lifted water in bulk packages and the same kind of canned drinks for everyone into the cart. Then we headed to the checkout.

Brent unloaded everything that I was to purchase first while I searched for my credit card. Then he slid his debit card in the reader faster than I could say "no way." I was stunned.

"Why did you do that? I was perfectly able to purchase this," I protested a little too loudly.

"Not in me to let a woman pay," he remarked.

Before I could respond, he said, "Stop right now, Hope! You won't win this argument. The Lord told me to do it."

I bit my tongue then said, "I'm sorry. Thanks." *And thank you, Lord*, I prayed mentally.

I was very glad that I'd cleaned my apartment Saturday because Brent helped me carry everything inside. I didn't know why it mattered so much, but it did. When he left, I felt strange.

Thursday was the fourth. I knew that packing each boy with a bag of extra clothes, swim trunks, snacks, and water would be hectic. I decided to make the sandwiches after church on Wednesday. It took me nearly an hour to make fifty. Instead of wrapping each sandwich individually, I took a shortcut and used two large plastic containers, making storage and transportation easier. It had been a long day, and I was worn-out.

I had just finished reading and talking with the Lord before turning out my light and sleeping when my landline phone rang. Who could be calling so late?

"Hello," I answered.

"Sorry I'm calling so late," Brent said.

Puzzled about his call, I asked, "What's the matter?"

"Nothing," he replied. "I just wanted to remind you to pack a swimsuit. You and I are responsible for overseeing the kids at the water park. Dad may help, but I don't want to assume, so I need your help."

"Why me?" I demanded.

"Remember, we are the younger escorts," he said.

"I'll bring a suit, but if your Dad is willing, don't expect me to help. I only want to be a spectator," I retorted.

"Come on, you'll be a lot prettier to look at in a suit than my dad," he joked.

I sternly answered, "That's the point! I don't want to be gawked at by a bunch of boys."

"Yes, ma'am! See you tomorrow." He laughed before hanging up.

I got up early to spend time with the Lord before preparing for the trip. The day was lovely, with no threat of rain. God provided a good day for our outing.

Reluctantly, I packed my bathing suit, knowing it might be necessary while praying that it wasn't. *Lord I don't want to be stared at. I will be the only female in our group wearing a bathing suit. It will make me uncomfortable, self-conscious, and nervous. Please intervene, Lord.*

Peace flooded my heart. I knew his compassionate nature was making arrangements to prevent me from being on display.

When I arrived at the Boys' Home around eleven, I was pleasantly surprised to find lasagna, garlic bread, and salad on the table, ready and waiting. The boys were almost out of control with anticipation. I had no idea lunch was on hold until I arrived. We planned to leave after lunch, so I wasn't in a hurry. As soon as everyone finished eating, people got busy.

Brent, his Dad, and Mr. Elder packed the school bus. There were two large coolers loaded with sandwich containers and canned drinks. There were bags of chips, bottles of water, plus four watermelons that the boys insisted on taking. Six blankets were also stowed to sit on if tables weren't available.

Olivia and Mrs. Elder prepared a backpack with swim trunks, towels, and extra clothes for each boy. I added an afternoon snack of jerky, cookies, and water to each backpack so they wouldn't have to go back to the bus. A large tote was loaded with four bottles of sunscreen and a first aid kit.

Our itinerary and schedule had been settled. After arriving, the boys would swim for a few hours, dry off, and eat their snacks. Next, they could enjoy various rides and visit the petting zoo. At picnic time, we'd go back to the bus to unload so we could eat. All of this had to coincide with the fireworks display and concert before returning home. We were in for a long day.

With so many boys, even though some were older, it was mandatory that we all stayed together. If something bad happened, it could jeopardize the privilege of getting to go somewhere special again.

The park was packed with people. It looked like thousands were there for the grand opening. Mr. Elder drove the bus around while the rest of us watched for a shaded picnic area near a parking place. God was smiling on us, giving us what we looked for. We found space a few feet away from several tables close to the restrooms—a perfect spot for groups like ours.

I clutched my bag with bathing suit, towel, and sunscreen, even though I had peace that I wouldn't need it. I wanted everyone to know I was willing to do my part if necessary.

At the swim park, Brent didn't request my assistance, confirming my answered prayer. When Mr. Arnold came out of the dressing area in his swim trunks, I wasn't surprised. What did surprise me, though, was Brent. The man was built! Who would have guessed under the business attire he always wore was a muscular tanned body? When did he find time? Ashamed of myself for staring, I quickly averted my eyes.

I sat on the sidelines with the other ladies, watching the kids—old and young—play on the water slides and swings. They were having a blast. A few times, I excused myself to cool off by sitting on the edge of the pool, dangling my feet and legs in the water. On one of those times, I was caught off guard when Greg did a cannonball real close to me. His splash totally drenched me from head to toe. I was cooled that time! I toweled off and sat in the sun until I was dry. It was all in good fun.

My eyes kept sliding back to Brent playing with the boys. He would make a good father someday. He loved kids, and they loved him. That's when I remembered Mr. Arnold saying he and Olivia prayed daily for Brent to find his soul mate. That afternoon, I added my prayer to theirs for Brent's sake.

When all had finished playing and eating, we used the blankets, even though we found tables. We stretched out and watched the fireworks not far from our bus. We listened to a few concert songs then noticed that Greg, Joey, and Harry had fallen asleep. We decided to pack up and leave. We were all very tired but had a wonderful day.

The Secrets Are Out

A few days after our great adventure, heavy rains came and flooded the area. Homes and businesses close to the river were destroyed, roads were washed away, many people were displaced and without work. Lakes in the area were running over, and the one near the Boys' Home caused the property to suffer some damage. The main house was spared, but the heavy rains and fierce winds made a mess of the barn. Olivia's garden was under water. At least most of the crop had been harvested, frozen, or canned for later use, so it wasn't a total devastation.

Due to a large hole in the roof, everything the boys had in the barn had to be cleaned or trashed. Power tools had to be cleaned and oiled before rust destroyed them. Everyone was busy and stressed out. The Labor Department was in turmoil, as people were lined up at the door, in need of assistance. The floodwaters hindered travel and people could not get to work causing some businesses to close. We were a lifeline to employees in this crisis. Help stations were set up all over town to assist the needy. Times were hard, and I'd never seen anything like it before. Frank, Amber, and I worked a lot of overtime, helping our office get through this disaster. Electrical power was out in many areas. People were hot, hungry, and dirty. It was so sad. I thanked the Lord constantly that He had spared me from some of this horror. I was grateful to Him that my mom, dad, and most of my church family had also been spared.

There was some relief when the water subsided and the power was restored. People could at least start the clean up until federal assistance arrived.

When I thought things were finally improving, Brent called me at home one afternoon, advising me that the Boys' Home was off-limits for a while. Several of the boys were very sick, and Mrs. Elder didn't want to take a chance of it spreading outside their place. He informed me that he wasn't allowed there since he also dealt with the public. The doctor had recommended that only staff, Mr. and Mrs. Elder, and Olivia could stay until they diagnosed the illness.

I was heartsick. My babies needed me, and I wasn't allowed to help. I started crying while talking with Brent on the phone. It upset him so much that he wanted to come over immediately. I assured him I was fine but just worried about boys.

He refused to listen. He told me earnestly, "Hope, we need to intercede now! I sense the urgency in my spirit, don't you?"

That jolted me out of my personal pity party. Indeed, I did sense urgency in my spirit. Immediately, I agreed, "Come now!"

I prayed the whole time I waited for Brent to arrive. The Lord showed me it was time, to be honest with Brent about my gifts. His suggestion alerted me instantly that the attack on the boys must be spiritual in nature, and the Lord wanted us to intervene.

When I let Brent in, I didn't know what he expected of me. He looked haggard and worried, which frightened me. We had only taken a few steps when he said, "We have to pray now! Something is sucking the life from the boys!"

His words caused violence to erupt in my spirit. We would restore what the enemy was stealing, by force if necessary. I knew demons had a grip on my babies! I knew if the demons could see me, they would flee! I was determined nothing or no one was stopping me from getting to them!

I demanded, "Stop it, Brent! I'll pray with you, but first, you are going to hear me out! I need to be on the premises now! I have abilities that I haven't told anyone about! God needs me there, and if I have to beat the gate down with my fist, I'll do it. Do you hear me?" I screamed.

He was shocked. I'd become a force to be reckoned with. He stood back and let me vent before asking, "What gifts?"

"Oh, you heard that, did you? Good! I want the world to know! Months ago, God granted me the ability to see and hear evil spirits and demons. I can watch the evil creatures doing their nasty deeds. Most run when I make them aware I can see them. Others, the Lord Himself must defeat. I'm trying to explain I know what is happening. If someone doesn't get over there that can see and stop what the damnable creatures are doing, the sickness will continue. Do you hear me?" I screamed impatiently.

Brent sputtered, "We need to pray first!"

I was shaking so hard that I could hardly answer him. "I've already prayed. I'm telling you, the Lord wants me there. Brent, you know me. I'm saner now than I've ever been. I'll pray with you on the way, I promise. Let's stop talking and get moving."

He hesitated. "But the doctor said not to go in."

"We don't have to go in. All I need is to look through a window. Take me over there or I'll drive myself," I responded. Brent agreed. In the car, we prayed in the Spirit, letting the Lord go before us.

I knew the minute I set foot on the property that evil was present. Hearing evil laughter coming from the barn's vicinity got my attention first.

"Lord, I need you. I need your armor. This may be a job for you, and I'm willing to fight alongside you." I had prayed aloud. I didn't care if anyone heard me at the moment. I was livid and ready to get these demons done.

Step inside me, Hope! I am ready and with you, the Lord replied.

I closed my eyes, mentally stepping into the Lord's presence as instructed. I wore Him like my skin. Then I proceeded toward the barn with Brent on my heels.

The ground was still wet and putrid-smelling. My shoes were muddy and ruined, but I didn't care. I was following a sound coming from the broadside of the barn. When I turned the corner, I wasn't shocked to see demons gathered around the water pump. They had overtaken the main water supply. Impure water might be making the boys sick.

The Lord and I pounded on the side of the barn, startling the foul creatures. Then he and I yelled, "We see you! You are commanded, in the name and by the blood of Christ Jesus, to restore what you have broken and stolen. Never return or suffer the wrath of God Almighty."

It was almost comical to see them scramble. The Lord let me watch. They were doing what was commanded of them—restoring what they destroyed, plus replacing what they had stolen. When the tasks were completed, they left as fast as they could.

Brent's eyes were wide with shock. I couldn't tell if he saw the demons or my actions, but I didn't care.

"It's almost over," I assured him. When he only blinked, I asked, "Are you okay?"

"Hope, is that you?" Brent stuttered.

"Yes, dummy, it's me.

Why?" I asked.

"You're glowing!" he exclaimed.

"Snap out of it!" I demanded. "It's me! I'm just in His armor. You glow when you're in the Spirit."

He looked at me, stupefied. "What?" he asked.

"We have work to do. I'll explain it later," I retorted. "We need to get to the house so I can look inside."

I marched toward the house without him. He was standing still in some kind of stupor. I didn't have time to worry about his reactions. I was on a mission and needed to see if other demons were attacking the house.

Peering through the front window, I observed Mrs. Elder and another lady talking. My heart sang! I had spiritual help on the inside. This beautiful black lady, dressed in a nurse's uniform had one of God's angels by her side. He was awesome! The angel had the face of a man. The one who followed me had the face of an eagle, and the one who followed Brent had the lion's face. I didn't recognize the nurse, but that didn't matter. She had the Lord's help. He had things under control. When Brent finally stood next to me, I asked who she was.

He replied, "Oh, that's Mamie Ross. She is a nurse from County Memorial Hospital. She is also a member of our church. Why?"

"I wish you could see what I'm seeing. She is so beautiful. She has an aura around her, and she's being followed by one of God's angels," I revealed.

"You can see that?" he queried.

"Yes, I can. We can relax now. God's got things under control on the inside. The boys are safe. I guess He just needed us to get things handled on the outside," I said.

"What do you mean?" he said in bewilderment.

I knew he was overwhelmed by all that had happened, so I calmly tried to reassure him all was well. "As soon as I opened the car door, I knew evil was here. I heard weird laughter coming from the barn. That's when I asked the Lord to help me. Soon after, He responded, letting me view what was going on. Demons had captured the water supply at the well. He commanded that they repair and restore what they had ravaged before they were banished. I think we'll learn that contaminated water is making the boys sick," I informed him.

He visibly relaxed after hearing things were going to get better. He was still awed by the experience and had every right to be. I hadn't intended for anyone to ever know that I had certain gifts. I was afraid if someone knew about my abilities, they might get confused or even be frightened of me.

"Brent, are you okay with this?" I asked cautiously.

He answered the best way he could, "I have read in the Word about your gifts, but I never dreamed that people saw things in the Spirit in this day and age. Elisha did, Daniel did, and many others, and God's not a respecter of persons. I'm just stunned at the moment."

I carefully responded, "I'm glad my gifts were revealed to you first. I've been afraid to tell anyone. If the kids hadn't gotten sick, I'd still have my secret. The threat to the boys motivated me. Does this change our relationship?"

He hugged me so hard that I thought my back would break. He whispered above my head, "Not in the least. If anything, my feelings for you have intensified."

Changing the subject, I stated, "I think we can leave now. Ms. Ross has things under control inside. Call your dad and let him know the well needs a proper overhaul."

When we got inside his BMW, Brent called his dad. I was grateful Brent was able to point suspicion to the water supply without telling his Dad what had happened. I didn't think many people would understand.

We were quiet during the ride to my apartment. We were physically and emotionally drained. When we arrived, Brent walked me to the front door, which he rarely did since we started riding together. When we got to the door, he turned me to face him. "Hope, I'm deeply in love with you," he declared before passionately kissing me.

Tears welled up in my eyes. I wasn't prepared for that at all. I couldn't reply to his declaration of love. I had to get away. I felt as if I'd betrayed my Lord. I lightly pushed Brent away before entering my apartment. I said softly, "I'm sorry. This is too much for me right now. I need some space. I need to think. Please understand." Then I closed the door in his face.

I left him on the doorstep. I knew I'd hurt him, but I needed the Lord immediately. I had to apologize. I never meant for things to change between Brent and me. I had physically responded to Brent's kiss. My body betrayed my heart, and now I felt ashamed.

Crouched in the bushes, Sam witnessed their kiss and gritted his teeth in fury. He wanted to kill the man for touching her. If he didn't do something to win Hope back soon, he would have to kill the man.

The Invitation

Jesus knew it was the time to meet with Hope. He commanded heaven to prepare for the visit. The coronation was about to take place. His chosen brides had to present themselves before the witness's one at a time. Hope had pledged herself, and it was time for the face-to-face commitment.

———∿∿∽∾⊙⊱⊰⊙∾∽∿∿———

I rushed to the bedroom, throwing myself across the bed sobbing, "Lord, I'm so sorry. I promised myself that I'd never let another man in my life, that you were all I'd ever need or want. You've been good to me. My body betrayed me tonight. I never meant for it to happen."

The Holy Spirit's voice was compassionate but firm. *Stop this immediately! You haven't betrayed me. If anything, you've confirmed your love. There has been a command given in heaven to prepare for a coronation ceremony. You are invited to meet Jesus face-to-face.*

I was flabbergasted. How could this be? Why does Jesus want to see me? Is my time on earth over? Have I died? I was confused and scared.

Stop it! You're worrying yourself sick. Do you remember the book of Esther? Many were called to meet the king. It's your time, Hope, that's all. He wants to see you. Confirm pledges to you and give you reassurance. I'm commanding your body to rest while I take you to meet your king, He informed me.

My body became heavy with exhaustion, and my eyes closed in sleep. Then my spirit was flying. I was on another marvelous journey, going to the heavenly palace.

When we arrived, the Holy Spirit bowed and left. Standing before me were many glorious angels, waving for me to follow them. Some introduced themselves while others only nodded, but I was totally accepted.

One of the head angels, who said his name was Shea, explained that I had to be purified and readied for the meeting. He opened a door that led into a chamber where beautiful female angels were gathered around an elegant marble bathing pool. The fragrance coming from the steaming was divine. Shea left me in their capable hands. I was bathed, pampered, massaged, and scrubbed. Oil was rubbed into my skin. My hair was washed then adorned with flowers. My covenant robe must have been cleaned because it had never radiated such beauty before. When they put it over my naked body, I felt a sense of shame. Why?

I was taken into a large dressing room filled with lovely garments of all shades. Gold robes, silver slippers, jewels were at my fingertips. I was surrounded by necklaces, earrings, rings, and small crowns in every stone or in pearl, ready for the picking. This was every girl's fantasy, a dream come true for most women, but I was turned off by it all. My heart didn't want any part of it. I didn't understand until I watched another lady dressed in finery coming from the main hall, looking depressed.

Instantly, I knew the cause. I remembered Vashti, from the book of Esther, who had chosen the company of her maids and the lovely possessions more than the king. Was this the reason the Holy Spirit reminded me about Esther? Did He reveal what I needed to do?

When it was time for my presentation, I rejected the lady angel's plea to dress. In fact, I stripped off my lovely covenant robe. Every other time I'd been here, I arrived naked. I didn't need anything or want anything. I only wanted my Jesus, Him only, with nothing in the way. Each time I'd stepped inside His armor, I'd been totally naked in my heart. It was no different this time. He was all and would be all I needed, and nothing would be between us.

I declared physically, even though I was in the spirit, that I was ready for love. I needed Jesus, and I was going to Him the way He created me—needy, lacking, and helpless.

When the large doors to the coronation hall opened, I stood in awe of the hundreds of witnesses who were present. Then my eyes fixed on Jesus's beautiful face. He was indescribable. I wanted to be ladylike, to walk steadily and confidently, but my heart urged me to run. I wanted to touch Him. I needed to feel His body.

With each step, angels flew around me. I was being covered with robes spun of real gold, arrayed in finery, even though I didn't want it; they mattered nothing to me. I could see by their frantic behavior that they had been commanded to dress me, so I stopped resisting and just humbled my heart. There was nothing in the dressings as beautiful or could compare to what I was being given.

I reached out my hands to grasp the only thing that mattered—my Jesus's hand. His touch was better than any physical contact I'd ever had. No other human experience produced the pleasure I was feeling. Joy surged throughout my body, my knees became weak, and I could no longer stand. I fell to my knees.

Humiliated at my response, I lowered my eyes and bowed my head in shame. I wanted to be a strong person who showed all of heaven how much He meant to me. Instead, I was a puddle of mush at His feet. I'd made a mockery of what I'd wanted to be for Him.

His kind and compassionate nature were overwhelming. He took me by my elbows and helped me to my feet. I couldn't believe Jesus was assisting me.

Then I heard His musical voice order me, "Look at me, Hope! I know your heart. You've made me very proud. Come, let me present you as a bride."

I looked into His gorgeous brown eyes as He commanded. He was exquisite, dressed in the most beautiful clothes imaginable. I couldn't speak. My tongue had no power to move. All I could do was turn and face the crowd behind me.

When I faced them, I felt something hard and heavy being placed on my head. I turned to look at Jesus. He was smiling. I reached up to touch whatever it was He had placed on my head. I was surprised to feel a very ornate jeweled crown.

"Yes, love, the Father has made you royal. You are my bride for eternity. Bow to your subjects," He whispered.

As directed, I bowed in every direction. I couldn't see faces through the tears streaming down my face. I was crying in heaven. I had been declared the wife of Jesus.

"It's time for us to be alone, Hope. We have much to discuss," He whispered in my ear.

We moved to a beautiful room with comfortable sofas and chairs. He beckoned me to sit. Sitting beside me, He took my hand, wiping away my tears with the other. I didn't know what to expect, but I was sure it would be good.

"You can speak to me, Hope. I haven't destroyed your tongue. I assure you that I'd love to hear what you have to say. I've listened to you for so long. Now I want you to speak directly to me," He shared.

I could only manage three words, "I love you!"

"I know you do. I love you as well," He said while continuing to wipe away my tears of joy. Then His face became serious, and He stood up. I didn't want Him to leave! Anxiously, I reached for His hand.

"I'm not going anywhere, Hope!" He assured. "I must share my heart with you. I needed to stand while making my request. I desire to have a family on earth, my children for generations. The only way that will happen is for my brides to continue the line."

I was mystified. Did He just say that I was pregnant and going to give birth to a child?

He stopped my confusion by stating His heart's desire. "Hear me out! To have children, I must share my brides with my brothers—men on earth who live in me, for me, and through me. I've chosen such a brother for you. I knew you wouldn't submit unless I made my pledge to you first. That was the reason for your coronation ceremony. Please do me the honor of giving me a family. Share my life with my brother. Learn to love him the way you love me. I'll never leave you, ever. You'll always be mine, and I'll always be yours."

"Will we still be able to communicate? Can we keep our relationship alive if I submit my heart to a man? I don't want to live unless you're with me in this all the way," I declared.

"I'll be with you forever. You can talk with me whenever you wish. Just like before, ask and I'll be there," He assured.

I agreed fearfully to His request. I would not let Him down. In my heart, I knew the brother that He had chosen. After I surrendered all to Him, we spent many hours pledging our hearts to each other until daybreak. Before it was time for me to awake physically, He showed me many wonders through His Word. The cycle of life was created for Him, and I was to be a part of it. He revealed I was already in love with Brent. I was just denying the fact. He was wholeheartedly in agreement because Brent was His chosen.

He instructed me to let Brent know as soon as I woke up. It was sweet being with Jesus. I would miss being face-to-face, but I was assured that we'd have other times together, just as special.

———❦———

The beeping alarm forced my eyes open. As always, I greeted the Lord first, only this time I thanked Him profusely for everything. Then I picked up my telephone. I wasn't giving my enemy, Satan, time to mess this up. I called Brent. I didn't care if it was six in the morning, he'd just have to deal with it. This was part of Jesus's plan, so he'd be ready for the assignment.

When he didn't answer right away, it frightened me. What could be wrong? I left voice mail instructions to call my cell or office phone as soon as he could because I needed to tell him something very important.

I ran to the kitchen where I'd left my purse to search for my cell phone. I needed it close if Brent called. I knew I wouldn't be able to hear the landline if I was showering.

I drank a cup of coffee then proceeded to get ready for work. My stomach was too nervous for food. Coffee was all I could handle at the moment.

I had slept all night fully clothed, shoes and all. I was badly in need of a shower. The moment I was stripped completely nude, ready to step into the shower, my cell phone rang. It was Brent's name on the display. Wouldn't you know it; the Lord connected the call when I was naked. I had to laugh at His sense of humor. I was ready again for love, but this time, pleasure was going to wait.

I answered the phone, "Hi, Brent! I love you too!"

I could have sworn I heard his phone drop. When he finally replied to my statement, he was breathing hard. "What did you say?" he stammered.

"I said I love you too!" I laughed.

"You scared me!" he choked. "You never call me this early. I thought something was wrong. You said you love me?"

"You heard me! I'm not repeating myself until I see your face," I said.

He replied swiftly, "I'm at the gym. I was about to get in the tanning booth when I saw your message. I'll be right there."

"No! Please give me a few minutes to shower and get dressed. Take your time. The Lord has assured me that we'll have a long time to get to know each other." Then I hung up my phone.

I barely had enough time to shower and dress. It was a good thing I usually didn't wear much makeup. I'd just finished putting the mascara wand back in the tube when my doorbell rang.

Looking out the window before opening the door, I saw a vision of grandeur. Brent was something to behold. He was dressed in a dark blue business suit with a pale-yellow shirt opened at the neck. He hadn't bothered to put on a tie yet. He was a fine-looking man, and he was mine! I could look at him now as much as I wanted.

When I opened the door, we just stared at each other a few seconds. He seemed to be searching my face before saying or doing anything. To break the ice, I reached up and took his handsome face in my hands. Looking him straight in the eyes, I said, "Brent Arnold, I, Hope Anderson, love you with all my heart. I'm sorry I've been so stubborn and hard to get along with. Until last night, I was afraid of giving my heart to another. When I said I needed time and space, I truly meant it. The Lord has assured me that I have His blessing with you. If you'll still have me, after all, I've put you through, I'm yours."

I felt one of his tears splash on my arm. He was crying. I hoped these were tears of joy, not heartache. Then he lifted me off my feet and kissed me passionately. It was so sweet that it caused me to cry too.

When we finally came up for air, he whispered, "I waited so long, Hope. I've prayed so hard for someone to love and who would love me. When you said we had the Lord's blessing, joy overflowed my heart. Will you marry me? Be my wife for as long as we live?"

"That's what I've been trying to tell you. I'm yours. Yes, I'll marry you. The sooner, the better," I exclaimed.

Neither of us wanted to work that day. We wanted to plan our wedding. But we both had obligations to honor.

Plans

Jesus met with the Holy Spirit and His personal angels. He shared what was about to happen and asked them to stay on high alert.

"I am aware Satan is planning to destroy Hope. He is using her ex-husband as a tool for his purpose. This battle is going to be hard to watch. I see in the future that problems in communication will arise, keeping us from helping her. Hope has everything she needs to be victorious but has to be the one to conquer her fears. If she is hurt in the process, we'll mend her. Giving my personal pledge to her caused a spiritual shift. Demons and evil angels have been dispatched against her. We already know the outcome. Satan's a fool."

―――

The previous night, Sam watched Brent's BMW drive away before making his move. He had to see her, talk with her in person. He had sense enough to know that if he went to her front door, she would freak out. Instead, he planned to trap her outside. Tampering with her vehicle was his first choice. She was unaware that he had made a copy of her SUV keys long before their divorce. He thought fate was on his side. He would use the keys to gain access and tamper with the electrical system to prevent it from starting. Once he had her inside the vehicle, he could talk with her after he calmed her down. He'd wait patiently the next morning for just the right time. He'd promise her anything. He would vow to change.

Hope always left for work around seven thirty every morning. Sam made sure that he was in place, leaning against her apartment, waiting for the perfect moment. What he hadn't planned on, though, was that rich man showing up again. The man always ruined everything!

Sam was furious watching the two of them walk out of the apartment hand in hand. Sam struggled to keep the upper hand.

He listened to their conversation, which made his blood boil. They were talking about getting married then embraced right in front of him. Sam almost rushed from his hiding place.

Sam stopped himself, deciding he might have a chance if the dude would leave. Then Hope got in her SUV. When she turned the key but nothing happened, the man returned to investigate. Hope left with the guy, and something in Sam snapped. He could only see red. Sam vowed the man had to die.

———w·o·o·o·o·o·o·w———

The angels of the Lord watched the drama unfold. They had strict orders just to observe. It was all they could do for the moment. The battle would be ninety percent Hope's.

———w·o·o·o·o·o·o·w———

"What do you think is wrong with your SUV?" Brent asked.

I shrugged. "Probably more water in the tank. It gave me problems weeks ago. Dad had it checked for me. The mechanic told him I had somehow gotten water in the gas line. I like buying gas at Ernie's because it is convenient and he pumps the gas for me. I guess I'll have to change service stations because this could get costly if I don't."

"Aren't you glad I was with you? You'd really be late for work otherwise," Brent joked.

"Yeah, yeah, I appreciate the lift. But if I had my way, I wouldn't be going to work. I'm too excited. I want to start planning our day, shopping, and telling everybody. Do you mind if I share our news without you?" I asked.

"Of course not! I want to shout from the rooftops myself," he declared.

Happily, I stated, "I can start with Amber and Frank at work. Then I can tell Mom and Dad when I call him about my vehicle again. They will be so excited. Mom loves you, and she's been teasing me about you anyway. When I tell her this news, she is going to freak out." I then turned to look at him. "What are your plans for today?" I asked.

"Try to function. Go through the motions at the moment because my mind isn't on the job," Brent admitted.

"Where is your mind?" I joked.

He parked the car close to my office door before answering. Then he looked at me with a wicked little grin on his face. "What's on my mind, Hope, is marrying you as soon as possible. How about planning it the weekend before Labor Day? Since the holiday is on a Tuesday, we can incorporate our day off, having a lovely celebration and honeymoon."

"That doesn't give me much time to plan, but I'll make it work. I don't require all the frills. Been there, done that already. What do you want?" I asked.

"I just want friends and family. I don't need anything fancy. Hope, look at the time! I need to go. Think about it today, make notes, and we'll talk in length tonight," he said before getting one last kiss in.

I felt like I was walking on air. Every step was almost a skip. Having the Lord's blessing this time around made everything special. I knew, without a doubt, this marriage would never fail for as long as we lived. I had to admit if Jesus hadn't sealed our covenant with the coronation ceremony, I would still resist marrying Brent. I had been fighting my emotions until Jesus explained everything so well. We were to live for Him by establishing a family.

Brent was everything I'd ever admired in a man. He was very handsome, honest, loyal, caring, compassionate, and a very hard worker. Mom even made the statement he was a fine catch and had all the amenities. This news was going to blow her mind. I could hardly wait to tell her and Dad.

I was in my office about two seconds when Amber rushed in with wonderful news. She and Lacey were happy. Her little girl was a joy. When her news received a halfhearted response, she became curious.

"What's wrong with you? You look spacey. You're here in body only. Spill! Something is on your mind," she jabbed.

I wanted to encourage her and give her support. She has waited long enough to have something good happen. I understood she was excited and wanted to share. But I couldn't contain myself. I had news, big news. I blurted out, "I'm getting married!"

She yelled, "What? Who? You haven't been dating anyone. Have you? You're fibbing! Who would have guessed? Are you a closet dater or something? No! Really, girl, who's the lucky guy?" "It's Brent Arnold," I replied.

"You go girl! He's a catch!" Amber squealed. "At one time, I thought about flirting with him. I could tell he only had eyes for you. You hardly gave him the time of day. What changed?"

"Let's say I had a wake-up call. The Lord showed me I was being a fool, ignoring a wonderful opportunity," I answered.

She was as excited as I was and kept chattering, "When's the day? Can I help with anything? I love weddings!"

Hearing all the fuss in my office, Frank walked in. "What are you two giggling about? "

"Hope's getting married!" Amber shouted.

I joked, "Hey! That's for me to tell."

"Sorry!" Amber apologized. "I'm just so happy for you!"

"Let me guess. I bet I know!" Frank kidded. "Could it be a tall domineering attorney that we both know and love?"

I couldn't help it! Smiling so big, it almost broke my face, I shouted, "Yes!"

"How did you know?" Amber asked.

"I've been babysitting that lovesick puppy for a while now. A lot of us have been praying Hope would see what a good thing she had. Just another witness that prayer works. Hope, I'm really happy for the two of you." Frank beamed.

When Joan and John hears the commotion, by 8:30 a.m., the news traveled throughout the office, then everyone expresses their congratulations.

I finally get everyone out of my office, so I can make a phone call to my parents. I knew they were early risers, and I did not worry about disturbing them. Even if I woke them, it was for a wonderful reason. I would be forgiven quickly.

When mom answered, I quickly spoke, "Hi, Mom! I need to tell you and Dad something. Is he near enough to hear us talking?"

"Sure, honey, is everything all right?" she queried.

"Everything is great! Get Dad so I can tell you," I prodded.

It wasn't long before Mom came back. "We're both here now, Hope. What is so important?"

"Mom, Dad, I'm getting married again!" I cried.

Mom was anxious, answering me with a question, "Is it, Brent? Lord, Hope, please tell me it is that nice young man! The two of you have been spending a lot of time together. We've been praying that you'd wake up and grab him before it was too late."

"Yes, Mom, it's Brent. You're getting your choice for a son-in-law this time," I joked.

Dad couldn't stand it. He wanted in on the conversation, so he took the phone away from Mom. "Honey, did I hear correctly?

You're getting married to Brent!"

"Yes, Sir!" I replied.

I was beginning to feel pressured, so I changed the subject, "Dad, I also called to ask for another favor. My SUV won't start. Do you think it may be water in the gas line again?"

He took the hint that I didn't want to talk marriage anymore. "It probably is. Where is your vehicle?" he asked.

"It's still at the apartment," I answered. "I caught a ride to work. Do you think you could have your mechanic check on it?"

He happily offered, "Anything for my little girl. Do you need me to take you home this afternoon after work?"

"No, sir. I'll catch a ride with a coworker. Thanks anyway," I responded.

After hanging up the phone, I proceeded to make sure I could ride with someone before I forgot. While searching for Amber, I learned she had appointments outside the office for the day. My other option was Frank. He was willing and happy to help.

Brent was going through the same thing at his office. All his coworkers were extremely happy for him and offering their congratulations. When he called his mom and dad, they were ecstatic. They had come to love Hope and were also praying that the two of them would get together. They could see Brent and Hope loved children, had the same faith, the same values, and were perfect for each other.

—————

Evil schemes were also being made. Sam was planning to kidnap Hope and murder her lover. Witnessing their kisses and hearing their marriage plans pushed him over the edge. Sam always carried a pistol in his vehicle. He had to make sure it was in working order. At the lake where he was staying, he fired a few rounds to test the accuracy. He didn't want to risk a misfire or have the gun's sight out of alignment. Killing what he aimed at was a priority. To make matters worse, he had purchased a large bottle of vodka and was proceeding to get drunk enough to have the nerve to carry out his plans.

Looking around the camper, he decided to at least pick up his trash. After all, Hope was coming to visit tonight. She would be his first guest in his new home.

Grimacing at the thought that she may fight him, he decided to make it hard for her to do much of anything but listen during her stay. Drugging her seemed the logical solution. He had been prescribed sleeping pills. He would make her take them. He would let her get hungry and thirsty then give her food and drink with the drug in them. She wouldn't even know what was going on.

Everything was set at the camper. Now all he had to do was find that pretty boy's car. He'd seen it before in the parking lot of Hope's place of business. He knew where to go to watch and wait.

—⁓⦿⦾⦿⦾⦿⦾⦿⁓—

Satan was overjoyed. If his puppet couldn't carry out the plan, Satan would just move in and possess Sam to make it happen. Having a compliant subject always made things easier. Sam was a prize. Murder and kidnapping! What could be more fun! Satan would convince Sam that Hope needed punishment. Maybe he would physically abuse her and rape her before her final demise. Satan hated Hope more than most. Sam had murder in his heart, and so did Satan.

Panic

Five o'clock wouldn't come fast enough. Working was a chore all day. I had better things to do. I caught myself daydreaming many times and had to retype or regroup in order to do things correctly.

When Frank stuck his head in my door and said, "Let's go," I couldn't shut down fast enough. I wasn't paying attention to my surroundings. I was too happy to be on alert for anything wicked.

We were in motion and just a few feet out of the parking lot when suddenly, a car rammed us in front. I knew who it was, but before I could scream for Frank to stay in the car, he had his door open and climbed out.

Then the unimaginable happened. Sam opened his car door with a pistol in hand, shooting Frank twice. I saw my friend hit the ground, blood spilling on his shirt and into the street. "Oh God! Don't let Frank die," I prayed.

I opened my door to run to Frank but came face-to-face with Sam. He was yelling, ordering me, "Get in the car! Loverboy is dead. If you don't do what I say, you're next."

I started screaming for help. I wasn't going anywhere with this maniac. When I wouldn't budge, he hit me on the side my head with the butt of his gun. I was swallowed by darkness as I fell into Sam's arms.

I regained consciousness in Sam's vehicle, dazed and scared. I looked around, trying to focus and regain control of my emotions. I considered opening the passenger side door, throwing myself onto the road. I'd risk bodily harm to get away from this murderer. I slowly slipped my hand onto the handle. It moved like it would open, but it didn't because he had locked the door. I reached slowly to the window, hoping in his drunken state that he wouldn't notice. I was heartsick when I couldn't find a lock release; he had removed the knob. I was trapped.

I began to sob loudly while hitting him. Even though we were traveling fast, I didn't care if we wrecked. I needed out of this car. "Let me out of this vehicle now, you jerk! This is kidnapping! I hate you! You've killed a decent man!" I screamed.

I clawed, scratched, punched, and kicked at him. I wanted blood! My sense of survival was fueled by panic and rage.

He got tired of my attempts to hurt him and pulled the car over. When he had the car in park, he backhanded me so hard it slammed my head into the passenger's window, breaking the glass and knocking me out again.

News spread fast about a shooting. Police and ambulances arrived on the scene, getting Frank to County Memorial Hospital's emergency center before he succumbed in the street. He needed surgery to remove two bullets from his body—one in his shoulder, and the other barely grazed one of his ribs, exiting cleanly out his back. His blood loss was severe, but no vital organs were damaged.

Bystanders who witnessed the shooting informed police that the lady passenger of the BMW was taken after being brutally beaten. Searching the vehicle for clues, the police found a lady's handbag. Inside the handbag was a wallet that identified the lady as Hope Anderson. Minutes later, they had a suspect. The witnesses' description along with the recorded court order Hope Anderson had against Sam Anderson gave credence to the identity of the kidnapper.

Twenty minutes later, the probation office was contacted, requesting an address for the suspect. Bonnie Fowler couldn't help. There wasn't a current address on file. Feeling horrible that her office had not located Sam Anderson for questioning after Brent had alerted her, she picked up the phone to call her friend. Telling Brent what happened to Hope was one of the hardest things she had done in her seventeen-year career.

When Brent answered his phone, he wasn't expecting to hear the voice of an anxious woman. "Brent Arnold?" the lady asked.

"Yes, can I help you?" he replied.

Keeping things professional, she calmly said, "Brent, this is Bonnie Fowler at probation. I have some very disturbing news."

"I'm listening," he prompted.

"This afternoon at approximately 5:20 p.m., Frank Addison was shot, and your girlfriend was kidnapped. The principle suspect is her ex-husband, Sam Anderson," she continued.

"No! No! This can't be happening." He'd just gotten her to admit her love for him. They were to be married. He thought frantically.

Getting himself together, he asked, "How is Frank?"

"Last report is that he is in surgery," Bonnie offered. "Brent, our office is doing everything humanly possible to locate Sam's whereabouts. I promise to keep you posted, but I'm sure you have other avenues you can pursue in the meantime."

He was glad he had an avenue to take, the most important route of all. He excused himself from their conversation, thanking her and hanging up his phone. Then he promptly fell to his knees on the floor of his office, going to the Lord in prayer.

"My Father, my God, I need you more now than I've ever needed you before. Our precious Hope is in danger. You've given me your spirit of justice, equipping me with your power of discernment. Move in me because I'm a mess. Even with these abilities, I am useless. My heart is too broken and full of rage. Please subdue this emotion. I can't. Fear is trying to dominate and seize my body. Hope needs us, yet I am nothing. With you, I've helped so many hurting and oppressed people. Now, please help me move out of your way so you can use me for the one I love. I admit it, Lord. I'm scared. I'm afraid for her physical safety. I know in my heart that she will be returned to me because you performed a miracle for me last night. You convinced her that she loves me. Sam has a history of violence and has hurt her before. Don't allow him to maim her beyond repair. I know she will be hurt, that's inevitable, but please don't let it be crippling. Find her! Help me find her, Lord."

Coming to his aid, the Lord replied, *Brent, rest in the covenant. I already know what is going on. The command for the enemy not to touch the anointed is still in force. When it is violated, things will change. Right now, Hope is operating in the flesh. Rest assured, it won't be long before her flesh gives up. Then it will be my turn to take the reproach, and the Father will get involved. Get up! Tell her parents, check on Frank, and get the church family to pray. Stay busy. Time will pass faster if you keep busy. Hope has been trained well and will give in soon. Patience! You'll be guided when the time is right. Operate with my authority like you've been trained!*

Brent physically sensed His presence. Brent felt peace overtake his soul. His mind was clear while his spiritual self was roaring like a lion. They would find Hope. She would be okay. He had to get to her parents and then call his. They were already family and needed to stay united.

———ᘀᕼᕼ◦ᘠᕼᕼ◦◦᙭ᘠᘠ᙭᙭◦ᘠᘀᘀᘀ———

Jesus smiled. Seeing that Brent recognized His presence allowed Him to empower the man with justice. The roaring lion was ordered to follow Brent, assisting through every turn.

———ᘀᕼᕼ◦ᘠᕼᕼ◦◦᙭ᘠᘠ᙭᙭◦ᘠᘀᘀᘀ———

When I came to this time, my head hurt so badly that I felt like vomiting. My mouth tasted like blood, and the taste of it was making me gag. I could tell that I was in some kind of trailer. Everything was crowded into a small area. Gathering my wits as much as possible, I realized I was bound on a bed, tied with

297

plastic construction ties like an animal. With that revelation, I rolled over and puked. "Let him clean up after me!" I rebelliously declared.

I felt a little better afterward. At least my stomach had quit rolling. I lay on my back, trying to make sense of my surroundings. I was in a pitifully small camper with rounded ceilings, on a small dirty double bed. The covers smelled like sweat and alcohol. Sam wasn't far from me. He was passed out in a lounge chair, probably from drinking too much, which was typical.

It took me a few minutes, but I managed to sit on the side of the bed. My head was pounding. My bladder hurt, and I was about to make another mess, one I'd have to wear unless I could wake him up. I started shouting at the jerk, "Sam! Wake up, you creep. I have to pee! Sam!"

He grunted. "What?"

I wanted to call him something far worse than jerk but bit my tongue. I screamed, "Get up, you jerk, I have to pee! Now!"

Waking enough to see my distress, he stumbled to the bed. By that time, I'd managed to stand, even with my feet tied. I needed to go to the bathroom. That's when he noticed the vomit on the floor. "You bitch! Why did you do that?" he shouted.

Then he side kicked me in the stomach with his booted foot. I fell in my own vomit, which caused me to vomit again.

He grabbed me under my arm, pulling me to my feet, screaming all kinds of obscenities. Then he said, "I'm going to untie your feet so you can walk to the bathroom, but I'm not untying your hands."

"How am I going to manage pulling down my panties and cleaning myself?" I asked furiously.

His demeanor changed. Evil enveloped him. He grinned, spitting out his intent, "That pleasure is all mine."

Since he had a knife ready to cut away the ties on my feet, he also cut away my clothes, bra, and panties. I was left totally nude in front of this madman.

He grabbed me by my hair, forcing me in the direction of the bathroom, and then shoving me onto the toilet. "Piss, damn you! Then you're taking a shower. I'm going to scrub every trace of that bastard off you."

He stood over me the whole time, so he knew when I finished. He handed me some toilet paper. Then he threw a wet towel at me. "What am I going to do with this?" I asked.

I missed a great opportunity to keep my mouth shut. I knew better! In the past, it only fueled his temper. He grabbed me by the hair again, steering me toward the bed. Then he pushed me onto my knees in front of the vomit, ordering me to clean it up. It was hard doing anything with tied hands, but I managed the best I could. I took it slow, dreading what was coming next. I needed time to think. What could I do or say that might delay or change his mind altogether?

I kept trying to determine what he meant by having a man on me. He was the last man I had sex with, and that was almost a year ago. What did he mean? Should I ask? It might cause another senseless beating. Did he mean Frank? I wasn't involved with Frank. Why had Sam killed him? I started crying. Frank had died because of me. What provoked Sam to shoot Frank? We were just friends. What was Sam thinking?

I looked up, indicating that my job had been accomplished, bracing for what was to come. By cleaning so slowly, I gave him time to undress. He took the towel, opened the small back door and threw it out. I thought about jumping. At that moment, the door was open to get outside. Shame from being naked was the least of my worries. If nothing else, maybe I could scream and get someone's attention. I started moving, but he realized what I was thinking and backhanded me again. Without hands to brace my fall, I toppled hard into a dresser.

299

"Bitch! Can't you even stand up! You fall at the slightest touch!" he spat.

An evil look came on his face. The inevitable time for my washing was here. Could I stand his hands scrubbing me, touching me in private areas that he no longer had claim over?

Could I endure being raped? My heart belonged to… And then I paused in mid-thought. I mentally called on my heart's desire. *Lord! Help me!*

I'm here, Hope! Do not fear! No matter what you have to go through, survive. Help is coming, He answered.

Survival

I had my order to survive. I had the assurance help was on the way. That meant, at least, that I wasn't going to die.

I tried to stay in contact with my Lord, but my head was snapped around again. Sam had me by the hair, dragging me to the shower. Thank God the space was extremely small. Two people couldn't fit, so he'd have to stay on the outside. Sam had more ties in the bathroom. He grabbed one, intertwining it with the one already holding my wrists together. I kicked, I screamed, I yanked my arms, trying to get away before he could push me in that shower. I did not want to be touched by Sam.

He fastened me to the shower head, but before turning on the water, he looked over my body. He ran his hands up and down my sides, roughly cupping my breast. Then he noticed something, and I watched him bend slightly to get a better look.

"Ha! I see you wear a brand from our last encounter. I claim that scar as my personal mark on your body. Must have hurt! All that hot grease spilling on your belly." He hissed, "This is also going to burn."

He turned on the water, and I knew my dreaded nightmare was about to begin. He had a look on his face that made me cringe inside. I know my suffering added to his pleasure. The water was scalding hot, making me scream in agony. I was being boiled alive. I kicked and fought. I shook the showerhead as hard as I could. Blood started trickling down my arms from the ties cutting my flesh. I knew I had to break the showerhead, so I kept tugging, squirming, and kicking. The kicking was laughable because the space in the stall didn't allow for much momentum. I tried to kick Sam, but he was too fast and anticipated my actions. I cracked the fiberglass and bent the shower nozzle, but it only caused more punishment. I heightened his fury with my efforts. He slapped me or punched me. Once, he punched me so hard that I thought he cracked one of my ribs.

When the water started to cool, he still wasn't finished. The next thing he did was unthinkable. I envisioned him fondling me while using soap. Instead, he took a toilet brush and covered it with abrasive cleanser and started scrubbing me. My body was on fire! I was raw from abrasions. I'd used facial scrubs before that were rough, but this chemical burned. I literally felt it taking my skin off.

My arms felt like they were being torn from their sockets with all the pulling and yanking. The fight in me was draining with the water. Sam slowed, and I thought he was finished. However, he was planning something even more sadistic. He was finished scrubbing my body, but he hadn't finished my bath. He put more cleanser on the brush and forced it between my legs. I couldn't believe his vile remarks. "Time to scrub and purify you. I've got to make sure all his seed is off of you."

"I haven't been with anybody!" I screamed.

He spat, "Shut up, bitch! I've been watching the two of you get together at night for weeks."

Even in my pain-induced stupor, I realized Sam had been watching me and Brent, not me and Frank. Sam had rammed Frank's car because he drove the same model and color as Brent's. These men were about the same size, composition, and color. Sam thought Frank was Brent! I wasn't about to give away my secret. Sam would never know. I would not lead Sam to my heart. Jesus had given me Brent. I would not let this madman harm Brent too.

The punishment was unbearable. Sam didn't care at all. I knew I must be bleeding between my legs from the force he was using to rub the brush back and forth. I focused on survival. I had to endure and survive. I had my orders. I could do it. Help was coming. Brent was coming. The Lord was helping him find me. The pain was overwhelming, and I blacked out again.

———wwↄ℮ⲧ©©ⲧ℮ↄↄww———

Jesus and the Holy Spirit watched as the horror was developing. Soon, children of God would arise, and they would be able to help.

———wwↄ℮ⲧ©©ⲧ℮ↄↄww———

At the Joiner's house, Brent assimilated information they divulged about Sam's family. Sam had a brother. If they could locate Marty Anderson, maybe he could tell them how to find Sam.

Next, he called the head intercessor, Mrs. Jonesboro, to request prayer. Nothing worked better for a cause than unified prayer. He was assured that everyone would be on top of the situation.

The Joiners, like most of the older generation, did not have a computer. Brent tried to make use of his iPhone. Frustrated, he decided to go home so he could pray, use his own computer, and work. Not knowing who to call after government offices were closed, he dialed Bonnie Fowler's home number. The hour was late, but he didn't care. Bonnie would sympathize and help if she could.

She answered after the second ring, and he said, "Bonnie, I know it's late, but I have information I need you to pursue. Sam has a brother who lives in Kentucky. His name is Marty Anderson. Hopefully, that is his real name. Is there any way you can locate him this evening? I'm on my way home. Call me if you find anything. I have a feeling if anyone knows where Sam is, it will be Marty."

"Sure thing!" she agreed. "I'm on it now. As soon as I have something, I'll call you back."

While driving home, his cell phone chimed, it was Bonnie. "Brent, we've located Paul Martin Anderson in Louisville. I will text his phone number so you can store it in your cell. Let us know if this is a good lead," Bonnie shared.

Seconds later, the text came through, so Brent could place the call. Not waiting to get home, Brent pulled his car onto the side of the road to place the call. Six rings but no answer. It was late in the evening, and most people would be in bed. He left an urgent message on a voice machine, asking the man to return his call at any hour.

Brent's body was extremely tired, even though his mind was overactive. He hadn't slept in almost forty hours. He had paced the night before, worried he had ruined his future with Hope. He had made progress in their relationship but had blown it with one kiss and his declaration of love. To get his mind off it, he'd gone to the gym. The gym catered to people working swing shifts by staying open twenty-four hours. When he had noticed on his cell display that Hope had called from home so early in the morning, he'd panicked. His heart had pounded so hard in his chest that it caused his words to falter. But praise God! He had received a miracle! Somehow, God had revealed Hope's hidden feelings for him. In moments, their relationship had been repaired, restored, and advanced.

In his apartment, he turned on the television, tuning to the local channel for news concerning the kidnapping. He wanted the world to know that his Hope had been taken. He suddenly felt very hungry and went to his refrigerator, which furnished a slice of cold pizza he'd purchased last Saturday. With food and drink in hand, he sat in his lounge chair to watch the news. When he finished eating, the food was heavy in his stomach. Due to a lack of sleep, he could no longer keep his eyes open. Sleep claimed him even though he fought it.

—⁓⁓∘◦◈◦◈◈◦◈◦∘⁓⁓—

I woke up again. I was in his dirty, smelly bed, suffering in agony. Another day was near because I could see faint light through the small camper window. I searched my mind, trying to decide if I'd been raped or not after I'd passed out. I was in terrible pain, but I wasn't sure Sam raped me. I simply prayed that he hadn't.

My feet were tied again to keep me from running. I had made it through the night. I'd survived. What wickedness would I face today? I didn't want to think about it, but I had to find a way to survive. My mouth was so dry that my lips were stuck together. I badly needed something to drink. I hadn't had anything since the water I had with lunch yesterday. I had to use the bathroom again but feared the pain if I somehow managed that.

Sam was sprawled in the lounge chair again, with a bottle of vodka cradled in his arm. At least he'd put his slacks on. The vision of him naked was too much under any circumstances.

I struggled to sit on the side of the bed. Then I managed to stand. I intended to hop or shuffle to the bathroom. I wanted Sam to stay asleep. Without clothes, I could sit on the toilet without assistance. I might be able to drink some water from the sink. Even though my hands were tied, they weren't immobile. I would look for his knife after I finished the tasks. Maybe I could get free.

I was about two feet from the bathroom door when Sam moved in his chair. I stopped and remained quiet, almost afraid to breathe for fear he'd hear me and wake up. When he continued to sleep, I shuffled on, making it just in time to relieve myself. Tears from excruciating pain ran down my cheeks as I bit back a moan. I had to be quiet. Patting myself with toilet paper was almost more that I could bear.

While still seated, I looked for the knife but I couldn't see it anywhere. It would have made things easier if only my hands were free. With that plan foiled, I decided to get a quick drink then try to make it to the back door and hop outside. A naked screaming woman in restraints could surely get somebody's attention. I was definitely in harm's way.

305

Shuffling to the bathroom sink didn't budge him, so I turned on the water. It made a horrible sputtering noise then spat out murky water. I was so thirsty that I didn't care. I was bending to put my mouth in the stream of water when Sam yanked my head up by my hair.

"What do you think you're doing? Can't you see the water is rusty?" he growled.

"I'm thirsty. I need water," I begged.

He pulled me back into the bedroom and pushed me on the bed face first. Then he grumbled, "I'll get you some tea. I make it from bottled water. You can't drink the water here because the pipes are rusty."

No water, but at least I was closer to the back door. I quickly maneuvered to sit and stand. Sam was several yards from me in the small kitchen area, so it was now or never. I hopped over to the little door and twisted the latch. Locked! Fumbling with the lock, I was losing precious time, but I couldn't figure out what was causing it to stick. Then thankfully, the door sprung open. I was about to jump when my head was jerked back again. I was able to scream while the door was open, "Help me! Somebody help me!"

I thrashed like a fish caught on a hook. Having my limbs bound made me feel helpless. I feared a booted kick or a punch in the gut, but neither came. That was a good sign. It usually meant Sam was somewhat sober. He picked me off the floor and placed me in the lounge chair he had previously occupied.

I could tell that he was suffering from a hangover. His brows were pinched together. Plus, he was acting funny. He didn't say anything either which was another good sign.

I watched as he walked to the refrigerator and retrieved a pitcher of tea. After he poured me a glass, he returned the pitcher and grabbed a beer. Great! My high hopes were shattered. He was starting his day early with alcohol. It wouldn't be long before he would be drinking the hard stuff again.

A Dance with the Devil

Brent was awakened by his cell phone ringing. He sat up, disoriented, trying to determine where the phone was. It rang several times before Brent remembered he'd left it to recharge on the bar in his kitchen.

He jumped up, turning over the plate balanced on his lap as he tried to get to the caller. He heard the voice mail alert sound, indicating whoever it was had given up and left a message. It was Bonnie.

She said in her message, "Brent, give me a call as soon as you hear this. We have a possible lead."

His fingers fumbled with the buttons on the phone, his hands shaking violently. What? What lead? His heart was fearfully pounding again. Recently, he needlessly feared rejection when Hope had called. This time, she really was in distress and at someone's mercy. His tango with fear had to stop! Surely, God had come to the rescue!

Bonnie answered her phone, and Brent urged, "Hi, Bonnie, it's me. What have you got?"

She recounted, "A domestic disturbance was just reported. A man witnessed a woman screaming for help at Russell Lake. The man stated she appeared to be naked and being violated. She had been forcibly pulled back into the camper. He said after the door slammed closed, the small camper rocked, which meant to him the tussle was ongoing. The sheriff's office is preparing to check out the situation. I thought I'd give you a call."

"I'm going with them," he insisted.

"I don't think that is wise Brent. First of all, it may not be Hope. Why not wait until they check it out?" she recommended.

"No! Something tells me this is the break we needed. I'm going with or without them," he vowed.

He couldn't tell her his spirit of justice had kicked into overdrive. The Lord was urging him on.

"Okay, I'll ask them to give you a few minutes before heading out. Your name has some pull, so maybe they'll wait," she agreed.

Brent didn't bother to tuck in his shirt. He was thankful he hadn't completely undressed but had fallen asleep with his clothes and shoes on. Grimy as he felt, he didn't care how he looked. Grabbing his cell, wallet, and keys, he rushed out the door.

On the way, he prayed in the Spirit, allowing the Lord to go before him. In his mind, he quoted scripture verses he'd memorized pertaining to God's goodness and justice. Brent recalled how he always vindicated the righteous and just. If any one person was righteous, it was Hope. He'd witnessed firsthand how she worked with the Lord.

Satan kept trying to tempt him with fear. Each time, he'd reject the attack with words of thanksgiving and praise to his God. "Hope is spared from evil's grasp. Hope has been vindicated in the name of the Lord. No weapons formed against her will prosper. Therefore, Satan, your evil tongue will be proved to be in the wrong. Our God has His vindication, and we are saved," he spoke aloud.

The Holy Spirit was ecstatic! The spirit of justice had been set free. The roaring lion was on the hunt! His prey did not have long to live.

In the camper, I watched Sam guzzle the beer then reach in the refrigerator for another. The tea he gave me was sickly sweet but wet.

I wanted to suck it down, but something in my spirit objected. *What is it, Lord?* I asked, remembering finally that He was always around when I needed Him.

Stop drinking! He demanded.

My body was craving the cold liquid, but I knew I needed to obey. He always had my best interest at heart. Something was wrong. Wanting to stay in touch with Him, I prayed silently, *Lord, how much longer? I know you've got a plan.*

Not long! He promised.

Our meeting was cut short. Sam had pulled a small chair in front of me and said, "We need to talk."

Now my focus was on this madman. I replied, "About what? How much pain you think you can inflict on me?"

"No, Hope! I don't know what got into me last night. I'm sorry. The thought of you being with another man was more than I could take. Yesterday morning, I'd planned to beg you to take me back. I missed and needed you. When I saw the two of you kissing and talking about marriage, I snapped. I'm not a fool. I know the cops are after me, so making amends now is out of the question," he spoke while drinking his third beer.

I knew better than to engage him in conversation. It wouldn't be long before his sobriety was replaced with his violent nature. I just listened and pretended to drink the tea. I didn't want him to know I had been ordered to stop drinking it.

I listened to him for a few minutes while he wallowed in pity. He was disgusting. He blamed me for everything. His six pack of beer was gone. He proceeded to break the seal off a fifth of vodka. Oh boy, here we go!

The television was on, but the mute button had been activated. When he reached for the bottle of vodka, something on the channel caught his eye. When he turned the volume up, I could see and hear a broadcast concerning what he'd done yesterday. Never grabbing a glass, he simply drank the vodka straight from the bottle.

Sam moved, blocking the television screen from my view. I had to be satisfied with audio only. What I heard made my heart sing. The newscaster said Frank Addison was in the hospital, recovering and out of danger. His wounds were not fatal. "Thank you, Jesus!" I whispered to my Lord. "Thank you, thank you, and thank you!"

Sam's chair slammed against the wall. I knew he was furious again. His mission had failed.

I tried to focus on him, but something was wrong with my eyes. Instinct prompted me to move away, but my body was heavy, numb, sluggish, and weak.

"What have you done to me?" I implored.

"Shut up, whore! I'm listening to this crap. I need to see if they know anything," he spat.

I must have been drugged. He'd planned it prior to my abduction. Why didn't I realize earlier the tea was a ploy? Sam didn't drink tea.

Lord, talk with me please, I mentally prayed. *Don't let me lose consciousness again.*

I'm here, Hope! Use your gift and focus. You can see me, He soothed.

He was right! Beside me stood my sweet Jesus, just as I remembered Him.

You're here! You're really here! I communicated within my mind.

Yes, love, I've been right here all along. You just couldn't call on me, He informed me.

Are you here to rescue me? I asked.

It won't be long now, but you need to do something first, He coaxed.

I was sad. I wanted my freedom, but I agreed by saying, *What, Lord?*

You need to forgive Sam, He urged.

I couldn't believe my ears! Couldn't He see what Sam had done to me? I was still bound and now drugged. *Why?* I whimpered.

Look at him with your spiritual sight. See the truth! Then you'll understand, He reassured.

I didn't want to look at Sam. Everything in me wanted to refuse. My eyes communicated that fact, causing the Lord to speak to me again.

Hope! Do you trust me? Don't you know I have your best interest at heart? If you don't do this before it's too late, you can't properly heal, He informed.

311

One thing I definitely knew was how much Jesus loved me. Obediently, I looked at Sam with my spiritual sight. What I saw explained everything. Sam was a human puppet. His puppeteer was the most hideous creature I'd ever seen. Every few seconds, I witnessed the true Sam try to escape its clutches, only to have the reins tightened. The creature had Sam pacing the camper, fearfully looking through every window. I watched as the creature physically took Sam's hand, making him grab the gun he'd stowed behind a table. Sam was a prisoner bound and no longer in control, just like me.

I conveyed to the Lord with my eyes that I knew what was happening to Sam.

Now you know, Hope. Sam is not the enemy. He is a victim. Doesn't this knowledge make it easier to forgive him?" Can you do it? Please try for me," He pleaded.

Staring into His lovely pleading eyes, I mentally handed Him all the rage and fear that I had against Sam. I gave Him my hurt, my grief, and my fear. Then I whispered, "Lord, in your name, I forgive my tormentor."

I spoke loud enough for Sam to hear, "I forgive you."

Chains fell from me. I had no substance. I was lighter than air but still grounded to the lounge chair. I knew that a spiritual bondage, which had me more restrained than the ties holding my limbs together, had been broken.

Sam's eyes were pleading with me, but shortly, I witnessed the creature force him to point the pistol at me. Sam's mouth was not his own. The creature was in control, and he said, "Sounds like we have company outside. I'd planned for us to have a pleasurable time today, but if we can't, oh well. I'm not going to jail. If I'm forced, I'll kill you before shooting myself."

I mentally squeezed the Lord's hand and kept repeating in my mind, *All is well*.

———∿∿◦◦◖◗◖◗◦◦∿∿———

Brent followed the sheriff's deputies to Russell Lake. On the way, his cell rang. When he answered, it was Marty Anderson.

312

"Mr. Arnold, I understand you have an emergency. I'm returning your call. What is this all about?" he inquired.

Brent demanded, "Do you have a brother by the name of Sam Anderson?"

"Yes, he's my brother. Why?" Marty asked.

"I'm an attorney with the District Attorney's office, and we are searching for his whereabouts." Brent then informed him, "Sam shot a man and abducted his ex-wife. Would you happen to know where he resides?"

Marty didn't hesitate. "At 102 Russell Lake Drive."

Brent was elated they were headed to the right place. "Thank you, Mr. Anderson. You've been most helpful. You may need to stay in touch with the county sheriff's office. Thanks again." Then he disconnected the call.

When Brent arrived at the address, the officers already had the place surrounded. He wanted to rush in, tear the door off, and rescue Hope. He knew he couldn't without violating protocol.

Then he heard assurance within his spirit. The Lord said, *Wait! My timing is perfect. Justice will prevail.*

Inside the camper, the creature was making Sam pace like a cat, snarling, and growling. My only guarantee of safety was standing beside me, holding my hands.

While Sam was focusing on the cops, Jesus was focusing on me. He soothed me by singing in my ear; *He will set me free and place in me in a large place. He is on my side. It is better to trust in the Lord and to take refuge in Him than to put confidence in man. What can man do to me?*

My heart made the connection. It understood what he was trying to convey. I needed to take refuge in Him. Why hadn't I done this earlier? I needed to put on His armor.

Lord, I understand. May I rest in your armor again? I asked.

You have something even better than my armor, Hope. Use it! You have My name. Remember who you are, He informed. Then He empowered my memory. *What did you and I do together recently?*

We got married! The coronation ceremony! God's acceptance of me as your bride! I exclaimed.

Yes, sweet! Wear your royalty proudly!" He said.

I remembered everything, accepting who I was. Instantly, I was surrounded by God's mighty angels. My friend the eagle was standing alongside the Lord Jesus. I was dressed in my royal clothes and crown. I had help of the most awesome kind. What could man do to me?

I was granted an awesome sight. I witnessed Satan's fear when he saw me sitting in the lounge chair with my body bound, dressed in my royal clothes and crown. The hideous creature left! He was not a fool! He knew my bindings were his idea, and he'd be facing judgment soon. Sam had not been released. The controlling reins had been given to a giant demon. Satan left one of his guards in command. It now ruled Sam with fear. I honestly felt sorry for the man who had been so mean to me. He'd never be free.

I heard the police screaming through a voice amplifier that the camper was surrounded. I knew my freedom was near. Then I saw the giant lean down and whisper in Sam's ear, causing Sam's eyes to get wide with fright. Immediately, he pointed the gun at me. He planned to kill me first.

The Lord squeezed my hand. I knew it was over. Sam had violated the ultimate rule. He'd come against God's child and His Son's bride. God didn't have any mercy. No one was pleading for Sam.

While Jesus and the angels watched motionlessly, I sat quietly. I watched as God's hand came down from heaven, twisting Sam's wrist, pointing the gun at him. The noise was deafening. The horrific sight made me scream at the top of my lungs. The next thing I saw was the door of the camper bursting open and two forms standing in the doorway. The lion angel leaped over Brent's head to subdue the demon giant that had controlled Sam before it could get away. My sweet Jesus killed the devilish thing.

I was finally in Brent's arms. I was so happy. I was naked to the human eye, covered in my own bloody filth. In Jesus's eyes, I was His queen. I'd made Him proud. I was free in more ways than most would ever know.

Restoring

I was transported by ambulance to County Memorial, with Brent following closely in his car. He wasn't about to let me out of his sight.

Over the next few days, I was under heavy sedation most of the time. The burns on my body required an extremely painful but necessary treatment for me to heal properly.

During the drug-induced coma, I had a sweet reunion with my Jesus. All things have to move forward, and it was time to get reacquainted with my future mate.

I woke to the sound of someone praying for me in the Spirit. I also heard my sweet Jesus verbally answering the prayers. The voice praying for me wasn't familiar.

When I finally opened my eyes, my spiritual sight was in full force. Standing over me was a large angel with the face of a man. Tending my wounds was a beautiful nurse Mamie Ross.

"Hello, child. I'm glad you've decided to join the land of the living again," she chirped. "My Jesus tells me that you have been healing with Him these many hours."

I knew I could be honest with her. She had all the evidence I needed. Her nurse's uniform was white and radiant. Her robe was far brighter than any bleached white garment. Her words were on target with what had happened, but the large angel standing next to her was the best proof.

"Yes, ma'am," I agreed. "He and I have been resting in God's house for a while. He said my body needed tending and suggested a short vacation in His presence while I healed. I took Him up on the offer. Am I okay?"

"Yes, child, you're going to be fine," she pledged.

"No, you don't understand. Was I violated sexually?" I timidly asked.

She smiled. "Your private parts were rubbed raw, but there was no evidence of penetration. You suffered chemical burns on most of your body, cuts, and bruises on your wrists and ankles, a cracked lower rib, and a lot of your hair has been pulled out. Never fear! Your hair will grow back, your rib will heal, and old Mamie loves to massage you with ointment so your skin will look like new."

Quietly, she added, "I lay hands on you, child. I pray in the Spirit while I minister. With each rub, I ask God to let the ointment soothe the pain away."

I knew what she was trying to tell me. She was testing my comprehension. "Your gift is healing. You minister love and care along with your gift. A beautiful angel stands by your side."

Her eyes lit up as she nodded in agreement. "Oh, you see him, do you? Good! He and I are going to take good care of you. Mr. Brent asked me personally to watch over you. I keep a foldout cot close by so I can be next to you. It allows me to tend you as much as possible during my time off."

"Time off? Do you mean Brent has you working a double shift for my benefit?" I asked, concerned.

"No problem, child. I wouldn't have it any other way. Even when I'm on duty, I check on you often. You're in my unit," she stated firmly.

"Are you on or off the clock?" I asked.

She acknowledged, "I'm off. I told your man if he wanted to see you, he'd better hurry. Mamie is tired. I need a nap. It looks like I'll be allowed to go home today since you're awake. Brent will want to be your caretaker. I hear you two need to do some planning."

Shortly, Brent knocked on the door, requesting permission to enter. He was a sight for my sore eyes. I truly loved him. I reached for him and grimaced. My whole body hurt. It appeared I was bandaged from head to foot.

Seeing my pain, he came to me quickly. "Don't move! I'm here," he urged. "How are you?"

"Mamie assures me that I'm going to mend with time. She's seeing to it," I said, rejoiced. "How's Frank?"

"Being stubborn and hardheaded. Frank wants to be released against the doctor's orders. If it weren't for Cindy keeping him straight and keeping continually updated, he would have flown the coop," answered Brent.

I mused, "I'm happy for them. He is good for her, and it seems she may be good for Frank."

Then I let my mind drift. What would have happened to Cindy's newly found faith if Frank had been killed? I shuddered at the thought. Instantly, I thanked the Lord for sparing her from that hell. I also thanked Him again for keeping Frank alive.

I realized Brent might not know the truth behind Sam's ugly deeds. I had to explain, "Brent, Frank took the bullets for you. Sam thought Frank was you."

Puzzled, he asked, "What makes you say that?"

I said, "Sam had been watching us for a while. The morning he shot Frank, he'd been hiding somewhere close and overheard us talking about getting married. The thought of me loving someone else put him over the edge. The rest of the day, he planned to kill you and kidnap me. He scrubbed me with bathroom cleaner because he thought we were already sexually involved."

"My God!" Brent exclaimed.

I continued, "I finally figured out that he went to my office to confront me and spotted Frank's car. He thought it was yours. Frank and you are similar, not your features, but your size and coloring. That's the reason Sam ambushed us at work."

Brent exclaimed angrily, "In light of what you're telling me, I think he must have been planning to abduct you that morning. That's probably why your vehicle wouldn't start. It had been tampered with."

"I think you may be right," I agreed.

I went on to explain to him something that would be hard for most to understand. "Brent, you know that I have extra gifts. Well, you, and now Mamie, but that is beside the point. Jesus helped me to see during my ordeal. Jesus showed me the real Sam loved me and didn't want to do those horrible things to me. He allowed me to see the cause. It was horrible. Sam was Satan's puppet. Every movement, every word, and most thoughts were being controlled by Satan. Sam didn't have free will. I watched Sam struggle with Satan, and I felt sorry for him. The truth set me free. All the hate and fear in me left as I emotionally and verbally forgave Sam. A few minutes after the gun went off, you were there. What I'm trying to say is that I had the chance to tell Sam I forgave him before he died."

Brent's face contorted. I could see he was having trouble accepting what I'd said. I squeezed his hand for reassurance. "I know you claim me as yours already. You also feel violated because of what happened. Trust me. If you don't find it in your heart to forgive Sam, anger will destroy you. For me, Brent, for Jesus, please let it go! Our marriage vows have to be free from stumbling blocks. If we are to be one, I can't bear the burden. I'd know why you were self-destructing. I would be the cause. Let it go! Please? Sam is dead! Don't keep beating up a dead man for Satan's actions," I begged.

I watched as Brent bowed his head and asked Jesus for his forgiveness. Then we both held each other and cried. At last, the stress and emotional pressure were being released.

That day, I ate and laughed, even though it was painful. The knowledge of being healed before it manifested was a heady thing. Time was on my side.

Visitors were kept to a minimum because I tired easily. Mom, Dad, Brent's parents, and Mark and Judy were the only ones allowed to see me that day. Frank politely rolled his wheelchair into my room unattended. When we laid eyes on each other for the first time since that fateful day, I felt even more stress drain away. My friend was healing too.

Frank made a joke of the situation, "I bet the office is in turmoil. Their best workers have been shelved for a bit. Hurry up and get mobile so we can race down the halls in our wheelchairs."

I laughed at Frank's remark then grimaced. Brent chased Frank out of my room. Laughing was painful for me, and Brent was trying to protect me.

News was spreading that I was awake. By afternoon, I had cards from all the boys and my room was wall-to-wall in flowers. Friends and church family were sending beautiful arrangements. They had waited until I could enjoy them. The room smelled divine. I could close my eyes and pretend I was in a flower garden instead of an antiseptic hospital.

The next morning, Joan came to see me. I was relieved she had placed me on family emergency leave so I wouldn't have to use all my sick leave. It also held my job for me, so I didn't have to worry about being unemployed. She assured me the office was dealing with my absence. She didn't stay long. I'd just returned from treatment, and Mamie was waiting for me.

Mamie's loving touch and encouraging prayers continued to heal me inside and out. I was glad Brent had hired her specifically to care for my wounds. I enjoyed our frank spiritual conversations, which were very refreshing. During our sessions, I could be honest and candid. I felt a deep bond with her. My intense feeling prompted me to go to the Lord in prayer about it.

"Lord, thank you for my new friend. Mamie is very special. With her, I can be myself. I sense something more, but I don't know what it is. Would you please enlighten me?" I prayed.

He responded, *Do you remember my four companions? My personal angels?*

"Yes, sir," I confirmed.

You've read about them and you have seen them. How did they present themselves in the script or in your vision? He asked.

I had to recall. When they were described in scripture, they were always together. The first time I actually saw them was at church, and they were all together and touching. That was my clue. I had the answer. I knew!

"Lord, they like to be connected to each other," I replied.

Yes! They work better as a team. That is why you feel such a bond with Mamie. The feeling is as intense as your bond with Brent but in a different way. Together, you are my harvesting machine. Separately, you come against evil, He informed me.

That was right! The three of us are followed by one of His angels. We are connected. It will be interesting to see how we work for the Lord.

"Thanks, Lord. It is good to know that my friendship with Mamie will continue outside of the hospital. She and I are part of your team, aren't we?" I inquired.

I have similar teams all over the world who are guided by my spirit and followed by these angels. Time and space don't matter

320

to us. We are all connected. When needs arise, hundreds of thousands of more angels can be dispatched. They are ordered by their commanding angels who are with me in heaven. Our enemy has similar angels. They are the giants you've seen who roam with Satan's followers, He shared.

It occurred to me that I hadn't met one of the four angels yet. I'd seen it but hadn't met its human companion. Part of our team was missing.

"Lord? Where's our other companion?" I inquired.

You met his commander in heaven with me. In time, you'll meet him too. The Ox is a very special angel. I will need the three of you by my side to be able to work efficiently. The angels following you, Brent, and Mamie are part of his team. They are my giants among men, who are commanded by their chiefs, who follow me around always. In time, this mighty giant angel will alert you, and you'll join forces. I will show you, Brent, and Mamie how to assist the Ox with its specific assignment. Don't fret, it will come, He informed me.

My curiosity was heightened. I wanted to know more, so I pressed Him with more questions. "I'm trying to understand the best way I can. Please tell me if I've got it right. You have commander angels in heaven with you like our defense secretary here in the States. They give direction to your giant angels who are like our generals here on earth. Then if the giants need help, they call others into service of a lesser rank. The same chain of command exists in our military on earth."

Yes! You've got it! How do you think man came up with ranks and divisions? Everything was my idea in the first place, He happily exclaimed.

I was enjoying our conversation, but Mamie had administered a sedative so I could rest. My body was feeling heavy, with uncontrollable sensations which forced me to sleep. Sometimes, I rested in the presence of the Lord, but other times, I just dreamed. I was happy with either because both were pleasant. I'd lived through a nightmare with eyes wide open, hopefully for the last time.

When I woke from my last sedation, I had company in my room. Brent had another man with him. I couldn't see who it was because he wasn't facing me. When he turned around, I gasped. It was Sam's brother, Marty.

Marty looked so much like Sam it was scary. I knew he was nothing like his brother, though. Marty was a good person who had made a good life for himself. Today, he looked worried and drawn. I assumed it was because he was in town to collect Sam's body for burial.

Marty spoke softly, "Hello, Hope. I'm so deeply sorry for what you had to endure. My brother had a mental challenge that he didn't control well. Due to his alcoholism, our parents didn't allow Sam to access his inheritance when they died. They put his share in a trust under my authority. I had specific instructions to give him what he desperately needed and only if he was sober. Now that he is dead, the balance comes to me. My conscience won't allow me to accept it, knowing what he did to you, Hope. You were his wife, and in his own perverted way, he loved you. I'm having my attorney draw up the necessary paperwork for Sam's share to be given to you. It will help with your expenses and give you a fresh start."

I stammered, "Marty, I don't know what to say. I'm grateful, but I don't feel right about your offer."

"Please, I insist. I've talked with your friend, and he assures me it can be done. It will give me peace, plus something good will come from Sam's death," Marty cried.

Marty leaned over and kissed me lightly on my forehead before leaving. After he was gone, I didn't know how to act or what to say. In an attempt to eliminate any painful movements, Brent took my hand, sitting beside me slowly on the bed. "The amount is staggering, Hope. It's over two million dollars."

I was astonished. "What? You're kidding?"

As I reminisced, I babbled, "I never met their parents. They both died the year before we got married. Sam never spoke of an inheritance. I remember Sam envied Marty. Sam even felt contempt for his brother at times. Now I understand. No wonder Marty had a good life. He didn't drink or gamble. He used his share wisely and formed a successful business. Wow! I'm overwhelmed."

Wedding Arrangements

I have been cooped up in the hospital for too long. I was going crazy. It had been three weeks, but some of my wounds still needed bandages. Every day, I could move a little easier, with less pain. My wrists looked horrible. I expect there will be ugly scars on them for the rest of my life. Struggling had caused the ties to cut me severely. My hair had to be cut extremely short. Mom's hairdresser advised that, with proper care and frequent haircuts, people wouldn't notice the large patches where hair had been pulled out. I was worried Brent wouldn't like it. He'd often commented on my long hair. When he saw my new haircut, he said he liked it and that it was cute.

My body was still red with patches where the scabs were slowly coming off. Mamie explained that those were the areas that had absorbed the most chemical. Thank God my private parts were healing quicker than others. I believed it had something to do with Mamie's specific style of caring. She had doubled and sometimes tripled the ointment in that area. I was mending.

The original wedding date I wanted had to be scrapped. I needed more time to heal emotionally and physically. Like any bride, I wanted to look pretty, but I wasn't there yet. Honeymoons should be special, but I wasn't ready for that either.

Amber came by regularly with loads of bride magazines for me to look through. My small quaint little ceremony was growing into something huge. Mom and Olivia were having fun planning a large reception. Our pastor visited me often while I was in the hospital. Once, when Brent and I were alone, he made a special visit for our marriage consultation.

Brent planned on having his dad as best man, with his brother and Frank as groomsmen. Since it was growing, I asked Judy to be my matron of honor and Amber to be my bridesmaid. My ring bearer had to be Greg. Lacey fit the bill perfectly for our flower girl. Dad would give me away one last time.

I wanted out of my cramped hospital room to look for a dress and choose bridesmaid dresses and clothes for the kids. It was my wedding, but everyone but me was having fun.

Brent noticed my blue mood when he came to see me. "What is wrong?" he asked.

I didn't have the heart to complain. Everyone was being so nice, trying to do something special for us. I just felt trapped. "I think I want to go home. No, to be honest, I want to go shopping," I replied.

My answer made him laugh out loud. He chuckled. "Is that all! I thought you were in pain or feeling sick. All you have is cabin fever!"

"Don't laugh! I am tired of looking at these same four walls. I want to join in the fun. It's my wedding too," I retorted.

Realizing my distress, he hugged me close. He whispered in my ear, "I've got a surprise for you. I have been carrying it for a while, and I think it's time to show you. You need to cheer up."

He reached inside his jacket pocket then handed me a beautiful small blue suede box. I knew what it contained, and I started crying. I opened the box and gasped at the lovely ring. The center stone was a carat-and-a-half diamond surrounded by small diamonds, creating a flower petal. The band was almost completely covered in small diamonds. It looked like a rose made of diamonds. I'd never seen anything like it before. I felt very special.

I shocked him when I gave the box back. Apparently, he thought for a moment that I didn't want it. I asked, "Will you put it on me? I don't want to touch it until you have placed in on my finger."

He graciously obliged. The ring fit perfectly, and it definitely brightened my day, my life.

"It looks good on you. Do you really like it?" Brent hesitated.

It felt like I had a baseball stuck in my throat. I could hardly speak. I was very emotional when I answered, "It's the most beautiful thing I've ever seen!"

"When I saw it, I thought of you. You're like a beautiful flower, with many layers precious to me," he stated.

"I can't wait to be your wife, Brent. You make me feel so special," I choked out.

Grinning, he said, "We need to set a date. The doctor thinks your skin will be healed and cleared soon, and the risk of infection is over. You should be released any day now. What about somewhere near the end of September since we missed Labor Day?"

I didn't want him to worry that I didn't want to rush to marry him, but I had some concerns. "Brent, I need to talk to my doctor about something first," I said shyly.

"Okay. What's the problem?" he inquired.

Biting my lip as I looked out the window to keep from crying, I whispered, "I'm still very sore, even though Mamie assures me I'm healing nicely."

"Oh! Honey, look at me! I want you. I can wait for your body. I need you to be my wife. I know you're healing, and if I have to wait for months, I can. I love you," he insisted.

I lost it! I sobbed inconsolably. This sweet man knew my heart and loved me for me.

"What did I say? I'm sorry if I upset you!" Brent exclaimed.

I blurted out, "Shut up! You didn't say anything wrong. You said everything right. Prior experiences made me afraid. Don't you understand? Both of my previous marriages were based on sex? I was worried sex was also on your mind."

"Don't get me wrong, Hope. Sex is on my mind. However, I've got sense enough to know marriage isn't just about sexual desire. Marriage is a commitment, sharing and building a home together. I want what our parents have. I think you do too. Sex is just a wonderful bonus. I'm sure when our time comes, it will be fabulous," he affirmed.

With all that settled, we decided to set our wedding date for September 30. I prayed a few more weeks of healing time would be enough.

———∽∽∾⊙∾⊙∾∽∽———

We were relaxing with the television when there was a slight knock on my door. When I bid whoever it was to enter, a small head poked around the door. It was Greg, followed by Olivia.

"Ms. Hope! Ms. Hope! Is that really you?" he squealed.

"Come here you!" I whooped.

Running up to the bed, he said, "You've cut off all your hair. It's like mine."

Brent helped him up onto the bed so we could hug. "I'm growing it long again," I confided. "I don't like it short. I had to cut it so the nurse could put medicine on my scalp."

"You okay now?" he asked anxiously. "I've been real worried."

Olivia chimed in, "This little tyke has worried himself sick and running us ragged. Last night, he cried so hard, thinking you weren't ever coming back. I had to promise to bring him to visit so he would go to bed."

"I love you, Ms. Hope," Greg whimpered.

To keep all of us from crying, I changed the subject. "Greg, would you like to be in my wedding? I need a ring bearer, and you'd be perfect."

"What's that?" he asked.

I explained, "It's a very special person who brings my new husband the ring to be placed on my finger, announcing we are married."

"You think I'm special?" he exclaimed.

"More than you know, kiddo, more than you know," I responded, hugging him tightly.

Observing our reunion gave Brent a wonderful idea. He knew in his heart what he was considering was right. That afternoon, he would research the matter.

Everyone's visit was cut short by the doctor coming in to examine Hope. Only family members could stay. Brent gave me a hug, vowing to see me later. Olivia and Greg left after I promised it wouldn't be long before I would see him again.

I took advantage of my time with the doctor by drilling him with all kinds of questions. Not only was I anxious about having sex, I was worried I might have other female issues. I had sustained punches and kicks to my midsection during my marriage as well as this last incident. Satan knew Jesus used His chosen to have a family. I was sure it was the reason for causing Sam to hit and kick me there. I wanted a family with Brent. The sooner I knew the truth, the faster I could relax. If I was damaged, I needed to know.

Dr. Jones was a wonderful man. He was kind, compassionate, and helpful. He couldn't answer my questions, though. He wasn't a gynecologist, but he did venture that he didn't think it should be a problem because I hadn't hemorrhaged. He asked if I needed my gynecologist to visit. He could schedule an examination at the hospital. Money wasn't a problem, so I asked Dr. Jones to please make the arrangements. I needed to know.

After that was resolved, he proceeded to inspect my wounds. The results were good news. I was elated to learn I could go home in two to three days.

Mamie came in as soon as Dr. Jones left. She had a few hours before her shift began. She wanted to apply more ointment. It was during her loving massage that I shared Brent's and my wedding plans. I invited her to come. After she washed her hands, she told me to bend my head so she could look at my scalp. I thought she was going to dab it with salve. She shocked me by stating, "I'm going to have my hairdresser look at your hair. It may be long enough by September 30 to add some extensions. Would you like that?"

"Extensions? You mean they can do that for white folks?" I joked.

"Sure! You'd look good with a short bob. Nothing too long. That wouldn't look natural under the circumstances, but just enough to make your hair look full for the wedding," she suggested.

"I'd love it!" I exclaimed. "I hadn't considered my hair, but you're right. I would prefer a feminine look for my wedding pictures. Thank you for being so considerate, Mamie."

Happy with my answer, Mamie offered, "Consider it my treat. I'll get Ellen to visit after you leave the hospital so she can practice."

I couldn't believe how this day had come full circle. I'd been depressed, but now, I was on cloud nine—officially engaged, going home in a few days, and getting a new do.

Most people would say they hit the floor running after being set free from a cage. This chick hit the floor shopping. I'd rested enough. Hours after I was released from the hospital, Mom took me to a wedding boutique.

On the way, I prayed, *Lord, please go before and pick your special dress. Let it catch my eye so I'll know it was handpicked by you. I want you in every part of my life, especially in this whirlwind of wedding plans. I can't waste time trying to find the right dress. I know firsthand you have exquisite taste."*

I heard Him laughing. *Your gown was my Father's concept. He ordered the angels to dress you. Not I. Look for something cheery. That will be the dress made especially for you. It represents this happy occasion.*

"Something cheery," I repeated aloud.

Mom asked, "What'd you say?"

I smiled. "I was thinking of a cheery dress, nothing too formal, and something lighthearted but elegant."

"So you aren't thinking white?" She hesitated.

"I don't think so. I'll know it when I see it." I answered confidently.

We looked and looked but didn't find anything cheery. I was beginning to think it wasn't at this store when the manager approached us. She informed us a new shipment had arrived yesterday that hadn't been unpacked yet. When I asked if one of the dresses was cheery-looking, her eyes lit up. She declared, "I've got just the ticket. It's a new design made with unusual fabric. I think you'll like it. I'll be right back."

I knew it was the perfect gown before she even returned with it. When she'd said "unusual fabric," my heart had soared.

The dress took my breath away. It was iridescent white, with hints of different colors almost too soft to see. The fabric was very sheer, requiring a lining. It was a replica of my convent robe, except it was fuller, with more material. When I tried it on, it fit like a glove. It had fitted sleeves that would cover my regenerating skin, a sweetheart neckline, a fitted waist, and a slightly flared skirt. It looked like a Cinderella dress. The gown was perfect. Mom agreed it was the one. Her eyes were bright with excitement.

When the manager asked if I was wearing a veil, I replied, "No." Then I asked, "Have you got a small tiara or a wreath like headpiece?"

She flew out of the room, reappearing with a box. When she showed me the headpiece, I gasped again. The box held a beautiful small crown of pearls—not a tiara, but a crown. It was perfect. I felt royal again.

While we were there, we also inspected bridesmaid dresses. I found two styles I liked. I asked the manager to mark them as my choices to show Judy and Amber when they came by. They could choose either style from my two selections. It didn't matter if they liked the same style or not, as long as the dresses were the same yellow color. My girls had to be dressed in sunshine. Next, I chose a flower girl dress for Lacey. It was a prissy little wedding dress with a yellow sash.

After all that excitement, I was worn-out. My body wasn't used to all the exercise. Mom promised to get Greg fitted in a suit or tux exactly like Brent's. All I had to worry about were the flowers.

That night, when Brent came in after work, I asked if he had made arrangements to use the church for our day. I didn't want to assume anything. He laughed and assured me all was ready. We were to be wed at 3:30 p.m. on Saturday, September 30. He had an announcement included in the bulletin, inviting everyone to attend. He added that our mothers were planning a big reception with all the fancy trimmings at the Boys' Home.

Everything was coming together nicely. I even convinced him to select yellow ties with whatever suit or tux he chose for his group.

My test results came back the next day from my gynecologist, informing me there was no damage to my reproductive system. He even stated I was healthy enough for a nice honeymoon if I were willing. Life couldn't be any better.

Every day, I expressed my gratitude to the Lord. I kept Him involved in everything—my worries, my joys, everything.

To keep from losing my mind, I went back to work during my second week home from the hospital. When I asked for three days off to go on a honeymoon, I was shocked it was approved. I had been thinking my request would be denied or I would be reprimanded. Either way, I was prepared to take leave, even if it was without pay. Working made the time fly. Days then weeks came and went. Suddenly, it was the Friday before our wedding day, the night of our rehearsal.

When five o'clock finally arrived, I was immediately out the door. I had to contact Ellen to verify if my extensions were ready. She would come to my apartment in the morning, and I needed everything in place. My coworkers loved my trial hairdo. The extensions were very natural-looking. Most people thought I had cut my hair instead of having hair weaved in.

We had fun that evening; no one was stressed. We just went with the flow. Afterward, Brent's parents paid for a nice rehearsal dinner at a local restaurant. We enjoyed the meal then said our good-byes. The wedding countdown was on.

Amber and Lacey spent the night so we could play. We painted each other's nails, ate, and enjoyed the night. The three of us ate a half gallon of butter pecan ice cream! Amber and I stayed up late; we were wired. Poor Lacey couldn't keep her eyes open. I was glad Amber and I had become close. She really was a fine, caring person under all her makeup and facade.

It felt like I had just gone to sleep when Ellen rang my doorbell at 6:30 a.m. It was early, and I was weary. She looked at me, shook her head, and frowned. "You need an espresso."

"Good morning to you too," I greeted. "Give me a few minutes to make some strong coffee please."

While we waited for the coffee to brew, I asked how long she thought my hairdo would take this time. I was shocked when she guessed, "About four hours."

"You've got to be kidding!" I flinched.

"Nope. Most of my customers try to sleep," she suggested.

Jokingly, I remarked, "Good. I'll do that."

I was grateful Ellen had a soft touch. Braiding the strands of real hair into my own hair was smooth and painless, so I was able to doze. It was a little tight when she finished but not uncomfortable. My pretty little bob cupped right under my chin. I was very pleased.

Amber and Lacey woke up about thirty minutes before Ellen finished. Even Amber said she couldn't tell it was a weave. It looked like my real hair.

Mom arrived shortly after Ellen left. She was also very complimentary. When she told me the reason she came by, I wanted to cry. She and Dad agreed that it was time I inherited something old from my grandmother. She handed me a jewelry case. When I opened it, her pearl necklace and earrings were cradled in soft satin. Even though they were old, they were the perfect shade to match my crown and dress.

Mom smiled. "Honey, when you put that pearl crown on your head the other day, I realized her set of pearls were a perfect finishing touch. I expressed my idea to your dad, and he went straight to our bank's safety deposit box to retrieve Grandma's pearls. We want you to have them."

"Thanks, Mom," I said as I tearfully hugged her.

United

I was gathering my things, preparing to leave for the church when my doorbell rang again. This time it was Mamie. I was glad she came but anxious about the reason.

She greeted me by hugging my neck. She looked me up and down then turned me around. She approved then stated what was on her mind. "Ellen did you up good. I think it's her best work yet. But that's not why I'm here. I came to loan you something."

"Loan me something? What is it?" I asked.

She answered, "It's not an it. I want to share my spiritual gift. Hope, Mamie is getting old, and I don't have any children to whom I can pass along this gift. Please give me the honor of sharing it with me until you have a child of your own to share it with. You already know my gift is healing and mercy. Join with me today and be part of it with me. The Lord has shown me we have connected already, and we need to be unified for Him this way."

I was confused because she was having a hard time expressing herself. I mentally asked the Lord for help to understand. *Lord, I know Mamie has come in your name. Help me understand. Please give me wisdom. I think I know, but I need full revelation.*

Remember the angels' wings touching? Mamie is trying to connect with you on a spiritual level by sharing her gifts of healing. Give her the honor and bestow your gift on her at the same time. In this manner, you can work together for me, He disclosed.

With revelation, I now responded to Mamie, "I'd love to share your gift. However, I'll only accept yours if you'll accept mine. The Lord just told me we need to share."

She grinned. "You're willing? I was afraid by the look on your face that you didn't want to take it."

She came near me just like the Holy Spirit did when He gave me my gifts. She placed her hands on my heart. That must be the place He touched her to give her the gift of healing. I decided to lay one of my hands on her eyes and the other on her right ear. Once we were touching, we both started praying in the Spirit. My chest felt warm, and my hands got hot. I was receiving, and she was accepting. The holy fire was being shared.

When we stopped praying, we both were overcome. I looked at Mamie, and she had an awestruck expression on her face. I knew what was happening. She was seeing angels.

"You've never seen them before?" I asked.

When she spoke, she exclaimed, "No! This is my first time. I knew they were around. I knew I had one following me. I never imagined they were so magnificent."

I was happy for her. "Are my hands hot because I have your gift?" I asked.

"Yes, child," she affirmed.

Because we were connected, I felt the need to warn her. "Mamie, you'll be able to see and hear evil as well as angels. Please be prepared. The Lord told me we are supposed to help each other with these gifts. I may not have your level of healing. You may not have my level of seeing or hearing. We might only have enough to assist when the need arises. We have awesome gifts!?" I said, hugging her.

"Sure do, child, sure do," she agreed.

"Mamie also came to help you get ready. I can see folks bailed out on you. I'm going with you to get you dressed," she said to change the subject.

I laughed. "It appears they have. My maid of honor and bridesmaid are going to meet me at the church. Mom had to get Dad and Greg ready. I am definitely on my own. I would love to have your assistance."

I was glad Mamie drove me to the church. It solved the problem of what to do with my SUV. After the ceremony, Brent and I would be leaving on our honeymoon. I would have to leave my vehicle at church or find someone to drive it home for me.

At the church, we lugged everything to the bridal suite where I would be getting ready. In less than an hour and a half, I would be Mrs. Brent Arnold. I couldn't wait. I had a flashback to both times I had feelings of apprehension prior to a marriage ceremony, but not joy. Even then the Lord was trying to derail my plans to keep me from heartache and pain, but I wouldn't listen. I was grateful that was no longer a problem. I listen and seek Him because I cannot bear not being in His presence.

My maids were lovely in their yellow dresses, and Lacey was a little doll. Amber had curled Lacey's hair into beautiful ringlets. When the florist came in with our bouquets, she had a crown of sweetheart yellow roses with hints of baby's breath and greenery made specifically for Lacey to wear. Now Lacey truly looked like a cherub.

I had no idea what Mom's florist, Doris, had designed for the church, the maids, the groomsmen or me. The flowers were another surprise. Doris allowed me two recommendations. First was color scheme, second was for Lacey's crown of flowers. She insisted the remainder had to be a surprise.

When she showed us our bouquets of roses in yellow and white, I was elated. My maids had white roses and greenery in small nosegays. I had both colors in a large bouquet adorned with baby's breath, greenery, and lace. They were breathtaking.

We were ready and about to walk to the sanctuary when Amber screeched, "Wait! I forgot your something blue."

She ran to her handbag and pulled out the cutest little blue garter. She knelt down, insisting I allow her to put it on my leg. When she did, I felt complete. I wore something old around my neck and on my ears. I had something new—my hair and gown. Mamie had given me the something borrowed, and Amber had given me something blue. All I needed now was the man.

The music was playing, everything was in place, and I was at Dad's left hand. I gently placed my right hand through his extended elbow as we waited for our cue. Maids walked down the aisle to the beat of the wedding march. Then Lacey followed and was accompanied by Greg, who looked so cute in his little blue tux. I watched them, gazed at the lovely room Doris had decorated with flowers, and then searched for Brent, who was patiently waiting for me.

He looked handsome in a dark blue tux and with a yellow tie. Yellow just did something for the man. When I saw him after my coronation, he'd been wearing a yellow shirt. His tanned skin, complimented by the yellow color, had made me soft inside then, but even more so now.

When Dad and I were cued to march, my heart started pounding. Holy matrimony would be mine at last. I was finally receiving my one true mate. Our eyes were locked on each other before our hands were joined. I saw those blue eyes I'd come to adore sparkle with tears, joy, and light of the Lord shining through. My smile was radiant. I've never been happier on earth. It will never compare with my heavenly experience, though.

When Dad placed my hand in Brent's, and we faced Pastor Craig, I had another surprise. Pastor Craig was radiating with the Holy Spirit like the first time I saw him. Brent and I were being married by the Lord's servant.

After we repeated our vows, exchanged rings, and kissed before all the witnesses in the room, I heard bells. I knew the sound wasn't coming from our church. Heaven must have been rejoicing with us.

The pastor introduced us as Mr. and Mrs. Brent Arnold, and guests were invited to the reception at the Boys' Home. Pictures were taken, and the wedding party gave Brent and me a proper send-off. His BMW had been decorated, complete with cans tied to the rear bumper.

Once we arrived at the Boys' Home, we took a few more pictures and greeted everyone. We were ushered to dressing rooms to change into more comfortable clothes.

The food, drinks, and cakes were wonderful. Our moms had outdone themselves. Brent and I enjoyed the party, but we were also eager to be alone. When the time came to excuse ourselves properly, we were sent off in style again. Bubbles were blown, birdseed was thrown, people cheered, and some cried while happiness ruled.

During our drive to our destination, I told Brent about the exchange of spiritual gifts between Mamie and me. I also shared with him everything the Lord told me about the three of us being connected. When I finished, he asked if I would share my gifts with him. Brent had been fascinated with my gifts since the night we came against evil at the Boys' Home. He wanted to experience what I did firsthand to understand better. I thought it was a wonderful idea and could hardly wait to get to the resort.

Once we arrived at our honeymoon suite, another surprise awaited me. Brent hadn't mentioned it, so when he sat me down on the bed and looked in my eyes, I thought, *here we go.* I was totally wrong. He sat me down to keep me from falling down.

He said, "Honey, I have something for you. A personal gift from my heart, but if you don't agree, I'll understand. Just know that I love you with all my being and want to make you happy. I promised God the day we connected at the barbecue that I would share you. However, I'll only share you this way."

Then he handed me an envelope. When I opened it, there was a form inside. I pulled the paper out with shaking hands. I didn't have a clue what this was all about. When I unfolded the form, my eyes couldn't believe what they read. It was an application for adoption. The section describing the child involved had a name already typed—Greg Hines.

I sobbed. "You want us to adopt Greg?"

He nodded. "Yes, honey. If I'm to share you with anyone, it will be with our children. In my own Father's honor, I felt it was the right thing to do. You love this little boy so much. If it hadn't been for Greg, I never would have fallen in love with you. It's only right to make him part of our family. Do you agree?"

"Yes! Yes!" I declared. "I love you more now than ever! I didn't think I could possibly love you more."

After the sweetest, the most passionate night of her life, Hope wanted Brent to experience her precious gifts. Not only would they be connected physically, they would be connected spiritually as well. She prayed, *Lord, I've given my heart to your brother. Let me share our precious gifts with him. This will allow me to be connected with Mamie and be connected with your spirit of authority and justice. I want this bond, and I know you do too. Bless Brent with the experience of holy fire exchange tonight.*

After asking for the Lord's blessing, I took Brent's handsome face in my hands. I placed a kiss on his lips and told him to be still. I explained, "Brent, I've asked the Lord to bless our spiritual

337

connection of gifts." Then I asked, "When he shared his gift of justice, how did he impart it to you?"

Brent answered, "He took my head in his hands and placed his forehead on mine. Why?"

I smiled, leaned forward placing my forehead against his. Then I placed my right hand over his left and my left hand over his right ear. I asked the Lord to make the exchange.

He and I sat on the bed engulfed with awesome sensations. Like before when Mamie received my gifts, I knew when Brent received them. He could see angels, and he was awestruck. My mind was filled with compassion, wisdom, and a strong sense of right and wrong.

Everything was complete. I had my wonderful life and family. God's harvesting machine was empowered and ready to help others.

Epilogue

My life was finally happy and complete, but my spirit wasn't totally satisfied. I developed a burden for God's children, for others in the community who didn't know Him, who were needy and lost without Him like I had been. Young adults searching for a better life were constantly on my mind.

I shared this burden with my husband, which empowered us to birth a new outreach. Brent totally agreed young adults out of college needed help to find their way. They needed guidance and role models. We were equipped to help them find their way. My testimonies would dissuade them from living apart from God.

Brent's testimony would encourage them to stay with God and wait for his blessing. God could use our life experiences like a guidebook to finding a deeper relationship with Jesus.

With the pastor's blessing, Brent and I started a singles' group at church. The group gave us another purpose beyond praying for those who need the Lord. We got to share firsthand our knowledge of Him.

My intercessory duties are far from over. The Lord has assured me I would be facing my old enemy, Satan, many more times, but I'll be hunting him.

Spiritual duties are never over. Mamie, Brent, and I have been connected to fulfill God's desires. We have not met the solitary fourth comrade—the Ox—yet. The Ox is still out there, finding fledglings being called into service.

One day soon, he will join us. Then we will work together becoming God's complete team in full operation, working together as a harvesting machine.

Bibliography

Bible: Zondervan Publishing
Amplified version references: Ezekiel 16:8; Matthew 23:37-38
and Proverbs 22:6

About the Author

Raven H. Price, is a Christian fiction writer who uses romance mixed with fantasy and supernatural events to intrigue her readers. She also enjoys devoting her time inspiring and encouraging people to believe in themselves and trusting in a loving God.

She is happily married to her husband, Ralph W. Price, III, and they live in Leesburg, Georgia with four cats. Since she is a cat lover, her Twitter handle is 'roaringpurr.' Her Facebook author page @Roaringpurr, is devoted not only to her books but as an outlet to encourage love, respect, and acceptance for all mankind.

Please consider leaving a review on Amazon by clicking on this, thank you.

www.ingramcontent.com/pod-product-compliance
Lightning Source LLC
Chambersburg PA
CBHW070207260626
47160CB00002B/470